CHRISTMAS PAST

The Christmas-Tree, from *Harper's Weekly*, January 2, 1869.

CHRISTMAS PAST

AN ANTHOLOGY OF SEASONAL STORIES FROM NINETEENTH-CENTURY AMERICA

EDITED BY **THOMAS RUYS SMITH**

LOUISIANA STATE UNIVERSITY PRESS
BATON ROUGE

Published with the assistance of the V. Ray Cardozier Fund

Published by Louisiana State University Press
www.lsupress.org

Manufactured in the United States of America
First printing

Designer: Barbara Neely Bourgoyne
Typeface: Calluna
Printer and binder: Sheridan Books

The jacket illustration and illustrations on the part dividers are taken from *Christmas Drawings for the Human Race* (1889), by Thomas Nast.

Library of Congress Cataloging-in-Publication Data
Names: Smith, Thomas Ruys, editor.
Title: Christmas past : an anthology of seasonal stories from nineteenth-century America / edited by Thomas Ruys Smith.
Description: Baton Rouge : Louisiana State University Press, 2021. | Includes bibliographical references.
Identifiers: LCCN 2021008034 (print) | LCCN 2021008035 (ebook) | ISBN 978-0-8071-7608-5 (cloth) | ISBN 978-0-8071-7652-8 (pdf) | ISBN 978-0-8071-7653-5 (epub)
Subjects: LCSH: Christmas stories, American. | Christmas—Literary collections. | American prose literature—19th century. | Christmas in literature. | Christmas—United States—History—19th century.
Classification: LCC PS648.C45 C455 2021 (print) | LCC PS648.C45 (ebook) | DDC 810.8/0334—dc23
LC record available at https://lccn.loc.gov/2021008034
LC ebook record available at https://lccn.loc.gov/2021008035

To my daughters, my wife, and my parents—

for Christmases past, present, and yet to come.

CONTENTS

III. CHRISTMAS REALITIES

IV. WRESTLING WITH THE REASON FOR THE SEASON

V. HAPPY CHRISTMAS TO ALL?

INTRODUCTION

Writing Christmas, Rewriting American Literature

Across the nineteenth century the modern celebration of Christmas took shape as rituals new, rediscovered, and revamped became such an intrinsic part of the rhythm of the year that they soon came to seem eternal. Above all, though, in ways that have hitherto gone unappreciated, the idea of an American Christmas came to life in the pages of books and magazines, where the surprising churn and turmoil of that creation story can still be vividly experienced. The front cover of the 1868 Christmas issue of *Harper's Weekly* magazine paints a telling picture (fig. 1). At the top of the frame all of the elements of an immediately recognizable seasonal scene are in evidence. Santa Claus strides across the rooftops, clutching a fully decorated Christmas tree, American flag prominent, toys swinging from his belt; his reindeer wait patiently behind him, flanked by a mirage of the wise men on camels, following the star. In the house below, however, a more domestic, though no less significant, tableau unfolds. A family sits reading—old and young, women and men, some to each other, some alone. One of them, conspicuously, is browsing an issue of *Harper's Weekly* itself. Reading, this image implies, is as central to the creation of Christmas spirit as the icons pictured above. Indeed, it suggests that the phantasmagoria depicted at the top of the illustration is really a vision conjured by the stories being avidly consumed by those below, a mélange of the sacred and secular narratives that make up this family's seasonal reading. Literature, this image tells us, was intimately connected to the

Figure 1. Front cover of the 1868 Christmas issue of *Harper's Weekly*, published January 2, 1869.

experience of Christmas. And that remains true. This illustration expresses a feedback loop with which we are still familiar: we experience Christmas by imagining Christmas through stories that inspire emulation in—and might equally serve as compensation for—our own festive celebrations. Like that image, this anthology is an attempt to explore the symbiotic relationship between Christmas and literature throughout the American nineteenth century, the implications and reverberations of which still intimately shape our own experience of the holidays.

Meditating on the season in 1889, the *Century Magazine* peremptorily declared that "the Christmas idea nowhere finds so full expression as in literature," noting the "absoluteness with which literature has indorsed Christmas."[1] Yet despite the centrality of reading and writing to the celebration of Christmas, then and now, American seasonal writing of the kind on display in this anthology has received surprisingly little attention, especially in comparison to the social history of the holidays. Most notably, Stephen Nissenbaum's *The Battle for Christmas* (1997), Penne L. Restad's *Christmas in America* (1995), and Karal Ann Marling's *Merry Christmas! Celebrating America's Greatest Holiday* (2000)—among many others—have given us a deep understanding of the social and material culture of American Christmases, particularly the "self-conscious" ways that Americans in the nineteenth century invented the modern celebration that we are still familiar with today, from Santa to Christmas trees and everything in between.[2] While they often draw from literary sources in their studies, the discrete literary history of the holidays remains untold. The venerable E. Douglas Branch's brief survey of the "literary success" of Christmas for the *Saturday Review of Literature* in 1937 still remains one of the most significant statements on this major strand of American writing.[3] Yet books were at the center of Christmas from the emergence of the modern form of the holiday to the end of the nineteenth century and beyond; books dominated the early Christmas gift market, and the stories contained within them disseminated the images and iconography that came to dominate the season. Still, the relationship between the development of American letters and the shaping of Christmas remains a profoundly understudied topic.

Of course, this was also a deeply transatlantic enterprise. Writing in 1890, George William Curtis explored the vital role that literature had long played in the generation of Christmas spirit. Imagining Christmas morning, he posed a question to his readers: "how is to-day different from yesterday?" The difference lay in "the power of association"—associations that were profoundly and primarily literary. To inspire the desired "feeling of rest or leisure, of bodily and spiritual refreshment," books were called for: "Shall we begin the day with a solemn service of Milton's 'Nativity,' or the Bible story of the manger and the star, or intone a Christmas carol, or read an old Christmas legend, or a tale of Dickens's, or Thackeray's tender lines, or Irving's cheery sketch?"[4] The prominence of British writers in Curtis's litany suggests another reason for the relative neglect of seasonal writing from America. While Dickens was hardly the first author to write about the season, his dominance has helped to obscure American literature's particular contribution to the culture of Christmas in this period and beyond. *A Christmas Carol* (1842) certainly left an indelible mark on festive literature; Scrooge and Tiny Tim still have a powerful grip on our imaginations. In a crowded field, Tara Moore's definitive *Victorian Christmas in Print* (2009)—as well as her collection of Victorian Christmas ghost stories—has given the most thorough and compelling account of the ways in which the work of "Dickens and his ilk" generated "reading materials that were to become as iconic as the Christmas feast." As the "consumption of seasonal print entered into the performance of the holiday," so too did this English Christmas canon instruct its home audience "in a newly codified national ritual."[5]

But what about America? For all that Dickens and his contemporaries had a profound impact on American readers and their festive reading habits, America had its own distinctive literature of Christmas before, during, and after Dickens's reign as the presiding spirit of the season. Christmas currents flowed back across the Atlantic, too, and when Christmas inspiration did arrive from the Old World, it always experienced an American translation. The most notorious example of that process can be found in the familiar shape of the Christmas tree. In 1848, the seasonal supplement of the *Illustrated London News* published a widely reproduced image of the Royal Family gathered around the Christmas tree at Windsor Castle. Accompanying the illustration was a detailed description of their seasonal traditions, and an account of "A German Christmas Tree" which promised to "throw some light upon the festive purposes for which they are employed," for the benefit of any readers who were still unfamiliar with the custom.[6] Equally keen to capitalize on the growing popularity of this seasonal fashion, Sarah Josepha Hale's influential American magazine

Godey's Lady's Book reprinted the image two years later. But in so doing, Hale Americanized the image, transforming the scene from regal splendor to bourgeois republican domesticity (fig. 2).[7] On the other hand, some elements of a British Christmas never got a firm foothold in the New World, even in translation. The Christmas pudding, for example, thrived in other British colonies. In Australia, for example, Nicole Anae has highlighted the ways in which it was not only a staple on the Christmas table but also provided "an enduring theme" in "popular, amateur and literary verse" in the nineteenth century, in ways that explored the ties between colony and motherland.[8] In America, though, the pudding was largely absent in the mouths of poets—and was hardly a staple of the season for their fellow citizens. As Natacha Chevalier has pointedly observed, "what is considered as the first cookbook published by an American author, *American Cookery* by Amelia Simmons in 1776, does not contain a plum pudding recipe."[9]

Figure 2. *The Christmas Tree at Windsor Castle,* from the *Illustrated London News* of 1848 (*left*), and as adapted for the American magazine *Godey's Lady's Book* two years later (*right*).

In truth, on the page, transatlantic differences ran deep during the holidays. While British writers tended to foreground seasonal spooks and spirits—as Tara Moore has noted, across the Atlantic "Christmas genres [. . .] regularly exploited the early association between the holiday and the ghost story"—American writers became far more concerned with the everyday, quotidian, domestic spaces of Christmas.[10] To use Gillian Avery's phrase, "Homely details were never so prominent in English books."[11] Moreover, far more than in Britain, American Christmas literature closely embroiled the festive season in a variety of distinctive political and social issues that ran through the nineteenth century, particularly sectional and sectarian arguments. This means that wars—cultural, cold, and the shooting kind—rage through these pages. We may assume that the Christmases documented in this collection emanate from a sacred, seasonal Golden Age, free from the stress and strife of modern life. Yet one of the most characteristic aspects of these American stories is the way in which, taken together, the only constant in this collaborative portrait of Christmas is flux and churn and conflict—up to and including Civil War. Even on a spiritual level, Christmas was riven by theological disagreement. Not until the latter part of the nineteenth century could Christmas come close to being considered a "national ritual." By 1883, George William Curtis, writing in *Harper's New Monthly Magazine,* might have felt able to pronounce Christmas a "universal holiday" that had been freed from the taint of "superstition," but the need for that assertion only highlights the degree to which, for most of the nineteenth century, celebrating Christmas was doctrinally suspect for many Americans. We may think of the idea of a "War on Christmas" as a contemporary phenomenon, but in the early nineteenth century it was a real conflict waged primarily by the faithful.[12] "Strange, indeed," marveled Susan Fenimore Cooper in 1850, when the matter was hardly settled, "that men, endowed with many Christian virtues, should have ever though it a duty to oppose so bitterly the celebration of a festival in honor of the Nativity of Christ!"[13]

This was a battle which also had deep sectional roots, palpable in the earliest expressions of Anglo-American literature. From the moment that English colonists arrived in the New World, Christmas was a holiday that was subject to significant regional variation, underpinned by religious and—increasingly—sociopolitical disagreements. Indeed, a succinct expression of these differences can be found in two of the earliest and most important accounts of colonial life in America. In December 1608, those who had crossed the Atlantic to establish an English foothold in Virginia were hardly having a festive time of it. Still, John Smith recorded that, reliant on the charity of their Native neighbors, they celebrated Christmas in the midst of their hardships: "the extreme wind, raine, frost, and snowy, caused us to keepe Christmas amongst the Salvages, where wee were never more merrie, nor fedde on more plentie of good oysters, fish, flesh, wild foule, and good bread, nor never had better fires in England."[14] Conversely, as Edward Everett Hale put it in 1868, "The first Christmas in New England was celebrated by some people who tried as hard as they could not to celebrate it at all."[15] In Pilgrim Plymouth, Christmas was cancelled. The lack of scriptural support for the festival combined with its associations with debauchery, excess, and the flavor of Rome meant that Puritans (on both sides of the Atlantic) were at pains to suppress seasonal celebrations. On their first December 25 in America in 1620, William Bradford pointedly recorded in his journal that, ignoring any other association the day might hold, he and his fellow colonists "begane to erecte ye first house for comone use to receive them and their goods."[16] The next year, however, Bradford—the governor of the colony—came into conflict with some new arrivals who were less spiritually committed and more attached to their Old World traditions:

> One ye day called Chrismas-day, ye Govr caled them out to worke [. . .] but ye most of this new-company excused them selves and said it wente against their consciences to work on ys day. So ye Govr tould them that if they made it mater of conscience, he would spare them till they were better informed. So he led-away ye rest and left them; but when they came home at noone from their worke, he found them in ye streets at play, openly; some pitching ye barr, & some at stoole-ball, and shuch like sports. So he went to them, and tooke away their implements, and tould them that was against his conscience, that they should play & others worke.[17]

These antipathies lasted much longer in New England than Old. Sitting at the heart of literary American Christmases, both of these archetypes echoed down the ages and left profound traces, as the texts in this collection amply demonstrate.

A vivid snapshot of the changing contours of belief and practice that characterized American Christmases in the nineteenth century can be traced in the literary lives of the famous Beecher family. Growing up under the strict spiritual regime of the formidable Lyman Beecher, freighted with the legacy of Puritan prejudices, the Beecher children were forbidden from enjoying seasonal celebrations. As his son—the charismatic, liberal, celebrity minister Henry Ward Beecher—would remember in 1874, "nobody talked to me about Christmas. I should have looked with wondering eyes to see what was meant if anybody had." He recalled passing by the local Episcopalian Church one Christmas morning, "and looking in I saw a number of people, with tallow candles, trying to put up some evergreens. I remember wondering why under the sun they were taking the woods into the church." But otherwise, "my youth was passed without any knowledge or associations of Christmas."[18] In his novel *Norwood* (1868), Beecher emphasized the ways in which Christmas was traditionally abjured: "New England has always been economical of holidays. Christmas she threw away with indignant emphasis, as stained and spattered with Papal superstition."[19] Still, Beecher did not count this absence in his spiritual calendar "as a blessing" and was open to change: "I should be glad if our children were brought up with associations such as would lead them to celebrate the anniversary day of the birth of our Lord." Yet he was also certain that he felt Christmas to be "a foreign day, and it will continue to be so till I die. [. . .] where a Christmas nerve ought to be in my nature, there is none."[20] And he was certainly not alone in that complicated response to the growing holiday.

Contrarily, his sister, the world-famous novelist Harriet Beecher Stowe, shared some of Henry's personal conflicts, but ultimately came to embrace the season and its potential, literary and social. She also fictionalized her youthful sense of estrangement from Christmas, but in so doing she explored the pain and confusion that it generated. In her last novel, *Poganuc*

People (1878), the character of Dolly is excluded from the seasonal festivities of her Episcopalian friends: "The world looked cold and dark and dreary[. . .]. She never felt injured; she never even in thought questioned that her parents were doing exactly right by her—she only felt that just here and now the right thing was very disagreeable." Yet Dolly's Christmas is saved, as Harriet's often were, by the arrival of presents from her mother's side of the family.[21] Inspired by the Christmas celebrations of her worldly Foote relatives—as early as the 1830s, her uncle Samuel was sending the family seasonal hopes for "good fires & plenty of apples & nuts—not to mention minced pyes & roasted Turkeys—long lives & Merry Evenings"—Harriet not only grew to celebrate Christmas, she mined its literary potential throughout her career.[22] *Uncle Tom's Cabin* itself contains multiple references to "Christmas holidays."[23] One of Stowe's earliest stories, "Christmas; or, The Good Fairy" (1850), is included in this collection.

Despite this contentious and conflicting position in America's spiritual life—and perhaps because of the uncertainties surrounding it—Christmas occupied an extraordinarily prominent place in nineteenth-century American literature. Yet seasonal sketches barely feature in most literary histories of this era. As Jana Tigchelaar has rightly argued, "In many cases, critics seem quick to dismiss Christmas stories [. . .] because these stories were often solicited for holiday themed magazine issues."[24] Moreover, as Susan Koppelman has noted, critics have also been apt to dismiss these kinds of "occasional stories" as "mawkish, whorish, trite, formulaic, and 'subliterary.'"[25] These remain viewpoints that still need to be challenged, not least because Christmas-themed stories and extracts remain some of the most visible pieces of nineteenth-century literature which remain in active circulation today. As this collection demonstrates, it is difficult to think of a theme that unites more significant American writers from this period. It was also a key ingredient of many of the biggest best sellers of these years. Many years ago, Katharine Allyn See suggested that the American Christmas story should be considered "an independent, minor literary genre unto itself."[26] Picking up that cue, we might also assert that it was a genre to which every major writer of this period contributed; as such, it was arguably *the* most important theme for nineteenth-century American writers. In many ways, the development of a distinctive American literature and a recognizably modern Christmas are coterminous. From early in the century, Christmas was a topic that gave space for continual invention and reinvention for American writers. In turn, the centrality of Christmas as a setting and a theme provides us with a new way to explore the development and growth of American literature in its most formative period. As well as telling us a great deal about Christmas and its place in the American imagination, this anthology can therefore also tell us a great deal about the development of American literature more broadly.

The ubiquity of Christmas as a subject, long hidden in plain sight, allows us to draw a line connecting romantics to realists, household names to the forgotten and the obscure. What becomes clear is that the changing image of Christmas traces the changing contours of American literature. When the first generation of American writers to achieve international renown were inventing a characteristic national literature, they turned to Christmas; when the wildly popular sentimental writers of mid-century were centering the domestic lives of American families in their work, they turned to Christmas; when writers were dealing with slavery, Civil War, and their aftermaths, they turned to Christmas; when a new generation of realists looked to reshape American literature, they turned to Christmas; and when a variety of writers on the margins of American life—the enslaved, Native Americans, newly arrived immigrants, women working for equality—looked to triangulate their own identity as Americans and to contest their ostracism, they too turned to Christmas. So before we get to the abundant festive feast that these writings represent, let us also turn to Christmas and briefly explore its extraordinary journey through nineteenth-century American literature.

OLD CHRISTMAS

In 1817, American writer Washington Irving made a house call that would have profound significance for himself, for the trajectory of American literature, and for our ongoing seasonal celebrations. He had arrived in England in 1815 as the world was in tumult—mere months after Britain and America had ended the War of 1812 and just as Napoleon was defeated at Waterloo. Obliged to work to rescue his family's failing merchant business, Irving was still on the lookout for literary inspiration. When not applying himself in desultory fashion to the mysteries of bookkeeping, he traveled around the Old World that had fascinated him since childhood. He made it to Scotland late in the summer of 1817. Clutching a letter of introduction from one Scottish poet—Thomas Campbell—he knocked on the door of another. As Irving put it in later years, the time he spent with Walter Scott at Abbotsford was idyllic: "The days thus spent, I shall ever look back to, as among the very happiest of my life. [. . .] it was, as if I were admitted to a social communion with Shakspeare."[27] Scott himself was charmed by his new American friend, describing him to Campbell as "one of the best and pleasantest acquaintances I have made this many a day."[28] In some ways they were a curious pairing. At this moment, Scott was more famous for his poetry than the novels that would cause an unparalleled sensation on both sides of the Atlantic—though those in the know were aware that he was the author of the Waverley novels. Irving had achieved some renown for his early writing, but life was hard for an American writer battling against transatlantic prejudices, the demands of business, and a frequently uninterested home crowd. Yet they shared one thing in common, a quirk that was unusual in their time but the significance of which would echo down the years: an antiquarian love of Christmas.

Even before their auspicious meeting, both men had already written about the season in ways that would prove prescient. That is not to say that they were complete pioneers. In Germany—in whose literature and folklore both men were well versed—Christmas had already experienced "intense emotional innovation" in the late eighteenth century when, as Joe Perry has elucidated, "The holiday as we know it took shape [. . .] in the family parlors of enlightened aristocrats and bourgeois intellectuals."[29] The was a trend that was readily discernible in early Romantic print culture. For example, in a pivotal scene in Goethe's epochal *Sorrows of Young Werther* (1774, published four times in America before 1800), Werther's unrequited love, Charlotte, prepares "little gifts for her brothers and sisters, which were to be distributed on Christmas-eve."[30] Whatever inspiration they may have received from their interests in German culture, Irving and Scott brought different sensibilities to bear on their literary engagements with Christmas.

Scott paved the way, as he did in so many things. In *Marmion* (1808), he had devoted one of the introductory poems which prefaced each of the six cantos to a nostalgic, historical celebration of the season which "Each age has deemed [. . .] The fittest time for festal cheer":

> England was merry England, when,
> Old Christmas brought his sports again.
> 'Twas Christmas broached the mightiest ale;
> 'Twas Christmas told the merriest tale;
> A Christmas gambol oft could cheer
> The poor man's heart through half the year.[31]

In a note to this section, Scott acknowledged his debts to one of Ben Jonson's Christmas masques for his portrait of celebrations in times gone by: from the start, the modern literary Christmas was a composite of previous paper visions. Still, Scott insisted that "Some remnants of the good old time [. . .] linger, in our northern clime." However much the season may have faded in significance elsewhere, he maintained that "my Christmas still I hold."[32] These were influential verses beyond their own moment: multiple, lush American gift editions of the Christmas verses from *Marmion* were still being published as late as the 1880s.[33] That Scott practiced what he preached we can prove thanks to an account of festivities at Abbotsford in December 1824 recorded by Basil Hall (a friend and fellow writer who would go on to publish a pioneering travel account of America). Hall was impressed with the "extraordinary splendour" he found there: "The whole establishment is on the same footing—I mean the attendance and entertainment—all is in good order, and an air of punctuality and method, without any waste or ostentation, pervades every thing. Every one seems at his ease; and although I have been in some big houses in my time, and amongst good folks who studied these sort of points not a little,

I don't remember to have any where met with things better managed in all respects."

Scott read his guests poetry, sang them ballads, regaled them with anecdotes, led the dance. Yet for all that, Hall himself was clearly not a fellow devotee of the season: "I confess, for my part, that your Christmas and New-years' parties seem generally dull." Hall found the "compulsion" to be merry wearing. Moreover, "it seldom happens that a party is quite well sorted"—even, apparently, at Abbotsford. For those and other reasons, Hall felt that the "fashion of keeping up old holidays [. . .] is surely decreasing."[34]

Irving, in contrast, deeply shared Scott's passion for "old holidays" and all that came with them. He was certainly familiar with Scott's portrait of Christmas in *Marmion*—he quoted some apposite lines from the poem in a letter to his brother Peter while sailing from Liverpool to Scotland.[35] Yet it should not be forgotten that Scott was also aware of Irving's own early—and distinctively American—literary evocations of the season. Before the two even met, one of Irving's friends had already presented Scott with a copy of Irving's satirical *History of New-York,* first published in 1809 before a revised version appeared in 1812. "I have been employed these few evenings in reading them aloud to Mrs Scott & two ladies who are our guests," Scott happily recounted, "and our sides have been absolutely sore with laughing."[36] In that book, Scott and his family circle would have encountered Irving's pioneering literary portrait of St. Nicholas. Throughout his comic and unreliable history, Irving positions him as the patron saint of New Amsterdam, from his presence as the figurehead of the ship carrying Dutch pioneers to the New World to his benevolent appearance in the dreams of early settlers. Indeed, in the "sylvan days" of New Amsterdam, Irving tells us, "St. Nicholas would often make his appearance in his beloved city, of a holiday afternoon, riding jollily among the tree tops, or over the roofs of the houses, now and then drawing forth magnificent presents from his breeches pockets, and dropping them down the chimnies of his favourites." In these "degenerate days," however, New Yorkers have to make do with a visitation only "one night in the year; when he rattles down the chimnies, of the descendants of the patriarchs, confining his presents merely to the children, in token of the degeneracy of the parents."[37] That vestigial and ironic portrait, a knowing American borrowing and updating of Old World traditions with little basis in local folk custom, was a significant step on the long road of the literary evolution of Santa Claus.

Other early American writers and artists, particularly those in Irving's New York circle, would also turn to St. Nicholas at this time, feeding into the modern vision of Santa which still dominates the season. Irving's brother-in-law James Kirke Paulding, for example, dedicated a whole book to him—"I have all my life been a sincere and fervent follower of the right reverend and jolly St. Nicholas," Paulding begins his portrait, "paying him my respectful devoirs on Christmas and Newyear's eve."[38] The popular versifier Samuel Woodworth similarly celebrated the delights of Christmas Eve in a poetic epistle written to accompany a Christmas gift in 1825:

> [. . .] the stocking, from each little leg,
> Must be suspended to a hook or peg,
> That *Santaclaus,* who travels all the night,
> Might, in the dark, bestow his favours right.[39]

No literary text did more to make the local cult of St. Nicholas into a national—indeed global—figure, and cement his burgeoning association with an American Christmas, than Clement Clarke Moore's still ubiquitous "Account of a Visit From St. Nicholas" when it appeared in the *Troy Sentinel* on December 23, 1823.[40] Whether Saint or Santa, writers—at least in and around New York—were clearly drawn to the creation of a distinctive American seasonal gift-bringer at this pivotal literary moment.

Yet Washington Irving still had plenty more to say about Christmas, particularly after his happy visit with Scott. When he published *The Sketch Book of Geoffrey Crayon, Gent.,* serially throughout 1819 and 1820, this beguiling blend of travel sketches and short stories caused a sensation on both sides of the Atlantic. The entire fifth installment, first published in America on January 1, 1820 (a week later than planned), Irving devoted to a rich evocation of the Old World Christmases lauded by Scott in *Marmion.* Deeply intertextual and peppered with references to seventeenth-century Christmas poems and plays, Irving's account immediately struck a tone of delight: "Of all the old festivals [. . .] that of Christmas awakens the strongest and most heartfelt associations."[41] It also cloaked itself in retrospection and nostalgia, beginning with an epigraph from an anti-Puritan pamphlet from the seventeenth century (fig. 3).[42] Like Scott, Irving mourned "the holyday customs and rural games of former times" which seemed to be fading in the face of "modern refinement."[43]

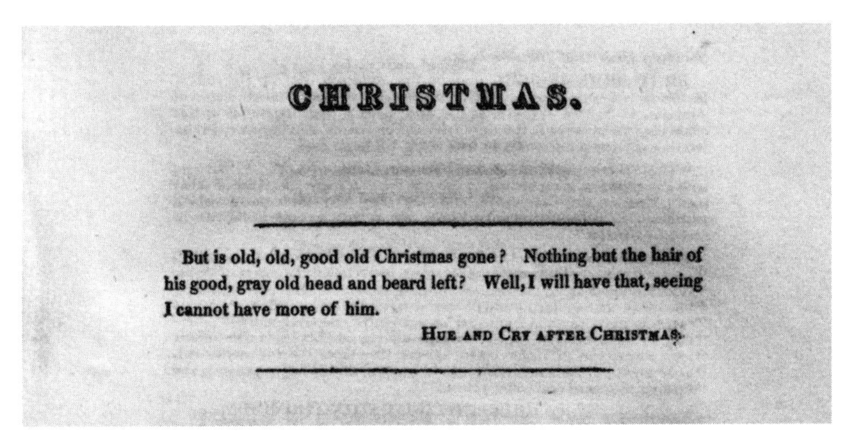

CHRISTMAS.

But is old, old, good old Christmas gone? Nothing but the hair of his good, gray old head and beard left? Well, I will have that, seeing I cannot have more of him.

HUE AND CRY AFTER CHRISTMAS.

Figure 3. Frontispiece to the Christmas number of Irving's *Sketch Book.*

Irving explored these central themes at length by imagining his narrator, Geoffrey Crayon, experiencing seasonal celebrations at Bracebridge Hall, the home of Squire Bracebridge. Both were fictional, and self-consciously intertextual, but Irving was inspired in his portraits by both his reading and his travels in the Old World. And as Brian Jay Jones has asserted, "perhaps the most important influence" on Irving's construction of Bracebridge was "Walter Scott's Abbotsford."[44] Like Scott—and like Irving—Bracebridge is markedly antiquarian in his tastes. As his son warns the narrator, amongst the Squire's "little eccentricities" he is a "strenuous advocate for the revival of the old rural games and holyday observances, and is deeply read in the writers, ancient and modern, who have treated of the subject."[45] What Irving presents in the *Sketch Book* is a knowingly ersatz Christmas, resurrected by Squire Bracebridge as a means of returning society to its former feudal glory: mistletoe hangs, the Yule log burns, the Wassail Bowl circulates, the Boar's Head is ceremonially serenaded as it takes its place on the Christmas dinner table. Though "joviality" is the order of the day, at points Bracebridge's attempts to turn back the clock lead to comic awkwardness.[46] Resurrecting the paternalism of former times, he "kept open house during the holydays in the old style," but the contemporary "country people did not understand how to play their parts in the scene of hospitality: many uncouth circumstances occurred."[47] Such misadventures were replaced with charitable gifts, bestowed at a distance. If Bracebridge's festive affectations are therefore partly played for knowing effect, the warmth and "delicious home feeling" of Irving's confabulation of Christmas ultimately triumph.[48] Such was the popularity of this section of the *Sketch Book* that Irving composed a sequel which took his narrator back for a longer stay at *Bracebridge Hall.* That book, too, ended with a poignant lament that inevitably the "old Hall will be modernised into a fashionable country-seat," and "Christmas [. . .] will be forgotten."[49] Again, after its initial success, this installment of the *Sketch Book* had a long half-life, reprinted frequently in seasonal gift books throughout the rest of the century.[50] As late as 1883, George William Curtis would declare Irving "the laureate of English Christmas. [. . .] the enduring popularity of his charming essays shows that this is the Christmas of the English-speaking race."[51]

Yet for some, that Englishness was a sticking point. Even at its genesis, literary Christmases proved to be a battleground for, among many other things, issues of politics and national identity. James Fenimore Cooper reviewed *Bracebridge Hall* and was quick to upbraid Irving's apparent affiliation with the likes of the Squire: "he eulogises the aristocracy of Great Britain; descants upon the dignity of descent, and the generous pride of illustrious ancestry!"[52] Setting his cap against this kind of apparently anti-Republican sentiment, Cooper set about crafting his own vision of a national literature—and to do so, he also gravitated toward the subject and setting of Christmas. In his pivotal novel *The Pioneers* (1823), Cooper offered readers an evocative and distinctively American Christmas on the early frontier. The book begins with a mountain sleigh ride "on a clear, cold day in December," and "thoughts of home and a Christmas fireside, with its Christmas frolics." There is the promise of "a visit from

Santaclaus," but there is also sectarian disagreement about the planned Episcopalian Christmas service. Over the succeeding chapters, a series of seasonal frontier genre scenes, undertaken by a representative miscellany of characters, unfolds for the reader—from an uproarious, bibulous Christmas Eve in the local tavern to "the old Christmas sport of shooting the turkey."[53] His daughter Susan kept up the family tradition, paying voluble tribute to the local Christmas culture around Cooperstown, New York, in *Rural Hours* (1850), her pioneering work of nature writing. "Christmas must always be a happy, cheerful day," she argued in a long and impassioned defense of its celebration in which she delighted in "the bright fires, the fresh and fragrant greens, the friendly gifts, and words of good-will."[54]

Nor was James Fenimore Cooper the only writer of his moment to translate the Christmas cues dropped by Scott and Irving and put them to use as distinctive matter for a new American literature. His contemporary Catherine Maria Sedgwick, best known for her historical novels, wrote one of the earliest literary descriptions of a Christmas tree (truly, a New Year's tree) in 1836. Inspired by their German maid, a family purchases "a fine tree of respectable growth" and "plant it in the library" where it is adorned with presents: "Never did Christmas tree bear more multifarious fruit,—for St. Nicholas, that most benign of all the saints of the Calendar, had, through the hands of many a ministering priest and priestess, showered his gifts."[55] In this anthology, British traveler Harriet Martineau provides another account of a pioneering American Christmas tree that she encountered earlier in the 1830s at the house of German émigré and abolitionist Charles Follen (potentially, the very same Christmas tree that inspired Sedgwick).

Yet the significance of Christmas to the development of American literature went deeper than simply providing distinctive subject matter. Sedgwick's Christmas tree sketch appeared in *The Token and Atlantic Souvenir: A Christmas and New Year's Present,* edited by Samuel Goodrich. As its name suggests, this was one of a multitude of gift books released in large numbers from the 1820s onwards. These were books which were expressly designed and released to serve as seasonal presents, and if they first originated in Britain they ultimately had more significance across the Atlantic. As Nissenbaum has described, American "publishers and booksellers were the shock troops in exploiting—and developing—a Christmas trade. [. . .] books were on the cutting edge of a commercial Christmas, making up more than half of the earliest items advertised as Christmas gifts."[56] Beyond inculcating the habits of seasonal present exchanges among the American populace, gift books were literary miscellanies which served as a truly vital publishing outlet for early American writers. In a preface to the 1836 edition of *The Token and Atlantic Souvenir* in which Sedgwick's Christmas tree appeared, Goodrich proudly proclaimed that his collection was "wholly an American production. It is the first annual, and the only highly embellished book, issued from the American press, which could claim entire independence of foreign aid."[57] In its pages, Sedgwick's story rubbed shoulders with contributions from Lydia Sigourney, James Fenimore Cooper, James Kirke Paulding, John Neal, Sarah Josepha Hale, Eliza Leslie, and Nathaniel Hawthorne—even if he would later abjure his many appearances in the "dingy pages" and "shabby morocco-covers of faded souvenirs."[58] Perhaps ironically, Hawthorne's allegorical story "The Christmas Banquet," which imagined a festive feast hosted for "ten of the most miserable persons that could be found," did not appear in a seasonal gift book.[59] The growth of Christmas and the development of American literature therefore walked hand in hand during the early decades of the nineteenth century, and are inextricable from each other. In this anthology, gift books are represented by a self-reflexive account of "Christmas" from the 1829 collection *The Pearl; or, Affection's Gift* (fig. 4).

Of course, the polite and picturesque Christmases that could be found in the pages of gift books and other sketches were in many ways an illusion, no less self-conscious than Irving's knowing antiquarian revival. In particular, they stood in stark contrast to the seasonal celebrations that bedeviled the streets of America's young cities. As Susan G. Davis has written about Philadelphia at this time, though her description is applicable far more broadly, "Christmas was then an essentially public celebration, unfolding in taverns, alleys, and squares[. . .]. Riot and revelry, disguise and debauch gave police and property owners reason to fear the approach of the holiday."[60] Vestigial traces of subversive Old World customs—like mumming and masking—carried with them a sense of misrule and vio-

Figure 4. Title page of *The Pearl; or, Affection's Gift.*

lence, implied and very real. Nor was drunken revelry confined to city streets. A young Nathaniel Parker Willis experienced seasonal high jinks at Yale in 1823. In a clear demonstration of lingering regional differences, southern students apparently bristled at the way in which their "Puritan college" refused "to make a holiday" of Christmas: "There were many of them drunk last evening," Willis wrote to his father, "Last night they barred the entry doors of the South College, to exclude the government, and then illuminated the building. This morning the recitation-room doors were locked and the key stolen, and we were obliged to knock down the doors to get in."[61] Out west, the rowdiness seems to have lingered longer. Traveling through Texas in 1856, Frederick Law Olmsted witnessed what he sardonically described as a "touching commemoration" on Christmas Eve in St Augustin: "A band of pleasant spirits started from the square, blowing tin horns, and beating tin pans, and visited in succession every house in the village, kicking in doors, and pulling down fences, until every male member of the family had appeared, with appropriate instruments, and joined the merry party."[62]

Despite the best efforts of genteel writers, domestic Christmases were still far from ubiquitous. While touring America in the early 1830s, popular British actress Fanny Kemble complained in her journal, published in 1835, "Here are comparatively no observances of tides and times. Christmas-day is no religious day, and hardly a holyday with them. New-year's day is perhaps a little, but only a little, more so. Twelfth-day, it is unknown." This she blamed on a relative paucity of "the blessed and holy influences of home" in America: "the young American leaves so soon the shelter of his home [. . .] that the happy and powerful associations of that word to him are hardly known."[63] But times were changing. Perhaps no American writer's engagement with Christmas at this moment was more telling than that of Lydia Maria Child. An influential writer and abolitionist, Child moved to New York to begin her editorship of the *National Anti-Slavery Standard* in the early 1840s. At the same time, she also began detailing her new experiences of life in that burgeoning urban environment, as unfamiliar to her as it was to many of her readers. The city's seasonal celebrations were one of the novel spectacles that she described in significant detail throughout her column, collected as *Letters from New York.* "To-day is Christmas," she addressed her readers on December 25, 1843, noting that, for "several days past, cartloads of evergreens have gone by my windows."[64] The season was already sufficiently commercial for Child to note that "the windows of New-York are to-day filled with all forms of luxury and splendour, to tempt the wealthy, who are making up Christmas boxes for family and friends [. . .] bestowed by affection or vanity." She certainly still had misgivings about the celebration—the arguments of the "learned" that "Christ was not born on that day," and her sense of its pagan roots in "the old Roman festival for the Birth of the Sun." Her Puritan hangover was still palpable, and she could never bring herself to raise a Christmas tree. Despite these uncertainties, Child was willing "to accept the wintry anniversary of Christmas and take it to my heart."[65]

Crucially, books had softened her suspicions of the season. As early as 1830, Child had clearly been aware of Samuel Taylor Coleridge's influential account of Christmas celebrations that he had experienced in Germany in the dying years of the eighteenth century.[66] She paraphrased Coleridge's description of the way that German children prepared presents for their parents and other family members in a Christmas gift book for children, *The Little Girl's Own Book,* declaring it to be "a most interesting and affectionate custom" that American girls might emulate.[67] In her Christmas column in 1843, Child quoted another popular European account of the season which had just been published—Frederika Bremer's "delightful picture of this Christian festival in the cold regions of the North," an account which provided a Utopian model for what the season could mean in the contemporary world, one far away from mean city streets: "Not alone in the houses of the wealthy blaze up fires of joy, and are heard the glad shouts of children. From the humblest cottages also resounds joy; in the prisons it becomes bright, and the poor partake of plenty. In the country, doors, hearths and tables, stand open to every wanderer [. . .]. And not only human beings, but animals also, have their good things at Christmas."[68]

Inspired by this festive reading, Child could turn to the meaning of Christmas as it played out in her adopted city, and ponder its potential for provoking amelioration. She cited the welcome example of a friend who, while not rich, "employed his Christmas more wisely" than the wealthy by filling a "large basket full of cakes [. . .] to distribute them among hungry children." After describing the "Christmas tour of observation" that she herself had taken among the tenements of the city's poorest inhabitants, and particularly the examples of charitable behavior that she had witnessed occurring between them, Child left her readers with a provoking question: "what exercise of the benevolent sympathies could a rich man enjoy, in making the most magnificent Christmas gift, compared with the beautiful self-denial which lends its last blanket, that another may sleep?" For Child, her troubling festive encounters were a rebuke to the very "structure of society, on this Christmas Day."[69] It was a moment to measure the distance between Christ's example, two thousands years ago, and the contemporary inequality that she saw around her in the modern city—just as it was a moment to note the gap between Bremer's literary evocation of Christmas in Sweden and the reality that Child uncovered in New York. Her readers, therefore, encountered a complex textual Christmas defined by these juxtapositions.

Nor was she finished with this theme. Six days before Child had written her Christmas day epistle, back across the Atlantic in London, Charles Dickens had just published *A Christmas Carol* on December 19, 1843. It was a book that had its own deep transatlantic inspirations. In a toast that Dickens gave at a literary dinner in New York during his trip to America in 1842, he offered a heartfelt tribute to the work of Washington Irving (who was himself in attendance, as was Catherine Maria Sedgwick): "I say, gentlemen, that I do not go to bed two nights out of any seven without taking Washington Irving under my arm up stairs to bed with me."[70] Where Irving's literary vision had already traveled, Dickens marveled, everyone else followed. This, of course, was particularly true of Christmas, a subject that Dickens famously turned to in earnest soon after his time in America in the company of Irving. Regardless, his concerns in *A Christmas Carol*—urban poverty, Christmas as a time of reformation and charity—were strikingly similar to Child's. She certainly noticed the resonances of their themes when she finally received a copy of Dickens's book early in 1844. Perhaps in contrast to our expectations, the book that continues to define the season in many imaginations was not an immediate success in America. On January 26, 1844, Child directed her readers' attention to Dickens's new work, noting that the newspapers "announce it merely as a 'ghost story,' and scarcely utter a word in its praise." The reason was plain: despite the warmth of his reception in America, Dickens had been famously rude about certain aspects of American life when he published a travel book about his experiences, *American Notes* (1842). Child was sure that his new Christmas book "would have met quite a different reception" if he hadn't "wounded our national vanity so deeply." Child herself found *A Christmas Carol* a "most genial production"—but more importantly, she already had evidence that it had shifted seasonal behavior. A friend had "proposed to give me a New-Year's present," she explained. Child asked her to give a charitable donation instead; disapproving of her choice of recipient, the friend had refused. But then, a neighbor sent Child's friend a copy of Dickens's new book. "I have read the Christmas Carol," Child's friend declared soon after, "and now I am *obliged* to give three dollars."[71]

Despite its apparently slow start, Americans came to embrace *A Christmas Carol.* In February 1844, *Magazine for the Million* bristled that Dickens had "unworthily repaid" the "unaffected friendship and affection" with which he had been greeted in America, but still begrudgingly accepted, "For all this, the Christmas Carol is a glorious good story, and will produce laughter and tears [. . .]. It is better than a sermon."[72] By 1862, Rebecca Harding Davis could use him as both touchstone and shorthand in a Christmas scene in her first novel: "As for the dinner, it was the essence of all Christmas dinners: Dickens himself, the priest of the genial day, would have been contented."[73] In 1873, Charles Dudley Warner would depict a couple with an ingrained ritual that placed Dickens at the center of their seasonal celebrations—where, for many, he still remains: "It is our custom on every Christmas eve [. . .] to read one of Dickens's Christmas stories."[74]

Dickens's literary domination of the festive season—whether alone or in collaboration with others in the Christmas numbers of *Household Words* and *All The Year Round* (released from 1850 to 1867)—undoubtedly cemented the close relationship between reading and the holiday season on both sides of the Atlantic. As John Drew has noted, both "in Britain and America" the Christmas numbers of Dickens' journals "had the highest circulation of any of Dickens's serial or periodical writings."[75] Undoubtedly, Dickens left a long literary shadow on the season, one that still lingers. He also inspired emulation among other writers and publishers who, to borrow Tara Moore's phrase, wanted to earn "a slice of the Christmas pudding."[76] A critic for *The Times* noted in 1866, speaking for the publishing situation in America as well as England, "Regularly as the year draws to a close we are inundated with a peculiar class of books which are supposed to be appropriate to the goodwill and joviality of the season. Most of these publications are quickly forgotten; and indeed, are so full of display that they deserve no better fate." Despite such lamentations about "the crowd of ostentatious and ephemeral works" that appeared at Christmastime, the seasonal story was firmly ensconced in the schedules of readers, writers, and editors alike.[77]

HOME FOR CHRISTMAS

Yet regardless of that crystallization of the literary marketplace, in the decades before the Civil War, Christmas was still a season in flux in America, and stories reflected and shaped those changes in distinctive ways. Early in the 1840s, Nathaniel Parker Willis (now a popular magazinist, as well as a former Christmas gift-book editor) still felt the need to complain, in the middle of a Christmas message to his readers, that Americans were "a monotonous people" who didn't pay enough regard to seasonal celebrations. As far as he was concerned, only New Year's Day was still widely recognized as a time away from business and worldly care. "We are sorry," he concluded, "we can not *paragraph* America into more feeling for holydays, but we may perhaps prevent a gradual desuetude of even keeping Christmas."[78] In the decades to come, American writers did exactly that, and much more besides. On the one hand, the gift book slowly fell out of favor. By 1853, *Putnam's Magazine* would offer a damning eulogy for the form: "It used to be the custom to issue, when Christmas approached, an almost endless variety of 'Gifts,' 'Remembrances,' 'Gems,' 'Tokens,' [. . .] ephemeral works, destined to perish in a few weeks; but that custom appears to be rapidly passing away."[79] Yet the scale and scope of American Christmas literature only grew, particularly in popular periodicals, and in the antebellum decades writers put Christmas to work in the service of an underpinning ideology that chimed with wider shifts in American culture.

While Lydia Maria Child may have spent her Christmas Day wandering the city streets, rhetorically and practically the season was becoming ever more focused on the home. As Stephen Nissenbaum has outlined, "What had changed [. . .] was not that the rowdier ways of celebrating Christmas had disappeared, or even that they had diminished, but that a new kind of holiday celebration, domestic and child-centered, had been fashioned and was now being claimed as the 'real' Christmas."[80] This, in turn, was of a piece with deeper changes in American culture. Christmas swiftly became emblematic of the so-called cult of domesticity which flourished in the antebellum years, just as it became a centerpiece of the enormously popular sentimental literature that promulgated its ethos to readers around the world. Susan Warner set the tone with publication of the era-defining novel *The Wide, Wide, World* (1850). The book went on sale in December, an ideal Christmas present, and alongside other sentimental tropes it featured its own lengthy depiction of its young heroine's novel experiences of a "very happy Christmas day."[81] The novel was an enormous popular success, and many of the sentimental texts that followed in its wake emulated its use of Christmas. Warner—in collaboration with her sister Anna Barlett—further compounded the link between sentimental literature and Christmas culture with the publication of *Carl Krinken: His Christmas Stocking* in 1854, an anthology for children in which Santa Claus—now established as the defining American gift-bringer—charms the toys in the stocking of a poor young boy so that each in turn can tell him a story.[82] Perhaps a little ironically, the most nakedly sentimental Christmas story featured in this collection comes from the pen of the frequently acerbic Fanny Fern, the most popular columnist of the 1850s—and Nathaniel Parker Willis's estranged sister.

As early as 1842, the popular literary newspaper *Brother Jonathan* had presented its readers with a surprisingly full account of the pleasures of a domestic American Christmas—conspicuously child-focused, with Santa at its heart—that even pre-empted Dickens:

> Tomorrow will be Christmas, jolly, rosy Christmas, the saturnalia of children. Ah! how the little rogues long for the advent of this day; for with it comes their generous friend Santa Claus, with his sleigh, like the purse of Fortunatus, even overrunning with treasures. Little sleep is had among the juveniles on the eve of Christmas, and the first sun beam, much to its surprise, peeping in at the chamber lattice, finds all astir. And then the shouts of joy as new treasures are fished up from

> the receptacle stocking, startle the elders from their morning naps, and then the embraces of love and gratitude from the little ones—surely the most cynical could not look upon such a pleasant scene as this and then join the family reunion at dinner, and the game of romp at night in the parlor without feeling the frost of his crabbedness gradually melting away before the warmth of such heart-feeling, and being ready to play leap frog with the masters, or forfeits with the misses, with all the ardor and abandon of his boyish days. All hail Christmas! say we.[83]

But how to achieve this idyll within your own home? Popular lifestyle periodicals like *Godey's Lady's Book,* edited by frequent gift-book contributor Sarah Josepha Hale, increasingly presented readers with a totalizing vision of what an idealized, domestic, middle-class Christmas should look like, a vision in which literature took a central role. Its December issue for 1857, for example, was announced as "the crowning beauty of the year." It was lavishly illustrated, boasting "*two* steel plates, never before equalled, 'The Night Before Christmas' and Christmas Morning."[84] Its fashion section offered a "charming home scene" depicting three styles suitable for children to wear on Christmas morning.[85] Its food column provided "a receipt for making Mince-pies, and several other valuable and seasonable receipts."[86] Alongside other Christmas stories and hymns, in one article the wise Aunt Sophie offered sage advice about the importance of planning this level of domestic perfection well ahead: "it is quite time, now, to begin to prepare your decorations for your tree, as it will take away from the happiness of the festive evening to know that you have neglected any duty for this pleasure." More than that, though, Aunt Sophie was keen to admonish, "you must not have one thought for your own pleasure in anything of this kind. Each must strive most earnestly to give happiness to all the rest."[87] If *Godey's* bracing juxtaposition of duty and pleasure makes the season seem like rather hard work, commentators at the time were quick to express some exasperation at these seasonal exertions. Harriet Beecher Stowe begins "The Good Fairy" (1850) with an exclamation of seasonal ennui that may still strike a chord: "Christmas is coming in a fortnight, and I have got to think up presents for every body! [. . .] Dear me, it's so tedious!"[88]

While these festive burdens fell heaviest on women, men also had to wrestle with the new demands of a domestic Christmas. In his essay "Gifts," published in 1844, Ralph Waldo Emerson pondered over "the difficulty experienced at Christmas and New Year [. . .] in bestowing gifts": "the impediment lies in the choosing. If, at any time, it comes into my head, that a present is due from me to somebody, I am puzzled what to give, until the opportunity is gone."[89] Indeed, the Transcendentalists do not seem to have been a very seasonal set, at least on the page. Margaret Fuller wished Christmas was a little "less selfish": "When shall we read of banquets prepared for the halt, the lame, and the blind, on the day that is said to have brought *their* friend into the world?"[90] The birth of her son brought about a change of heart, however: "The Christmas holidays interest me now, through my child, as they never did for myself." "You would laugh," she wrote after seeing his delight on Christmas morning, not long before both of their deaths by drowning, "to know how much remorse I feel that I never gave children more toys in the course of my life."[91] Henry David Thoreau encountered a beautiful frost on the window of Stacy's store in Concord on a November morning in 1857. He marveled at the "fancy articles and toys for Christmas and New-Year's presents," but he was adamant that "this delicate and graceful outside frosting surpassed them all infinitely."[92]

In equal contrast to the domestic cult of Christmas that dominated the antebellum years, it is on "a short, cold Christmas" day that Herman Melville sends the Pequod and its crew on their hunt for Moby Dick.[93] Yet it would be wrong to assume that the popular literature of domestic Christmases ignored the world beyond its front door any more than the wider aesthetic of which it was a part. Nina Baym's influential definition still holds true: in these texts, domesticity "is set forth as a value scheme for all of life, in competition with the ethos of money and exploitation that is perceived to prevail in American society."[94] It built a fictional world which mapped out and promoted "the whole network of human attachments based on love, support, and mutual responsibility."[95] It also allowed for visions of Christmas outside of *Godey's* normative, hermetic ideal.

A perfect example of the complex intertwining of these elements can be found in Maria Susanna Cummins's enormous best seller *The Lamp-*

lighter (1854). One of the most widely read books of the antebellum years on both sides of the Atlantic, Cummins's novel follows its orphaned heroine, Gerty, from poverty to eventual bourgeois respectability. Early in the book, Gerty is rescued from a childhood of abuse by the eponymous lamplighter, the heroic Trueman Flint—on Christmas Eve, no less. Together with his widowed neighbor Mrs. Sullivan, and her son Willie—Gerty's future husband—the four form a makeshift, alternative, improvised domestic unit that is the moral center of the novel. They celebrate Christmas together, something that is relatively new to all of them, especially the previously unloved orphan. Luckily, books are on hand to help with their sentimental education: "Gerty did not know anything about Santa Claus, that special friend of children; and Willie, who had only lately read about him in some book, undertook to tell her what he knew of the veteran toy-dealer."[96] Gerty herself is also the recipient of a gift. It is another suitably festive book which contains a frontispiece with a portrait of Santa himself in which Gerty discerns a resemblance between her rescuer and the seasonal saint: "a fur cap, a pipe, and just such a pleasant face; oh Uncle True," Gerty declares, "if you only had a sack of toys over your shoulder, instead of your lantern and that great turkey, you would be a complete Santa Claus." Thus, with the help of some seasonal reading, Gerty is acculturated simultaneously into the sensibilities of domesticity, its idealized "network of human attachments," and the ways of Christmas by those sentimental souls who have spirited her away from deprivation—and so, too, were Cummins's readers.

Christmas, therefore, became a prime moment in which to celebrate the potential of the domestic at the apex of its significance, but it was also—as Child had indicated—a time to direct its potent emotive energies for reformist purposes in the literary service of various causes. For the likes of Scott and Irving, Christmas was essentially a conservative, backward-looking celebration, embedded in times, and social orders, past; in the antebellum years, though, it was frequently put to progressive work in the present with hope for Christmases yet to come. Timothy Shay Arthur, for example—author of the hugely popular temperance novel *Ten Nights in a Bar Room* (1854)—released *A Christmas Box for the Sons and Daughters of*

Temperance in 1847. But it was the issue of abolitionism that had the strongest connection to antebellum Christmas literature. On the one hand, this was a manifestation of what P. Gabrielle Foreman has termed "sentimental abolition"—a mode that "coincides with, and borrows from the power of, the extended domestic spheres popularized in reformist communities and culture in the 1830s and 1840s; it stresses the affectional over the authoritative, emphasizing that the heart is the only true site of change and redemption."[97] It is therefore unsurprising that many of those figures closely associated with the intersection of sentimental domesticity, abolition, and other reform movements—Lydia Maria Child and Harriet Beecher Stowe in particular—were also significant promulgators of Christmas stories.

By the far the most potent juxtaposition of abolition and slavery came in the pages of the narratives written by those men and women who had themselves previously been enslaved. Christmas was a staple feature of slave narratives as Black abolitionists also sought to leverage the emotive power of the season. As Foreman has noted, if sentimental literature's insistence on the "affectional" frequently "distances it from political reform," the work of formerly enslaved authors like Frederick Douglass could exploit the mode "to explore emotive arenas in order to energise political protest."[98] The hypocrisies of the nominally Christian South were laid particularly bare at Christmastime (and not just the South: when he wrote his pivotal account of jolly St. Nick, for example, Clement Clarke Moore held five people in slavery).[99] And while fellow enslavers pointed to the days of holiday that some of the enslaved were granted at this time of year as evidence of the essential benevolence of the system, many were quick to highlight the ways in which this, too, was a coercive tool. In Frederick Douglass's famous formulation: "The holidays are part and parcel of the gross fraud, wrong, and inhumanity of slavery [. . .]. Were the slaveholders at once to abandon this practice, I have not the slightest doubt it would lead to an immediate insurrection among the slaves. These holidays serve as conductors, or safety-valves, to carry off the rebellious spirit of enslaved humanity."[100]

Conversely, the centrality of Christmas to the slave narrative often lay in its practical potential to those who worked to escape from bondage.

William and Ellen Craft, for example, explained the way that they exploited their "few days' holiday at Christmas time" to make their flight from slavery. When they arrived in Philadelphia, "we knelt down, on this Sabbath, and Christmas-day,—a day that will ever be memorable to us,—and poured out our heartfelt gratitude to God."[101] Henry Bibb, on the other hand, noted that his marriage to a woman named Malinda "took place one night during the Christmas holydays," but lamented: "Our Christmas holydays were spent in matrimonial visiting among our friends, while it should have been spent in running away to Canada, for our liberty."[102] He later used the season to attempt his own escape. Henry Box Brown was alienated from Christianity when his wife and children were sold away from him, but when he attended a service on Christmas Day, 1848, he was inspired to "snap in sunder those bonds by which I was held body and soul as the property of a fellow man" and make his own bid for freedom.[103] The three excerpts included in this anthology from works by Douglass, Harriet Jacobs, and Solomon Northup present a poignant panorama of what it meant to be enslaved at Christmastime in the antebellum South.

The intertwining of literature and abolitionism also had a tangible, physical embodiment at Christmas. First, special editions of best-selling antislavery texts like *Uncle Tom's Cabin* comprised a significant portion of the Christmas gift-book market in the 1850s. Marveling at the apparently unstoppable global progress of the book, Charles Frederick Briggs joked in *Putnam's Monthly* that "future generations of Terra-del Fuegians and Esquimaux will be making Christmas presents at this season of the year, of Uncle Tom's Cabin in holiday bindings."[104] In 1834, Lydia Maria Child edited a Christmas gift book, *The Oasis,* explicitly to support the cause.[105] At the other end of the book market, a similar intersection was discernible in the pages of sensational dime novels: Metta Victor's pioneering *Maum Guinea* (1861), Beadle and Company's "Holiday Offering" for that season, was a fictional exploration of Nat Turner's rebellion set at Christmastime on a Louisiana plantation.[106] Teresa Goddu has also highlighted the way that a new and related form of "sentimental consumerism" played out at antislavery fairs: "Held at Christmastime for the express purpose of providing presents for the holiday season, fairs [. . .] configured consumption itself as emancipatory."[107] Central to their merchandise were—almost inevitably—specially produced gift books, "among the most revered objects at antislavery fairs," which served as "tokens of friendship (exchanged as Christmas and New Year's gifts)."[108]

Keenly attuned to the shifts in Christmas culture, the 1842 Boston Anti-Slavery Fair even featured the novelty of a Christmas tree. Prominent abolitionist Maria Weston Chapman breathlessly described the spectacle in the pages of the *Liberator,* looping the innovation back into textual culture: "A young pine-tree of the exact height of the Hall was brought triumphantly in, and hung with gilded apples, glittering strings of nuts and almonds, tissue paper purses of the gayest dyes filled with glittering egg-baskets and crystals of many coloured sugar—with every possible needlebook, pincushion, bag, basket, cornucopia, pen-wiper, book-mark, box and doll, that could be afforded for ninepence." So eager were the Boston crowds to catch a sight of this spectacle that "thousands, it is said, went away disappointed. But to those who did obtain entrance, the blaze of the Christmas Tree was a spectacle even beyond the bright expectations they had formed." Chapman ended her description with an exhortation to "KEEP NEXT CHRISTMAS IN MIND, YOUNG FRIENDS," promising another Christmas tree which would "flame like a new constellation in the moral firmament."[109]

Yet the power of Christmas to sway hearts and minds could cut both ways. Its potential was also understood by those white southern writers who attempted to push back against abolitionist rhetoric. Increasingly, the South prided itself on the apparent longevity of its Christmas celebrations, especially when contrasted with the lingering Puritanical squeamishness of its northern neighbors, and claimed it as a mark of both regional distinctiveness and sectional superiority. In his account of *Social Relations in Our Southern States* (1860), Daniel Hundley proclaimed that Christmas "has always been a day of much greater renown in the South than in the North. Of late years, 'tis true, the Free States are changing in this regard very much, but still there is not in them that general *abandon,* that universal merry-making which always characterises Christmas in the slave states."[110] These partisan myths of southern Christmases created their own distinctive print culture. Prominent antebellum southern writer William

Gilmore Simms, for example, released the short novel *The Golden Christmas* in 1852, at the same moment that Harriet Beecher Stowe was serializing *Uncle Tom's Cabin.* A comic account of festivities in the Old South, Simms's book was also an explicit defense of the region, picturing Christmas as a time which exemplified the way that "the institution of Southern slavery" was marked by "charity" and "permitted play and pleasure" and was therefore ultimately "agreeable."[111] Simms's Christmas propaganda even extended to a sectional blast about the presiding spirit of the season. In the South, Simms asserted, children were visited by Father Christmas: "Our saint is an English, not a Dutch saint," he explained, "a much more respectable person, in our imagination, than the dapper little Manhattan goblin whom they call Santa Claus."[112] Not that these views were contained within the region. In 1847, for example, *Godey's Lady's Book* had published another Christmas story by Simms—"Maize In Milk, A Christmas Story of the South"—which promoted the same racist fictions about the season and its relationship to slavery.[113]

When Civil War came, both North and South conscripted Christmas and its popular avatars for literary service. It is telling that Christmas was sufficiently embedded in national life and literary culture that, even in the midst of war, Americans tried to celebrate. As *Harper's New Monthly Magazine* noted in January 1864, "the Christmas holidays are here. Holidays they still are, although they come while the war rages." Indeed, according to *Harper's,* Christmas now took on a new significance: "The ancient hilarity of Christmas should take—it does take—a deeper, brighter glow."[114] That same Christmas, what might be considered the first modern Santa, as depicted by illustrator Thomas Nast, made his debut appearance on the cover of *Harper's Weekly,* decked out in Stars and Stripes and giving presents to Union soldiers (fig. 5).[115] For men fighting away from home, Christmas was rarely so jolly. In one of the few accounts of front-line soldiering actually published contemporaneously, Ebenezer Hannaford lamented: "Christmas came to us in camp at last. Christmas-day, but not good old Christmas times—social, generous, 'merry Christmas!' To us it was only December 25, 1862."[116] In the ensuing battle of Stones River, which commenced on New Year's Eve, Hannaford was wounded and hospitalized. Perhaps if he was

Figure 5. Thomas Nast, *Santa in Camp,* from *Harper's Weekly,* January 3, 1863.

lucky, he ended up in a ward of the sort that Louisa May Alcott described in "A Hospital Christmas," a story included in this collection. Alcott's vision of seasonal celebrations in a Civil War sanatorium, based on her own experiences of nursing, is a potent one: as Elizabeth Young has described, it levers the emotive power of the season during wartime to propose "a systematic model of female governance in which men are not only led by female authority but are taught to internalise female virtues of sympathy, sacrifice, and self-restraint." It was, in many ways, a last Utopian hurrah for the all-encompassing "triumph of domesticity."[117]

Perhaps the most radical changes that the war brought to American print culture were in the realm of children's literature. Both sides weaponized the season as it bore on the reading habits of the young. As James Marten has described, "Whether it was seen as an evil or as an inspiration, the Civil War penetrated, invigorated, and politicized children's magazines, North and South."[118] In "Christmas, After All," published in *The Little Pilgrim* in April 1862, for example, a group of siblings who are "tired to death of Christmas presents" club together to help the escape from slavery of the daughter of their "dear old negro nurse," Aunt Thula.[119] At the same time, as Alice Fahs has described, "war novels [. ..] also became popular with children." At Christmastime, this had a significant effect on youthful literary culture. Fahs gives the example of Grenville Norcross, who kept a journal of his wartime reading: "For Christmas in 1863 [. . .] Grenville received the war correspondent Charles Carleton Coffin's *My Days and Nights on the Battlefield.* For Christmas in 1864, he received Oliver Optic's novel *The Sailor Boy* from his father as well as its companion volume, *The Soldier Boy,* from his aunt."[120] In the South, where resources and publishers were scarcer, these trends were still present. But to rationalize sparsely filled stockings, some further rhetorical gestures were also required. The *Richmond Examiner* informed its young readers, echoing Simms's comments from before the war, that Santa Claus was nothing more than "a dutch-toy monger, an immigrant from England, a transflated scrub into New York and New England."[121] Yet it was also in a children's magazine—*Our Young Folks,* which launched during the war—that Longfellow chose to publish "Christmas Bells," his prescient celebration of the end of the conflict, a few months before the cessation of hostilities:

> I heard the bells on Christmas Day
> Their old, familiar carols play,
> And wild and sweet
> The words repeat
> Of peace on earth, good-will to men![122]

This was not the only way that Longfellow would feature in the nation's Christmas celebrations: in the 1880s his image appeared on a Christmas card released by Louis Prang's pioneering company as part of an American literature series, also featuring tributes to Whittier and Bryant.[123]

In 1866, the war over, Lydia Maria Child returned to the subject of Christmas. For the same children's magazine where Longfellow had published his hopes for peace, she told a tale of "The Two Christmas Evenings." Twenty years after she had introduced her readers to the modernizing and unfamiliar celebration that she found in the streets of New York, Child marked the literary changes by crafting a story that contained all of the tropes of a now-established sentimental, domestic Christmas. The story opens on Christmas Eve; while a "light snow" falls outside, Mrs. Rich's parlor is brilliantly ornamented by "an Evergreen Tree, with a sparkling crown of little lamps, and gay with festoons of ribbons and trinkets."[124] Children and parents gather around the tree, and presents are exchanged—a now common scene, richly illustrated. Of course, there are lessons to be learned—the blessing of giving rather than receiving, particularly to orphans and "the freed children"; the joy of making rather than consuming; and above all, in this postwar moment, the importance of understanding that "Liberty ought to be proclaimed to all."[125] Yet what might appear to have been settled was really in flux again: as America reshaped itself in the wake of the Civil War, the way it told its Christmas stories would also change accordingly.

RECONSTRUCTING CHRISTMAS

When Charles Dickens died in 1870—the same year that Ulysses Grant officially signed Christmas into existence as a federal holiday—American writers offered up appropriately seasonal elegies. Before his death, the man himself had apparently tired of the merry monster that he had created. In 1868, he grumbled to a correspondent, "I have invented so many of these Christmas Nos, and they are so profoundly unsatisfactory [. . .] that I fear I am sick of the thing."[126] Countless others were ready to pick up his mantle.

In the year of Dickens's death, Constance Fenimore Woolson paid poetic tribute to the "one who told the Christmas story / With matchless loving art" for *Harper's Bazaar:*

> The kindly heart is still; the voice is silent;
> No more we wait to hear
> The magic accents of the Great Enchanter,
> The story-teller dear;
> But from the stormy shore of dark Atlantic
> To fair Pacific's wave
> Thousands of hearts will send a Christmas blessing
> To rest on Dickens' grave.[127]

A year later, she included another eulogy in her intertextual seasonal story, "A Merry Christmas": "on this Christmas-day," one of her characters declares, "there will be many a sigh over the missing Christmas story, and many a kindly memory of the man to whom Christmas was a real festival, full of love, peace, and good-will toward men. Friends, let us drink to the genius of Christmas—to the memory of our dear lost friend, Charles Dickens."[128] The significance of a Dickensian Christmas for Woolson was apparently more than just literary artifice. Declining an invitation from friends, she spent Christmas Day 1893 alone in Venice, rereading *A Christmas Carol,* less than a month before her apparent suicide.[129]

In a clear tribute to Dickens, children's magazine *Our Boys and Girls* published a brief dramatization of *A Christmas Carol* suitable "for home representation" in its 1870 Christmas issue.[130] Yet at the same time, veneration was not universal. For *Scribner's* 1871 Christmas number, magazinist Frank Stockton published what was a clear burlesque of Dickens's most famous Christmas story, and the genre more broadly, in a story which featured the moral reform of an "unsympathetic, selfish" landlord called "Stephen Skarridge" who is prompted to a new sense of charity by the visitation of a fairy, a giant, a dwarf, and a talking mackerel.[131] Reviewing the issue, the *Nation* noted that, more broadly, "the Scrooge and Marley, Tiny Tim and Bob Cratchit, variety of Christmas makes rather less of a figure in the

January magazines than it has made in some years," and pondered whether the vital presence of Dickens himself and his "effusiveness of sentiment" had been needed to "keep in countenance the kind-hearted writers whose milk of human kindness it must have been a somewhat discouraging business to set out in such quantities before the uneffusive American."[132]

The postwar years were, then, a time of change for the relationship between Christmas and American writers. Two of the most important developments can be found in the juxtaposition of the two excerpts above. On the one hand, the postwar years were an explosive moment for the development of American children's writing, and Christmas helped to power that boom. As Eugene Giddens has asserted, "The Christmas market played a large part in the emergence of the 'golden age' of children's literature."[133] Fresh from writing her iconic vision of Christmas in a military hospital during the Civil War, Louisa May Alcott helped to inspire the deep connection between children's literature and the holiday season with the preliminary scenes of *Little Women* (1868). Its opening line remains one of the most resonant in American literary history: "'Christmas won't be Christmas without any presents,' grumbled Jo, lying on the rug."[134] Taking up the mantle of the antebellum domestic sentimentalists, those writing for American children understood its profound appeal to the young and seized upon the spiritual, moral, and literary potential of Christmas. Festive scenes feature in all of the best-selling children's books of this era. In the wake of *Little Women, What Katy Did* (1872) features "a pleasant Christmas [. . .] the nicest they had ever had."[135] (Amongst other gifts, Katy herself receives a copy of Susan Warner's *The Wide, Wide World,* cementing the literary legacies inherent in these scenes.) In Martha Finley's *Elsie Dinsmore* (1867), which generated twenty-eight sequels over the next four decades, her heroine is also given a book at Christmas—though Elsie's domineering father rules that Elsie must be content "with looking at the pictures; [. . .] the stories are very unsuitable for a little girl of your age."[136] In the equally significant *Five Little Peppers and How They Grew* (1881), another children's best seller that spawned a raft of sequels well into the twentieth century, a long sequence dominates the heart of the book in which the poverty-stricken Peppers attempt to "try Christmas" for the first time.[137] An excerpt is included in this collection. And one of the first books written by Kate Douglas Wiggin, author of *Rebecca of Sunnybrook Farm* (1903), was *The Birds' Christmas Carol* (1888), a popular seasonal story about a dying child.

No less important was Mary Mapes Dodge's establishment of *St Nicholas Magazine* in November 1873: the most prestigious children's periodical of the late nineteenth century carried a name that kept Christmas in the minds of its young readers all year long. Dodge explained the rationale for this decision in her opening editorial. St Nicholas's brand values—whether her readers knew him as "Santa Claus, Kriss Kringle, St. Nick" or any of his other "pet names"—were an important marketing tool:

> Hurrah for dear St. Nicholas! He has made us friends in a moment. And no wonder. Is he not the boys' and girls' own Saint, the especial friend of young Americans? [. . .] Another thing you know: He is fair and square. He comes when he says he will. At the very outset he decided to visit our boys and girls every Christmas; and doesn't he do it? [. . .] What a host of wonderful stories are told about him—you may hear them all some day—and what loving, cheering thoughts follow in his train! He has attended so many heart-warmings in his long, long day that he glows without knowing it, and, coming as he does, at a holy time, casts a light upon the children's faces that lasts from year to year. Never to dim this light, young friends, by word or token, to make it even brighter, when we can, in good, pleasant, helpful ways, and to clear away clouds that sometimes shut it out, is our aim and prayer.[138]

In turn, children's magazines like *St. Nicholas* became a regular venue for the distribution of new seasonal stories and articles which helped to develop a potent Christmas sensibility in young readers (fig. 6).

On the other hand, the rather more cynical trends discernible in "Stephen Skarridge" were crucial to the shifting landscape of American literature at this time of change. As literary realism came to challenge sentiment's domination of the textual marketplace, it may be expected that Christmas became less significant as a subject, so closely associated was it with the elevation of the domestic and the emotive. In part, this was

SANTA CLAUS AND HIS MEN.

By C. A. Lynde.

A curious place is Old Santa Claus' den,
All stor'd full of treasures ; where queer little men,
No larger than drumsticks, yet active and bright,
Are busily working from morning till night.

These queer little fellows, these workmen so small,
All answer with pleasure Old Santa Claus' call
For " Fifty more bonbons, one hundred more toys !
More names on my list of good girls and good boys ! "

" Here, merrily ho ! " he gleefully cries ;
" My sled is all ready—make haste, the time flies !
My reindeer are prancing and pawing the snow ;
Make haste there, make haste, we're impatient to go ! "

Soon the bundles are packed with the greatest of care.
Then off spring the reindeer, on ! on ! thro' the air,
Till they stop at some home, where snug in their bed
Sleep Cora and Mabel, or Willie and Fred.

When the children awake at dawn's early light,
And steal from their beds, how they 'll scream with delight
On beholding their stockings, they hung on the wall,
With treasures o'erflowing, and something for all.

Figure 6. Christmas content for children from *St. Nicholas Magazine*, January 1875.

the case, and—fresh from battlefields of the Civil War—Christmas was conscripted again into the literary wars that erupted in the postwar decades. The issue of Christmas sat right at the heart of transatlantic debates circulating at this time, particularly as they played out in the thinking of William Dean Howells. As editor and writer, Howells did more than anyone to promote the realist aesthetic in America. He also spent more time than most contemplating the significance of the relationship between literature and Christmas, thereby centering it in both the literary arguments surrounding realism and a war of words taking place between American and Britain at this moment.

Howells had already upset the English a few years earlier when, in a profile of Henry James, he had made an unflattering comparison between his American contemporaries and a previous generation of writers back across the Atlantic: "The art of fiction has [. . .] become a finer art in our day than it was with Dickens and Thackeray."[139] His Christmas cogitations were a continuation of that argument. In January 1887, for example, Howells surveyed the "widely established [. . .] literary worship of Christmas." While he credited Irving and "his New World love of the past" for laying the groundwork, he also admitted that it was Dickens who "divined its immense advantage as a literary occasion." But that was as far as the praise went. Indeed, despite allowing for Dickens's "great talent," Howells forcefully blamed him for "the creation of holiday literature as we have known it for the last half-century." Looking back over Dickens's Christmas books, Howells discovers a catalog of literary sins that seem to exemplify all that he was attempting to abolish from American letters: "The pathos appears false and strained; the humor largely horse-play; the character theatrical; the joviality pumped; the psychology commonplace; the sociology alone funny." The stories at least had "ethical dignity"—something which his "circle of imitators" had apparently abandoned. According to Howells, in Dickens's wake holiday literature had been "abandoned" to "a whole school of unrealities so ghastly that one can hardly recall without a shudder those sentimentalities at second-hand." This, too, was another sign of America's literary superiority over the Old World. While festive short stories still abounded in America, the Christmas book was no longer a phenomenon—Howells asserted, as an example, "we cannot conceive of Mark Twain's writing a holiday opuscule for the subscription trade."[140] In this respect, at least, Howells wasn't wrong. Outside of his family circle, where he was known to write letters from Santa to his daughters, Twain's cynical pronouncement on the season in *Following the Equator* (1897) chimed with Howells's conclusions: "The approach of Christmas brings harrassment and dread to many excellent people. They have to buy a cart-load of presents, and they never know what to buy to hit the various tastes; they put in three weeks of hard and anxious work, and when Christmas morning comes they are so dissatisfied with the result, and so disappointed that they want to sit down and cry. Then they give thanks that Christmas comes but once a year."[141] Howells himself was not above writing a Christmas story, though, and his gently satirical "Christmas Every Day" is included in this collection.

In *Harper's New Monthly Magazine* in December 1889, Howells put forward another suggestion designed to reform the Christmas literary landscape. Striving to promote the idea of a truly distinctive American seasonal canon, Howells drew some lines of comparison between Thanksgiving and Christmas stories. "Generally," he asserted, "the Thanksgiving story is cheerfuler in its drama and simpler in its persons than the Christmas story." Still, it was also "more restricted in its range; the scene is still mostly in New England." One was provincial and Puritan, the other universal and with strong roots in the South. Howells was still even tempted to see the Christmas story as, truly, an "English cousin," "transplanted" rather than fully American. Howells therefore put forward the suggestion of "a gradual fusion of the literature proper to Christmas and the literature proper to Thanksgiving in a literature proper to both"—something that took in the sensibilities and traditions of both holidays. In part, he presumed to speak on behalf of the wider publishing world with this novelty: "We think every editor will agree with us that some such combine, or rather pooling of issues, is desirable, for [. . .] it is plain that there must soon come a moment of absolute dearth in the material unless it is more carefully husbanded." In short, as far as Howells was concerned, the ubiquitous sentimental seasonal story was exhausted. As he saw it, in Gilded Age America, "the chance of reforming a stony-hearted miser through the influence of a Christmas dinner, with any decent degree of probability, is growing so small that it must be more sparingly taken in the future, if any hold is to be kept upon even the easy credulity of the average story-reader." The larger goal was of a piece with Howells's wider literary ambitions: American writers, he argued, should "turn to human life and observe how it is really affected on these holidays, and be tempted to present some of its actualities. This would be a great thing to do, and would come home to readers with surprise."[142]

While the hybrid Thanksgiving-Christmas story never caught on,

American writers undoubtedly did infuse the Christmas literary landscape with a new realist impetus in the latter decades of the nineteenth century. Proving to be a surprisingly resilient and adaptable genre, Christmas stories took on new forms and were put to a variety of purposes—stimulated, no doubt, by the boom in magazine publishing across this period. As early as 1884, looking back over the annals of Christmas, Charles Dudley Warner—writer, editor, Mark Twain's neighbor and collaborator—could note the abundance of "Christmas literature in the past dozen years," and conclude, with another implicit transatlantic swipe, "We have saved out of the past nearly all that was good in it, and the revived Christmas of our time is no doubt better than the old. [. . .] never before in history was Christmas kept so truly and heartily in the spirit of the day as it is now."[143]

Certainly, American writers did not retreat from the subject, and many of them took up Howells's challenge to attend to the "actualities" of the season. Henry James had rather more affection for the season and its literature than Howells, one which lay deep at the root of his Anglophilia. "In those days," James remembered of his childhood, "in America, the manufacture of children's picture-books was an undeveloped industry." Even as a child, James felt "the best things came from London, and brought with them the aroma of a richer civilization." In particular, he remembered "the dazzling tone of a little Christmas book"—John Leech's *Young Troublesome; or, Master Jacky's Holidays* (circa 1850)—whose scapegrace protagonist "seemed to lead a life all illumined with rosy Christmas fire."[144] In later life, having crossed the Atlantic himself, James remained alive to the literary associations of Christmas. After all, *The Turn of the Screw* (1898) was James's own contribution to the genre of the Christmas ghost story. Yet he also celebrated "the social desolation of Christmas week" in London, when "the country-houses are filled at the expense of the metropolis," and hymned the delights of the "friendly fog" and the "big fires" in the city's clubs. "Then it is," he confessed, "that I am most haunted with the London of Dickens, feel most as if it were still recoverable, still exhaling its queerness in patches perceptible to the appreciative." It was also, he thought, "the best time for writing."[145] In this volume, however, we take a trip out of the city with James, as he reflects on a rather less cheery festive season in England in 1879—a negative image of Irving's antiquarian delights in the *Sketch Book.*

The transition between sentiment and realism can also be traced in the stories in this volume by Rebecca Harding Davis and Bret Harte. In these sketches, sitting on the cusp of literary realism, these writers push Christmas into new dimensions both geographical—Harte's enormously popular take on the West—and social—Davis's bleak, hard-edged portrait of poverty, prostitution, and seasonal suffering. Harte's western Christmas also points to a literary lineage that includes the pioneering work of Owen Wister who, not long before the genre-defining publication of *The Virginian* in 1902, published a cowboy Christmas story, "A Journey in Search of Christmas," in 1898. A gift edition lavishly illustrated by Frederic Remington was released in 1904.[146] Another facet of literary realism can be found in the work of local color writers, here represented by Mary Wilkins Freeman and Alice Dunbar-Nelson. If the local colorists were partial heirs to the sentimentalists, they were also part of the realist project, and their distinctive, regional Christmas visions were uniquely positioned between those poles in the postwar years. Jana Tigchelaar has compellingly argued, in her analysis of some of the many Christmas stories of Freeman and her contemporary Sarah Orne Jewett, that these sketches actually imagined "an alternative" to the "specific national narrative" of the "domestic Christmas" forged in the antebellum years. What Tigchelaar terms the "neighborly Christmas" refocuses readers' attention "to the needs of the community (both economic and social) and the moral obligation to recognise those who fall outside of the domestic family unit."[147]

Literary debates, implicit and explicit, were hardly the only controversies which animated Christmas literature in the Gilded Age. Longstanding arguments, stretching back to the first Christmases in America, continued apace. The religious controversy over the reason for the season was powerfully enlivened in the last decades of the century. In the 1890s, Robert G. Ingersoll—the famous orator and writer known as "The Great Agnostic" for his attacks on organized religion—stirred up controversy by writing a number of articles attempting to wrestle the season away from the faithful entirely, two of which are reproduced in this anthology. In

1891, he entered the fray by publishing an alternative, secular Christmas sermon which began by proclaiming, "The good part of Christmas is not always Christian—it is generally Pagan; that is to say, human, natural." Not that Ingersoll objected to the holiday itself: "I believe in Christmas," he proclaimed, "and in every day that has been set apart for joy. We in America have too much work and not enough play." Moreover, Christmas was a moment "to forgive and forget [. . .] to throw away prejudices and hatred."[148] The ensuing controversy—threats to boycott the newspaper that published it, accusations that Ingersoll was "dropping [. . .] poison" in the cup of "Christian family joys," but also support for his position—was sufficiently protracted to result in the publication of a collection of the voluminous correspondence generated by Ingersoll's sermon.[149] Undeterred, he returned to his theme in ensuing festive seasons. In 1897, for example, Ingersoll published "What I Want for Christmas," a list which started with the abdication of all kings, emperors, and priests and ended with a desire "to see the whole world free—free from injustice—free from superstition." At least, Ingersoll concluded, "This will do for next Christmas. The following Christmas, I may want more."[150]

Yet despite Ingersoll's best efforts—and in part because of them, and others like him—the last decades of the century were also the moment that the faithful came to enjoy a reinvigorated relationship with Christmas. Of course, sectarian strife aside, religion had always been part of the American idea of Christmas, and devotional poems and hymns littered popular journals in the antebellum years. Harriet Prescott Spofford, for example, published a nativity poem—"Ah! Said the lowly shepherd then / The Seraph sang good-will to men"—in *Our Young Folks* in December 1865.[151] But the lingering denominational disagreements about the probity of winter festivities meant that the sacred had previously been less centered in American seasonal literature than the domestic, the familial, the human. Increasingly, though, religion, and particularly the story of the Nativity, became newly central to the popular literature of Christmas.

With no little irony, Ingersoll himself was personally responsible for this revival. In 1876, when both men were traveling to a Civil War reunion, Ingersoll struck up a conversation with General Lew Wallace. Inevitably, the talk turned to religion. Confronted with the frankness of Ingersoll's controversial agnosticism, Wallace was thrown into a spiritual crisis, one which had profound consequences for the direction of the relationship between literature, religion, and Christmas. As he recalled in his autobiography:

> I had been listening to discussion which involved such elemental points as God, heaven, life hereafter, Jesus Christ, and His divinity. Trudging on in the dark, alone except as one's thoughts may be company, good or bad, a sense of the importance of the theme struck me for the first time with a force both singular and persistent. My ignorance of it was painfully a spot of deeper darkness in the darkness. I was ashamed of myself, and make haste now to declare that the mortification of pride I then endured, or if it be preferred, the punishment of spirit, ended in a resolution to study the whole matter, if only for the gratification there might be in having convictions of one kind or another.[152]

The direct result of Wallace's ensuing studies was the novel *Ben Hur* (1880)—alongside Stowe's *Uncle Tom's Cabin,* one of the great American best sellers of all time. The first section of Wallace's book, initially conceived and later released as a volume in and of itself, was a profoundly influential retelling of the Nativity, a portion of which is included in this volume. By transforming the first Christmas into literary fiction, Wallace set a recognizable template that lives with us today. This was a timely endeavor. As Barbara Ryan and Milette Shamir have noted, "The postbellum era was a time of huge ferment for the Bible and of marvelous artistic creativity in relation to it."[153] Writers both sacred and profane were responding to the emergence of higher biblical criticism earlier in the century—works like Ernest Renan's best seller *Vie de Jésus* (1863) which attempted to empirically uncover the historical underpinnings of the Gospels and the real man behind the biblical Jesus. The Christmas story did not fare well in Renan's hands: he stated unequivocally that "Jesus was born at Nazareth," assigning the Bethlehem Nativity story the status of "awkward [. . .] legend."[154] While many of the faithful responded with horror at these apparently heretical endeavors, the approach of the higher biblical critics was impossible to entirely ignore. In particular, literary accounts of the life of Jesus—sacred and secular—became an increasingly popular and fraught literary subject. Yet the paucity of biblical material relating to the Nativity was a problem for these writers, too. When Henry Ward Beecher joined the throng with his popular *The Life of Jesus, The Christ,* in 1871, he covered the first Christmas in ten relatively unromantic pages. "The laying of the little babe in the manger," Beecher explained, "is not to be regarded then as an extraordinary thing, or a positive hardship. It was merely subjecting the child to a custom which peasants frequently practised." After all, Beecher noted, "our own children have slept there in our rude summer retreats on the mountain."[155] But then, he never was a fan of Christmas anyway.

Wallace's innovation in *Ben Hur* was to use the brief canonical accounts of Christ's birth as a springboard for his own fiction. Conjuring up an immersive biblical landscape, Wallace gave readers a fully realized world in which they could experience the Nativity on a rich, textured, human level. As Jefferson J. A. Gatrall has noted, Wallace "transforms seven verses from Matthew into a novella-length narrative through the aid of biblical geography, ethnography, astronomy, and comparative religion, among other academic disciplines."[156] In so doing, he found an enormous audience for decades to come. Wallace opened the doors of still suspicious homes to the celebration of Christ's birth at Christmastime and reestablished the icons of the Nativity in the minds of Americans. And Wallace wasn't done with Christmas either. In December 1886, he published "The Boyhood of Christ" in the Christmas issue of *Harper's*—a tale, set on Christmas Eve, which delved into the youthful experiences of Jesus in similar style.[157]

Wallace's deep influence can be found in a diverse range of literary Christmases. In "A Christmas Guest," first published in the *Century* in December 1894, Ruth McEnery Stuart leavened a comic monologue with gentle allusions to the Nativity. The narrator—a rustic father whose first child has just been born—marvels that his son has arrived on such an auspicious day: "laws-a-mercy me! Ef-to-day-ain't been Christmas! [. . .] I've had many a welcome Christmas-gif' in my life, but the idee o' the good Lord a-timin' *this* like that." At the end of the story, the proud father falls asleep next to his new arrival, drowsily favored with a Christmas vision: "Blest ef I don't hear singing—an' how white the moonlight is! They's angels all over the house—an' their robes is breshin' the roof whiles they sing."[158] In this collection, Wallace's influence can be seen in Frank Norris's curiosity "Miracle Joyeux," from the Christmas issue of *McClure's Magazine* in 1898. Norris is best known as a literary naturalist, and this sketch of Christ's boyhood may seem an unlikely choice of subject for him. Yet as Steven Bembridge has demonstrated, Norris was in direct conversation with Wallace in this sketch. On the one hand, he felt *Ben Hur* was the best novel "yet produced by an American author," though he also lamented that "nothing is more unoriginal and hackneyed than the narrative of the New Testament."[159] In an early version of this story, the boyish Christ—as in apocryphal infancy gospels—was capricious and cruel in his use of his powers. *McClure's* asked for a rewrite before agreeing to publish it. Even then, those tensions are still discernible in the idiosyncrasy of Norris's contribution to the Christmas genre.

Southern writers continued to lean heavily on the emotive, nostalgic powers of Christmas in order to promote a certain vision of the region. Just as the season had been used as propaganda for the system of slavery in the antebellum years, so Christmas was exploited in the promotion of Lost Cause mythology—the attempt to portray the defeated Old South and the carceral landscape of the plantation in a nostalgic and benevolent light. As Robert E. May has highlighted, "Between Reconstruction's end in the mid-1870s and the Roaring Twenties, a veritable legion of southern white memoirists, essayists, novelists, folklorists, children's writers and editorialists [. . .] forged a genre of stereotypical slave Christmas idylls glorifying the coercive labour system that lay at the root of their antebellum society and the recent Civil War. [. . .] Appearing in works aimed at children readers and listeners as well as in adult magazines and books, they had a cradle-to-grave impact."[160] The South may have lost the war, but it could be argued that it won this Christmas battle.

Irwin Russell's vernacular poem "Christmas-Night in the Quarters" was one of the harbingers when it was published in *Scribner's Monthly* in January 1878. Accompanied by minstrel illustrations and written in comic dialect, it depicted "high carnival" on a benevolent plantation on Christmas night and imagined even Santa Claus "grieving" to be "His own dear Land of Cotton leaving" at the end of the celebrations.[161] Arch Lost-Causer John Esten Cooke lauded "Christmas Time in Old Virginia" for the *Magazine of American History* in December 1883, laying a claim for the soul of the season while spreading racist tropes: "Each and all seem to have greeted it as a time of mirth and good will to men, and this influence of the season is perhaps as strong in the nineteenth century as the olden time"—for even "the poor African, with no intelligence whatever," he explained, will "still cling with obstinate tenacity to the old Christmas legend."[162] Susan Dabney Smedes's sentimental, nostalgic, and very popular *Memories of a Southern Planter* (1887) contained numerous seasonal reminiscences of Christmas on her father's plantation: "It was as looked forward to not only by the family and by friends in the neighborhood and at a distance, but by the house and plantation servants."[163] Joel Chandler Harris concluded *Nights with Uncle Remus* (1883) with a wistful sketch of "The Night Before Christmas" on the plantation: "There was pleasure in the big house, and pleasure in the humble cabins in the quarters." Rebecca Cameron evoked "Christmas On An Old Plantation" for the *Ladies' Home Journal* in 1891.[164] Thomas Nelson Page, whose stories and novels were central to the widespread popularity of the plantation myth, wrote multiple seasonal stories that ventriloquized the formerly enslaved in their effusions for the memory of a "Christmas so long ago [. . .] a Christmas like you been read 'bout!"[165] And there were, indeed, many to read about. These were the visions of southern Christmases that circulated widely through mainstream, national publications at the end of the nineteenth century—and well beyond.

Just as in the antebellum years, though, Black American writers pushed back against that overwhelming tide. As Bettye Collier-Thomas has noted, "Journalists, intellectuals, and various activists perceived Christmas as a perfect time to capture the attention of black readers," particularly to question "America's commitment to its black citizens."[166] In this collection, Pauline Hopkins's story "General Washington" uses an act of racial violence on Christmas Day to explicitly attack white supremacy—and imagine its possible rehabilitation. But Hopkins was not alone. It is a sign of Christmas literature's significance in this arena that one of the few pieces of fiction written by the activist and reformer Ida B. Wells was "Two Christmas Days" (1899), a holiday romance infused with hopeful racial uplift. In another Christmas essay written for the *New York Freeman,* Wells roused her fellow women to "help men" to better understand the purpose of the festive season: "to feel that there is a [. . .] purer, nobler, more fitting way of celebrating this anniversary of His birth, than in drunken debauchery and midnight carousals; recall to their minds the poor and needy, the halt and blind that are always with us and who stand in need of Christmas cheer."[167] As the century drew to a close, other groups who were excluded from the dominant narratives of an American Christmas staked a claim to the rhetorical power of the season. In this collection, Charles Alexander Eastman, born into the Santee Sioux tribe in 1858, remembers his experiences of the massacre at Wounded Knee at Christmastime in 1890; Abraham Cahan explores the difficult questions of accommodation that the holiday posed for its new Jewish citizens; and Jacob Riis, perhaps best known for his muckraking photographs of urban poverty, crafts a tale of Christmas in the heterogenous tenements of immigrant New York that evokes Lydia Maria Child's pedestrian tour of the city fifty years previously. So much had changed, and so much, including the urban deprivation, remained the same. But it was still Christmas, Riis noted, "with the old cheer, the old message of good-will, the old royal road to the heart."[168]

GHOSTS OF CHRISTMAS PAST

This account of Christmas literature's extraordinary transformations across the nineteenth century began with a house call between two antiquarians intent on reimagining a lost Golden Age of seasonal festivities back into existence. It ends with a house party, and an equally transatlantic and allusive collaboration. In 1899, Stephen Crane moved to Brede Place, a crumbling medieval pile in East Sussex. Though debt-ridden and dying, he and his companion Cora Stewart hosted an elaborate Christmas celebration that drew in their literary friends and neighbors from both sides of the Atlantic: Henry James, Joseph Conrad, H. G. Wells, H. Rider Haggard, and many more. "Surely there has never been such a house party," remembered the British journalist Charles Lewis Hind. "The ancient house, in spite of its size, was taxed to the uttermost."[169] H. G. Wells and his wife were grateful to secure "a room over the main gateway in which there was a portcullis and an owl's nest." It was, he recalled, "an extraordinary lark."[170] In a setting fit for the kind of festivities imagined by Irving and Scott decades before, their literary heirs undertook an extraordinary, ephemeral piece of Christmas writing that marked an end to the century. Having gathered so many extraordinary talents under one leaky roof, Crane set them to work on a collaborative play he called—with a suitable nod to Dickens—"The Ghost." Crane had been preparing for months: in November, he had sent out letters to the great and the good, asking them "to write a mere word—any word 'it,' 'they,' 'you,'—any word and thus identify themselves with this crime." The list of collaborating authors printed on the final program would therefore be a "terrible [. . .] distinguished rabble." Crane combined their efforts, however meager, with his own. The ensuing "awful rubbish," full of in-jokes and allusions, was performed—for one night only—as "a free play to the villagers at Christmas time in the school-house" at Brede on the evening of December 28, 1899.[171] Unpublished and unrepeated—if not unrepeatable—the play itself now only exists in fragments, and most of the contributions are unidentifiable. "It amused its authors and cast vastly," Wells concluded, "What the Brede people made of it is not on record."[172] The next evening, the Christmas party was broken up when Crane's health deteriorated and he suffered a tubercular hemorrhage, a prelude of his death a few months later. And so, with a last hurrah, the last literary Christmas of the 1800s faded into memory.

In this collection, however, the ghosts of Christmas past live again. What I hope emerges from this festive chorus is much more than the ossified seasonal scene that we might expect: dusty ornaments, faded cards, stale feasts from yesteryear. Rather, I hope readers will be surprised at the multiplicity of perspectives on display. Those modern readers looking for antiquarian pleasures beyond Dickens will find much to enjoy here. But these stories also provide a shock of recognition—and perhaps reassurance—that the same concerns and tensions that animate the festive season today were equally felt by those living in the nineteenth century. In these stories, people lament the commercialization of the season, agonize about selecting presents for loved ones, argue about its spiritual significance, flagrantly politicize the holidays, and use this time of year to highlight inequities that seemed even more stark when displayed against a festive backdrop. I hope, too, it will help to reshape our understanding of the relationship between Christmas and literature as it developed across the American nineteenth century—and beyond. Far from being peripheral or occasional, Christmas sat at the heart of the changing literary landscape in America throughout this crucial period. In 1888, in the "Editor's Drawer" of *Harper's New Monthly Magazine,* Charles Dudley Warner declared that Christmas was "one of the most serious events of modern life." He also worried that its now firmly established popularity meant that America ran the characteristic risk of "running a thing into the ground"—which would be a pity, "because it would be next to impossible to make another holiday as good as Christmas."[173] He needn't have worried. The Christmas forged in these stories is the foundation for our own contemporary Christmas culture in ways both big and small. Still today, we are haunted by the ghosts of Christmas past conjured up by the writers in this volume. They come with tidings of comfort and joy, but they also, like any good Christmas spirits, offer lessons from which we can learn.

NOTES

1. "Topics of the Time: Christmas," *Century Magazine,* December 1888, 311–12.

2. Penne L. Restad, *Christmas in America: A History* (New York: Oxford University Press, 1995), viii. See also Stephen Nissenbaum, *The Battle for Christmas* (New York: Vintage Books, 1997); Karal Ann Marling's *Merry Christmas! Celebrating America's Greatest Holiday* (Cambridge, MA: Harvard University Press, 2000).

3. E. Douglas Branch, "Jingle Bells: Notes on Christmas in American Literature," *Saturday Review of Literature,* December 4, 1937, 3–4, 20, 24, 28.

4. George William Curtis, "Editor's Easy Chair," *Harper's New Monthly Magazine,* December 1890, 152–55, 152.

5. Tara Moore, *Victorian Christmas in Print* (New York: Palgrave Macmillan, 2009), 2–3, 6. See also Tara Moore, ed., *The Valancourt Book of Victorian Christmas Ghost Stories* (Richmond, VA: Valancourt Books, 2016).

6. "The Christmas Tree at Windsor Castle" and "A German Christmas Tree," *Illustrated London News,* December 23, 1848, 409–10.

7. "The Christmas Tree," *Godey's Lady's Book,* December 1850, n.p.

8. Nicole Anae, "'101 in the Shade': Christmas Pudding in Australian Popular Literary Verse, 1830–1900," in Lorna Piatti-Farnell and Donna Lee Brien, eds, *The Routledge Companion to Literature and Food* (New York: Routledge, 2018), 113–26, 113.

9. Natacha Chevalier, "Iconic dishes, culture and identity: The Christmas pudding and its hundred years' journey in the USA, Australia, New Zealand and India," *Food, Culture & Society* 21, no. 3 (2018): 367–83, 374.

10. Moore, *Victorian Christmas,* 81. While the Christmas ghost story was never dominant in America, Christopher Philippo has gathered some compelling examples of the form in *The Valancourt Book of Victorian Christmas Ghost Stories,* vol. 4 (Richmond, VA: Valancourt Books, 2020).

11. Gillian Avery, "Home and Family: English and American Ideals in the Nineteenth Century," in Dennis Butts, ed., *Stories and Society: Children's Literature in its Social Context* (New York: Palgrave Macmillan, 1992), 37–49, 44.

12. George William Curtis, "Christmas," *Harper's New Monthly Magazine,* December 1883, 3–16, 3, 16. For more on the contentious history of Christmas celebrations, see Gerry Bowler, *Christmas in the Crosshairs: Two Thousand Years of Denouncing and Defending the World's Most Celebrated Holiday* (New York: Oxford University Press, 2017).

13. Susan Fenimore Cooper, *Rural Hours* (New York: George P. Putnam, 1850), 300.

14. Captain John Smith, *A Select Edition of His Writings,* ed. Karen Ordahl Kupperman (Chapel Hill: University of North Carolina Press, 1988), 172.

15. Edward Everett Hale, "The Same Christmas in Old England and New," *Galaxy,* January 1868, 47–59, 47.

16. William Bradford, *History of Plymouth Plantation* (Boston: privately printed, 1856), 88.

17. Bradford, *History,* 112.

18. Henry Ward Beecher, "Religious Anniversaries," *Christian Union,* December 30, 1874, 522–23, 523.

19. Henry Ward Beecher, *Norwood; or, Pastoral Life in New England* (New York: Charles Scribner & Co., 1868), 231.

20. Beecher, "Religious Anniversaries," 522–23.

21. Harriet Beecher Stowe, *Poganuc People: Their Loves and Lives* (London: Sampson Low, Marston, Searle, & Rivington, 1878), 193.

22. Joan D. Hedrick, *Harriet Beecher Stowe: A Life* (New York: Oxford University Press, 1995), 73.

23. Harriet Beecher Stowe, *Uncle Tom's Cabin* (Boston: John P. Jewett & Company, 1852), vol. 1: 60.

24. Jana Tigchelaar, "The Neighborly Christmas: Gifts, Community, and Regionalism in the Christmas Stories of Sarah Orne Jewett and Mary Wilkins Freeman," *Legacy* 31, no. 2 (2014): 236–57, 238.

25. Susan Koppelman, *"May Your Days Be Merry and Bright": Christmas Stories by Women* (New York: Mentor, 1991), 254.

26. Katharine Allyn See, "The Christmas Story in American Literature," MA thesis, University of Louisville, 1943, 94.

27. Washington Irving, *Abbotsford and Newstead Abbey* (Philadelphia: Carey, Lea & Blanchard, 1835), 86–87.

28. John Gibson Lockhart, *Memoirs of the Life of Sir Walter Scott* (Edinburgh: Robert Cadell, 1839), vol. 5: 243.

29. Joe Perry, *Christmas in Germany: A Cultural History* (Chapel Hill: University of North Carolina Press, 2010), 17, 2.

30. [Johann Wolfgang von Goethe], *The Sorrows of Werter: A German Story* (London: J. Dodsley, 1780), vol. 2: 117.

31. Walter Scott, *Marmion; a Tale of Flodden Field* (Edinburgh: J. Ballantyne and Co., 1808), 299, 303, cii.

32. Scott, *Marmion,* 303–4.

33. See, for example, Sir Walter Scott, *The Olden Christmas from Marmion* (Boston: D. Lothrop & Co., 1886); Sir Walter Scott, *Christmas in the Olden Time* (New York: Cassell and Co., 1887).

34. Lockhart, *Memoirs of the Life of Sir Walter Scott* 7: 285, 293.

35. Pierre M. Irving, ed., *The Life and Letters of Washington Irving* (New York: G. Putnam, 1864), vol. 1: 377.

36. Henry Brevoort, *Letters of Henry Brevoort to Washington Irving,* ed. George S. Hellman (New York: G. P. Putnam's Sons, 1916), vol. 2: 203.

37. Washington Irving, *A History of New-York* (New York: Inskeep and Bradford, 1812), vol. 2: 145.

38. James Kirke Paulding, *The Book of Saint Nicholas* (New York: Harper & Brothers, 1836), vii.

39. Samuel Woodworth, *Melodies, Duets, Trios, Songs and Ballads* (New York: James M. Campbell, 1826), 154.

40. "Account of a Visit from St. Nicholas," *Troy Sentinel,* December 23, 1823, 3.

41. Washington Irving, *The Sketch Book of Geoffrey Crayon, Gent., No. V: Christmas* (New York: C. S. Van Winkle, 1819), 342.

42. Irving, *The Sketch Book, No. V,* title page.

43. Irving, *The Sketch Book, No. V,* 341, 347.

44. Brian Jay Jones, *Washington Irving: An American Original* (New York: Arcade Publishing, 2008), 204.

45. Irving, *The Sketch Book, No. V,* 372–73.

46. Irving, *The Sketch Book, No. V,* 434.

47. Irving, *The Sketch Book, No. V,* 419.

48. Irving, *The Sketch Book, No. V,* 376.

49. Washington Irving, *Bracebridge Hall* (London: John Murray, 1822), vol. 2: 391–92.

50. See, amongst many others, *Christmas Stories from the "Sketch Book"* (Philadelphia: J. B. Lippincott & Co., 1863); *Old Christmas from Washington Irving's Sketch-Book* (London: Macmillan & Co., 1882).

51. Curtis, "Christmas," 3–16, 15.

52. "Bracebridge Hall," *Literary and Scientific Repository,* May 1822, 422–32, 429.

53. James Fenimore Cooper, *The Pioneers* (New York: Charles Wiley, 1823), vol. 1: 3, 5, 52, 233.

54. Cooper, *Rural Hours,* 442.

55. Catharine Maria Sedgwick, "New Year's Day," *The Token and Atlantic Souvenir, A Christmas and New Year's Present* (Boston: Charles Bowen, 1836), 11–31, 14.

56. Nissenbaum, *Battle for Christmas,* 140.

57. "Preface," *The Token and Atlantic Souvenir,* iii.

58. Nathaniel Hawthorne, "Preface," *Twice-Told Tales* (Boston: Ticknor and Fields, 1851), vol. 1: 6.

59. Nathaniel Hawthorne, *Mosses From An Old Manse* (New York: Wiley and Putnam, 1846), vol. 2: 39.

60. Susan G. Davis, "'Making Night Hideous': Christmas Revelry and Public Order in Nineteenth-Century Philadelphia," *American Quarterly* 34, no. 2 (Summer 1982): 185–99, 15.

61. Henry A. Beers, *Nathaniel Parker Willis* (Boston: Houghton, Mifflin and Co., 1896), 36–37.

62. Frederick Law Olmsted, *A Journey Through Texas; or, A Saddle-Trip on the Southwestern Frontier* (New York: Dix, Edwards & Co., 1857), 68–69.

63. Frances Anne Butler, *Journal* (London: John Murray, 1835), vol. 2: 68–69.

64. Lydia Maria Child, *Letters from New York: Second Series* (New York: C. S. Francis & Co., 1846), 13.

65. Child, *Letters,* 16–18.

66. Nissenbaum, *Battle for Christmas,* 200.

67. Lydia Maria Child, *The Little Girl's Own Book* (Boston: Clark Austin & Co., 1833), 287.

68. Child, *Letters,* 18. The quotation is from Mary Howitt's translation of Frederika Bremer's *Strife and Peace* (1844).

69. Child, *Letters,* 19, 21.

70. "Mr. Dickens Speech," *Brother Jonathan,* February 26, 1842, 242–43.

71. Child, *Letters,* 65–66.

72. "A Christmas Carol," *Magazine For The Million,* February 17, 1844, 18.

73. Rebecca Harding Davis, *Margret Howth* (Boston: Ticknor and Fields, 1862), 249.

74. Charles Dudley Warner, *Backlog Studies* (Boston: James R. Osgood and Co., 1873), 266.

75. John M. L. Drew, *Dickens the Journalist* (New York: Palgrave Macmillan, 2003), 148.

76. Moore, *Victorian Christmas,* 3.

77. "Muggy Junction," *The Times,* December 5, 1866, 5.

78. Nathaniel Parker Willis, *Dashes at Life With a Free Pencil: Part IV; Ephemera* (New York: J. S. Redfield, 1845), 181.

79. "Editorial Notes," *Putnam's Magazine,* February 1853, 230.

80. Nissenbaum, *Battle for Christmas,* 99.

81. Elizabeth Wetherell [Susan Warner], *The Wide, Wide World* (New York: George P. Putnam, 1851), vol. 2: 10.

82. [Susan and Anna Bartlett Warner], *Carl Krinken: His Christmas Stocking* (New York: G. P. Putnam, 1854).

83. "Our Weekly Gossip," *Brother Jonathan,* December 24, 1842, 494–95.

84. "Godey's Arm-Chair," *Godey's Lady's Book,* December 1857, 563–65, 563.

85. "Novelties for December," *Godey's Lady's Book,* December 1857, 541–42.

86. "Receipts, &c.," *Godey's Lady's Book,* December 1857, 553–56, 553.

87. Lucy N. Godfrey, "Aunt Sophie's Visits—No. II," *Godey's Lady's Book,* December 1857, 519–24, 521.

88. Harriet Beecher Stowe, "Christmas, or The Good Fairy," *National Era,* December 26, 1850, 1.

89. Ralph Waldo Emerson, *Essays: Second Series* (Boston: James Munro and Co., 1844), 173.

90. Margaret Fuller Ossoli, *Woman in the Nineteenth Century, and Kindred Papers* (Boston: John P. Jewett & Co., 1855), 302.

91. Margaret Fuller, *Memoirs of Margaret Fuller Ossoli,* ed. R. W. Emerson, W. H. Channing, and J. F. Clarke (Boston: Roberts Brothers, 1874), vol. 2: 309, 271.

92. Henry David Thoreau, *The Journal of Henry David Thoreau, 1837–1861,* ed. Damion Searls (New York: New York Review Books, 2009), 481.

93. Herman Melville, *Moby-Dick; or, The Whale* (New York: Harper & Brothers, 1851), 114.

94. Nina Baym, *Woman's Fiction: A Guide to Novels by and about Women in America, 1820–1870* (Urbana: University of Illinois Press, 1993), 27.

95. Baym, *Woman's Fiction,* 27.

96. Maria Susanna Cummins, *The Lamplighter* (Boston: John P. Jewett & Co., 1854), 106–7.

97. P. Gabrielle Foreman, "Sentimental Abolition in Douglass's Decade: Revision, Erotic Conversion, and the Politics of Witnessing in *The Heroic Slave* and *My Bondage and My Freedom,*" in Mary Chapman and Glenn Hendler, eds., *Sentimental Men: Masculinity and the Politics of Affect in American Culture* (Berkeley: University of California Press, 1999), 149–62, 150.

98. Foreman, "Sentimental Abolition," 150.

99. Nissenbaum, *Battle for Christmas,* 67.

100. Frederick Douglass, *Narrative of the Life of Frederick Douglass* (Boston: Anti-Slavery Office, 1845), 74–75.

101. Ellen and William Craft, *Running a Thousand Miles for Freedom* (London: William Tweedie, 1860), 31, 80.

102. Henry Bibb, *Narrative of the Life and Adventures of Henry Bibb* (New York: Henry Bibb, 1849), 40–1.

103. Henry Box Brown, *Narrative of the Life of Henry Box Brown* (Manchester, England: Lee and Glynn, 1851), 49.

104. Charles Frederick Briggs, "Uncle Tomitudes," *Putnam's Monthly,* January 1853, 97–102, 100.

105. Lydia Maria Child, ed., *The Oasis* (Boston: Benjamin C. Bacon, 1834).

106. Metta Victor, *Maum Guinea, and Her Plantation 'Children'; or, Holiday-Week on a Louisiana Estate* (New York: Beadle and Co., 1861).

107. Teresa Goddu, *Selling Antislavery: Abolition and Mass Media in Antebellum America* (Philadelphia: University of Pennsylvania Press, 2020), 89, 92.

108. Goddu, *Selling Antislavery,* 124.

109. Maria Weston Chapman, "Sketches of the Fair—No. II, The Christmas Tree," *Liberator,* January 27, 1843, 15.

110. Daniel Hundley, *Social Relations in Our Southern States* (New York: Henry B. Price, 1860), 359.

111. William Gilmore Simms, *The Golden Christmas* (Charleston, SC: Walker, Richards and Co., 1852), 153.

112. Simms, *Golden Christmas,* 150.

113. William Gilmore Simms, "Maize in Milk, A Christmas Story of the South," *Godey's Lady's Book,* January 1847, 62–67.

114. "Editor's Easy Chair" *Harper's New Monthly Magazine,* January 1864, 275–79, 278.

115. Thomas Nast, "Santa in Camp," *Harper's Weekly,* January 3, 1863, 1.

116. Ebenezer Hannaford, "In the Ranks at Stone River," *Harper's New Monthly Magazine,* November 1863, 809–15, 809.

117. Elizabeth Young, *Disarming the Nation: Women's Writing and the American Civil War* (Chicago: University of Chicago, 1999), 98–99.

118. James Marten, *Lessons of War: The Civil War in Children's Magazines* (Lanham, MD: SR Books, 1999), xvii.

119. Marten, *Lessons,* 185, 182.

120. Alice Fahs, *The Imagined Civil War* (Chapel Hill: University of North Carolina Press, 2001), 256, 258.

121. James Marten, *The Children's Civil War* (Chapel Hill: University of North Carolina Press, 1998), 120.

122. Henry Wadsworth Longfellow, "Christmas Bells," *Our Young Folks,* February 1865, 123.

123. Marling, *Merry Christmas!* 291–92.

124. Lydia Maria Child, "The Two Christmas Evenings," *Our Young Folks,* January 1866, 3.

125. Child, "The Two Christmas Evenings," 10–11.

126. Graham Storey, ed., *The Letters of Charles Dickens: Volume Twelve, 1868–1870* (Oxford, UK: Oxford University Press, 2002), 159.

127. Constance Fenimore Woolson, "Charles Dickens, Christmas, 1870," *Harper's Bazar* [*sic*], December 30, 1870, 842.

128. Constance Fenimore Woolson, "A Merry Christmas," *Harper's Monthly,* January 1872, 231–43, 233.

129. Anne Boyd Rioux, *Constance Fenimore Woolson: Portrait of a Lady Novelist* (New York: W. W. Norton & Co., 2016), 298.

130. "Original Dialogue: A Christmas Carol, Arranged as an Entertainment," *Our Boys and Girls,* January 1871, 48–53.

131. Frank R. Stockton, "Stephen Skarridge's Christmas," *Scribner's Monthly,* January 1872, 279–87, 280.

132. "The Magazines for January," *Nation,* January 4, 1872, 13–16.

133. Eugene Giddens, *Christmas Books for Children* (Cambridge, UK: Cambridge University Press, 2019), 1.

134. Louisa May Alcott, *Little Women, or, Meg, Jo, Beth, and Amy* (Boston: Roberts Brothers, 1868), 7.

135. Susan Coolidge, *What Katy Did, A Story* (Boston: Roberts Brothers, 1873), 203.

136. Martha Farquharson [Martha Finley], *Elsie Dinsmore* (New York: M. W. Dodd, 1867), 333.

137. Margaret Sidney, *Five Little Peppers and How They Grew* (Boston: Lothrop Publishing Co., 1881), 204.

138. Mary Mapes Dodge, "Dear Girl and Boy," *St Nicholas Magazine,* November 1873, 1.

139. William Dean Howells, "Henry James, Jr.," *Century,* November 1882, 24–29, 28.

140. William Dean Howells, "Editor's Study," *Harper's New Monthly Magazine,* January 1887, 321–25.

141. Mark Twain, *Following the Equator* (Hartford, CT: American Publishing Co., 1897), 163.

142. William Dean Howells, "Editor's Study," *Harper's New Monthly Magazine,* December 1889, 155–59.

143. Charles Dudley Warner, "Christmas Past," *Harper's New Monthly Magazine,* December 1884, 3–17, 3, 6, 17.

144. Henry James, "Du Maurier and London Society," *Century Magazine,* May 1883, 48–64.

145. Henry James, "London," *Century Magazine,* December 1888, 219–39, 234.

146. The story was first included in *Lin McLean* (New York: Harper & Brothers, 1898); see also *A Journey in Search of Christmas* (New York: Harper & Brothers, 1904).

147. Tigchelaar, "Neighborly Christmas," 237.

148. *The Great Ingersoll Controversy, Beginning with the Celebrated 'Christmas Sermon'* (New York: J. Buckley, n.d.), 5–6.

149. *Great Ingersoll Controversy,* 14.

150. Robert Ingersoll, "What I Want for Christmas," in *The Works of Robert Ingersoll* (New York: Dresden Publishing Co., 1912), vol. 11: 375–76.

151. Harriet E. Prescott, "Christmas," *Our Young Folks,* December 1865, 50.

152. Lew Wallace, *An Autobiography* (New York: Harper and Brothers, 1906), vol. 2: 929–30.

153. Barbara Ryan and Milette Shamir, "Introduction: The *Ben Hur* Tradition," in Ryan and Shamir, eds., *Bigger Than Ben-Hur: The Book, Its Adaptations, and Their Audiences* (Syracuse, NY: Syracuse University Press, 2016), 1–17, 9.

154. Ernest Renan, *The Life of Jesus* (New York: G. W. Dillingham, 1891), 65.

155. Henry Ward Beecher, *The Life of Jesus, The Christ* (New York: J. B. Ford and Co., 1871), 30.

156. Jefferson J. A. Gatrall, "Retelling and Untelling the Christmas Story: *Ben Hur,* Uncle Midas and the Sunday-School Movement," in Ryan and Shamir eds, *Bigger Than Ben-Hur,* 52–73, 64.

157. Lew Wallace, "The Boyhood of Christ," *Harper's New Monthly Magazine,* December 1886, 3–18.

158. Ruth McEnery Stuart, "A Christmas Guest," *Century Magazine,* December 1894, 198–201, 199, 201.

159. Steven Bembridge, "Frank Norris's 'Miracle Joyeux': A Biographical Exploration of Apocryphal, Islamic, and Nineteenth-Century Cultural Sources," *Studies in American Naturalism* 13: 2 (Winter 2018): 109–29, 109.

160. Robert E. May, *Yuletide in Dixie: Slavery, Christmas, and Southern Memory* (Charlottesville: University of Virginia Press, 2019), 198.

161. Irwin Russell, "Christmas-Night in the Quarters," *Scribner's Monthly,* January 1878, 445–48.

162. John Esten Cooke, "Christmas Time in Old Virginia," *Magazine of American History,* December 1883, 443–59, 443, 447–48.

163. Susan Dabney Smedes, *Memorials of a Southern Planter* (Baltimore: Cushing & Bailey, 1887), 160.

164. Joel Chandler Harris, *Nights with Uncle Remus, Myths and Legends of the Old Plantation* (Boston: James R. Osgood & Co., 1883), 408; Rebecca Cameron, "Christmas On An Old Plantation," *Ladies' Home Journal,* December 1891, 5.

165. Thomas Nelson Page, "'Unc' Edinburg's Drowndin', A Plantation Echo," *Harper's New Monthly Magazine,* January 1886, 304–15, 307, 313.

166. Bettye Collier-Thomas, ed., *A Treasury of African American Christmas Stories* (Boston: Beacon Press, 2018), ii.

167. Ida B. Wells, "Woman's Mission: A Beautiful Christmas Essay on the Duty of Woman in the World's Economy," in Mia Bay, ed., *The Light of Truth: Writings of an Anti-Lynching Crusader* (New York: Penguin Classics, 2014), 13–16, 16.

168. Jacob A. Riis, "Merry Christmas in the Tenements," *Century Magazine,* December 1897, 163–82, 164.

169. C. Lewis Hind, *Authors and I* (New York: John Lane Co., 1921), 72.

170. H. G. Wells, *Experiment in Autobiography* (London: Victor Gollancz, 1934), vol. 2: 613.

171. Crane quoted in John D. Gordan, "*The Ghost* at Brede Place," *Bulletin of the New York Public Library* 56, no. 12 (December 1952): 591–95, 593. Crane was also the author of a Christmas story, "Christmas Dinner Won in Battle," published, perhaps surprisingly, in the *Plumbers' Trade Journal* in January 1895.

172. Wells, *Experiment* 2: 614.

173. Charles Dudley Warner, "Editor's Drawer," *Harper's New Monthly Magazine,* December 1888, 160–61.

I

Old Christmas, New Christmas

CHRISTMAS

WASHINGTON IRVING

From *The Sketch Book of Geoffrey Crayon, Gent. No. V* (New York: C. S. Van Winkle, 1819), 341–52.

Washington Irving's evocation of Christmas past in the Old World—self-consciously antiquarian, gently ironic, knowingly idyllic—had an enormous impact on both sides of the Atlantic that lingered well into the nineteenth century. In this opening section of the Christmas number of his miscellaneous Sketch Book, *first published in January 1819, Irving sets the tone of nostalgia and escapism that characterized his pioneering literary resurrection of the season.*

A man might then behold
At Christmas, in each hall,
Good fires to curb the cold,
And meat for great and small:
The neighbours were friendly bidden,
And all had welcome true,
The poor from the gates were not chidden
When this old cap was new.

—OLD SONG.

There is nothing in England that exercises a more delightful spell over my imagination than the lingerings of the holyday customs and rural games of antiquity. They recal the fond picturings of an ideal state of things, which I was wont to indulge in the May morning of life, when as yet I only knew the world through books, and believed it to be all that poets had painted it; and they bring with them the flavour of those good old times, in which, perhaps with equal fallacy, I am apt to think the world was more homebred, social, and joyous, than at present. I regret to say that they are daily growing more and more faint, being gradually worn away by time, but still more obliterated by modern fashion. They resemble those picturesque morsels of Gothic architecture, which we see crumbling in various parts of the country, partly dilapidated by the waste of ages, and partly lost in the additions and alterations of latter days. Poetry, however, clings with cherishing fondness about the rural game and holyday revel, from which it has derived so many of its themes—as the ivy winds its rich foliage about the gothic arch and mouldering tower, gratefully repaying their support, by clasping together their tottering remains, and, as it were, embalming them in verdure.

Of all the old festivals, however, that of Christmas awakens the strongest and most heartfelt associations. There is a tone of solemn and sacred feeling that blends with our conviviality, and lifts the spirit to a state of hallowed and elevated enjoyment. The services of the church about this season are extremely tender and inspiring. They dwell on the beautiful story of the origin of our faith, and the pastoral scenes that accompanied its announcement. They gradually increase in fervour and pathos during the season of Advent, until they break forth in full jubilee on the morning that brought peace and good will to men. I do not know a grander effect of music on the moral feelings, than to hear the full choir and the pealing organ performing a Christmas anthem in a cathedral, and filling every part of the vast pile with triumphant harmony.

It is a beautiful arrangement, also, derived from days of yore, that this festival, which commemorates the announcement of the religion of peace and love, has been made the season for gathering together of family connexions, and drawing closer again those bands of kindred hearts, which the cares and pleasures and sorrows of the world are continually operating to cast loose; of calling back the children of a family, who have launched forth in life, and wandered widely asunder, once more to assemble about the paternal hearth, that rallying place of the affections, there to grow young and loving again among the endearing mementos of childhood.

There is something in the very season of the year that gives a charm to the festivity of Christmas. At other times we derive a great portion of our pleasures from the mere beauties of nature. Our feelings sally forth and dissipate themselves over the sunny landscape, and we "live abroad and every where." The song of the bird, the murmur of the stream, the breathing fragrance of spring, the soft voluptuousness of summer, the golden pomp of autumn, earth with its mantle of refreshing green, and heaven with its deep delicious blue and cloudy magnificence, all fill us with mute but exquisite delight, and we revel in the luxury of mere sensation. But in the depth of winter, when nature lies despoiled of every charm, and wrapped in her shroud of sheeted snow, we turn for our gratifications to moral sources. The dreariness and desolation of the landscape, the short gloomy days and darksome nights, while they circumscribe our wanderings, shut in our feelings also from rambling abroad, and make us more keenly disposed for the pleasures of the social circle. Our thoughts are more concentrated, our friendly sympathies more aroused. We feel more sensibly the charm of each other's society, and are brought more closely together by dependence on each other for enjoyment. Heart calleth unto heart, and we draw our pleasures from the deep wells of living kindness which lie in the quiet recesses of our bosoms, and which, when resorted to, furnish forth the pure element of domestic felicity.

The pitchy gloom without, makes the heart dilate on entering the room filled with the glow and warmth of the evening fire. The ruddy blaze diffuses an artificial summer and sunshine through the room, and lights up each countenance into a kindlier welcome. Where does the honest face of hospitality expand into a broader and more heart-felt smile—where is the shy glance of love more sweetly eloquent—than by the winter fireside;—and as the hollow blast of wintry wind rushes through the hall, claps the distant door, whistles about the casement, and rumbles down the chimney—

what can be more grateful than that feeling of sober and sheltered security, with which we look round upon the comfortable chamber, and the scene of domestic hilarity.

The English, from the great prevalence of rural habits throughout every class of society, have been extremely fond of those festivals and holydays which agreeably interrupt the stillness of country life, and, in former days, were particularly observant of the religious and social rites of Christmas. It is inspiring to read even the dry details which some antiquarians have given of the quaint humours, the burlesque pageants, the complete abandonment to mirth and good fellowship, with which this festival was celebrated. It seemed to throw open every door, and unlock every heart. It brought the peasant and the peer together, and blended all ranks in one warm generous flow of joy and kindness. The old halls of castles and manor houses resounded with the harp and the Christmas carol, and their ample boards groaned under the weight of hospitality. Even the poorest cottage welcomed the festive season with green decorations of bay and holly—the cheerful fire glanced its rays through the lattice, inviting the passenger to raise the latch, and join the gossip knot huddled round the hearth, beguiling the long evening with legendary jokes, and oft-told Christmas tales.

One of the least pleasing effects of modern refinement is the havoc it has made among the hearty old holyday customs. It has completely taken off the fine edge, the sharp touchings and spirited reliefs of these embellishments of life, and has worn down society into a more smooth—and polished, but certainly a less characteristic surface. Many of the games and ceremonials of Christmas have entirely disappeared, and, like the sherris sack of old Falstaff, are matters of speculation and dispute among commentators. They flourished in times full of spirit and lustihood, when men enjoyed life roughly, but heartily and vigorously: times wild and picturesque, which have furnished poetry with its richest materials, and the drama with its greatest variety of characters and manners. The world has become more worldly. There is more of dissipation, and less of enjoyment. Pleasure has expanded into a broader, but a shallower stream, and has forsaken many of those deep and quiet channels where it flowed sweetly through the calm bosom of domestic life. Society has a more enlightened and general tone; but it has lost many of its strong local peculiarities, its homebred feelings, its honest fireside delights. The traditionary customs of golden hearted antiquity, its feudal hospitalities, and lordly wassailings, have passed away with the baronial castles and stately manor houses in which they were celebrated. They comported with the shadowy hall, the great oaken gallery, and the tapestried parlour, but were unfitted for the light showy saloons and gay drawing rooms of the modern villa.

Shorn, however, as it is, of its ancient and festive honours, Christmas is still a period of delightful excitement in England. It is gratifying to see that home feeling completely aroused which seems to hold so powerful a place in every English bosom. The preparations making on every side for the social board that is again to unite friends and kindred—the presents of good cheer passing and repassing, those tokens of regard and quickeners of kind feelings—the evergreens distributed about houses and churches, emblems of peace and gladness—all these have the most pleasing effect in producing fond associations, and kindling benevolent sympathies. Even the sound of the Waits,* rude as may be their minstrelsy, breaks upon the midwatches of a winter night with the effect of perfect harmony. As I have been awakened by them in that still and solemn hour "when deep sleep falleth upon man," I have listened with a hushed delight, and connecting them with the sacred and joyous occasion, have almost fancied them into another celestial choir, announcing peace and good will to mankind. How delightfully the imagination, when wrought upon by these moral influences, turns everything to melody and beauty. The very crowing of the cock, who is sometimes heard in the profound repose of the country, "telling the night watches to his feathery dames," was thought by the common people to announce the approach of this sacred festival:

> Some say that ever 'gainst that season comes
> Wherein our Saviour's birth is celebrated,

*Musical bands that go about the towns and villages of England, serenading for several nights preceding Christmas. They call, on that day, for a Christmas-box (that is, present) at the houses before which they have played.

This bird of dawning singeth all night long:
And then, they say, no spirit dares stir abroad;
The nights are wholesome—then no planets strike,
No fairy takes, no witch hath power to charm,
So hallowed and so gracious is the time.

Amidst the general call to happiness, the bustle of the spirits, and stir of the affections, which prevail at this period, what bosom can remain insensible? It is, indeed, the season of regenerated feeling—the season for kindling not merely the fire of hospitality in the hall, but the genial flame of charity in the heart. The scene of early love again rises green to memory beyond the sterile waste of years, and the idea of home, fraught with the fragrance of home dwelling joys, reanimates the drooping spirit—as the Arabian breeze will sometimes waft the freshness of the distant fields to the weary pilgrim of the desert.

Stranger and sojourner as I am in the land—though for me no social hearth may blaze, no hospitable roof throw open its doors, nor the warm grasp of friendship welcome me at the threshold—yet I feel the influence of the season beaming into my soul from the happy looks of those around me. Surely happiness is reflective, like the light of heaven; and every countenance bright with smiles, and glowing with innocent enjoyment, is a mirror transmitting to others the rays of a supreme and ever shining benevolence. He who can turn churlishly away from contemplating the felicity of his fellow beings, and sit down darkling and repining in his loneliness when all around is joyful, may have his moments of strong excitement and selfish gratification, but wants the genial and social sympathies which constitute the charm of a merry Christmas.

CHRISTMAS

From *The Pearl; or, Affection's Gift*
(Philadelphia: Thomas T. Ash, 1829), 53–58.

Gift books containing a miscellany of prose and poetry by a wide variety of authors became an important part of seasonal life in America at the same moment that Christmas was developing a new significance in American life. These fashionable literary annuals originated in England in the early 1820s, and Philadelphia publishers Carey and Lea brought them to America in 1825 with the release of The Atlantic Souvenir: A Christmas and New Year's Offering. *Many imitators soon followed, providing a vital cyclical outlet for American writers, as well as handy gifts for those exchanging presents. This gift-book essay—unusually seasonal in its concerns—provides a fascinating snapshot of the developing and regionally diverse expression of Christmas in American life in 1829, a moment when local folk traditions had not yet been homogenized into a national standard.*

Come hither, come hither, 'tis merry day all;
Saint Nicholas rides—he will make you a call.
Here's a stocking—a shoe—for you, Mary and Ann,
Place both in the corner;—be sad now, who can?

The approach of Christmas is hailed annually, by the youthful part of the community especially, as a season of gaiety and joy. As the holidays approach, even the very hours are counted which intervene between *merry-day* and the present. Gifts are anticipated in rich profusion, and all hearts seem light and buoyant with cheerfulness and excitement.

This festival is of very ancient origin; but I do not purpose now to enter into its history, neither the various modes of celebrating its arrival by different nations, in different parts of the Christian world.

Every people hold some peculiarities, even in the different states of our own country the forms of observing this festival vary widely.

I am told that it is but few years since Christmas in Philadelphia was to the children their day of days through all the year. It was anticipated with an impatience that disregarded control, and was welcomed with noisy joy.

Saint Nicholas, by some means, has come to be patron saint to all good children on this memorable day; and it seems his employment, the night before Christmas, is riding through the air laden with gifts: he descends the chimney silently, and those who have had the providence to hang a stocking in the flue, or deposit a shoe in the corner, find their pains rewarded (and very lavishly, too, judging from all I have seen) by the receipt of books, toys, comfits, and bon-bons, which are not sooner discovered than the happy receiver is proclaimed a favourite of the kind-hearted saint.

Such are some of the innocent amusements of the early day:—the remaining time is as variously disposed almost as there are children to please and be pleased. But all the truth should be told:—the day really ends, like all seasons of great excitement, in weariness, and many a little head is willingly laid early upon its pillow.

The Germans introduced into Pennsylvania a diversion for this day, which, though now passing, in many villages, into utter forgetfulness, for a long time maintained such a place as to be worthy of record.

The frolic of the *Krish-Krinkle* is in amount this.

A party of gay young people, habited in grotesque garments, and wearing frightfully ugly masks, go from house to house, leaving sweet meats at some, nuts and cakes at others, and nut shells and false-cake at others. Occasionally they demand entrance, with much noisy vociferation, and require a contribution from those they visit, fit for a hideous figure stuffed with straw, which they carry about and call the Krish-Krinkle: if they cannot obtain what they ask, they feel authorized to take what they can; and sometimes carry their joke too far to be agreeable to those on whom they practise.

It is not uncommon in the country, to find a tree planted directly against your door in the morning, or an immense heap of potatoes which come rolling in over the floors as soon as the doors are opened. Then again the outer passages are barricadoed with cabbages: but it is deemed the best joke of all, to enter the vegetable gardens, and remove all things left in them from the place where the owner intended they should remain;—nay, sometimes transporting the whole to a remote house, incommoding the receiver of these mischief-made presents, as much as the owner of the property—or I might say the involuntary donor: and all this wild work is called "fun," "frolic," "a good joke," and any thing rather than unlawful infringement of a neighbour's rights. We sober New Englanders should almost regard such pranks a breaking of the sixth Mosaic commandment.

In general, we know more of Christmas held as a religious festival—and very proper is it that all sects of religionists who call themselves Christians, should unitedly celebrate this season by public worship and hymns of joy.

It is at this time that so much pains is taken to ornament our churches with verdant boughs, fragrant evergreens, and the wild trailing moss-pine. This is symbolical of joy no doubt, and teaches a simple silent lesson, to him who will accept its "still small teachings."

The hilarity of this period is considerably increased by the near approach of New-Years',—when the young and joyous again find ample occasion to indulge their mirth, and

Yield the full heart to gladness.

But perhaps these periods are most valued as seasons of social intercourse. Visits are paid and received with less ceremony now than at other times: *good feeling* seems to be more alive; *kind feeling* is on the alert; and *generous feeling* never wearies or retires from the scene.

The young and old, of both sexes, mingle with less of that artificial manner that binds society in fetters of iron, and which shuts out most of the better emotions and impulses of social life, giving in their place a cold false manner, which has nothing of worth or interest, or, what is equally as bad, an abrupt freedom, which disgusts rather than pleases.

I would not be thought severe, especially by the more youthful portion of my readers, but I do lament to see so little simplicity of mind and manner; so much of acquirement; so much "show-off appearance," which but betrays its own falsity, as a pewter ring washed with gold lacker soon shows its real worthlessness.

I should be glad to see all affectation, and a thousand little modes of fashion, fall into their deserved oblivion, and witness in young gentlemen and ladies that respect for themselves, and each other individually, which alone gives evidence of true good-breeding, elevated sentiments, and refined manners.

But this is felt and known—why should I repeat it? may it be so appreciated, as that more of sincere politeness, added to genuine kindness, be seen among us, in the place of that heartless intercourse which but too often attends on fortune and fashion. Minds, good and beautiful minds, how many possess, yet bury them amidst pride and frivolity.

EXCERPT FROM

RETROSPECT OF WESTERN TRAVEL

HARRIET MARTINEAU

From *Retrospect of Western Travel*
(London: Saunders & Otley, 1838), vol. 3: 182–85.

Harriet Martineau was a remarkable polymath: though beset by ill health and disability from an early age, she was a world traveler, an influential political and social theorist, a prolific writer, and much more besides. In 1834, she made a lengthy visit to America which resulted in a number of high-profile and controversial accounts of what she found in the New World—contentious, particularly, because of the close relationship she developed with members of the abolitionist movement. Those connections also resulted in her encounter, detailed below, with one of the first Christmas trees erected in America, at the residence of German émigré Charles Follen, professor of German literature at Harvard until his radical abolitionism resulted in his dismissal. Below, Martineau describes the effects of this new seasonal delight on Follen's son Charley.

I was present at the introduction into the new country of the spectacle of the German Christmas tree. My little friend Charley, and three companions, had been long preparing for this pretty show. The cook had broken her eggs carefully in the middle for some weeks past, that Charley might have the shells for cups; and these cups were gilt and coloured very prettily. I rather think it was, generally speaking, a secret out of the house; but I knew what to expect. It was a New-Year's tree, however; for I could not go on Christmas-eve; and it was kindly settled that New-Year's-eve would do as well. We were sent for before dinner; and we took up two round-faced boys by the way. Early as it was, we were all so busy that we could scarcely spare a respectful attention to our plum-pudding. It was desirable that our preparations should be completed before the little folks should begin to arrive; and we were all engaged in sticking on the last of the seven dozen of wax-tapers, and in filling the gilt egg-cups, and gay paper cornucopiae with comfits, lozenges, and barley-sugar. The tree was the top of a young fir, planted in a tub, which was ornamented with moss. Smart dolls, and other whimsies, glittered in the evergreen; and there was not a twig which had not something sparkling upon it. When the sound of wheels was heard, we had just finished; and we shut up the tree by itself in the front drawing-room, while we went into the other, trying to look as if nothing was going to happen. Charley looked a good deal like himself, only now and then twisting himself about in an unaccountable fit of giggling. It was a very large party; for besides the tribes of children, there were papas and mammas, uncles, aunts, and elder sisters. When all were come, we shut out the cold: the great fire burned clearly; the tea and coffee were as hot as possible, and the cheeks of the little ones grew rosier, and their eyes brighter every moment. It had been settled that, in order to cover our designs, I was to resume my vocation of teaching Christmas games after tea, while Charley's mother and her maids went to light up the front room. So all found seats, many of the children on the floor, for Old Coach. It was difficult to divide even an American stage-coach into parts enough for every member of such a party to represent one: but we managed it without allowing any of the elderly folks to sit out. The grand fun of all was to make the clergyman and an aunt or two get up and spin round. When they were fairly practised in the game, I turned over my story to a neighbour, and got away to help to light up the tree.

It really looked beautiful; the room seemed in a blaze; and the ornaments were so well hung on that no accident happened, except that one doll's petticoat caught fire. There was a sponge tied to the end of a stick to put out any supernumerary blaze; and no harm ensued. I mounted the steps behind the tree to see the effect of opening the doors. It was delightful. The children poured in; but in a moment, every voice was hushed. Their faces were upturned to the blaze, all eyes wide open, all lips parted, all steps arrested. Nobody spoke; only Charley leaped for joy. The first symptom of recovery was the children's wandering round the tree. At last, a quick pair of eyes discovered that it bore something eatable; and from that moment the babble began again. They were told that they might get what they could without burning themselves; and we tall people kept watch, and helped them with good things from the higher branches. When all had had enough, we returned to the larger room, and finished the evening with dancing. By ten o'clock, all were well warmed for the ride home with steaming mulled wine, and the prosperous evening closed with shouts of mirth. By a little after eleven, Charley's father and mother and I were left by ourselves to sit in the New Year. I have little doubt the Christmas-tree will become one of the most flourishing exotics of New England.

II

Sentiment, Slavery, and War at Christmas

CHRISTMAS, OR THE GOOD FAIRY

HARRIET BEECHER STOWE

From *National Era,* December 26, 1850, 1.

*Harriet Beecher Stowe remains famous as the author of one of the most important novels of the nineteenth century—*Uncle Tom's Cabin *(1852), a book that was first serialized in the abolitionist newspaper, the* National Era. *But not long before she embarked on that landmark project, Stowe published this early sketch in the very same newspaper. A lesson in the importance of charity at Christmas, it is characterized by Stowe's typical humor and keen eye for social observation. Given the theological strictness of her upbringing, Stowe's embrace of Christmas and her frequent return to it in her writing positions her as a bellwether in the reshaping of the season in American life and literature.*

"Oh, dear! Christmas is coming in a fortnight, and I have got to think up presents for everybody!" said young Ellen Stuart, as she leaned languidly back in her chair. "Dear me, it's so tedious! Everybody has got everything that can be thought of."

"Oh, no!" said her confidential adviser, Miss Lester, in a soothing tone. "You have means of buying everything you can fancy, and, when every shop and store is glittering with all manner of splendors, you cannot surely be at a loss."

"Well, now, just listen. To begin with, there's mamma! what can I get for her? I have thought of ever so many things. She has three card cases, four gold thimbles, two or three gold chains, two writing desks of different patterns; and then as to rings, brooches, boxes, and all other things, I should think she might be sick of the sight of them. I am sure I am," said she, languidly gazing on her white and jewelled fingers.

This view of the case seemed rather puzzling to the adviser, and there was silence for a few moments, when Eleanor, yawning, resumed—

"And then there's Cousins Ellen and Mary—I suppose they will be coming down on me with a whole load of presents; and Mrs. B. will send me something—she did last year; and then there's Cousins William and Tom—I must get them something, and I would like to do it well enough, if I only knew what to get!"

"Well," said Eleanor's aunt, who had been sitting quietly rattling her knitting needles during this speech, "it's a pity that you had not such a subject to practice on as I was when I was a girl—presents did not fly about in those days as they do now. I remember when I was ten years old, my father gave sister Mary and me a most marvellously ugly sugar dog for a Christmas gift, and we were perfectly delighted with it—the very idea of a present was so new to us."

"Dear aunt, how delighted I should be if I had any such fresh, unsophisticated body to get presents for! but to get and get for people that have more than they know what to do with now—to add pictures, books, and gilding when the centre tables are loaded with them now—and rings and jewels when they are a perfect drug! I wish myself that I were not sick, and sated, and tired with having everything in the world given me!"

"Well, Eleanor," said her aunt, "if you really do want unsophisticated subjects to practise on, I can put you in the way of it. I can show you more than one family to whom you might seem to be a very good fairy, and where such gifts as you could give with all ease would seem like a magic dream."

"Why, that would really be worth while, aunt."

"Look right across the way," said her aunt. "You see that building."

"That miserable combination of shanties? Yes."

"Well, I have several acquaintances there who have never been tired of

Christmas gifts, or gifts of any other kind. I assure you, you could make quite a sensation over there."

"Well, who is there? Let us know!"

"Do you remember Owen, that used to make your shoes?"

"Yes, I remember something about him."

"Well, he has fallen into a consumption, and cannot work any more, and he and his wife and three little children live in one of the rooms over there."

"How DO they get along?"

"His wife takes in sewing sometimes, and sometimes goes out washing. Poor Owen! I was over there yesterday; he looks thin and wistful, and his wife was saying that he was parched with constant fever, and had very little appetite. She had, with great self-denial, and by restricting herself almost of necessary food, got him two or three oranges, and the poor fellow seemed so eager after them."

"Poor fellow!" said Eleanor, involuntarily.

"Now," said her aunt, "suppose Owen's wife should get up on Christmas morning and find at the door a couple of dozen of oranges and some of those nice white grapes, such as you had at your party last week, don't you think it would make a sensation?"

"Why, yes, I think very likely it might; but who else, aunt? You spoke of a great many."

"Well, on the lower floor there is a neat little room, that is always kept perfectly trim and tidy; it belongs to a young couple who have nothing beyond the husband's day wages to live on. They are, nevertheless, as cheerful and chipper as a couple of wrens, and she is up and down half a dozen times a day, to help poor Mrs. Owen. She has a baby of her own, about five months old, and of course does all the cooking, washing, and ironing for herself and husband; and yet, when Mrs. Owen goes out to wash, she takes her baby, and keeps it whole days for her."

"I'm sure she deserves that the good fairies should smile on her," said Eleanor; "one baby exhausts my stock of virtue very rapidly."

"But you ought to see her baby," said Aunt E., "so plump, so rosy, and good-natured, and always clean as a lily. This baby is a sort of household shrine; nothing is too sacred and too good for it; and I believe the little, thrifty woman feels only one temptation to be extravagant, and that is to get some ornaments to adorn this little divinity."

"Why, did she ever tell you so?"

"No; but one day, when I was coming down stairs, the door of their room was partly open, and I saw a pedlar there with open box. John, the husband, was standing with a little purple cap on his hand, which he was regarding with mystified, admiring air, as if he didn't quite comprehend it, and trim little Mary gazing at it with longing eyes."

"I think we might get it," said John.

"'Oh, no,' said she, regretfully; "yet I wish we could, it's *so pretty!*"

"Say no more, aunt. I see the good fairy must pop a cap into the window on Christmas morning. Indeed, it shall be done. How they will wonder where it came from, and talk about it for months to come!"

"Well, then," continued her aunt, "in the next street to ours there is a miserable building, that looks as if it were just going to topple over; and away up in the third story, in a little room just under the eaves, live two poor, lonely old women. They are both nearly on to ninety. I was in there day before yesterday. One of them is constantly confined to her bed with rheumatism; the other, weak and feeble, with failing sight and trembling hands, totters about, her only helper; and they are entirely dependent on charity."

"Can't they do anything? Can't they knit?" said Eleanor.

"You are young and strong, Eleanor, and have quick eyes and nimble fingers; how long would it take you to knit a pair of stockings?"

"I?" said Eleanor. "What an idea! I never tried, but I think I could get a pair done in a week, perhaps!"

"And if somebody gave you twenty-five cents for them, and out of this you had to get food, and pay room rent, and buy coal for your fire, and oil for your lamp"—

"Stop, aunt, for pity's sake!"

"Well, I will stop; but they can't: they must pay so much every month for that miserable shell they live in, or be turned into the street. The meal and flour that some kind person sends goes off for them just as it does for others, and they must get more or starve; and coal is now scarce and high priced."

"Oh, aunt, I'm quite convinced, I'm sure; don't run me down and annihilate me with all these terrible realities. What shall I do to play good fairy to these poor old women?"

"If you will give me full power, Eleanor, I will put up a basket to be sent to them, that will give them something to remember all winter."

"Oh, certainly I will. Let me see if I can't think of something myself."

"Well, Eleanor, suppose, then, some fifty or sixty years hence, if you were old, and your father, and mother, and aunts, and uncles, now so thick around you, laid cold and silent in so many graves—you have somehow got away off to a strange city, where you were never known—you live in a miserable garret, where snow blows at night through the cracks, and the fire is very apt to go out in the old cracked stove; you sit crouching over the dying embers the evening before Christmas—nobody to speak to you, nobody to care for you, except another poor old soul who lies moaning in the bed—now, what would you like to have sent you?"

"Oh, aunt, what a dismal picture!"

"And yet, Ella, all poor, forsaken old women are made of young girls, who expected it in their youth as little as you do, perhaps."

"Say no more, aunt. I'll buy—let me see—a comfortable warm shawl for each of these poor women; and I'll send them—let me see—oh! some tea—nothing goes down with old women like tea; and I'll make John wheel some coal over to them; and, aunt, it would not be a very bad thought to send them a new stove. I remember, the other day, when mamma was pricing stoves, I saw some such nice ones for two or three dollars."

"For a new hand, Ella, you work up the idea very well," said her aunt.

"But how much ought I to give, for any one case, to these women, say?"

"How much did you give last year for any single Christmas present?"

"Why, six or seven dollars, for some; those elegant souvenirs were seven dollars; that ring I gave Mrs. B—— was ten."

"And do you suppose Mrs. B—— was any happier for it?"

"No, really, I don't think she cared much about it; but I had to give her something, because she had sent me something the year before, and I did not want to send a paltry present to one in her circumstances."

"Then, Ella, give the same to any poor, distressed, suffering creature who really needs it, and see in how many forms of good such a sum will appear. That one hard, cold, glittering diamond ring, that now cheers nobody, and means nothing, that you give because you must, and she takes because she must, might, if broken up into smaller sums, send real warm and heart-felt gladness through many a cold and cheerless dwelling, through many an aching heart."

"You are getting to be an orator, aunt; but don't you approve of Christmas presents, among friends and equals?"

"Yes, indeed," said her aunt, fondly stroking her head. "I have had some Christmas presents that did me a world of good—a little book mark, for instance, that a certain niece of mine worked for me, with wonderful secrecy, three years ago, when she was not a young lady with a purse full of money—that book mark was a true Christmas present; and my young couple across the way are plotting a profound surprise to each other on Christmas morning. John has contrived, by an hour of extra work every night, to lay by enough to get Mary a new calico dress; and she, poor soul, has bargained away the only thing in the jewelry line she ever possessed, to be laid out on a new hat for him."

"I know, too, a washerwoman who has a poor, lame boy—a patient, gentle little fellow—who has lain quietly for weeks and months in his little crib, and his mother is going to give him a splendid Christmas present."

"What is it, pray?"

"A whole orange! Don't laugh. She will pay ten whole cents for it; for it shall be none of your common oranges, but a picked one of the very best going! She has put by the money, a cent at a time, for a whole month; and nobody knows which will be happiest in it, Willie or his mother. These are such Christmas presents as I like to think of—gifts coming from love, and tending to produce love; these are the appropriate gifts of the day."

"But, don't you think that it's right for those who *have* money to give expensive presents, supposing always, as you say, they are given from real affection?"

"Sometimes, undoubtedly. The Savior did not condemn her who broke an alabaster box of ointment—*very precious*—simply as a proof of love, even although the suggestion was made, 'this might have been sold for three hundred pence, and given to the poor.' I have thought he would regard with sympathy the fond efforts which human love sometimes makes to express itself by gifts, the rarest and most costly. How I rejoiced with all my heart, when Charles Elton gave his poor mother that splendid Chinese shawl and gold watch—because I knew they came from the very fullness of his heart to a mother that he could not do too much for—a mother that has done and suffered everything for him. In some such cases, when resources are ample, a costly gift seems to have a graceful appropriateness; but I cannot approve of it, if it exhausts all the means of doing for the poor; it is better, then, to give a simple offering, and to do something for those who really need it."

Eleanor looked thoughtful; her aunt laid down her knitting, and said, in a tone of gentle seriousness:

"Whose birth does Christmas commemorate, Ella?"

"Our Saviour's, certainly, aunt."

"Yes," said her aunt. "And when and how was he born? in a stable! laid in a manger; thus born, that in all ages he might be known as the brother and friend of the poor. And surely it seems but appropriate to commemorate His birthday by an especial remembrance of the lowly, the poor, the outcast, and distressed; and if Christ should come back to our city on a Christmas day, where should we think it most appropriate to his character to find him? Would he be carrying splendid gifts to splendid dwellings, or would he be gliding about in the cheerless haunts of the desolate, the poor, the forsaken, and the sorrowful?"

And here the conversation ended.

* * *

"What sort of Christmas presents is Ella buying?" said Cousin Tom, as the waiter handed in a portentous-looking package, which had been just rung in at the door.

"Let's open it," said saucy Will. "Upon my word, two great gray blanket shawls! These must be for you and me, Tom! And what's this? A great bolt of cotton flannel and gray yarn stockings!"

The door bell rang again, and the waiter brought in another bulky parcel, and deposited it on the marble-topped centre table.

"What's here?" said Will, cutting the cord. "Whew! a perfect nest of packages! oolong tea! oranges! grapes! white sugar! Bless me, Ella must be going to housekeeping!"

"Or going crazy!" said Tom; "and on my word," said he, looking out of the window, "there's a drayman ringing at our door, with a stove, with a tea-kettle set in the top of it!"

"Ella's cook stove, of course," said Will; and just at this moment the young lady entered, with her purse hanging gracefully over her hand.

"Now, boys, you are too bad!" she exclaimed, as each of the mischievous youngsters were gravely marching up and down, attired in a gray shawl.

"Didn't you get them for us? We thought you did," said both.

"Ella, I want some of that cotton flannel, to make me a pair of pantaloons," said Tom.

"I say, Ella," said Will, "when are you going to housekeeping? Your cooking stove is standing down in the street; 'pon my word, John is loading some coal on the dray with it."

"Ella, isn't that going to be sent to my office?" said Tom; "do you know I do so languish for a new stove with a tea-kettle in the top, to heat a fellow's shaving water!"

Just then, another ring at the door, and the grinning waiter handed in a small brown paper parcel for Miss Ella. Tom made a dive at it, and staving off the brown paper, developed a jaunty little purple velvet cap, with silver tassels.

"My smoking cap! as I live," said he; "only I shall have to wear it on my thumb, instead of my head—too small entirely," said he, shaking his head gravely.

"Come, you saucy boys," said aunt E——, entering briskly, "what are you teasing Ella for?"

"Why, do see this lot of things, aunt? What in the world is Ella going to do with them?"

"Oh! I know!"

"You know; then I can guess, aunt, it is some of your charitable works. You are going to make a juvenile Lady Bountiful of El, eh?"

Ella, who had colored to the roots of her hair at the exposé of her very unfashionable Christmas preparations, now took heart, and bestowed a very gentle and salutary little cuff on the saucy head that still wore the purple cap, and then hastened to gather up her various purchases.

"Laugh away," said she, gaily; "and a good many others will laugh, too, over these things. I got them to make people laugh—people that are not in the habit of laughing!"

"Well, well, I see into it," said Will; "and I tell you I think right well of the idea, too. There are worlds of money wasted at this time of the year, in getting things that nobody wants, and nobody cares for after they are got; and I am glad, for my part, that you are going to get up a variety in this line; in fact, I should like to give you one of these stray leaves to help on," said he, dropping a $10 note into her paper. I like to encourage girls to think of something besides breastpins and sugar candy."

But our story spins on too long. If anybody wants to see the results of Ella's first attempts at *good fairyism,* they can call at the doors of two or three old buildings on Christmas morning, and they shall hear all about it.

MERRY CHRISTMAS!—HAPPY CHRISTMAS!

FANNY FERN

From *Fern Leaves from Fanny's Port-Folio* (Auburn, NY: Derby and Miller, 1853), 295–97.

Fanny Fern was a formidable presence in American literary life in the middle of the nineteenth century. Following an education at the hands of Catharine Beecher (Harriet's sister) and much personal sadness (her first husband died young, her second marriage was deeply unhappy), for a time she was the highest-paid columnist in America. A collection of her newspaper work, from which this short sketch is taken, was an enormous best seller. Frequently conversational and frank, and never shying away from controversial topics, Fanny Fern commanded a wide variety of styles and tones—from scathing satire and righteous protest to broad comedy and emotive sentiment. This sweet seasonal miniature falls firmly into the latter group.

How it flew from one laughing lip to another!—trembling on the tongue of decrepitude; lisped by prattling infancy, and falling like a funeral knell on the ear of the grief-stricken!

Little, busy feet were running to and fro, trumpeting the fame of "good Santa Claus." The pretty blue-eyed maiden blushed, as she placed her Christmas gift on the betrothal finger. Yes, it might have been ten times colder than it was, and nobody would have known it, every body's heart was so warm.

See that great house opposite! How bright the fire-light falls on those rare old pictures; on marble, and damask, and gold and silver! Now they are decking a Christmas-tree. Never a diamond sparkled brighter than those children's eyes. 'Tis all sunshine at the great house.

Kathleen sits at her low, narrow window. She sees it all. There are no pictures on her walls; though she has known the time when they were decked with the rarest. There is nothing there, now, that the eye would look twice upon, save the fair, sad face of its inmate. But it is not of gilded splendor she is thinking.

Last Christmas the wealth of a noble heart was laid at her feet. Now she is written widow! How brief a word to express such a far-reaching sorrow! Walter and she were so happy! "Only one voyage more, dear Katie, and then I will turn landsman, and stay with you on shore"; and so Kathleen clung, weeping, to his neck, and bade him a silent farewell. And since ! * * * Oh, how wearily pass time's leaden footsteps to the watchful eye and the listening ear of love! "Her eyes were with her heart, and that was far away."

Day after day crept on. Then came, at last, these crushing words,—"All on board perished!"

With that short sentence, the light of hope died out in her heart, and the green earth became one wide sepulchre. The blight fell early on so fair a flower. There were many who would gladly have lit again the love-light in those soft, blue eyes; but from all Kathleen turned, heart-sick, away to her little, lonely room, to toil, and dream, and weep, and pray.

And now the twilight has faded away, and the holy stars, one by one, have come stealing out to witness her sorrow. There she sits, with a filling eye and an aching heart, and watches the merry group yonder. Life is so bright to them; so weary to her, without that dear arm to lean upon. Could she but have pillowed that dying head; heard him say but once more, "I love you, Kathleen." But that despairing struggle with those dark, billowy waves; that shriek for "help," where no help could come; that strong arm and brave heart so stricken down! Poor Kathleen!

Blessed sleep! touch those sad eyes lightly. Torture not that troubled heart with mocking dreams. See, she smiles!—a warm flush creeps to her cheek and dries away the tear. Sleep has restored the dear one to her. Dream on while you may, sweet Kathleen!

* * *

"That is the house, sir. God bless me, that you should be alive! That one, sir, with the small windows. No light there. Find the way, sir?"

Tap, tap on the window! Kathleen wakes from that sweet dream to listen. She does not tremble, for grief like hers knows neither hope nor fear. She is soon apparelled, and, shading the small lamp with her little hand, advances to the door. Its flickering ray falls upon the stalwart form before her. What is there in its outline to palsy her tongue, and blanch her cheek? This torturing suspense! If the stranger would but speak!

"Kathleen!"

With one wild cry of joy, she falls upon his neck. Ah, little Katie! Dreams are not always a mockery. A merry Christmas to you!

Illustration accompanying "Merry Christmas!—Happy Christmas!" in *Fern Leaves from Fanny's Port-Folio.*

CHRISTMAS IN SLAVERY

Christmas was put to potent use by abolitionists in the antebellum decades. Exploiting the dominant associations of the season—Christianity, charity, family—abolitionists, particularly those Black activists who had liberated themselves from slavery, frequently focused on the festive to highlight the hypocrisies and cruelties of the enslavers of the South. In the excerpts below, taken from some of the most important accounts written by fugitives from slavery in the antebellum years, Frederick Douglass, Solomon Northup, and Harriet Jacobs present very different accounts of what Christmas meant to the enslaved. While Douglass emphasizes the cruel ironies of the season, Northup (referred to as Platt Epps during his time in bondage) describes some of the important pleasures that the season could still offer even to those in the depths of slavery—Christmas as resistance. Harriet Jacobs, hiding in her grandmother's roof space for an extended period of time at this point in her narrative, articulates the pain generated by her separation from her children at Christmastime, as well as describing the distinctive festive phenomenon of the "Johnkannaus" which spread across the Black Atlantic.

EXCERPT FROM
NARRATIVE OF THE LIFE OF FREDERICK DOUGLASS

FREDERICK DOUGLASS

From *Narrative of the Life of Frederick Douglass* (Boston: Anti-Slavery Office, 1845), 74–77.

The days between Christmas and New Year's day are allowed as holidays; and, accordingly, we were not required to perform any labor, more than to feed and take care of the stock. This time we regarded as our own, by the grace of our masters; and we therefore used or abused it nearly as we pleased. Those of us who had families at a distance, were generally allowed to spend the whole six days in their society. This time, however, was spent in various ways. The staid, sober, thinking and industrious ones of our number would employ themselves in making corn-brooms, mats, horse-collars, and baskets; and another class of us would spend the time in hunting opossums, hares, and coons. But by far the larger part engaged in such sports and merriments as playing ball, wrestling, running foot-races, fiddling, dancing, and drinking whisky; and this latter mode of spending the time was by far the most agreeable to the feelings of our masters. A slave who would work during the holidays was considered by our masters as scarcely deserving them. He was regarded as one who rejected the favor of his master. It was deemed a disgrace not to get drunk at Christmas; and he was regarded as lazy indeed, who had not provided himself with the necessary means, during the year, to get whisky enough to last him through Christmas.

From what I know of the effect of these holidays upon the slave, I believe them to be among the most effective means in the hands of the slaveholder in keeping down the spirit of insurrection. Were the slaveholders at once to abandon this practice, I have not the slightest doubt it would lead to an immediate insurrection among the slaves. These holidays serve as conductors, or safety-valves, to carry off the rebellious spirit of enslaved humanity. But for these, the slave would be forced up to the wildest desperation; and woe betide the slaveholder, the day he ventures to remove or hinder the operation of those conductors! I warn him that, in such an event, a spirit will go forth in their midst, more to be dreaded than the most appalling earthquake.

The holidays are part and parcel of the gross fraud, wrong, and inhumanity of slavery. They are professedly a custom established by the benevolence of the slaveholders; but I undertake to say, it is the result of selfishness, and one of the grossest frauds committed upon the downtrodden slave. They do not give the slaves this time because they would not like to have their work during its continuance, but because they know it would be unsafe to deprive them of it. This will be seen by the fact, that the slaveholders like to have their slaves spend those days just in such a manner as to make them as glad of their ending as of their beginning. Their object seems to be, to disgust their slaves with freedom, by plunging them into the lowest depths of dissipation. For instance, the slaveholders not only like to see the slave drink of his own accord, but will adopt various plans to make him drunk. One plan is, to make bets on their slaves, as to who can drink the most whisky without getting drunk; and in this way they succeed in getting whole multitudes to drink to excess. Thus, when the slave asks for virtuous freedom, the cunning slaveholder, knowing his ignorance, cheats him with a dose of vicious dissipation, artfully labelled with the name of liberty. The most of us used to drink it down, and the result was just what might be supposed: many of us were led to think that there was little to choose between liberty and slavery. We felt, and very properly too, that we had almost as well be slaves to man as to rum. So, when the holidays ended, we staggered up from the filth of our wallowing, took a long breath, and marched to the field,—feeling, upon the whole, rather glad to go, from what our master had deceived us into a belief was freedom, back to the arms of slavery.

I have said that this mode of treatment is a part of the whole system of fraud and inhumanity of slavery. It is so. The mode here adopted to disgust the slave with freedom, by allowing him to see only the abuse of it, is carried out in other things. For instance, a slave loves molasses; he steals some. His master, in many cases, goes off to town, and buys a large quantity; he returns, takes his whip, and commands the slave to eat the molasses, until the poor fellow is made sick at the very mention of it. The same mode is sometimes adopted to make the slaves refrain from asking for more food than their regular allowance. A slave runs through his allowance, and applies for more. His master is enraged at him; but, not willing to send him off without food, gives him more than is necessary, and compels him to eat it within a given time. Then, if he complains that he cannot eat it, he is said to be satisfied neither full nor fasting, and is whipped for being hard to please! I have an abundance of such illustrations of the same principle, drawn from my own observation, but think the cases I have cited sufficient. The practice is a very common one.

EXCERPT FROM
TWELVE YEARS A SLAVE

SOLOMON NORTHUP

From *Twelve Years a Slave* (Auburn, NY: Derby and Miller, 1853), 213–18.

The only respite from constant labor the slave has through the whole year, is during the Christmas holidays. Epps allowed us three—others allow four, five and six days, according to the measure of their generosity. It is the only time to which they look forward with any interest or pleasure. They are glad when night comes, not only because it brings them a few hours repose, but because it brings them one day nearer Christmas. It is hailed with equal delight by the old and the young; even Uncle Abram ceases to glorify Andrew Jackson, and Patsey forgets her many sorrows amid the general hilarity of the holidays. It is the time of feasting, and frolicking, and fiddling—the carnival season with the children of bondage.

They are the only days when they are allowed a little restricted liberty, and heartily indeed do they enjoy it.

It is the custom for one planter to give a "Christmas supper," inviting the slaves from neighboring plantations to join his own on the occasion; for instance, one year it is given by Epps, the next by Marshall, the next by Hawkins, and so on. Usually from three to five hundred are assembled, coming together on foot, in carts, on horseback, on mules, riding double and triple, sometimes a boy and girl, at others a girl and two boys, and at others again a boy, a girl and an old woman. Uncle Abram astride a mule, with Aunt Phebe and Patsey behind him, trotting towards a Christmas supper, would be no uncommon sight on Bayou Boeuf.

Then, too, "of all days i' the year," they array themselves in their best attire. The cotton coat has been washed clean, the stump of a tallow candle has been applied to the shoes, and if so fortunate as to possess a rimless or a crownless hat, it is placed jauntily on the head. They are welcomed with equal cordiality, however, if they come bare-headed and bare-footed to the feast. As a general thing, the women wear handkerchiefs tied about their heads, but if chance has thrown in their way a fiery red ribbon, or a cast-off bonnet of their mistress' grandmother, it is sure to be worn on such occasions. Red—the deep blood red—is decidedly the favorite color among the enslaved damsels of my acquaintance. If a red ribbon does not encircle the neck, you will be certain to find all the hair of their woolly heads tied up with red strings of one sort or another.

The table is spread in the open air, and loaded with varieties of meat and piles of vegetables. Bacon and corn meal at such times are dispensed with. Sometimes the cooking is performed in the kitchen on the plantation, at others in the shade of wide branching trees. In the latter case, a ditch is dug in the ground, and wood laid in and burned until it is filled with glowing coals, over which chickens, ducks, turkeys, pigs, and not unfrequently the entire body of a wild ox, are roasted. They are furnished also with flour, of which biscuits are made, and often with peach and other preserves, with tarts, and every manner and description of pies, except the mince, that being an article of pastry as yet unknown among them. Only the slave who has lived all the years on his scanty allowance of meal and bacon, can appreciate such suppers. White people in great numbers assemble to witness the gastronomical enjoyments.

They seat themselves at the rustic table—the males on one side, the females on the other. The two between whom there may have been an exchange of tenderness, invariably manage to sit opposite; for the omnipresent Cupid disdains not to hurl his arrows into the simple hearts of slaves. Unalloyed and exulting happiness lights up the dark faces of them all. The ivory teeth, contrasting with their black complexions, exhibit two long, white streaks the whole extent of the table. All round the bountiful board a multitude of eyes roll in ecstacy. Giggling and laughter and the clattering of cutlery and crockery succeed. Cuffee's elbow hunches his neighbor's side, impelled by an involuntary impulse of delight; Nelly shakes her finger at Sambo and laughs, she knows not why, and so the fun and merriment flows on.

When the viands have disappeared, and the hungry maws of the children of toil are satisfied, then, next in the order of amusement, is the Christmas dance. My business on these gala days always was to play on the violin. The African race is a music-loving one, proverbially; and many there were among my fellow-bondsmen whose organs of tune were strikingly developed, and who could thumb the banjo with dexterity; but at the expense of appearing egotistical, I must nevertheless, declare, that I was considered the Ole Bull of Bayou Boeuf. My master often received letters, sometimes from a distance of ten miles, requesting him to send me to play at a ball or festival of the whites. He received his compensation, and usually I also returned with many picayunes jingling in my pockets—the extra contributions of those to whose delight I had administered. In this manner I became more acquainted than I otherwise would, up and down the bayou. The young men and maidens of Holmesville always knew there was to be a jollification somewhere, whenever Platt Epps was seen passing through the town with his fiddle in his hand. "Where are you going now, Platt?" and "What is coming off tonight, Platt?" would be interrogatories issuing from every door and window, and many a time when there was no special hurry, yielding to pressing importunities, Platt would draw his bow, and sitting astride his mule, perhaps, discourse musically to a crowd of delighted children, gathered around him in the street.

Alas! had it not been for my beloved violin, I scarcely can conceive how I could have endured the long years of bondage. It introduced me to great houses—relieved me of many days' labor in the field—supplied me with conveniences for my cabin—with pipes and tobacco, and extra pairs of shoes, and oftentimes led me away from the presence of a hard master, to witness scenes of jollity and mirth. It was my companion—the friend of my bosom—triumphing loudly when I was joyful, and uttering its soft, melodious consolations when I was sad. Often, at midnight, when sleep had fled affrighted from the cabin, and my soul was disturbed and troubled with the contemplation of my fate, it would sing me a song of peace. On holy Sabbath days, when an hour or two of leisure was allowed, it would accompany me to some quiet place on the bayou bank, and, lifting up its voice, discourse kindly and pleasantly indeed. It heralded my name round the country—made me friends, who, otherwise would not have noticed me—gave me an honored seat at the yearly feasts, and secured the loudest and heartiest welcome of them all at the Christmas dance. The Christmas dance! Oh, ye pleasure-seeking sons and daughters of idleness, who move with measured step, listless and snail-like, through the slow-winding cotillon, if ye wish to look upon the celerity, if not the "poetry of motion"—upon genuine happiness, rampant and unrestrained—go down to Louisiana, and see the slaves dancing in the starlight of a Christmas night.

CHRISTMAS FESTIVITIES

HARRIET JACOBS

From *Incidents in the Life of a Slave Girl* (Boston, 1863), 179–82.

Christmas was approaching. Grandmother brought me materials, and I busied myself making some new garments and little playthings for my children. Were it not that hiring day is near at hand and many families are fearfully looking forward to the probability of separation in a few days, Christmas might be a happy season for the poor slaves. Even slave mothers try to gladden the hearts of their little ones on that occasion. Benny and Ellen had their Christmas stockings filled. Their imprisoned mother could not have the privilege of witnessing their surprise and joy. But I had the pleasure of peeping at them as they went into the street with their new suits on. I heard Benny ask a little playmate whether Santa Claus brought him any thing. "Yes," replied the boy; "but Santa Claus ain't a real man. It's the children's mothers that put things into the stockings." "No, that can't be," replied Benny, "for Santa Claus brought Ellen and me these new clothes, and my mother has been gone this long time."

How I longed to tell him that his mother made those garments, and that many a tear fell on them while she worked!

Every child rises early on Christmas morning to see the Johnkannaus. Without them, Christmas would be shorn of its greatest attraction. They consist of companies of slaves from the plantations, generally of the lower class. Two athletic men, in calico wrappers, have a net thrown over them, covered with all manner of bright-colored stripes. Cows' tails are fastened to their backs, and their heads are decorated with horns. A box, covered with sheepskin, is called the gumbo box. A dozen beat on this, while others strike triangles and jawbones, to which bands of dancers keep time. For a month previous they are composing songs, which are sung on this occasion. These companies, of a hundred each, turn out early in the morning, and are allowed to go round till twelve o'clock, begging for contributions. Not a door is left unvisited where there is the least chance of obtaining a penny or a glass of rum. They do not drink while they are out, but carry the rum home in jugs, to have a carousal. These Christmas donations frequently amount to twenty or thirty dollars. It is seldom that any white man or child refuses to give them a trifle. If he does, they regale his ears with the following song:—

"Poor massa, so dey say;
Down in de heel, so dey say;
Got no money, so dey say;

Not one shillin, so dey say;
God A' mighty bress you, so dey say."

Christmas is a day of feasting, both with white and colored people. Slaves, who are lucky enough to have a few shillings, are sure to spend them for good eating; and many a turkey and pig is captured, without saying, "By your leave, sir." Those who cannot obtain these, cook a 'possum, or a raccoon, from which savory dishes can be made. My grandmother raised poultry and pigs for sale; and it was her established custom to have both a turkey and a pig roasted for Christmas dinner.

On this occasion, I was warned to keep extremely quiet, because two guests had been invited. One was the town constable, and the other was a free colored man, who tried to pass himself off for white, and who was always ready to do any mean work for the sake of currying favor with white people. My grandmother had a motive for inviting them. She managed to take them all over the house. All the rooms on the lower floor were thrown open for them to pass in and out; and after dinner, they were invited up stairs to look at a fine mocking bird my uncle had just brought home. There, too, the rooms were all thrown open, that they might look in. When I heard them talking on the piazza, my heart almost stood still. I knew this colored man had spent many nights hunting for me. Every body knew he had the blood of a slave father in his veins; but for the sake of passing himself off for white, he was ready to kiss the slaveholders' feet. How I despised him! As for the constable, he wore no false colors. The duties of his office were despicable, but he was superior to his companion, inasmuch as he did not pretend to be what he was not. Any white man, who could raise money enough to buy a slave, would have considered himself degraded by being a constable; but the office enabled its possessor to exercise authority. If he found any slave out after nine o' clock, he could whip him as much as he liked; and that was a privilege to be coveted. When the guests were ready to depart, my grandmother gave each of them some of her nice pudding, as a present for their wives. Through my peep-hole I saw them go out of the gate, and I was glad when it closed after them. So passed the first Christmas in my den.

A HOSPITAL CHRISTMAS

LOUISA MAY ALCOTT

From *Hospital Sketches and Camp and Fireside Stories* (Boston: Roberts Brothers, 1869), 317–44.

The opening section of Little Women *(1868–69) alone guarantees Louisa May Alcott a place in the Christmas literary pantheon. But the March sisters' donation of their Christmas breakfasts was hardly Alcott's only seasonal sketch, and festive offerings peppered her prolific career. This early sketch from 1864 is one of the most remarkable. Based on Alcott's experiences as a nurse during the Civil War, it presents a unique portrait of Christmas in an army hospital. Under the command of the capable Miss Hale, aided by the beatific Big Ben, miscellaneous assorted wounded Union soldiers manage to find some Christmas cheer in the face of their physical and emotional sufferings. It is a vivid example of the ways in which the season was intimately implicated in the conflict engulfing America.*

"Merry Christmas!" "Merry Christmas!" "Merry Christmas, and lots of 'em, ma'am!" echoed from every side, as Miss Hale entered her ward in the gray December dawn. No wonder the greetings were hearty, that thin faces brightened, and eyes watched for the coming of this small luminary more eagerly than for the rising of the sun; for when they woke that morning, each man found that in the silence of the night some friendly hand had laid a little gift beside his bed. Very humble little gifts they were, but well chosen and thoughtfully bestowed by one who made the blithe anniversary pleasant even in a hospital, and sweetly taught the lesson of the hour—Peace on earth, good-will to man.

"I say, ma'am, these are just splendid. I've dreamt about such for a week, but I never thought I'd get 'em," cried one poor fellow, surveying a fine bunch of grapes with as much satisfaction as if he had found a fortune.

"Thank you kindly, Miss, for the paper and the fixings. I hated to keep borrowing, but I hadn't any money," said another, eying his gift with happy anticipations of the home letters with which the generous pages should be filled.

"They are dreadful soft and pretty, but I don't believe I'll ever wear 'em out; my legs are so wimbly there's no go in 'em," whispered a fever patient, looking sorrowfully at the swollen feet ornamented with a pair of carpet slippers gay with roses, and evidently made for his especial need.

"Please hang my posy basket on the gas-burner in the middle of the room, where all the boys can see it. It's too pretty for one alone."

"But then you can't see it yourself, Joe, and you are fonder of such things than the rest," said Miss Hale, taking both the little basket and the hand of her pet patient, a lad of twenty, dying of rapid consumption.

"That's the reason I can spare it for a while, for I shall feel 'em in the room just the same, and they'll do the boys good. You pick out the one you like best, for me to keep, and hang up the rest till by-and-by, please."

She gave him a sprig of mignonette, and he smiled as he took it, for it reminded him of her in her sad-colored gown, as quiet and unobtrusive, but as grateful to the hearts of those about her as was the fresh scent of the flower to the lonely lad who never had known womanly tenderness and care until he found them in a hospital. Joe's prediction was verified; the flowers did do the boys good, for all welcomed them with approving glances, and all felt their refining influence more or less keenly, from cheery Ben, who paused to fill the cup inside with fresher water, to surly Sam, who stopped growling as his eye rested on a geranium very like the one blooming in his sweetheart's window when they parted a long year ago.

"Now, as this is to be a merry day, let us begin to enjoy it at once. Fling up the windows, Ben, and Barney, go for breakfast while I finish washing faces and settling bed-clothes."

With which directions the little woman fell to work with such infectious energy that in fifteen minutes thirty gentlemen with spandy clean faces and hands were partaking of refreshment with as much appetite as their various conditions would permit. Meantime the sun came up, looking bigger, brighter, jollier than usual, as he is apt to do on Christmas days. Not a snow-flake chilled the air that blew in as blandly as if winter had relented, and wished the "boys" the compliments of the season in his mildest mood; while a festival smell pervaded the whole house, and appetizing rumors of turkey, mince-pie, and oysters for dinner, circulated through the wards. When breakfast was done, the wounds dressed, directions for the day delivered, and as many of the disagreeables as possible well over, the fun began. In any other place that would have been considered a very quiet morning; but to the weary invalids prisoned in that room, it was quite a whirl of excitement. None were dangerously ill but Joe, and all were easily amused, for weakness, homesickness and *ennui* made every trifle a joke or an event.

In came Ben, looking like a "Jack in the Green," with his load of hemlock and holly. Such of the men as could get about and had a hand to lend, lent it, and soon, under Miss Hale's direction, a green bough hung at the head of each bed, depended from the gas-burners, and nodded over the fireplace, while the finishing effect was given by a cross and crown at the top and bottom of the room. Great was the interest, many were the mishaps, and frequent was the laughter which attended this performance; for wounded men, when convalescent, are particularly jovial. When "Daddy Mills," as one venerable volunteer was irreverently christened, expatiated learnedly upon the difference between "sprewce, hemlock and pine," how they all listened, each thinking of some familiar wood still pleasantly haunted by boyish recollections of stolen gunnings, gum-pickings, and bird-nestings. When quiet Hayward amazed the company by coming out strong in a most unexpected direction, and telling with much effect the story of a certain "fine old gentleman" who supped on hemlock tea and died like a hero, what commendations were bestowed upon the immortal heathen in language more hearty than classical, as a twig of the historical tree was passed round like a new style of refreshment, that inquiring parties might satisfy themselves regarding the flavor of the Socratic draught. When Barney, the colored incapable, essayed a grand ornament above the door, and relying upon one insufficient nail, descended to survey his success with the proud exclamation, "Look at de neatness of dat job, gen'l'men,"—at which point the whole thing tumbled down about his ears,—how they all shouted but Pneumonia Ned, who, having lost his voice, could only make ecstatic demonstrations with his legs. When Barney cast himself and his hammer despairingly upon the floor, and Miss Hale, stepping into a chair, pounded stoutly at the traitorous nail and performed some miracle with a bit of string which made all fast, what a burst of applause arose from the beds. When gruff Dr. Bangs came in to see what all the noise was about, and the same intrepid lady not only boldly explained, but stuck a bit of holly in his button-hole, and wished him a merry Christmas with such a face full of smiles that the crabbed old doctor felt himself giving in very fast, and bolted out again, calling Christmas a humbug, and exulting over the thirty emetics he would have to prescribe on the morrow, what indignant denials followed him. And when all was done, how everybody agreed with Joe when he said, "I think we are coming Christmas in great style; things look so green and pretty, I feel as I was settin' in a bower."

Pausing to survey her work, Miss Hale saw Sam looking as black as any thunder-cloud. He bounced over on his bed the moment he caught her eye, but she followed him up, and gently covering the cold shoulder he evidently meant to show her, peeped over it, asking, with unabated gentleness,—

"What can I do for you, Sam? I want to have all the faces in my ward bright ones to-day."

"My box ain't come; they said I should have it two, three days ago; why don't they do it, then?" growled Ursur Major.

"It is a busy time, you know, but it will come if they promised, and patience won't delay it, I assure you."

"My patience is used up, and they are a mean set of slow coaches. I'd get it fast enough if I wore shoulder straps; as I don't, I'll bet I sha'n't see it till the things ain't fit to eat; the news is old, and I don't care a hang about it."

"I'll see what I can do; perhaps before the hurry of dinner begins some one will have time to go for it."

"Nobody ever does have time here but folks who would give all they are worth to be stirring round. You can't get it, I know; it's my luck, so don't you worry, ma'am."

Miss Hale did not "worry," but worked, and in time a messenger was found, provided with the necessary money, pass and directions, and despatched to hunt up the missing Christmas-box. Then she paused to see what came next, not that it was necessary to look for a task, but to decide which, out of many, was most important to do first.

"Why, Turner, crying again so soon? What is it now? the light head or the heavy feet?"

"It's my bones, ma'am. They ache so I can't lay easy any way, and I'm so tired I just wish I could die and be out of this misery," sobbed the poor ghost of a once strong and cheery fellow, as the kind hand wiped his tears away, and gently rubbed the weary shoulders.

"Don't wish that Turner, for the worst is over now, and all you need is to get your strength again. Make an effort to sit up a little; it is quite time you tried; a change of posture will help the ache wonderfully, and make this 'dreadful bed,' as you call it, seem very comfortable when you come back to it."

"I can't, ma'am, my legs ain't a bit of use, and I ain't strong enough even to try."

"You never will be if you don't try. Never mind the poor legs, Ben will carry you. I've got the matron's easy-chair all ready, and can make you very cosy by the fire. It's Christmas-day, you know; why not celebrate it by overcoming the despondency which retards your recovery, and prove that illness has not taken all the manhood out of you?"

"It has, though, I'll never be the man I was, and may as well lay here till spring, for I shall be no use if I do get up."

If Sam was a growler this man was a whiner, and few hospital wards are without both. But knowing that much suffering had soured the former and pitifully weakened the latter, their nurse had patience with them, and still hoped to bring them round again. As Turner whimpered out his last dismal speech she bethought herself of something which, in the hurry of the morning, had slipped her mind till now.

"By the way, I've got another present for you. The doctor thought I'd better not give it yet, lest it should excite you too much; but I think you need excitement to make you forget yourself, and that when you find how many blessings you have to be grateful for, you will make an effort to enjoy them."

"Blessings, ma'am? I don't see 'em."

"Don't you see one now?" and drawing a letter from her pocket she held it before his eyes. His listless face brightened a little as he took it, but gloomed over again as he said fretfully,—

"It's from wife, I guess. I like to get her letters, but they are always full of grievings and groanings over me, so they don't do me much good."

"She does not grieve and groan in this one. She is too happy to do that, and so will you be when you read it."

"I don't see why,—hey?—why you don't mean—"

"Yes I do !" cried the little woman, clapping her hands, and laughing so delightedly that the Knight of the Rueful Countenance was betrayed into a broad smile for the first time in many weeks.

"Is not a splendid little daughter a present to rejoice over and be grateful for?"

"Hooray! hold on a bit,—it's all right,—I'll be out again in a minute."

After which remarkably spirited burst, Turner vanished under the bedclothes, letter and all. Whether he read, laughed or cried, in the seclusion of that cotton grotto, was unknown; but his nurse suspected that he did all three, for when he reappeared he looked as if during that pause he had dived into his "sea of troubles," and fished up his old self again.

"What *will* I name her?" was his first remark, delivered with such vivacity that his neighbors began to think he was getting delirious again.

"What is your wife's name?" asked Miss Hale, gladly entering into the domesticities which were producing such a salutary effect.

"Her name's Ann, but neither of us like it. I'd fixed on George, for I wanted my boy called after me; and now you see I ain't a bit prepared for this young woman." Very proud of the young woman he seemed, nevertheless, and perfectly resigned to the loss of the expected son and heir.

"Why not call her Georgiana then? That combines both her parents' names, and is not a bad one in itself."

"Now that's just the brightest thing I ever heard in my life!" cried Turner, sitting bolt upright in his excitement, though half an hour before he would have considered it an utterly impossible feat. "Georgiana Butterfield Turner,—it's a tip-top name, ma'am, and we can call her Georgie just the same. Ann will like that, it's so genteel. Bless 'em both! don't I wish I was at home." And down he lay again, despairing.

"You can be before long, if you choose. Get your strength up, and off you go. Come, begin at once,—drink your beef-tea, and sit up for a few minutes, just in honor of the good news, you know."

"I will, by George—no, by Georgiana! That's a good one, ain't it?" and the whole ward was electrified by hearing a genuine giggle from the "Blueing-bag."

Down went the detested beef-tea, and up scrambled the determined drinker with many groans, and a curious jumble of chuckles, staggers, and fragmentary repetitions of his first, last, and only joke. But when fairly settled in the great rocking-chair, with the gray flannel gown comfortably on, and the new slippers getting their inaugural scorch, Turner forgot his bones, and swung to and fro before the fire, feeling amazingly well, and looking very like a trussed fowl being roasted in the primitive fashion. The languid importance of the man, and the irrepressible satisfaction of the parent, were both laughable and touching things to see, for the happy soul could not keep the glad tidings to himself. A hospital ward is often a small republic, beautifully governed by pity, patience, and the mutual sympathy which lessens mutual suffering. Turner was no favorite; but more than one honest fellow felt his heart warm towards him as they saw his dismal face kindle with fatherly pride, and heard the querulous quaver of his voice soften with fatherly affection, as he said, "My little Georgie, sir."

"He'll do now, ma'am; this has given him the boost he needed, and in a week or two he'll be off our hands."

Big Ben made the remark with a beaming countenance, and Big Ben deserves a word of praise, because he never said one for himself. An ex-patient, promoted to an attendant's place, which he filled so well that he was regarded as a model for all the rest to copy. Patient, strong, and tender, he seemed to combine many of the best traits of both man and woman; for he appeared to know by instinct where the soft spot was to be found in every heart, and how best to help sick body or sad soul. No one would have guessed this to have seen him lounging in the hall during one of the short rests he allowed himself. A brawny, six-foot fellow, in red shirt, blue trousers tucked into his boots, an old cap, visor always up, and under it a roughly-bearded, coarsely-featured face, whose prevailing expression was one of great gravity and kindliness, though a humorous twinkle of the eye at times betrayed the man, whose droll sayings often set the boys in a roar. "A good-natured, clumsy body" would have been the verdict passed upon him by a casual observer; but watch him in his ward, and see how great a wrong that hasty judgment would have done him.

Unlike his predecessor, who helped himself generously when the meals came up, and carelessly served out rations for the rest, leaving even the most helpless to bungle for themselves or wait till he was done, shut himself into his pantry, and there,—to borrow a hospital phrase,—gormed, Ben often left nothing for himself, or took cheerfully such cold bits as remained when all the rest were served; so patiently feeding the weak, being hands and feet to the maimed, and a pleasant provider for all that, as one of the boys said,—"It gives a relish to the vittles to have Ben fetch 'em." If one were restless, Ben carried him in his strong arms; if one were undergoing the sharp torture of the surgeon's knife, Ben held him with a touch as firm as kind; if one were homesick, Ben wrote letters for him with great hearty blots and dashes under all the affectionate or important words. More than one poor fellow read his fate in Ben's pitiful eyes, and breathed his last breath away on Ben's broad breast,—always a quiet pillow till its work was done, then it would heave with genuine grief, as his big hand softly closed the tired eyes, and made another comrade ready for the last review. The war shows us many Bens,—for the same power of human pity which makes women brave also makes men tender; and each is the womanlier, the manlier, for these revelations of unsuspected strength and sympathies.

At twelve o'clock dinner was the prevailing idea in ward No. 3, and when the door opened every man sniffed, for savory odors broke loose from the kitchens and went roaming about the house. Now this Christmas dinner had been much talked of; for certain charitable and patriotic persons had endeavored to provide every hospital in Washington with materials for this time-honored feast. Some mistake in the list sent to head-quarters, some unpardonable neglect of orders, or some premeditated robbery, caused the long-expected dinner in the —— Hospital to prove a dead failure; but to which of these causes it was attributable was never known, for the deepest mystery enveloped that sad transaction. The full weight of the dire disappointment was mercifully lightened by premonitions of the impending blow. Barney was often missing; for the attendants were to dine *en masse* after the patients were done, therefore a speedy banquet for the latter parties was ardently desired, and he probably devoted his energies to goading on the cooks. From time to time he appeared in the doorway, flushed and breathless, made some thrilling announcement, and vanished, leaving ever-increasing appetite, impatience and expectation, behind him.

Dinner was to be served at one; at half-past twelve Barney proclaimed, "Dere ain't no vegetables but squash and pitaters." A universal groan arose; and several indignant parties on a short allowance of meat consigned the defaulting cook to a warmer climate than the tropical one he was then enjoying. At twenty minutes to one, Barney increased the excitement by whispering, ominously, "I say, de puddins isn't plummy ones."

"Fling a piller at him and shut the door, Ben," roared one irascible being, while several others *not* fond of puddings received the fact with equanimity. At quarter to one Barney piled up the agony by adding the bitter information, "Dere isn't but two turkeys for dis ward, and dey's little fellers."

Anxiety instantly appeared in every countenance, and intricate calculations were made as to how far the two fowls would go when divided among thirty men; also friendly warnings were administered to several of the feebler gentlemen not to indulge too freely, if at all, for fear of relapses. Once more did the bird of evil omen return, for at ten minutes to one Barney croaked through the key-hole, "Only jes half ob de pies has come, gen'l'men." That capped the climax, for the masculine palate has a predilection for pastry, and mince-pie was the sheet-anchor to which all had clung when other hopes went down. Even Ben looked dismayed; not that he expected anything but the perfume and pickings for his share, but he had set his heart on having the dinner an honor to the institution and a memorable feast for the men, so far away from home, and all that usually makes the day a festival among the poorest. He looked pathetically grave as Turner began to fret, Sam began to swear under his breath, Hayward to sigh, Joe to wish it was all over, and the rest began to vent their emotions with a freedom which was anything but inspiring. At that moment Miss Hale came in with a great basket of apples and oranges in one hand, and several convivial-looking bottles in the other.

"Here is our dessert, boy! A kind friend remembered us, and we will drink her health in her own currant wine."

A feeble smile circulated round the room, and in some sanguine bosoms hope revived again. Ben briskly emptied the basket, while Miss Hale whispered to Joe,—

"I know you would be glad to get away from the confusion of this next hour, to enjoy a breath of fresh air, and dine quietly with Mrs. Burton round the corner, wouldn't you?"

"Oh, ma'am, so much! the noise, the smells, the fret and flurry, make me sick just to think of! But how can I go? that dreadful ambulance 'most killed me last time, and I'm weaker now."

"My dear boy, I have no thought of trying that again till our ambulances are made fit for the use of weak and wounded men. Mrs. Burton's carriage is at the door, with her motherly self inside, and all you have got to do is to let me bundle you up, and Ben carry you out."

With a long sigh of relief Joe submited to both these processes, and when his nurse watched his happy face as the carriage slowly rolled away, she felt well repaid for the little sacrifice of rest and pleasure so quietly made; for Mrs. Burton came to carry her, not Joe, away.

"Now, Ben, help me to make this unfortunate dinner go off as well as we can," she whispered. "On many accounts it is a mercy that the men are spared the temptations of a more generous meal; pray don't tell them so, but make the best of it, as you know very well how to do."

"I'll try my best, Miss Hale, but I'm no less disappointed, for some of 'em, being no better than children, have been living on the thoughts of it for a week, and it comes hard to give it up."

If Ben had been an old-time patriarch, and the thirty boys his sons, he could not have spoken with a more paternal regret, or gone to work with a better will. Putting several small tables together in the middle of the room, he left Miss Hale to make a judicious display of plates, knives and forks, while he departed for the banquet. Presently he returned, bearing the youthful turkeys and the vegetables in his tray, followed by Barney, looking unutterable things at a plum-pudding baked in a milk-pan, and six very small pies. Miss Hale played a lively tattoo as the procession approached, and, when the viands were arranged, with the red and yellow fruit prettily heaped up in the middle, it really did look like a dinner.

"Here's richness! here's the delicacies of the season and the comforts of life!" said Ben, falling back to survey the table with as much apparent satisfaction as if it had been a lord mayor's feast.

"Come, hurry up, and give us our dinner, what there is of it!" grumbled Sam.

"Boys," continued Ben, beginning to cut up the turkeys, "these noble birds have been sacrificed for the defenders of their country; they will go as far as ever they can, and, when they can't go any farther, we shall endeavor to supply their deficiencies with soup or ham, oysters having given out unexpectedly. Put it to vote; both have been provided on this joyful occasion, and a word will fetch either."

"Ham! ham!" resounded from all sides. Soup was an every-day affair, and therefore repudiated with scorn; but ham, being a rarity, was accepted as a proper reward of merit and a tacit acknowledgment of their wrongs.

The "noble birds" did go as far as possible, and were handsomely assisted by their fellow martyr. The pudding was not as plummy as could have been desired, but a slight exertion of fancy made the crusty knobs do duty for raisins. The pies were small, yet a laugh added flavor to the mouthful apiece, for, when Miss Hale asked Ben to cut them up, that individual regarded her with an inquiring aspect as he said, in his drollest tone,—

"I wouldn't wish to appear stupid, ma'am, but, when you mention 'pies,' I presume you allude to these trifles. 'Tarts,' or 'patties,' would meet my views better, in speaking of the third course of this lavish dinner. As such I will do my duty by 'em, hoping that the appetites is to match."

Carefully dividing the six pies into twenty-nine diminutive wedges, he placed each in the middle of a large clean plate, and handed them about with the gravity of an undertaker. Dinner had restored good humor to many; this hit at the pies put the finishing touch to it, and from that moment an atmosphere of jollity prevailed. Healths were drunk in currant wine, apples and oranges flew about as an impromptu game of ball was got up, Miss Hale sang a Christmas carol, and Ben gambolled like a sportive giant as he cleared away. Pausing in one of his prances to and fro, he beckoned the nurse out, and, when she followed, handed her a plate heaped up with good things from a better table than she ever sat at now.

"From the matron, ma'am. Come right in here and eat it while it's hot; they are most through in the diningroom, and you'll get nothing half so nice," said Ben, leading the way into his pantry and pointing to a sunny window-seat.

"Are you sure she meant it for me, and not for yourself, Ben?"

"Of course she did Why, what should I do with it, when I've just been feastin' sumptuous in this very room?"

"I don't exactly see what you have been feasting on," said Miss Hale, glancing round the tidy pantry as she sat down.

"Havin' eat up the food and washed up the dishes, it naturally follows that you don't see, ma'am. But if I go off in a fit by-and-by you'll know what it's owin' to," answered Ben, vainly endeavoring to look like a man suffering from repletion.

"Such kind fibs are not set down against one, Ben, so I will eat your dinner, for if I don't I know you will throw it out of the window to prove that you can't eat it."

"Thankee ma'am, I'm afraid I should; for, at the rate he's going on, Barney wouldn't be equal to it," said Ben, looking very much relieved, as he polished his last pewter fork and hung his towels up to dry.

A pretty general siesta followed the excitement of dinner, but by three o'clock the public mind was ready for amusement, and the arrival of Sam's box provided it. He was asleep when it was brought in and quietly deposited at his bed's foot, ready to surprise him on awaking. The advent of a box was a great event, for the fortunate receiver seldom failed to "stand treat," and next best to getting things from one's own home was the getting them from some other boy's home. This was an unusually large box, and all felt impatient to have it opened, though Sam's exceeding crustiness prevented the indulgence of great expectations. Presently he roused, and the first thing his eye fell upon was the box, with his own name sprawling over it in big black letters. As if it were merely the continuance of his dream, he stared stupidly at it for a moment, then rubbed his eyes and sat up, exclaiming,—

"Hullo! that's mine!"

"Ah! who said it wouldn't come? who hadn't the faith of a grasshopper? and who don't half deserve it for being a Barker by nater as by name?" cried Ben, emphasizing each question with a bang on the box, as he waited, hammer in hand, for the arrival of the wardmaster, whose duty it was to oversee the opening of such matters, lest contraband articles should do mischief to the owner or his neighbors.

"Ain't it a jolly big one? Knock it open, and don't wait for anybody or anything!" cried Sam, tumbling off his bed and beating impatiently on the lid with his one hand.

In came the ward-master, off came the cover, and out came a motley collection of apples, socks, dough-nuts, paper, pickles, photographs, pocket-handkerchiefs, gingerbread, letters, jelly, newspapers, tobacco, and cologne. "All right, glad it's come,—don't kill yourself," said the ward-master, as he took a hasty survey and walked off again. Drawing the box nearer the bed, Ben delicately followed, and Sam was left to brood over his treasures in peace.

At first all the others, following Ben's example, made elaborate pretences of going to sleep, being absorbed in books, or utterly uninterested in the outer world. But very soon curiosity got the better of politeness, and one by one they all turned round and stared. They might have done so from the first, for Sam was perfectly unconscious of everything but his own affairs, and, having read the letters, looked at the pictures, unfolded the bundles, turned everything inside out and upside down, tasted all the eatables and made a spectacle of himself with jelly, he paused to get his breath and find his way out of the confusion he had created. Presently he called out,—

"Miss Hale, will you come and right up my duds for me?" adding, as her woman's hands began to bring matters straight, "I don't know what to do with 'em all, for some won't keep long, and it will take pretty steady eating to get through 'em in time, supposin' appetite holds out."

"How do the others manage with their things?"

"You know they give 'em away; but I'll be hanged if I do, for they are always callin' names and pokin' fun at me. Guess they won't get anything out of me now."

The old morose look came back as he spoke, for it had disappeared while reading the home letters, touching the home gifts. Still busily folding and arranging, Miss Hale asked,—

"You know the story of the Three Cakes; which are you going to be—Harry, Peter, or Billy?"

Sam began to laugh at this sudden application of the nursery legend; and, seeing her advantage, Miss Hale pursued it:

"We all know how much you have suffered, and all respect you for the courage with which you have borne your long confinement and your loss; but don't you think you have given the boys some cause for making fun of you, as you say? You used to be a favorite, and can be again, if you will only put off these crusty ways, which will grow upon you faster than you think. Better lose both arms than cheerfulness and self-control, Sam."

Pausing to see how her little lecture was received, she saw that Sam's better self was waking up, and added yet another word, hoping to help a mental ailment as she had done so many physical ones. Looking up at him with her kind eyes, she said, in a lowered voice,—

"This day, on which the most perfect life began, is a good day for all of us to set about making ourselves readier to follow that divine example. Troubles are helpers if we take them kindly, and the bitterest may sweeten us for all our lives. Believe and try this, Sam, and when you go away from us let those who love you find that two battles have been fought, two victories won."

Sam made no answer, but sat thoughtfully picking at the half-eaten cookey in his hand. Presently he stole a glance about the room, and, as if all helps were waiting for him, his eye met Joe's. From his solitary corner by the fire and the bed he would seldom leave again until he went into his grave, the boy smiled back at him so heartily, so happily, that something gushed warm across Sam's heart as he looked down upon the faces of mother, sister, sweetheart, scattered round him, and remembered how poor his comrade was in all such tender ties, and yet how rich in that beautiful content, which, "having nothing, yet hath all." The man had no words in which to express this feeling, but it came to him and did him good, as he proved in his own way. "Miss Hale," he said, a little awkwardly, "I wish you'd pick out what you think each would like, and give 'em to the boys."

He got a smile in answer that drove him to his cookey as a refuge, for his lips would tremble, and he felt half proud, half ashamed to have earned such bright approval.

"Let Ben help you,—he knows better than I. But you must give them all yourself, it will so surprise and please the boys; and then to-morrow we will write a capital letter home, telling what a jubilee we made over their fine box."

At this proposal Sam half repented; but, as Ben came lumbering up at Miss Hale's summons, he laid hold of his new resolution as if it was a sort of shower-bath and he held the string, one pull of which would finish the baptism. Dividing his most cherished possession, which (alas for romance!) was the tobacco, he bundled the larger half into a paper, whispering to Miss Hale,—

"Ben ain't exactly what you'd call a ministerin' angel to look at, but he is amazin' near one in his ways, so I'm goin' to begin with him."

Up came the "ministering angel," in red flannel and cow-hide boots; and Sam tucked the little parcel into his pocket, saying, as he began to rummage violently in the box,—

"Now jest hold your tongue, and lend a hand here about these things."

Ben was so taken aback by this proceeding that he stared blankly, till a look from Miss Hale enlightened him; and, taking his cue, he played his part as well as could be expected on so short a notice. Clapping Sam on the shoulder,—not the bad one, Ben was always thoughtful of those things,—he exclaimed heartily,

"I always said you'd come round when this poor arm of yours got a good start, and here you are jollier'n ever. Lend a hand 1 so I will, a pair of 'em. What's to do? Pack these traps up again?"

"No; I want you to tell what *you'd* do with 'em if they were yours. Free, you know,—as free as if they really was."

Ben held on to the box a minute as if this second surprise rather took him off his legs; but another look from the prime mover in this resolution steadied him, and he fell to work as if Sam had been in the habit of being "free."

"Well, let's see. I think I'd put the clothes and sich into this smaller box that the bottles come in, and stan' it under the table, handy. Here's newspapers—pictures in 'em, too! I should make a circulatin' lib'ry of them; they'll be a real treat. Pickles—well, I guess I should keep them on the winder here as a kind of a relish dinnertimes, or to pass along to them as longs for 'em. Cologne—that's a dreadful handsome bottle, ain't it? That, now, would be fust-rate to give away to somebody as was very fond of it,—a kind of a delicate attention, you know, if you happen to meet such a person anywheres."

Ben nodded towards Miss Hale, who was absorbed in folding pocket-handkerchiefs. Sam winked expressively, and patted the bottle as if congratulating himself that it *was* handsome, and that he *did* know what to do with it. The pantomime was not elegant, but as much real affection and respect went into it as if he had made a set speech, and presented the gift upon his knees.

"The letters and photographs I should probably keep under my piller for a spell; the jelly I'd give to Miss Hale, to use for the sick ones; the cake-stuff and that pot of jam, that's gettin' ready to work, I'd stand treat with for tea, as dinner wasn't all we could have wished. The apples I'd keep to eat, and fling at Joe when he was too bashful to ask for one, and the *tobaccer* I would *not* go lavishin' on folks that have no business to be enjoyin' luxuries when many a poor feller is dyin' of want down to Charlestown. There, sir! that's what *I'd* do if any one was so clever as to send me a jolly box like this."

Sam was enjoying the full glow of his shower-bath by this time. As Ben designated the various articles, he set them apart; and when the inventory ended, he marched away with the first instalment: two of the biggest, rosiest apples for Joe, and all the pictorial papers. Pickles are not usually regarded as tokens of regard, but as Sam dealt them out one at a time,—for he would let nobody help him, and his single hand being the left, was as awkward as it was willing,—the boys' faces brightened; for a friendly word accompanied each, which made the sour gherkins as welcome as sweetmeats. With every trip the donor's spirits rose; for Ben circulated freely between whiles, and, thanks to him, not an allusion to the past marred the satisfaction of the present. Jam, soda-biscuits, and cake, were such welcome additions to the usual bill of fare, that when supper was over a vote of thanks was passed, and speeches were made; for, being true Americans, the ruling passion found vent in the usual "Fellow-citizens!" and allusions to the "Star-spangled Banner." After which Sam subsided, feeling himself a public benefactor, and a man of mark.

A perfectly easy, pleasant day throughout would be almost an impossibility in any hospital, and this one was no exception to the general rule; for, at the usual time, Dr. Bangs went his rounds, leaving the customary amount of discomfort, discontent and dismay behind him. A skilful surgeon and an excellent man was Dr. Bangs, but not a sanguine or conciliatory individual; many cares and crosses caused him to regard the world as one large hospital, and his fellow-beings all more or less dangerously wounded patients in it. He saw life through the bluest of blue spectacles, and seemed to think that the sooner people quitted it the happier for them. He did his duty by the men, but if they recovered he looked half disappointed, and congratulated them with cheerful prophecies that there would come a time when they would wish they hadn't. If one died he seemed relieved, and surveyed him with pensive satisfaction, saying heartily,—

"He's comfortable, now, poor soul, and well out of this miserable world, thank God!"

But for Ben the sanitary influences of the doctor's ward would have been small, and Dante's doleful line might have been written on the threshold of the door,—

"Who enters here leaves hope behind."

Ben and the doctor perfectly understood and liked each other, but never agreed, and always skirmished over the boys as if manful cheerfulness and medical despair were fighting for the soul and body of each one.

"Well," began the doctor, looking at Sam's arm, or, rather, all that was left of that member after two amputations, "we shall be ready for another turn at this in a day or two if it don't mend faster. Tetanus sometimes follows such cases, but that is soon over, and I should not object to a case of it, by way of variety." Sam's hopeful face fell, and he set his teeth as if the fatal symptoms were already felt.

"If one kind of lockjaw was more prevailing than 'tis, it wouldn't be a bad thing for some folks I could mention," observed Ben, covering the well-healed stump as carefully as if it were a sleeping baby; adding, as the doctor walked away, "There's a sanguinary old sawbones for you! Why, bless your buttons, Sam, you are doing splendid, and he goes on that way because there's no chance of his having another cut at you! Now he's squenchin' Turner, jest as we've blowed a spark of spirit into him. If ever there was a born extinguisher its Bangs!"

Ben rushed to the rescue, and not a minute too soon; for Turner, who now labored under the delusion that his recovery depended solely upon his getting out of bed every fifteen minutes, was sitting by the fire, looking up at the doctor, who pleasantly observed, while feeling his pulse,—

"So you are getting ready for another fever, are you? Well, we've grown rather fond of you, and will keep you six weeks longer if you have set your heart on it."

Turner looked nervous, for the doctor's jokes were always grim ones; but Ben took the other hand in his, and gently rocked the chair as he replied, with great politeness,—

"This robust convalescent of ourn would be happy to oblige you, sir, but he has a pressin' engagement up to Jersey for next week, and couldn't stop on no account. You see Miss Turner wants a careful muss for little Georgie, and he's a goin' to take the place."

Feeling himself on the brink of a laugh as Turner simpered with a ludicrous mixture of pride in his baby and fear for himself, Dr. Bangs said, with unusual sternness and a glance at Ben,—

"You take the responsibility of this step upon yourself, do you? Very well; then I wash my hands of Turner; only, if that bed is empty in a week, don't lay the blame of it at my door."

"Nothing shall induce me to do it, sir," briskly responded Ben. "Now then, turn in my boy, and sleep your prettiest, for I wouldn't but disappoint that cheerfulest of men for a month's wages; and that's liberal, as I ain't likely to get it."

"How is this young man after the rash dissipations of the day?" asked the doctor, pausing at the bed in the corner, after he had made a lively progress down the room, hotly followed by Ben.

"I'm first-rate, sir," panted Joe, who always said so, though each day found him feebler than the last. Every one was kind to Joe, even the gruff doctor, whose manner softened, and who was forced to frown heavily to hide the pity in his eyes.

"How's the cough?"

"Better, sir; being weaker, I can't fight against it as I used to do, so it comes rather easier."

"Sleep any last night?"

"Not much; but it's very pleasant laying here when the room is still, and no light but the fire. Ben keeps it bright; and, when I fret, he talks to me, and makes the time go telling stories till he gets so sleepy he can hardly speak. Dear old Ben I hope he'll have some one as kind to him, when he needs it as I do now."

"He will get what he deserves by-and-by, you may be sure of that," said the doctor, as severely as if Ben merited eternal condemnation.

A great drop splashed down upon the hearth as Joe spoke; but Ben put his foot on it, and turned about as if defying any one to say he shed it.

"Of all the perverse and reckless women whom I have known in the course of a forty years' practice, this one is the most perverse and reckless," said the doctor, abruptly addressing Miss Hale, who just then appeared, bringing Joe's "posy-basket" back. "You will oblige me, ma'am, by sitting in this chair with your hands folded for twenty minutes; the clock will then strike nine, and you will go straight up to your bed."

Miss Hale demurely sat down, and the doctor ponderously departed, sighing regretfully as he went through the room, as if disappointed that the whole thirty were not lying at death's door; but on the threshold he turned about, exclaimed "Good-night, boys! God bless you!" and vanished as precipitately as if a trap-door had swallowed him up.

Miss Hale was a perverse woman in some things; for, instead of folding her tired hands, she took a rusty-covered volume from the mantle-piece, and, sitting by Joe's bed, began to read aloud. One by one all other sounds grew still; one by one the men composed themselves to listen; and one by one the words of the sweet old Christmas story came to them, as the woman's quiet voice went reading on. If any wounded spirit needed balm, if any hungry heart asked food, if any upright purpose, newborn aspiration, or sincere repentance wavered for want of human strength, all found help, hope, and consolation in the beautiful and blessed influences of the book, the reader, and the hour.

The bells rung nine, the lights grew dim, the day's work was done; but Miss Hale lingered beside Joe's bed, for his face wore a wistful look, and he seemed loath to have her go.

"What is it, dear?" she said; "what can I do for you before I leave you to Ben's care?"

He drew her nearer, and whispered earnestly, "It's something that I know you'll do for me, because I can't do it for myself, not as I want it done, and you can. I'm going pretty fast now, ma'am; and when—when some one else is laying here, I want you to tell the boys,—every one, from Ben to Barney,—how much I thanked 'em, how much I loved 'em, and how glad I was that I had known 'em, even for such a little while."

"Yes, Joe, I'll tell them all. What else can I do, my boy?"

"Only let me say to you what no one else must say for me, that all I want to live for is to try and do something in my poor way to show you how I thank you, ma'am. It isn't what you've said to me, it isn't what you've done for me alone, that makes me grateful; it's because you've learned me many things without knowing it, showed me what I ought to have been before, if I'd had any one to tell me how, and made this such a happy, home-like place, I shall be sorry when I have to go."

Poor Joe! it must have fared hardly with him all those twenty years, if a hospital seemed home-like, and a little sympathy, a little care, could fill him with such earnest gratitude. He stopped a moment to lay his cheek upon the hand he held in both of his, then hurried on as if he felt his breath beginning to give out:

"I dare say many boys have said this to you, ma'am, better than I can, for I don't say half I feel; but I know that none of 'em ever thanked you as I thank you in my heart, or ever loved you as I'll love you all my life. To-day I hadn't anything to give you, I'm so poor; but I wanted to tell you this, on the last Christmas I shall ever see."

It was a very humble kiss he gave that hand; but the fervor of a first love warmed it, and the sincerity of a great gratitude made it both a precious and pathetic gift to one who, half unconsciously, had made this brief and barren life so rich and happy at its close. Always womanly and tender, Miss Hale's face was doubly so as she leaned over him, whispering,—

"I have had my present, now. Good-night, Joe."

EXCERPT FROM

FIVE LITTLE PEPPERS AND HOW THEY GREW

MARGARET SIDNEY

From *Five Little Peppers and How They Grew* (Boston: Lothrop Publishing Co., 1881).

When Harriet Lothrop (writing as Margaret Sidney) published the short story "Polly Pepper's Chicken Pie" in the children's magazine Wide Awake *in 1877, readers were introduced to a cast of characters who would capture the hearts of generations of young Americans. Capitalizing on the popularity of this short sketch, Lothrop released the best-selling* Five Little Peppers and How They Grew *in 1881; she was still writing sequels in 1916. The Peppers in question were the five children of the widowed and impoverished Mrs. Pepper: Ben, Polly, Joel, Davie, and Phronsie. They befriend a young boy called Jasper King—known to them as "Jappy"—whose wealthy father becomes their benefactor, eventually hiring Mrs. Pepper as a housekeeper and welcoming the entire Pepper family into his home. In this excerpt, the Peppers are still resident in their "little brown house" and, inspired by Jasper's example, the children attempt to have their first Christmas—a key trope in children's literature in this formative period.*

CHAPTER XVI: GETTING A CHRISTMAS FOR THE LITTLE ONES

And so October came and went. The little Peppers were very lonely after Jasper had gone; even Mrs. Pepper caught herself looking up one day when the wind blew the door open suddenly, half expecting to see the merry whole-souled boy, and the faithful dog come scampering in.

But the letters came—and that was a comfort; and it was fun to answer them. The first one spoke of Jasper's being under a private tutor, with his cousins; then they were less frequent, and they knew he was studying hard. Full of anticipations of Christmas himself, he urged the little Peppers to try for one. And the life and spirit of the letter was so catching, that Polly and Ben found their souls fired within them to try at least to get for the little ones a taste of Christmastide.

"Now, mammy," they said at last, one day in the latter part of October, when the crisp, fresh air filled their little healthy bodies with springing vitality that must bubble over and rush into something, "we don't want a Thanksgiving—truly we don't. But may we try for a Christmas—just a *little* one," they added, timidly, "for the children?" Ben and Polly always called the three younger ones of the flock "the children."

To their utter surprise, Mrs. Pepper looked mildly assenting, and presently she said, "Well, I don't see why you can't try; 'twon't do any harm, I'm sure."

You see Mrs. Pepper had received a letter from Jasper, which at present she didn't feel called upon to say anything about.

"Now," said Polly, drawing a long breath, as she and Ben stole away into a corner to "talk over" and lay plans, "what does it mean?"

"Never mind," said Ben; "as long as she's given us leave I don't *care* what it is."

"I neither," said Polly, with the delicious feeling as if the whole world were before them where to choose; "it'll be just *gorgeous,* Ben!"

"What's that?" asked Ben, who was not as much given to long words as Polly, who dearly loved to be fine in language as well as other things.

"Oh, it's something Jappy said one day; and I asked him, and he says it's fine, and lovely, and all that," answered Polly, delighted that she knew something she could really tell Ben.

"Then why not *say* fine?" commented Ben, practically, with a little upward lift of his nose.

"Oh, I'd know, I'm sure," laughed Polly. "Let's think what'll we do for Christmas—how many weeks are there, anyway, Ben?" And she began to count on her fingers.

"That's no way," said Ben, "I'm going to get the Almanac."

So he went to the old clock where hanging up by its side, was a "Farmer's Almanac."

"Now, we'll know," he said, coming back to their corner. So with heads together they consulted and counted up till they found that eight weeks and three days remained in which to get ready.

"Dear me!" said Polly. "It's most a year, isn't it, Ben?"

"'Twon't be much time for us," said Ben, who thought of the many hours to be devoted to hard work that would run away with the time. "We'd better begin right away, Polly."

"Well, all right," said Polly, who could scarcely keep her fingers still, as she thought of the many things she should so love to do if she could. "But first, Ben, what let's do?"

"Would you rather hang up their stockings?" asked Ben, as if he had unlimited means at his disposal; "or have a tree?"

"Why," said Polly, with wide open eyes at the two magnificent ideas, "we haven't got anything to put in the stockings when we hang 'em, Ben."

"That's just it," said Ben. "Now, wouldn't it be better to have a tree, Polly? I can get that easy in the woods, you know."

"Well," interrupted Polly, eagerly, "we haven't got anything to hang on that, either, Ben. You know Jappy said folks hang all sorts of presents on the branches. So I don't see," she continued, impatiently, "as that's any good. We can't do anything, Ben Pepper, so there! there isn't anything to do anything with," and with a flounce Polly sat down on the old wooden stool, and folding her hands looked at Ben in a most despairing way.

"I know," said Ben, "we haven't got much."

"We haven't got anything," said Polly, still looking at him.

"Why, we've got a tree," replied Ben, hopefully.

"Well, what's a tree," retorted Polly, scornfully. "Anybody can go out and look at a tree outdoors."

"Well, now, I tell you, Polly," said Ben, sitting down on the floor beside her, and speaking very slowly and decisively, "we've got to do something 'cause we've begun; and we might make a tree real pretty."

"How?" asked Polly, ashamed of her ill-humor, but not in the least seeing how anything could be made of a tree. "How, Ben Pepper?"

"Well," said Ben, pleasantly, "we'd set it up in the corner—"

"Oh, no, not in the corner," cried Polly, whose spirits began to rise a little as she saw Ben so hopeful. "Put it in the middle of the room, *do!*"

"I don't care where you put it," said Ben, smiling, happy that Polly's usual cheerful energy had returned, "but I thought—'twill be a little one, you know, and I thought 'twould look better in the corner."

"What else?" asked Polly, eager to see how Ben would dress the tree.

"Well," said Ben, "you know the Henderson boys gave me a lot of corn last week."

"I don't see as that helps much," said Polly, still incredulous. "Do you mean hang the cobs on the branches, Ben? That would be just dreadful!"

"I should think likely," laughed Ben. "No, indeed, Polly Pepper! but if we should pop a lot, oh! a bushel, and then we should string 'em, we could wind it all in and out among the branches, and—"

"Why, wouldn't that be pretty?" cried Polly, "real pretty—and we can do that, I'm sure."

"Yes," continued Ben; "and then, don't you know, there's some little candle ends in that box in the Provision Room, maybe mammy'd give us them."

"I don't believe but she would," cried Polly; "'twould be just like Jappy's if she would! Let's ask her now—this very same minute!"

And they scampered hurriedly to Mrs. Pepper, who to their extreme astonishment, after all, said "yes," and smiled encouragingly on the plan.

"Isn't mammy good?" said Polly, with loving gratitude, as they seated themselves again.

"Now we're all right," exclaimed Ben, "and I tell you we can make the tree look perfectly *splendid,* Polly Pepper!"

"And I'll tell you another thing, Ben," Polly said, "oh! something elegant! You must get ever so many hickory nuts; and you know those bits of bright paper I've got in the bureau drawer? Well, we can paste them on to the nuts and hang 'em on for the balls Jappy tells of."

"Polly," cried Ben, "it'll be such a tree as never was, won't it?"

"Yes; but dear me," cried Polly, springing up, "the children are coming! Wasn't it good, grandma wanted 'em to come over this afternoon, so's we could talk! Now *hush!*" as the door opened to admit the noisy little troop.

"If you think of any new plan," whispered Ben, behind his hand, while Mrs. Pepper engaged their attention, "you'll have to come out into the wood-shed to talk after this."

"I know it," whispered Polly back again; "oh! we've got just heaps of things to think of, Bensie!"

Such a contriving and racking of brains as Polly and Ben set up after this! They would bob over at each other, and smile with significant gesture as a new idea would strike one of them, in the most mysterious way that, if observed, would drive the others almost wild. And then, frightened lest in some hilarious moment the secret should pop out, the two conspirators would betake themselves to the wood-shed as before agreed on. But Joel, finding this out, followed them one day—or, as Polly said, tagged—so that was no good.

"Let's go behind the wood-pile," she said to Ben, in desperation; "he can't hear there, if we whisper real soft."

"Yes, he will," said Ben, who knew Joel's hearing faculties much better. "We'll have to wait till they're a-bed."

So after that, when nightfall first began to make its appearance, Polly would hint mildly about bedtime.

"You hustle us so!" said Joel, after he had been sent off to bed for two or three nights unusually early.

"Oh, Joey, it's good for you to get to bed," said Polly, coaxingly; "it'll make you grow, you know, real fast."

"Well, I don't grow a-bed," grumbled Joel, who thought something was in the wind. "You and Ben are going to talk, I know, and wink your eyes, as soon as we're gone."

"Well, go along, Joe, that's a good boy," said Polly, laughing, "and you'll know some day."

"What'll you give me?" asked Joel, seeing a bargain, his foot on the lowest stair leading to the loft, "say, Polly?"

"Oh, I haven't got much to give," she said, cheerily; "but I'll tell you what, Joey—I'll tell you a story every day that you go to bed."

"Will you?" cried Joe, hopping back into the room. "Begin now, Polly, begin now!"

"Why, you haven't been to bed yet," said Polly, "so I can't till to-morrow."

"Yes, I have—you've made us go for three—no, I guess fourteen nights," said Joel, indignantly.

"Well, you were *made* to go," laughed Polly. "I said if you'd go good, you know; so run along, Joe, and I'll tell you a nice one to-morrow."

"It's got to be long," shouted Joel, when he saw he could get no more, making good time up to the loft.

To say that Polly, in the following days, was Master Joel's slave, was stating the case lightly. However, she thought by her story-telling she got off easily, as each evening saw the boys drag their unwilling feet to-bedward, and leave Ben and herself in peace to plan and work undisturbed. There they would sit by the little old table, around the one tallow candle, while Mrs. Pepper sewed away busily, looking up to smile or to give some bits of advice; keeping her own secret meanwhile, which made her blood leap fast, as the happy thoughts nestled in her heart of her little ones and their coming glee. And Polly made the loveliest of paper dolls for Phronsie out of the rest of the bits of bright paper; and Ben made windmills and whistles for the boys; and a funny little carved basket with a handle, for Phronsie, out of a hickory nut shell; and a new pink calico dress for Seraphina peered out from the top drawer of the old bureau in the bedroom, whenever anyone opened it—for Mrs. Pepper kindly let the children lock up their treasures there as fast as completed.

"I'll make Seraphina a bonnet," said Mrs. Pepper, "for there's that old bonnet-string in the bag, you know, Polly, that'll make it beautiful."

"Oh, do, mother," cried Polly, "she's been wanting a new one awfully."

"And I'm going to knit some mittens for Joel and David," continued Mrs. Pepper; "'cause I can get the yarn cheap now. I saw some down at the store yesterday I could have at half price."

"I don't believe anybody'll have as good a Christmas as we shall," cried Polly, pasting on a bit of trimming to the gayest doll's dress; "no, not even Jappy."

An odd little smile played around Mrs. Pepper's mouth, but she said not a word, and so the fun and the work went on.

The tree was to be set up in the Provision Room; that was finally decided, as Mrs. Pepper showed the children how utterly useless it would be to try having it in the kitchen.

"I'll find the key, children," she said, "I think I know where 'tis, and then we can keep them out."

"Well, but it looks so," said Polly, demurring at the prospect.

"Oh, no, Polly," said her mother; "at any rate it's *clean.*"

"Polly," said Ben, "we can put evergreen around, you know."

"So we can," said Polly, brightly; "oh, Ben, you do think of the *best* things; we couldn't have had *them* in the kitchen."

"And don't let's hang the presents on the tree," continued Ben; "let's have the children hang up their stockings; they want to, awfully—for I heard David tell Joel this morning before we got up—they thought I was asleep, but I wasn't—that he did so wish they could, but, says he, 'Don't tell mammy, 'cause that'll make her feel bad.'"

"The little dears!" said Mrs. Pepper, impulsively; "they shall have their stockings, too."

"And we'll make the tree pretty enough," said Polly, enthusiastically; "we shan't want the presents to hang on; we've got so many things. And then we'll have hickory nuts to eat; and perhaps mammy'll let us make some molasses candy the day before," she said, with a sly look at her mother.

"You may," said Mrs. Pepper, smiling.

"Oh, goody!" they both cried, hugging each other ecstatically.

"And we'll have a frolic in the Provision Room afterwards," finished Polly; "oh! ooh!"

And so the weeks flew by—one, two, three, four, five, six, seven, eight! till only the three days remained, and to think the fun that Polly and Ben had had already!

"It's better'n a Christmas," they told their mother, "to get ready for it!"

"It's too bad you can't hang up *your* stockings," said Mrs. Pepper, looking keenly at their flushed faces and bright eyes; "you've never hung 'em up."

"That isn't any matter, mamsie," they both said, cheerily; "it's a great deal better to have the children have a nice time—oh, won't it be elegant! p'r'aps we'll have ours next year!"

For two days before, the house was turned upside down for Joel to find the biggest stocking he could; but on Polly telling him it must be his own, he stopped his search, and bringing down his well-worn one, hung it by the corner of the chimney to be ready.

"You put yours up the other side, Dave," he advised.

"There isn't any nail," cried David, investigating.

"I'll drive one," said Joel, so he ran out to the tool-house, as one corner of the wood-shed was called, and brought in the hammer and one or two nails.

"Phronsie's a-goin' in the middle," he said, with a nail in his mouth.

"Yes, I'm a-goin' to hang up my stockin'," cried the child, hopping from one toe to the other.

"Run get it, Phronsie," said Joel, "and I'll hang it up for you."

"Why, it's two days before Christmas yet," said Polly, laughing; "how they'll look hanging there so long."

"I don't care," said Joel, giving a last thump to the nail; "we're a-goin' to be ready. Oh, dear! I wish 'twas to-night!"

"Can't Seraphina hang up her stocking?" asked Phronsie, coming up to Polly's side; "and Baby, too?"

"Oh, let her have part of yours," said Polly, "that'll be best—Seraphina and Baby, and you have one stocking together."

"Oh, yes," cried Phronsie, easily pleased; "that'll be best."

So for the next two days, they were almost distracted; the youngest ones asking countless questions about Santa Claus, and how he possibly could get down the chimney, Joel running his head up as far as he dared, to see if it was big enough.

"I guess he can," he said, coming back in a sooty state, looking very much excited and delighted.

"Will he be black like Joey?" asked Phronsie, pointing to his grimy face.

"No," said Polly; "he don't ever get black."

"Why?" they all asked; and then, over and over, they wanted the delightful mystery explained.

"We never'll get through this day," said Polly in despair, as the last one arrived. "I wish 'twas to-night, for we're all ready."

"Santy's coming! Santy's coming!" sang Phronsie, as the bright afternoon sunlight went down over the fresh, crisp snow, "for it's night now."

"Yes, Santa is coming!" sang Polly; and "Santa Claus is a-coming," rang back and forth through the old kitchen, till it seemed as if the three little old stockings would hop down and join in the dance going on so merrily.

"I'm glad mine is red," said Phronsie, at last, stopping in the wild jig, and going up to see if it was all safe, "'cause then Santy'll know it's mine, won't he, Polly?"

"Yes, dear," cried Polly, catching her up. "Oh, Phronsie! you *are* going to have a Christmas!"

"Well, I wish," said Joel, "I had my name on mine! I know Dave'll get some of my things."

"Oh, no, Joe," said Mrs. Pepper, "Santa Claus is smart; he'll know yours is in the left-hand corner."

"Will he?" asked Joel, still a little fearful.

"Oh, yes, indeed," said Mrs. Pepper, confidently. "I never knew him to make a mistake."

"Now," said Ben, when they had all made a pretence of eating supper, for there was such an excitement prevailing that no one sat still long enough to eat much, "you must every one fly off to bed as quick as ever can be."

"Will Santa Claus come faster then?" asked Joel.

"Yes," said Ben, "just twice as fast."

"I'm going, then," said Joel; "but I ain't going to sleep, 'cause I mean to hear him come over the roof; then I'm going to get up, for I do so want a squint at the reindeer!"

"I am, too," cried Davie, excitedly. "Oh, do come, Joe!" and he began to mount the stairs.

"Good night," said Phronsie, going up to the centre of the chimney-piece, where the little red stocking dangled limpsily, "lift me up, Polly, do."

"What you want to do?" asked Polly, running and giving her a jump. "What you goin' to do, Phronsie?"

"I want to kiss it good night," said the child, with eyes big with anticipation and happiness, hugging the well worn toe of the little old stocking affectionately. "I wish I had something to give Santa, Polly, I *do!*" she cried, as she held her fast in her arms.

"Never mind, Pet," said Polly, nearly smothering her with kisses; "if you're a good girl, Phronsie, that pleases Santa the most of anything."

"Does it?" cried Phronsie, delighted beyond measure, as Polly carried her into the bedroom, "then I'll be good always, I *will!*"

CHAPTER XVII: CHRISTMAS BELLS!

In the middle of the night Polly woke up with a start.

"What in the world!" said she, and she bobbed up her head and looked over at her mother, who was still peacefully sleeping, and was just going to lie down again, when a second noise out in the kitchen made her pause and lean on her elbow to listen. At this moment she thought she heard a faint whisper, and springing out of bed she ran to Phronsie's crib—it was empty! As quick as a flash she sped out into the kitchen. There, in front of the chimney, were two figures. One was Joel, and the other, unmistakably, was Phronsie!

"What are you doing?" gasped Polly, holding on to a chair.

The two little night-gowns turned around at this.

"Why, I thought it was morning," said Joel, "and I wanted my stocking. Oh!" as he felt the toe, which was generously stuffed, "give it to me, Polly Pepper, and I'll run right back to bed again!"

"Dear me!" said Polly; "and you, too, Phronsie! Why, it's the middle of the night! Did I ever!" and she had to pinch her mouth together tight to keep from bursting out into a loud laugh. "Oh, dear, I shall laugh! don't look so scared, Phronsie, there won't anything hurt you." For Phronsie who, on hearing Joel fumbling around the precious stockings, had been quite willing to hop out of bed and join him, had now, on Polly's saying the dire words "in the middle of the night," scuttled over to her protecting side like a frightened rabbit.

"It never'll be morning," said Joel taking up first one cold toe and then the other; "you *might* let us have 'em now, Polly, *do!*"

"No," said Polly sobering down; "you can't have yours till Davie wakes up, too. Scamper off to bed, Joey, dear, and forget all about 'em—and it'll be morning before you know it."

"Oh, I'd rather go to bed," said Phronsie, trying to tuck up her feet in the little flannel night-gown, which was rather short, "but I don't know the way back, Polly. Take me, Polly, do," and she put up her arms to be carried.

"Oh, *I* ain't a-goin' back alone, either," whimpered Joel, coming up to Polly, too.

"Why, you came down alone, didn't you?" whispered Polly, with a little laugh.

"Yes, but I thought 'twas morning," said Joel, his teeth chattering with something beside the cold.

"Well, you must think of the morning that's coming," said Polly, cheerily. "I'll tell you—you wait till I put Phronsie into the crib, and then I'll come back and go half-way up the stairs with you."

"I won't never come down till it's mornin' again," said Joel, bouncing along the stairs, when Polly was ready to go with him, at a great rate.

"Better not," laughed Polly, softly. "Be careful and not wake Davie nor Ben."

"I'm *in,*" announced Joel, in a loud whisper; and Polly could hear him snuggle down among the warm bedclothes. "Call us when 'tis mornin', Polly."

"Yes," said Polly, "I will; go to sleep."

Phronsie had forgotten stockings and everything else on Polly's return, and was fast asleep in the old crib. The result of it was that the children slept over, when morning did really come; and Polly had to keep her promise, and go to the foot of the stairs and call—

"MERRY CHRISTMAS! oh, Ben! and Joel! and Davie!"

"Oh!—oh!—oo-h!" and then the sounds that answered her, as with smothered whoops of expectation they one and all flew into their clothes!

Quick as a flash Joel and Davie were down and dancing around the chimney.

"Mammy! mammy!" screamed Phronsie, hugging her stocking, which Ben lifted her up to unhook from the big nail, "Santy did *come,* he *did!*" and then she spun around in the middle of the floor, not stopping to look in it.

"Well, open it, Phronsie," called Davie, deep in the exploring of his own; "oh! isn't that a splendid wind-mill, Joe?"

"Yes," said that individual, who, having found a big piece of molasses candy, was so engaged in enjoying a huge bite that, regardless alike of his other gifts or of the smearing his face was getting, he gave himself wholly up to its delights.

"Oh, Joey," cried Polly, laughingly, "molasses candy for breakfast!"

"That's *prime!*" cried Joel, swallowing the last morsel. "Now I'm going to see what's this—oh, Dave, see here! see here!" he cried in intense excitement, pulling out a nice little parcel which, unrolled, proved to be a bright pair of stout mittens. "See if you've got some—look quick!"

"Yes, I have," said David, picking up a parcel about as big. "No, that's molasses candy."

"Just the same as I had," said Joel; "do look for the mittens. P'r'aps Santa Claus thought you had some—oh, dear!"

"Here they are!" screamed Davie. "I *have* got some, Joe, just exactly like yours! See, Joe!"

"Goody!" said Joel, immensely relieved; for now he could quite enjoy his to see a pair on Davie's hands, also. "Look at Phron," he cried, "she hasn't got only half of her things out!"

To tell the truth, Phronsie was so bewildered by her riches that she sat on the floor with the little red stocking in her lap, laughing and cooing to herself amid the few things she had drawn out. When she came to Seraphina's bonnet she was quite overcome. She turned it over and over, and smoothed out the little white feather that had once adorned one of Grandma Bascom's chickens, until the two boys with their stockings, and the others sitting around in a group on the floor watching them, laughed in glee to see her enjoyment.

"Oh, dear," said Joel, at last, shaking his stocking; "I've got all there is. I wish there were forty Christmases coming!"

"I haven't!" screamed Davie; "there's some thing in the toe."

"It's an apple, I guess," said Joel; "turn it up, Dave."

"'Tisn't an apple," exclaimed Davie, "'tisn't round—it's long and thin; here 'tis." And he pulled out a splendid long whistle on which he blew a blast long and terrible, and Joel immediately following, all quiet was broken up, and the wildest hilarity reigned.

"I don't know as you'll want any breakfast," at last said Mrs. Pepper, when she had got Phronsie a little sobered down.

"I do, I do!" cried Joel.

"Dear me! after your candy?" said Polly.

"That's all gone," said Joel, tooting around the table on his whistle. "What are we going to have for breakfast?"

"Same as ever," said his mother; "it can't be Christmas all the time."

"I wish 'twas," said little Davie; "forever and ever!"

"Forever an' ever," echoed little Phronsie, flying up, her cheeks like two pinks, and Seraphina in her arms with her bonnet on upside down.

"Dear, dear," said Polly, pinching Ben to keep still as they tumbled down the little rickety steps to the Provision Room, after breakfast. The children, content in their treasures, were holding high carnival in the kitchen. "Suppose they *should* find it out now—I declare I should feel most awfully. Isn't it *elegant?*" she asked, in a subdued whisper, going all around and around the tree, magnificent in its dress of bright red and yellow balls, white festoons, and little candle-ends all ready for lighting. "Oh, Ben, did you lock the door?"

"Yes," he said. "That's a mouse," he added, as a little rustling noise made Polly stop where she stood back of the tree and prick up her ears in great distress of mind. "'Tis elegant," he said, turning around in admiration, and taking in the tree which, as Polly said, was quite "gorgeous," and the evergreen branches twisted up on the beams and rafters, and all the other festive arrangements. "Even Jappy's isn't better, I don't believe!"

"I wish Jappy was here," said Polly with a small sigh.

"Well, he isn't," said Ben; "come, we must go back into the kitchen, or all the children will be out here. Look your last, Polly; 'twon't do to come again till it's time to light up."

"Mammy says she'd rather do the lighting up," said Polly.

"Had she?" said Ben, in surprise; "oh, I suppose she's afraid we'll set somethin' a-fire. Well, then, we shan't come in till we *have* it."

"I can't bear to go," said Polly, turning reluctantly away; "it's most beautiful—oh, Ben," and she faced him for the five-hundredth time with the question, "is your Santa Claus dress all safe?"

"Yes," said Ben, "I'll warrant they won't find that in one hurry! Such a time as we've had to make it!"

"I know it," laughed Polly; "don't that cotton wool look just like bits of fur, Ben?"

"Yes," said Ben, "and when the flour's shaken over me it'll be Santa himself."

"We've got to put back the hair into mamsie's cushion the first thing to-morrow," whispered Polly anxiously, "and we mustn't forget it, Bensie."

"I want to keep the wig awfully," said Ben. "You did make that just magnificent, Polly!"

"If you could see yourself," giggled Polly; "did you put it in the straw bed? and are you sure you pulled the ticking over it smooth?"

"Yes, *sir,*" replied Ben, "sure's my name's Ben Pepper! if you'll only keep them from seeing me when I'm in it till we're ready—that's all I ask."

"Well," said Polly a little relieved, "but I hope Joe won't look."

"Come on! they're a-comin'!" whispered Ben; "quick!"

"Polly!" rang a voice dangerously near; so near that Polly, speeding over the stairs to intercept it, nearly fell on her nose.

"Where you been?" asked one.

"Let's have a concert," put in Ben; Polly was so out of breath that she couldn't speak. "Come, now, each take a whistle, and we'll march round and round and see which can make the biggest noise."

In the rattle and laughter which this procession made all mystery was forgotten, and the two conspirators began to breathe freer.

Five o'clock! The small ones of the Pepper flock, being pretty well tired out with noise and excitement, all gathered around Polly and Ben, and clamored for a story.

"Do, Polly, do," begged Joel. "It's Christmas, and 'twon't come again for a year."

"I can't," said Polly, in such a twitter that she could hardly stand still, and for the first time in her life refusing, "I can't think of a thing."

"I will then," said Ben; "we must do something," he whispered to Polly.

"Tell it good," said Joel, settling himself.

So for an hour the small tyrants kept their entertainers well employed.

"Isn't it growing awful dark?" said Davie, rousing himself at last, as Ben paused to take breath.

Polly pinched Ben.

"Mammy's a-goin' to let us know," he whispered in reply. "We must keep on a little longer."

"Don't stop," said Joel, lifting his head where he sat on the floor. "What you whisperin' for, Polly?"

"I'm not," said Polly, glad to think she hadn't spoken.

"Well, do go on, Ben," said Joel, lying down again.

"Polly'll have to finish it," said Ben; "I've got to go up-stairs now."

So Polly launched out into such an extravagant story that they all, perforce, *had* to listen.

All this time Mrs. Pepper had been pretty busy in *her* way. And now she came into the kitchen and set down her candle on the table. "Children," she said. Everybody turned and looked at her—her tone was so strange; and when they saw her dark eyes shining with such a new light, little Davie skipped right out into the middle of the room. "What's the matter, mammy?"

"You may all come into the Provision Room," said she.

"What for?" shouted Joel, in amazement; while the others jumped to their feet, and stood staring.

Polly flew around like a general, arranging her forces. "Let's march there," said she; "Phronsie, you take hold of Davie's hand, and go first."

"I'm goin' first," announced Joel, squeezing up past Polly.

"No, you mustn't, Joe," said Polly decidedly; "Phronsie and David are the youngest."

"They're *always* the youngest," said Joel, falling back with Polly to the rear.

"*Forward!* MARCH!" sang Polly. "Follow mamsie!"

Down the stairs they went with military step, and into the Provision Room. And then, with one wild look, the little battalion broke ranks, and tumbling one over the other in decidedly unmilitary style, presented a very queer appearance!

And Captain Polly was the queerest of all; for she just gave one gaze at the tree, and then sat right down on the floor, and said, "OH! OH!"

Mrs. Pepper was flying around delightedly, and saying, "Please to come right in," and "How do you do?"

And before anybody knew it, there were the laughing faces of Mrs. Henderson and the Parson himself, Doctor Fisher and old Grandma Bascom; while the two Henderson boys, unwilling to be defrauded of any of the fun, were squeezing themselves in between everybody else, and coming up to Polly every third minute, and saying, "There—aren't you surprised?"

"It's Fairyland!" cried little Davie, out of his wits with joy; "Oh! aren't we in Fairyland, ma?"

The whole room was in one buzz of chatter and fun; and everybody beamed on everybody else; and nobody knew what they said, till Mrs. Pepper called, "*Hush!* Santa Claus is coming!"

Illustration from *Five Little Peppers and How They Grew.*

A rattle at the little old window made everybody look there, just as a great snow-white head popped up over the sill.

"*Oh!*" screamed Joel, "'*tis Santy!*"

"He's a-comin' in!" cried Davie in chorus, which sent Phronsie flying to Polly. In jumped a little old man, quite spry for his years; with a jolly, red face and a pack on his back, and flew into their midst, prepared to do his duty; but what should he do, instead of making his speech, "this jolly Old Saint"—but first fly up to Mrs. Pepper, and say—"*Oh, mammy how did you do it?*"

"It's Ben!" screamed Phronsie; but the little Old Saint didn't hear, for he and Polly took hold of hands, and pranced around that tree while everybody laughed till they cried to see them go!

And then it all came out!

"*Order!*" said Parson Henderson in his deepest tones; and then he put into Santa Claus' hands a letter, which he requested him to read. And the jolly Old Saint, although he was very old, didn't need any spectacles, but piped out in Ben's loudest tones:

"Dear Friends—A Merry Christmas to you all! And that you'll have a good time, and enjoy it all as much as I've enjoyed my good times at your house, is the wish of your friend,

JASPER ELYOT KING"

"Hurrah for Jappy!" cried Santa Claus, pulling his beard; and "Hurrah for Jasper!" went all around the room; and this ended in three good cheers—Phronsie coming in too late with her little crow—which was just as well, however!

"Do your duty now, Santa Claus!" commanded Dr. Fisher as master of ceremonies; and everything was as still as a mouse!

And the first thing she knew, a lovely brass cage, with a dear little bird with two astonished black eyes dropped down into Polly's hands. The card on it said: "*For Miss Polly Pepper, to give her music everyday in the year.*"

"Mammy," said Polly; and then she did the queerest thing of the whole! she just burst into tears! "I never thought I should have a bird for *my very own!*"

"Hulloa!" said Santa Claus, "I've got something myself!"

"Santa Claus' clothes are too old," laughed Dr. Fisher, holding up a stout, warm suit that a boy about as big as Ben would delight in.

And then that wonderful tree just rained down all manner of lovely fruit. Gifts came flying thick and fast, till the air seemed full, and each one was greeted with a shout of glee, as it was put into the hands of its owner. A shawl flew down on Mrs. Pepper's shoulders; and a work-basket tumbled on Polly's head; and tops and balls and fishing poles, sent Joel and David into a corner with howls of delight!

But the climax was reached when a large wax doll in a very gay pink silk dress, was put into Phronsie's hands, and Dr. Fisher, stooping down, read in loud tones: "FOR PHRONSIE, FROM ONE WHO ENJOYED HER GINGERBREAD BOY."

After that, nobody had anything to say! Books jumped down unnoticed, and gay boxes of candy. Only Polly peeped into one of her books, and saw in Jappy's plain hand—"*I hope we'll both read this next summer.*" And turning over to the title-page, she saw "A Complete Manual of Cookery."

"The best is to come," said Mrs. Henderson in her gentle way. When there was a lull in the gale, she took Polly's hand, and led her to a little stand of flowers in the corner concealed by a sheet—pinks and geraniums, heliotropes and roses, blooming away, and nodding their pretty heads at the happy sight—Polly had her flowers.

"Why didn't we know?" cried the children at last, when everybody was tying on their hoods, and getting their hats to leave the festive scene, "how *could* you keep it secret, mammy?"

"They all went to Mrs. Henderson's," said Mrs. Pepper; "Jasper wrote me, and asked where to send 'em, and Mrs. Henderson was so kind as to say that they might come there. And we brought 'em over last evening, when you were all abed. I couldn't have done it," she said, bowing to the Parson and his wife, "if 'twasn't for their kindness—never, in all this world!"

"And I'm sure," said the minister, looking around on the bright group, "if we can help along a bit of happiness like this, it is a blessed thing!"

And here Joel had the last word. "You said 'twan't goin' to be Christmas always, mammy. I say," looking around on the overflow of treasures and the happy faces—"it'll be just *forever!*"

III

Christmas Realities

THE PROMISE OF THE DAWN: A CHRISTMAS STORY

REBECCA HARDING DAVIS

From *Atlantic Monthly*, January 1863, 10–25.

When Rebecca Harding Davis published her debut story, "Life in the Iron Mills," in the Atlantic *in 1861 (Emily Dickinson was a fan), it was a sign that a new literary aesthetic was on the march. With her concern for the grim lives of industrial workers, Davis was a harbinger of a new self-conscious interest in realism in American literature. Those same preoccupations are in evidence in this Christmas story, also published while the Civil War raged. As Davis put it in the* Atlantic *in October 1861, "common, every-day drudgery" could also be akin to "great warfare" for those who lived on the wrong side of the poverty line. In that vein, this seasonal story fearlessly takes on a number of hard-hitting issues, particularly prostitution, which is alluded to throughout. Here, the domestic and sentimental home proves to be little insulation from the "brutal cry of pain" that emanates from those suffering outside its walls.*

A winter's evening. Do you know how that comes here among the edges of the mountains that fence in the great Mississippi valley? The sea-breath in the New-England States thins the air and bleaches the sky, sucks the vitality out of Nature, I fancy, to put it into the brains of the people: but here, the earth every day in the year pulses out through hill or prairie or creek a full, untamed animal life,—shakes off the snow too early in spring, in order to put forth untimed and useless blossoms, wasteful of her infinite strength. So when this winter's evening came to a lazy town bedded in the hills that skirt Western Virginia close by the Ohio, it found that the December air, fiercely as it blew the snow-clouds about the hill-tops, was instinct with a vigorous, frosty life, and that the sky above the clouds was not wan and washed-out, as farther North, but massive, holding yet a sensuous yellow languor, the glow of unforgotten autumn days.

The very sun, quite certain of where he would soonest meet with gratitude, gave his kindliest good-night smile to the great valley of the West, asleep under the snow: very kind to-night, just as calm and loving, though he knew the most plentiful harvest which the States had yielded that year was one of murdered dead, as he gave to the young, untainted world, that morning, long ago, when God blessed it, and saw that it was good. Because, you see, this was the eve of a more helpful, God-sent day than that, in spite of all the dead: Christmas eve. To-morrow Christ was coming,—whatever He may be to you,—Christ. The sun knew that, and glowed as cheerily, steadily, on blood as water. Why, God had the world! Let them fret, and cut each other's throats, if they would. God had them: and Christ was coming. But one fancied that the earth, not quite so secure in the infinite Love that held her, had learned to doubt, in her six thousand years of hunger, and heard the tidings with a thrill of relief. Was the Helper coming? Was it the true Helper? The very hope, even, gave meaning to the tender rose-blush on the peaks of snow, to the childish sparkle on the grim rivers. They heard and understood. The whole world answered.

One man, at least, fancied so: Adam Craig, hobbling down the frozen streets of this old-fashioned town. He thought, rubbing his bony hands together, that even the wind knew that Christmas was coming, the day that Christ was born: it went shouting boisterously through the great mountain-gorges, its very uncouth soul shaken with gladness. The city itself, he fancied, had caught a new and curious beauty: this winter its mills were stopped, and it had time to clothe the steep streets in spotless snow and icicles; its windows glittered red and cheery out into the early night: it looked just as if the old burgh had done its work, and sat down, like one of its own mill-men, to enjoy the evening, with not the cleanest face in the world, to be sure, but with an honest, jolly old heart under all, beating rough and glad and full. That was Adam Craig's fancy: but his head was full of queer fancies under the rusty old brown wig: queer, maybe, yet as pure and childlike as the prophet John's: coming, you know, from the same kinship. Adam had kept his fancies to himself these forty years. A lame old chap, cobbling shoes day by day, fighting the wolf desperately from the door for the sake of orphan brothers and sisters, has not much time to put the meanings God and Nature have for his ignorant soul into words, has he? But the fancies had found utterance for themselves, somehow: in his hatchet-shaped face, even, with its scraggy gray whiskers; in the quick, shrewd smile; in the eyes, keen eyes, but childlike, too. In the very shop out there on the creek-bank you could trace them. Adam had cobbled there these twenty years, chewing tobacco and taking snuff, (his mother's habit, that,) but the little shop was pure: people with brains behind their eyes would know that a clean and delicate soul lived there; they might have known it in other ways too, if they chose: in his gruff, sharp talk, even, full of slang and oaths; for Adam, invoke the Devil often as he might, never took the name of Christ or a woman in vain. So his foolish fancies, as he called them, cropped out. It must be so, you know: put on what creed you may, call yourself chevalier or Sambo, the speech your soul has held with God and the Devil will tell itself in every turn of your head, and jangle of your laugh: you cannot help that.

But it was Christmas eve. Adam took that in with keener enjoyment, in every frosty breath he drew. Different from any Christmas eve before: pulling off his scuffed cap to feel the full strength of the "nor'rer." Whew! how it blew! straight from the ice-fields of the Pole, he thought. So few people there were up there to be glad Christ was coming! But those filthy little dwarfs up there needed Him all the same: every man of them had a fiend tugging at his soul, like us, was lonely, wanted a God to help him, and—a wife to love him. Adam stopped short here a minute, something choking in his throat. "Jinny!" he said, under his breath, turning to some new hope in his heart, with as tender, awe-struck a touch as one lays upon a newborn infant. "Jinny!" praying silently with blurred eyes. I think Christ that moment came very near to the woman who was so greatly loved, and took her in His arms, and blessed her. Adam jogged on, trying to begin a whistle, but it ended in a miserable grunt: his heart was throbbing under his smoke-dried skin, silly as a woman's, so light it was, and full.

"Get along, Old Dot, and carry one!" shouted the boys, sledding down the icy sidewalk.

"Yip! you young devils, you!" stopping to give them a helping shove and a cheer: loving little children always, but never as to-day.

Surely there never was such a Christmas eve before! The frozen air glistened grayly up into heaven itself, he thought; the snow-covered streets were alive, noisy,—glad into their very cellars and shanties; the sun was sorry to go away. No wonder. His heartiest ruby-gleam lingered about the white Virginia heights behind the town, and across the river quite glorified the pale stretch of the Ohio hills. Free and slave. (Adam was an Abolitionist.) Well, let that be. God's hand of power, like His sunlight, held the master and the slave in loving company. Tomorrow was the sign.

The cobbler stopped on the little swinging foot-bridge that crosses the creek in the centre of the city. The faint saffron sunset swept from the west over the distant wooded hills, the river, the stone bridge below him, whose broad gray piers painted perpetual arches on the sluggish, sea-colored water. The smoke from one or two far-off foundries hung just above it, motionless in the gray, in tattered drifts, dyed by the sun, clear drab and violet. A still picture. A bit of Venice, poor Adam thought, who never had been fifty miles out of Wheeling. The quaint American town was his world: he brought the world into it. There were relics of old Indian forts and mounds, the old times and the new. The people, too, though the cobbler only dimly saw that, were as much the deposit and accretion of all dead ages as was the coal that lay bedded in the fencing hills. Irish, Dutch, whites, blacks, Moors, old John Bull himself: you can find the dregs of every day of the world in any milltown of the States. Adam had a dull perception of this. Christmas eve came to all the world, coming here.

Leaning on the iron wires, while the unsteady little bridge shook under him, he watched the stunned beams of the sun urging themselves through the smoke-clouds. He thought they were like "the voice of one crying in the wilderness, 'Prepare ye the way of the Lord, make His paths straight.'" It wakened something in the man's hackneyed heart deeper even than the thought of the woman he had prayed for. A sudden vision that a great Peace held the world as did that glow of upper light: he rested in its calm. Up the street a few steps rose the walls of the old theatre, used as a prison now for captured Confederates: it was full now; he could see them looking out from behind the bars, grimy and tattered. Far to the north, on Mount Woods, the white grave-stones stood out clear in the darkening evening. His enemies, the busy streets, the very war itself, the bones and souls of the dead yonder,—the great Peace held them all. We might call them evil, but they were sent from God, and went back to God. All things were in Him.

I tell you, that when this one complete Truth got into this poor cobbler's brain,—in among its vulgar facts of North and South, and patched shoes, and to-morrow's turkey,—a great poet-insight looked out of his eyes for the minute. Saint John looked thus as he wrote that primitive natal word, "God is love." Cobblers, as well as Saint John, or the dying Herder, need great thoughts, and water from God to refresh them, believe me.

Trotting on, hardly needing his hickory stick, Adam could see the little brown shop yonder on the creek-bank. All dark: but did you ever see anything brighter than the way the light shone in the sitting-room, behind the Turkey-red curtains? Such a taste that little woman had! Two years ago the cobbler finished his life-work, he thought: he had been mother and father both to the orphans left with him, faithful to them, choking down the hungry gnawing within for something nearer than brother or sister. Two years ago they had left him, struck out into the world for themselves.

"Then, you see," Adam used to say, "I was settlin' down into an old man; dryin' up, d' ye see? thinkin' the Lord had forgotten me, when He said to other men, 'Come, it's *your* turn now for home and lovin'.' Them young ones was dear enough, but a man has a cravin' for somethin' that's his own. But it was too late, I thought. Bitter; despisin' the Lord's eyesight; thinkin'

He didn't see or care what would keep me from hell. I believed in God, like most poor men do, thinkin' Him coldblooded, not hearin' when we cry out for work, or a wife, or child. I didn't cry. I never prayed. But look there. Do you see—*her?* Jinny?" It was to the young Baptist preacher Adam said this, when he came to make a pastoral visit to Adam's wife. "That's what He did. I'm not ashamed to pray now. I ask Him every hour to give me a tight grip on her so that I kin follow her up, and to larn me some more of His ways. That's my religious 'xperience, Sir."

The young man coughed weakly, and began questioning old Craig as to his faith in immersion. The cobbler stumped about the kitchen a minute before answering, holding himself down. His face was blood-red when he did speak, quite savage, the young speaker said afterward.

"I don't go to church, Sir. My wife does. I don't say *now,* 'Damn the churches!' or that you, an' the likes of you, an' yer Master, are all shams an' humbugs. I know Him now. He's 'live to me. So now, when I see you belie Him, an' keep men from Him with yer hundreds o' wranglin' creeds, an' that there's as much honest love of truth outside the Church as in it, I don't put yer bigotry an' foulness on Him. I on'y think there's an awful mistake: just this: that the Church thinks it is Christ's body an' us uns is outsiders, an' we think so too, an' despise Him through you with yer stingy souls an' fights an' squabblins; not seein' that the Church is jes' an hospital, where some of the sickest of God's patients is tryin' to get cured."

The preacher never went back; spoke in a church-meeting soon after of the prevalence of Tom Paine's opinions among the lower classes. Half of our sham preachers take the vague name of "Paine" to cover all of Christ's opponents,—not ranking themselves there, of course.

Adam thought he had won a victory. "Ef you'd heard me flabbergast the parson!" he used to say, with a jealous anxiety to keep Christ out of the visible Church, to shut his eyes to the true purity in it, to the fact that the Physician was in His hospital. To-night some more infinite gospel had touched him. "Good evenin', Mr. Pitts," he said, meeting the Baptist preacher. "Happy Christmas, Sir!" catching a glance of his broken boots. "Danged ef I don't send that feller a pair of shoes unbeknownst, to-morrow! He's workin' hard, an' it's not for money."

The great Peace held even its erring Church, as Adam dully saw. The streets were darkening, but full even yet of children crowding in and out of the shops. Not a child among them was more busy or important, or keener for a laugh than Adam, with his basket on his arm and his hand in his pocket clutching the money he had to lay out. The way he had worked for that! Over-jobs, you know, done at night when Jinny and the baby were asleep. It was carrying him through splendidly, though: the basket was quite piled up with bundles: as for the turkey, had n't he been keeping that in the back-yard for weeks, stuffing it until it hardly could walk? That turkey, do you know, was the first thing Baby ever took any notice of, except the candle? Jinny was quite opposed to killing it, for that reason, and proposed they should have ducks instead; but as old Jim Farley and Granny Simpson were invited for dinner, and had been told about the turkey, matters must stay as they were.

"Poor souls, they'll not taste turkey agin this many a day, I'm thinkin', Janet. When we give an entertainment, it's allus them-like we'll ask. That's the Master's biddin', ye know."

But the pudding was yet to buy. He had a dirty scrap of paper on which Jinny had written down the amount. "The hand that woman writes!" He inspected it anxiously at every streetlamp. Did you ever see anything finer than that tongue, full of its rich brown juices and golden fat? or the white, crumbly suet? Jinny said veal: such a saving little body she was but we know what a pudding ought to be. Now for the pippins for it, yellow they are, holding summer yet; and a few drops of that brandy in the window, every drop shining and warm: that'll put a soul into it, and—He stopped before the confectioner's: just a moment, to collect himself; for this was the crowning point, this. There they were, in the great, gleaming window below: the rich Malaga raisins, bedded in their cases, cold to the lips, but within all glowing sweetness and passion; and the cool, tart little currants. If Jinny could see that window! and Baby. To be sure, Baby mightn't appreciate it, but—White frosted cakes, built up like fairy palaces, and mountains of golden oranges, and the light trembling through delicate candies, purple and rose-color. "Let's have a look, boys!"—and Adam crowded into the swarm outside.

Over the shops there was a high brick building, a concert-hall. You could hear the soft, dreamy air floating down from it, made vocal into a wordless love and pathos. Adam forgot the splendors of the window, listening; his heart throbbed full under his thin coat; it ached with an infinite tenderness. The poor old cobbler's eyes filled with tears: he could have taken Jesus and the great world all into his arms then. How loving and pure it was, the world! Christ's footsteps were heard. The eternal stars waited above; there was not a face in the crowd about him that was not clear and joyous. These delicate, pure women flitting past him up into the lighted hall,—it made his nerves thrill into pleasure to look at them. Jesus' world! His creatures.

He put his hand into the basket, and shyly took out a bunch of flowers he had bought,—real flowers, tender, sweet-smelling little things. Wouldn't Jinny wonder to find them on her bureau in the morning? Their fragrance, so loving and innocent, filled the frosty air, like a breath of the purity of this Day coming. Just as he was going to put them back carefully, a hand out of the crowd caught hold of them, a dirty hand, with sores on it, and a woman thrust her face from under her blowzy bonnet into his: a young face, deadly pale, on which some awful passion had cut the lines; lips dyed scarlet with rank blood, lips, you would think, that in hell itself would utter a coarse jest.

"Give 'em to me, old cub!" she said, pulling at them. "I want 'em for a better nor you."

"Go it, Lot!" shouted the boys.

He struck her. A woman? Yes; if it had been a slimy eel standing upright, it would have been less foul a thing than this.

"Damn you!" she muttered, chafing the hurt arm. Whatever words this girl spoke came from her teeth out,—seemed to have no meaning to her.

"Let's see, Lot."

She held out her arm, and the boy, a black one, plastered it with grime from the gutter. The others yelled with delight. Adam hurried off. A pure air? God help us! He threw the flowers into the gutter with a bitter loathing. *Her* fingers would be polluted, if they touched them now. He would not tell her of this: he would cut off his hand rather than talk to her of this,—let her know such things were in the world. So pure and saintly she was, his little wife! a homely little body, but with the cleanest, most loving heart, doing her Master's will humbly. The cobbler's own veins were full of Scotch blood, as pure indignant as any knight's of the Holy Greal. He wiped his hand, as though a leper had tainted it.

Passing down Church Street, the old bell rang out the hour. All day he had fancied its tone had gathered a lighter, more delicate sweetness with every chime. The Christ-child was coming; the world held up its hands adoring; all that was needed of men was to love Him, and rejoice. Its tone was different now: there was a brutal cry of pain in the ponderous voice that shook the air,—a voice saying something to God, unintelligible to him. He thrust out the thought of that woman with a curse: he had so wanted to have a good day, to feel how great and glad the world was, and to come up close to Christ with Jinny and the baby! He did soon forget the vileness there behind, going down the streets; they were so cozy and friendly-hearted, the parlor-windows opening out red and cheerfully, as is the custom in Southern and Western towns; they said "Happy Christmas" to every passer-by. The owners, going into the houses, had a hearty word for Adam. "Well, Craig, how goes it?" or, "Fine, frosty weather, Sir." It quite heartened the cobbler. He made shoes for most of these people, and whether men are free and equal or not, any cobbler will have a reverence for the man he has shod.

So Adam trotted on, his face a little redder, and his stooped chest, especially next the basket, in quite a glow. There she was, clear out in the snow, waiting for him by the curb-stone. How she took hold of the basket, and Adam made believe she was carrying the whole weight of it! How the fire-light struck out furiously through the Turkey-red curtains, so as to show her to him quicker!—to show him the snug coffee-colored dress, and the bits of cherry ribbon at her throat,—to show him how the fair curly hair was tucked back to leave the rosy ears bare he thought so dainty,—to show him how young she was, how faded and worn and tired-out she was, how hard the years had been,—to show him how his great love for her was thickening the thin blood with life, making a child out of the thwarted woman,—to show him—this more than all, this that his soul watched for, breathless, day and night—that she loved him, that she knew nothing better than the ignorant, loving heart, the horny hands that had taken her hungry fate to hold, and made of it a color and a fragrance. "Christmas is coming, little woman!" Of course it was. If it had not taken the whole world into its embrace yet, there it was compacted into a very glow of love and warmth and coziness in that snuggest of rooms, and in that very Jinny and Baby,—Christmas itself,—especially when he kissed her, and she blushed and laughed, the tears in her eyes, and went fussing for that queer roll of white flannel.

Adam took off his coat: he always went at the job of nursing the baby in his shirt-sleeves. The anxious sweat used to break on his forehead before he was through. He got its feet to the fire. "I'm dead sure that much is right," he used to say. Jinny put away the bundles, wishing to herself Mrs. Perkins would happen in to see them: one didn't like to be telling what they had for dinner, but if it was known accidentally—You poets, whose brains have quite snubbed and sent to Coventry your stomachs, never could perceive how the pudding was a poem to the cobbler and his wife,—how a very actual sense of the live goodness of Jesus was in it,—how its spicy steam contained all the cordial cheer and jollity they had missed in meaningless days of the year. Then she brought her sewing-chair, and sat down, quite idle.

"No work for to-night! I'll teach you how to keep Christmas, Janet, woman!'"

It was her first, one might say. Orphan girls that go about from house to house sewing, as Jinny had done, don't learn Christmas by heart year by year. It was a new experience: she was taking it in, one would think, to look at her, with all her might, with the earnest blue eyes, the shut-up brain behind the narrow forehead, the loving heart: a contracted tenement, that heart, by-the-by, adapted for single lodgers. She wasn't quite sure that Christmas was not, after all, a relic of Papistry,—for Jinny was a thorough Protestant: a Christian, as far as she understood Him, with a keen interest in the Indian missions. "Let us begin in our own country," she said, and always prayed for the Sioux just after Adam and Baby. In fact, if we are all parts of God's temple, Jinny was a very essential, cohesive bit of mortar. Adam had a wider door for his charity: it took all the world in, he thought,—though the preachers did enter with a shove, as we know. However, this was Christmas: the word took up all common things, the fierce wind without, the clean hearth, the modest color on her cheek, the very baby, and made of them one grand, sweet poem, that sang to the man the same story the angels told eighteen centuries ago: "Glory to God in the highest, and on earth peace, good-will toward men."

Sitting there in the evenings, Adam was the talker: such a fund of anecdote he had! Jinny never could hear the same story too often. To-night there was a bit of a sigh in them: his heart was tender: about the Christmases at home, when he and Nelly were little chubs together, and hung up their stockings regularly every Christmas eve.

"Twins, Nelly an' me was, oldest of all. When I was bound to old Lowe, it went hard, ef I couldn't scratch together enough for a bit of ribbon-bow or a ring for Nell, come Christmas. She used to sell the old flour-barrels an' rags, an' have her gift all ready by my plate that mornin': never missed. I never hed a sweetheart then."

Jinny laid her hand on his knee.

"Ye 'r' glad o' that, little woman? Well, well! I didn't care for women, only Ellen. She was the only livin' thing as come near me. I gripped on to her like death, havin' only her. But she—hed more nor me."

Jinny knew the story well.

"She went away with him?" softly.

"Yes, she did. I don't blame her. She was young, unlarned. No man cared for our souls. So, when she loved him well, she thort God spoke to her. So she was tuk from me. She went away."

He patted the baby, his skinny hand all shaking. Jinny took it in hers, and, leaning over, stroked his hair.

"You've hed hard trouble, to turn it gray like this."

"No trouble like that, woman, when he left her."

"Left her! An' then she was tired of God, an' of livin', or dyin'. So as she loved him! You know, my husband. As I love you. An' he left her! What wonder *what* she did? All alone! So as she loved him still! God shut His eyes to what she did."

The yellow, shaggy face was suddenly turned from her. The voice choked.

"Did He, little woman? *You* know."

"So, when she was a-tryin' to forget, the only way she knew, God sent an angel to bring her up, an' have her soul washed clean."

Adam laughed bitterly.

"That's not the way men told the story, child. I got there six months after: to New York, you know. I found in an old paper jes' these words: 'The woman, Ellen Myers, found dead yesterday on one of the docks, was identified. Died of starvation and whiskey.' That was Nelly, as used to hang up her stockin' with me. Christian people read that. But nobody cried but me."

"They're tryin' to help them now at the Five Points there."

"God help them as helps others this Christmas night! But it's not for such as you to talk of the Five Points, Janet," rousing himself. "What frabbit me to talk of Nelly the night? Someways she's been beside me all day, as if she was grippin' me by the sleeve, beggin', dumb-like."

The moody frown deepened.

"The baby! See, Adam, it'll waken! Quick, man!"

And Adam, with a start, began hushing it after the fashion of a chimpanzee. The old bell rang out another hour: how genial and loving it was!

"Nine o'clock! Let me up, boys!—and Lot Tyndal hustled them aside from the steps of the concert-hall. They made way for her: her thin, white arms could deal furious blows, they knew from experience. Besides, they had seen her, when provoked, fall in some cellar-door in a livid dead spasm. They were afraid of her. Her filthy, wet skirt flapped against her feet, as she went up; she pulled her flaunting bonnet closer over her head. There was a small room at the top of the stairs, a sort of greenroom for the performers. Lot shoved the door open and went in. Madame —— was there, the prima-donna, if you chose to call her so: the rankest bloom of fifty summers, in white satin and pearls: a faded dahlia. Women hinted that the fragrance of the dahlia had not been healthful in the world; but they crowded to hear her: such a wonderful contralto! The manager, a thin old man, with a hook-nose, and kindly, uncertain smile, stood by the stove, with a group of gentlemen about him. The wretch from the street went up to him, unsteadily.

"Lot's drunk," one door-keeper whispered to another.

"No; the Devil's in her, though, like a tiger, to-night."

Yet there was a certain grace and beauty in her face, as she looked at the manager, and spoke low and sudden.

"I'm not a beggar. I want money,—honest money. It's Christmas eve. They say you want a voice for the chorus, in the carols. Put me where I'll be hid, and I'll sing for you."

The manager's hand fell from his watch-chain. Storrs, a young lawyer of the place, touched his shoulder.

"Don't look so aghast, Pumphrey. Let her sing a ballad to show you. Her voice is a real curiosity."

Madame —— looked dubiously across the room; her black maid had whispered to her. Lot belonged to an order she had never met face to face before: one that lives in the suburbs of hell.

"Let her sing, Pumphrey."

"If"—looking anxiously to the lady.

"Certainly," drawled that type of purity. "If it is so curious, her voice."

"Sing, then," nodding to the girl.

There was a strange fierceness under her dead, gray eye.

"Do you mean to employ me tonight?"

Her tones were low, soft, from her teeth out, as I told you. Her soul was chained, below: a young girl's soul, hardly older than your little daughter's there, who sings Sunday-school hymns for you in the evenings. Yet one fancied, if this girl's soul were let loose, it would utter a madder cry than any fiend in hell.

"Do you mean to employ me?" biting her finger-ends until they bled.

"Don't be foolish, Charlotte," whispered Storrs. "You may be thankful you're not sent to jail instead. But sing for him. He'll give you something, may-be."

She did not damn him, as he expected, stood quiet a moment, her eye-lids fallen, relaxed with an inexpressible weariness. A black porter came to throw coals into the stove: he knew "dat debbil, Lot," well: had helped drag her drunk to the lock-up a day or two before. Now, before the white folks, he drew his coat aside, loathing to touch her. She followed him with a glazed look.

"Do you see what I am?" she said to the manager.

Nothing pitiful in her voice. It was too late for that.

"He wouldn't touch me: I'm not fit. I want help. Give me some honest work."

She stopped and put her hand on his coat-sleeve. The child she might have been, and never was, looked from her face that moment.

"God made me, I think," she said, humbly.

The manager's thin face reddened.

"God bless my soul! what shall I do, Mr. Storrs?"

The young man's thick lip and thicker eyelid drooped. He laughed, and whispered a word or two.

"Yes," gruffly, being reassured. "There's a policeman outside. Joe, take her out, give her in charge to him."

The negro motioned her before him with a billet of wood he held. She laughed. Her laugh had gained her the name of "Devil Lot."

"Why,"—fires that God never lighted blazing in her eyes,—"I thought you wanted me to sing! I'll sing. We'll have a hymn. It's Christmas, you know."

She staggered. Liquor, or some subtler poison, was in her veins. Then, catching by the lintel, she broke into that most deep of all adoring cries,—

"I know that my Redeemer liveth."

A strange voice. The men about her were musical critics: they listened intently. Low, uncultured, yet full, with childish grace and sparkle; but now and then a wailing breath of an unutterable pathos.

"Git out wid you," muttered the negro, who had his own religious notions, "pollutin' de name ob de Lord in *yer* lips!"

Lot laughed.

"Just for a joke, Joe. *My* Redeemer!"

He drove her down the stairs.

"Do you want to go to jail, Lot?" he said, more kindly. "It's orful cold out to-night."

"No. Let me go."

She went through the crowd out into the vacant street, down to the wharf, humming some street-song,—from habit, it seemed; sat down on a pile of lumber, picking the clay out of the holes in her shoes. It was dark: she did not see that a man had followed her, until his white-gloved hand touched her. The manager, his uncertain face growing red.

"Young woman"—

Lot got up, pushed off her bonnet. He looked at her.

"My God! No older than Susy," he said.

By a gas-lamp she saw his face, the trouble in it.

"Well?" biting her finger-ends again.

"I'm sorry for you, I—"

"Why?" sharply. "There's more like me. Fifteen thousand in the city of New York. I came from there."

"Not like you, child."

"Yes, like me," with a gulping noise in her throat. "I'm no better than the rest."

She sat down and began digging in the snow, holding the sullen look desperately on her face. The kind word had reached the tortured soul beneath, and it struggled madly to be free.

"Can I help you?"

No answer.

"There's something in your face makes me heart-sick. I've a little girl of your age."

She looked up quickly.

"Who are you, girl?"

She stood up again, her child's face white, the dark river rolling close by her feet.

"I'm Lot. I always was what you see. My mother drank herself to death in the Bowery dens. I learned my trade there, slow and sure."

She stretched out her hands into the night, with a wild cry,—

"My God! I had to live!"

What was to be done? Whose place was it to help her? he thought. He loathed to touch her. But her soul might be as pure and groping as little Susy's.

"I wish I could help you, girl," he said. "But I'm a moral man. I have to be careful of my reputation. Besides, I couldn't bring you under the same roof with my child."

She was quiet now.

"I know. There's not one of those Christian women up in the town yonder 'ud take Lot into their kitchens to give her a chance to save herself from hell. Do you think I care? It's not for myself I'm sorry. It's too late."

Yet as this child, hardly a woman, gave her soul over forever, she could not keep her lips from turning white.

"There's thousands more of us. Who cares? Do preachers and them as sits in the grand churches come into our dens to teach us better?"

Pumphrey grew uneasy.

"Who taught you to sing?" he said.

The girl started. She did not answer for a minute.

"What did you say?" she said.

"Who taught you?"

Her face flushed warm and dewy; her eyes wandered away, moistened and dreamy; she curled her hair-softly on her finger.

"I'd—I'd rather not speak of that," she said, low. "He's dead now. *He* called me—Lottie," looking up with a sudden, childish smile. "I was only fifteen then."

"How old are you now?"

"Four years more. But I tell you I've seen the world in that time."

It was Devil Lot looked over at the dark river now.

He turned away to go up the wharf. No help for so foul a thing as this. He dared not give it, if there were. She had sunk down with her old, sullen glare, but she rose and crept after him. Why, this was her only chance of help from all the creatures God had made!

"Let me tell you," she said, holding by a fire-plug. "It's not for myself I care. It's for Benny. That's my little brother. I've raised him. He loves me; *he don't know.* I've kept him alone allays. I don't pray, you know; but when Ben puts his white little arms about me 't nights and kisses me, somethin' says to me, 'God loves you, Lot.' So help me God, that boy shall never know what his sister was! He's gettin' older now. I want work, before he can know. Now, will you help me?"

"How can I?"

The whole world of society spoke in the poor manager.

"I'll give you money."

Her face hardened.

"Lot, I'll be honest. There's no place for such as you. Those that have made you what you are hold good stations among us; but when a woman's once down, there's no raising her up."

"*Never?*"

"Never."

She stood, her fair hair pushed back from her face, her eye deadening every moment, quite quiet.

"Good bye, Lot."

The figure touched him somehow, standing alone in the night there.

"It wasn't my fault at the first," she wandered. "Nobody teached me better."

"*I*'m not a church-member, thank God!" said Pumphrey to himself, and so washed his hands in innocency.

"Well, good bye, girl," kindly. "Try and lead a better life. I wish I could have given you work."

"It was only for Benny that I cared, Sir."

"You're sick? Or"—

"It'll not last long, now. I only keep myself alive eating opium now and then. D'ye know? I fell by your hall to-day; had a fit, they said. It wasn't a fit; it was death, Sir."

He smiled.

"Why did n't you die, then?"

"I would n't. Benny would have known then. I said,—"I will not. I must take care o' him first.' Good bye. You'd best not be seen here."

And so she left him.

One moment she stood uncertain, being alone, looking down into the seething black water covered with ice.

"There's one chance yet," she muttered. "It's hard; but I'll try,"—with a shivering sigh; and went dragging herself along the wharf, muttering still something about Benny.

As she went through the lighted streets, her step grew lighter. She lifted her head. Why, she was only a child yet, in some ways, you know;

and this was Christmas-time; and it wasn't easy to believe, that, with the whole world strong and glad, and the True Love coming into it, there was no chance for her. Was it? She hurried on, keeping in the shadow of the houses to escape notice, until she came to the more open streets,—the old "commons." She stopped at the entrance of an alley, going to a pump, washing her face and hands, then combing her fair, silky hair.

"I'll try it," she said again.

Some sudden hope had brought a pink flush to her cheek and a moist brilliance to her eye. You could not help thinking, had society not made her what she was, how fresh and fair and debonair a little maiden she would have been.

"He's my mother's brother. He'd a kind face, though he struck me. I'll kill him, if he strikes me agin," the dark trade-mark coming into her eyes. "But mebbe," patting her hair, "he'll not. Just call me Charley, as Ben does: help me to be like his wife: I'll hew a chance for heaven at last."

She turned to a big brick building and ran lightly up the stairs on the outside. It had been a cotton-factory, but was rented in tenement-rooms now. On the highest porch was one of Lot's rooms: she had two. The muslin curtain was undrawn, a red fire-light shone out. She looked in through the window, smiling. A clean, pure room: the walls she had whitewashed herself; a white cot-bed in one corner; a glowing fire, before which a little child sat on a low cricket, building a house out of blocks. A brave, honest-faced little fellow, with clear, reserved eyes, and curling golden hair. The girl, Lot, might have looked like that at his age.

"Benny" she called, tapping on the pane.

"Yes, Charley!" instantly, coming quickly to the door.

She caught him up in her arms.

"Is my baby tired waiting for sister? I'm finding Christmas for him, you know."

He put his arms about her neck, kissing her again and again, and laying his head down on her shoulder.

"I'm so glad you've come, Charley! so glad! so glad!"

"Has my boy his stocking up? Such a big boy to have his stocking up!"

He put his chubby hands over her eyes quickly, laughing.

"Don't look, Charley! don't! Benny's played you a trick now, I tell you!" pulling her towards the fire. "Now look! Not Benny's stocking: Charley's, *I* guess."

The girl sat down on the cricket, holding him on her lap, playing with the blocks, as much of a child as he.

"Why, Bud! Such an awful lot of candies that stocking'll hold!" laughing with him. "It'll take all Kriss Kringle's sack."

"*Kriss Kringle!* Oh, Charley I'm too big; I'm five years now. You can't cheat me."

The girl's very lips went white. She got up at his childish words, and put him down.

"No, I'll not cheat you, Benny, never, any more."

"Where are you going, Charley?"

"Just out a bit," wrapping a plain shawl about her. "To find Christmas, you know. For you—and me."

He pattered after her to the door.

"You'll come put me to bed, Charley dear? I'm so lonesome!"

"Yes, Bud. Kiss me. One,—two,—three times,—for God's good-luck."

He kissed her. And Lot went out into the wide, dark world,—into Christmas night, to find a friend.

She came a few minutes later to a low frame-building, painted brown: Adam Craig's house and shop. The little sitting-room had a light in it: his wife would be there with the baby. Lot knew them well, though they never had seen her. She had watched them through the window for hours in winter nights. Some damned soul might have thus looked wistfully into heaven: pitying herself, feeling more like God than the blessed within, because she knew the pain in her heart, the struggle to do right, and pitied it. She had a reason for the hungry pain in her blood when the kind-faced old cobbler passed her. She was Nelly's child. She had come West to find him.

"Never, that he should know *me!* never that! but for Benny's sake."

If Benny could have brought her to him, saying, "See, this is Charley, my Charley!" But Adam knew her by another name,—Devil Lot.

While she stood there, looking in at the window, the snow drifting on her head in the night, two passers-by halted an instant.

"Oh, father, look!" It was a young girl spoke. "Let me speak to that woman."

"What does thee mean, Maria?"

She tried to draw her hand from his arm. "Let me go,—she's dying, I think. Such a young, fair face. She thinks God has forgotten her. Look!"

The old Quaker hesitated.

"Not thee, Maria. Thy mother shall find her to-morrow. Thee must never speak to her. Accursed! 'Her house is the way to hell, going down to the chambers of death.'"

They passed on. Lot heard it all. God had offered the pure young girl a chance to save a soul from death; but she threw it aside. Lot did not laugh: looked after them with tearless eyes, until they were out of sight. She went to the door then. "It's for Benny," she whispered, swallowing down the choking that made her dumb. She knocked and went in.

Jinny was alone: sitting by the fire, rocking the baby to sleep, singing some child's hymn: a simple little thing, beginning,—

"Come, let us sing of Jesus,
Who wept our path along:
Come, let us sing of Jesus,
The tempted, and the strong."

Such a warm, happy flush lightened in Charley's heart at that! She did not know why; but her fear was gone. The baby, too, a white, pure little thing, was lying in the cradle, cooing softly to itself. The mother-instinct is nearest the surface in a loving woman; the girl went up quickly to it, and touched its cheek, with a smile: she could not help it.

"It's so pretty!" she said.

Jinny's eyes glowed.

"*I* think so," she said, simply. "It's my baby. Did you want me?"

Lot remembered then. She drew back, her face livid and grave.

"Yes. Do you know me? I'm Lot Tyndal. Don't jerk your baby back! Don't! I'll not touch it. I want to get some honest work. I've a little brother."

There was a dead silence. Jinny's brain, I told you, was narrow, her natural heart not generous or large in its impulse; the kind of religion she learned did not provide for anomalies of work like this. (So near at hand, you know. Lot was neither a Sioux nor a Rebel.)

"I'm Lot,"—desperately. "You know what I am. I want you to take us in, stop the boys from hooting at me on the streets, make a decent Christian woman out of me. There's plain words. Will you do it? I'll work for you. I'll nurse the baby, the dear little baby."

Jinny held her child tighter to her breast, looking at the vile clothes of the wretch, the black marks which years of crime had left on her face. Don't blame Jinny. Her baby was God's gift to her: she thought of that, you know. She did not know those plain, coarse words were the last cry for help from a drowning soul, going down into depths whereof no voice has come back to tell the tale. Only Jesus. Do you know what message He carried to those "spirits in prison"?

"I daren't do it. What would they say of me?" she faltered.

Lot did not speak. After a while she motioned to the shop. Adam was there. His wife went for him, taking the baby with her. Charley saw that, though everything looked dim to her; when Adam came in, she knew, too, that his face was angry and dark.

"It's Christmas eve," she said.

She tried to say more, but could not.

"You must go from here!" speaking sharp, hissing. "I've no faith in the whinin' cant of such as you. Go out, Janet. This is no place for you or the child."

He opened the street-door for Lot to go out. He had no faith in her. No shrewd, common-sense man would have had. Besides, this was his Christmas night: the beginning of his new life, when he was coming near to Christ in his happy home and great love. Was this foul worm of the gutter to crawl in and tarnish it all? She stopped one instant on the threshold. Within was a home, a chance for heaven; out yonder in the night—what?

"You will put me out?" she said.

"I know your like. There's no help for such as you"; and he closed the door.

She sat down on the curb-stone. It was snowing hard. For about an hour she was there, perfectly quiet. The snow lay in warm, fleecy drifts about her: when it fell on her arm, she shook it off: it was so pure and clean, and *she*—She could have torn her flesh from the bones, it seemed so foul to her that night. Poor Charley! If she had only known how God loved something within her, purer than the snow, which no foulness of flesh or circumstance could defile! Would you have told her, if you had been there? She only muttered, "Never," to herself now and then, "Never."

A little boy came along presently, carrying a loaf of bread under his arm,—a manly, gentle little fellow. She let Benny play with him sometimes.

"Why, Lot," he said. "I'll walk part of the way home with you. I'm afraid."

She got up and took him by the hand. She could hardly speak. Tired, worn-out in body and soul; her feet had been passing for years through water colder than the river of death: but it was nearly over now.

"It's better for Benny it should end this way," she said.

She knew how it would end.

"Rob," she said, when the boy turned to go to his own home, "you know Adam Craig? I want you to bring him to my room early to-morrow morning,—by dawn. Tell him he'll find his sister Nelly's child there: and never to tell that child that his 'Charley' was Lot Tyndal. You'll remember, Rob?"

"I will. Happy Christmas, Charley!"

She waited a minute, her foot on the steps leading to her room.

"Rob!" she called, weakly, "when you play with Ben, I wish you'd call me Charley to him, and never—that other name."

"I'll mind," the child said, looking wistfully at her.

She was alone now. How long and steep the stairs were! She crawled up slowly. At the top she took a lump of something brown from her pocket, looked at it long and steadily. Then she glanced upward.

"It's the only way to keep Benny from knowing," she said. She ate it, nearly all, then looked around, below her, with a strange intentness, as one who says good-bye. The bell tolled the hour. Unutterable pain was in its voice,—may-be dumb spirits like Lot's crying aloud to God.

"One hour nearer Christmas," said Adam Craig, uneasily. "Christ's coming would have more meaning, Janet, if this were a better world. If it wasn't for these social necessities that"—

He stopped. Jinny did not answer.

Lot went into her room, roused Ben with a kiss. "His last remembrance of me shall be good and pleasant," she said. She took him on her lap, untying his shoes.

"My baby has been hunting eggs today in Rob's stable," shaking the hay from his stockings.

"Why, Charley! how could you know?" with wide eyes.

"So many things I know! Oh, Charley's wise! To-morrow, Bud will go see new friends,—such kind friends! Charley knows. A baby, Ben. My boy will like that: he's a big giant beside that baby. *Ben* can hold it, and touch it, and kiss it."

She looked at his pure hands with hungry eyes.

"Go on. What else but the baby?"

"Kind friends for Ben, better and kinder than Charley."

"That's not true. Where are you going, Charley? I hate the kind friends. I'll stay with you,"—beginning to cry.

Her eyes sparkled, and she laughed childishly.

"Only a little way, Bud, I'm going. You watch for me,—all the time you watch for me. Some day you and I'll go out to the country, and be good children together."

What dawning of a new hope was this? She did not feel as if she lied. Some day,—it might be true. Yet the vague gleam died out of her heart, and when Ben, in his white night-gown, knelt down to say the prayer his mother had taught him, it was "Devil Lot's" dead, crime-marked face that bent over him.

"God bless Charley!" he said.

She heard that. She put him into the bed, then quietly bathed herself, filled his stocking with the candies she had bought, and lay down beside him,—her limbs growing weaker, but her brain more lifeful, vivid, intent.

"Not long now," she thought. "Love me, Benny. Kiss me good-night."

The child put his arms about her neck, and kissed her forehead.

"Charley's cold," he said. "When we are good children together, let's live in a tent. Will you, Sis? Let's make a tent now."

"Yes, dear."

She struggled up, and pinned the sheet over him to the head-board; it was a favorite fancy of Ben's.

"That's a good Charley," sleepily.

"Good night. I'll watch for you all the time, all the time."

He was asleep,—did not waken even when she strained him to her heart, passionately, with a wild cry.

"Good bye, Benny." Then she lay quiet. "We might have been good children together, if only—I don't know whose fault it is," throwing her thin arms out desperately. "I wish—oh, I do wish somebody had been kind to me!"

Then the arms fell powerless, and Charley never moved again. But her soul was clear. In the slow tides of that night, it lived back, hour by hour, the life gone before. There was a skylight above her; she looked up into the great silent darkness between earth and heaven,—Devil Lot, whose soul must go out into that darkness alone. She said that. The world that had held her under its foul heel did not loathe her as she loathed herself that night. *Lot.*

The dark hours passed, one by one. Christmas was nearer, nearer,—the bell tolled. It had no meaning for her: only woke a weak fear that she should not be dead before morning, that any living eye should be vexed by her again. Past midnight. The great darkness slowly grayed and softened. What did she wait for? The vile worm Lot,—who cared in earth or heaven when she died? *Then the Lord turned, and looked upon Charley.* Never yet was the soul so loathsome, the wrong so deep, that the loving Christ has not touched it once with His hands, and said, "Will you come to me?" Do you know how He came to her? how, while the unquiet earth needed Him, and the inner deeps of heaven were freshening their fairest morning light to usher in the birthday of our God, He came to find poor Charley, and, having died to save her, laid His healing hands upon her? It was in her weak, ignorant way she saw Him. While she, Lot, lay there corrupt, rotten in soul and body, it came to her how, long ago, Magdalene, more vile than Lot, had stood closest to Jesus. Magdalene loved much, and was forgiven.

So, after a while, Charley, the child that might have been, came to His feet humbly, with bitter sobs. "Lord, I'm so tired!" she said. "I'd like to try again, and be a different girl." That was all. She clung close to His hand as she went through the deep waters.

Benny, stirring in his sleep, leaned over, and kissed her lips. "So cold!" he whispered, drowsily. "God—bless—Charley!" She smiled, but her eyes were closed.

The darkness was gone: the gray vault trembled with a coming radiance; from the East, where the Son of Man was born, a faint flush touched the earth: it was the promise of the Dawn. Lot's foul body lay dead there with the Night: but Jesus took the child Charley in His arms, and blessed her.

Christmas evening. How still and quiet it was! The Helper had come. Not to the snow-covered old earth, falling asleep in the crimson sunset mist: it did not need Him. Not an atom of its living body, from the granite mountain to the dust on the red sea-fern, had failed to perform its work: taking time, too, to break forth in a wild luxuriance of beauty as a psalm of thanksgiving. The Holy Spirit you talk of in the churches had been in the old world since the beginning, since the day it brooded over the waters, showing itself as the spirit of Life in granite rock or red sea-fern,—as the spirit of Truth in every heroic deed, in every true word of poet or prophet,—as the spirit of Love as—Let your own hungry heart tell how. To-day it came to man as the Helper. We all saw that dimly, and showed that we were glad, in some weak way. God, looking down, saw a smile upon the faces of His people.

The fire glowed redder and cheerier in Adam's little cottage; thy lamp was lighted; Jinny had set out a wonderful table, too. Benny had walked around and around it, rubbing his hands slowly in dumb ecstasy. Such oranges! and frosted cakes covered with crushed candy! Such a tree in the middle, hung with soft-burning tapers, and hidden in the branches the white figure of the loving Christ-child. That was Adam's fancy. Benny sat in Jinny's lap now, his head upon her breast. She was rocking him to sleep, singing some cheery song for him, although that baby of hers lay broad awake in the cradle, aghast and open-mouthed at his neglect. It had been just "Benny" all day,—Benny that she had followed about, uneasy lest the wind should blow through the open door on him, or the fire be too hot, or that every moment should not be full to the brim with fun and pleasure, touching his head or hand now and then with a woful tenderness, her throat choked, and her blue eyes wet, crying in her heart incessantly, "Lord, forgive me!"

"Tell me more of Charley," she said, as they sat there in the evening.

He was awake a long time after that, telling her, ending with,—

"She said, 'You watch for me, Bud, all the time.' That's what she said. So she'll come. She always does, when she says. Then we're going to the country to be good children together. I'll watch for her."

So he fell asleep, and Jinny kissed him,—looking at him an instant, her cheek growing paler.

"That is for you, Benny," she whispered to herself,—"and this," stooping to touch his lips again, "this is for Charley. Last night," she muttered, bitterly, "it would have saved her."

Old Adam sat on the side of the bed where the dead girl lay.

"Nelly's child!" he said, stroking the hand, smoothing the fair hair. All day he had said only that,—"Nelly's child!"

Very like her she was,—the little Nell who used to save her cents to buy a Christmas-gift for him, and bring it with flushed cheeks, shyly, and slip it on his plate. This child's cheeks would have flushed like hers—at a kind word; the dimpled, innocent smile lay in them,—only a kind word would have brought it to life. She was dead now, and he—he had struck her yesterday. She lay dead there with her great loving heart, her tender, childish beauty,—a harlot,—Devil Lot. No more.

The old man pushed his hair back, with shaking hands, looking up to the sky. "Lord, lay not this sin to my charge!" he said. His lips were bloodless. There was not a street in any city where a woman like this did not stand with foul hand and gnawing heart. They came from God, and would go back to Him. To-day the Helper came; but who showed Him to them, to Nelly's child?

Old Adam took the little cold hand in his: he said something under his breath: I think it was, “Here am I, Lord, and the wife that Thou hast given,” as one who had found his life’s work, and took it humbly. A sworn knight in Christ’s order.

Christmas-day had come,—the promise of the Dawn, sometime to broaden into the full and perfect day. At its close now, a still golden glow, like a great Peace, filled the earth and heaven, touching the dead Lot there, and the old man kneeling beside her. He fancied that it broke from behind the dark bars of cloud in the West, thinking of the old appeal, “Lift up your heads, O ye gates, and the King of Glory shall come in.” Was He going in, yonder? A weary man, pale, thorn-crowned, bearing the pain and hunger of men and women vile as Lot, to lay them at His Father’s feet? Was he to go with loving heart, and do likewise? Was that the meaning of Christmas-day? The quiet glow grew deeper, more restful; the bell tolled: its sound faded, solemn and low, into the quiet, as one that says in his heart, Amen.

That night, Benny, sleeping in the still twilight, stirred and smiled suddenly, as though some one had given him a happy kiss, and, half waking, cried, “Oh, Charley! Charley!”

HOW SANTA CLAUS CAME TO SIMPSON'S BAR

BRET HARTE

From *Mrs. Skagg's Husbands, and Other Sketches* (Boston: James R. Osgood and Co., 1873), 55–79.

Bret Harte's rise to literary prominence in the wake of the Civil War was meteoric. A New Yorker by birth, Harte moved to California in the 1850s, and his tales of life in the West captured the imagination of American readers looking for distraction from the aftermath of the recent national conflict. Mixing rough emotion with earthy realism, Harte's stories of mining life established his fame around the world—much to the chagrin of his sometime friend and frequent enemy Mark Twain. This Christmas sketch is a perfect example of Harte's talents: his portrait of motley miners mixes broad comedy and seasonal pathos in equal measure. Its reference to Jim Smiley as a "fool" and a "skunk" is also a knowing dig in Twain's ribs—Smiley was one of Twain's most famous literary creations at this time.

It had been raining in the valley of the Sacramento. The North Fork had overflowed its banks and Rattlesnake Creek was impassable. The few boulders that had marked the summer ford at Simpson's Crossing were obliterated by a vast sheet of water stretching to the foothills. The up stage was stopped at Grangers; the last mail had been abandoned in the *tules,* the rider swimming for his life. "An area," remarked the "Sierra Avalanche," with pensive local pride, "as large as the State of Massachusetts is now under water."

Nor was the weather any better in the foothills. The mud lay deep on the mountain road; wagons that neither physical force nor moral objurgation could move from the evil ways into which they had fallen, encumbered the track, and the way to Simpson's Bar was indicated by broken-down teams and hard swearing. And farther on, cut off and inaccessible, rained upon and bedraggled, smitten by high winds and threatened by high water, Simpson's Bar, on the eve of Christmas day, 1862, clung like a swallow's nest to the rocky entablature and splintered capitals of Table Mountain, and shook in the blast.

As night shut down on the settlement, a few lights gleamed through the mist from the windows of cabins on either side of the highway now crossed and gullied by lawless streams and swept by marauding winds. Happily most of the population were gathered at Thompson's store, clustered around a red-hot stove, at which they silently spat in some accepted sense of social communion that perhaps rendered conversation unnecessary. Indeed, most methods of diversion had long since been exhausted on Simpson's Bar; high water had suspended the regular occupations on gulch and on river, and a consequent lack of money and whiskey had taken the zest from most illegitimate recreation. Even Mr. Hamlin was fain to leave the Bar with fifty dollars in his pocket,—the only amount actually realized of the large sums won by him in the successful exercise of his arduous profession. "Ef I was asked," he remarked somewhat later,—"ef I was asked to pint out a purty little village where a retired sport as didn't care for money could exercise hisself, frequent and lively, I'd say Simpson's Bar; but for a young man with a large family depending on his exertions, it don't pay." As Mr. Hamlin's family consisted mainly of female adults, this remark is quoted rather to show the breadth of his humor than the exact extent of his responsibilities.

Howbeit, the unconscious objects of this satire sat that evening in the listless apathy begotten of idleness and lack of excitement. Even the sudden splashing of hoofs before the door did not arouse them. Dick Bullen alone paused in the act of scraping out his pipe, and lifted his head, but no other one of the group indicated any interest in, or recognition of, the man who entered.

It was a figure familiar enough to the company, and known in Simpson's Bar as "The Old Man." A man of perhaps fifty years; grizzled and scant of hair, but still fresh and youthful of complexion. A face full of ready, but not very powerful sympathy, with a chameleon-like aptitude for taking on the shade and color of contiguous moods and feelings. He had evidently just left some hilarious companions, and did not at first notice the gravity of the group, but clapped the shoulder of the nearest man jocularly, and threw himself into a vacant chair.

"Jest heard the best thing out, boys! Ye know Smiley, over yar,—Jim Smiley,—funniest man in the Bar? Well, Jim was jest telling the richest yarn about—"

"Smiley's a —— fool," interrupted a gloomy voice.

"A particular —— skunk," added another in sepulchral accents.

A silence followed these positive statements. The Old Man glanced quickly around the group. Then his face slowly changed. "That's so," he said reflectively, after a pause, "certingly a sort of a skunk and suthin of a fool. In course." He was silent for a moment as in painful contemplation of the unsavoriness and folly of the unpopular Smiley. "Dismal weather, ain't it?" he added, now fully embarked on the current of prevailing sentiment. "Mighty rough papers on the boys, and no show for money this season. And tomorrow's Christmas."

There was a movement among the men at this announcement, but whether of satisfaction or disgust was not plain. "Yes," continued the Old Man in the lugubrious tone he had, within the last few moments, unconsciously adopted,—"yes, Christmas, and to-night's Christmas eve. Ye see, boys, I kinder thought—that is, I sorter had an idee, jest passin' like, you know—that may be ye'd all like to come over to my house to-night and have a sort of tear round. But I suppose, now, you wouldn't? Don't feel like it, may be?" he added with anxious sympathy, peering into the faces of his companions.

"Well, I don't know," responded Tom Flynn with some cheerfulness. "P'r'aps we may. But how about your wife, Old Man? What does *she* say to it?"

The Old Man hesitated. His conjugal experience had not been a happy one, and the fact was known to Simpson's Bar. His first wife, a delicate, pretty little woman, had suffered keenly and secretly from the jealous suspicions of her husband, until one day he invited the whole Bar to his house to expose her infidelity. On arriving, the party found the shy, *petite* creature quietly engaged in her household duties, and retired abashed and discomfited. But the sensitive woman did not easily recover from the shock of this extraordinary outrage. It was with difficulty she regained her equanimity sufficiently to release her lover from the closet in which he was concealed and escape with him. She left a boy of three years to comfort her bereaved husband. The Old Man's present wife had been his cook. She was large, loyal, and aggressive.

Before he could reply, Joe Dimmick suggested with great directness that it was the "Old Man's house," and that, invoking the Divine Power, if the case were his own, he would invite whom he pleased, even if in so doing he imperilled his salvation. The Powers of Evil, he further remarked, should contend against him vainly. All this delivered with a terseness and vigor lost in this necessary translation.

"In course. Certainly. Thet's it," said the Old Man with a sympathetic frown. "Thar's no trouble about *thet.* It's my own house, built every stick on it myself. Don't you be afeard o' her, boys. She *may* cut up a trifle rough,—ez wimmin do,—but she'll come round." Secretly the Old Man trusted to the exaltation of liquor and the power of courageous example to sustain him in such an emergency.

As yet, Dick Bullen, the oracle and leader of Simpson's Bar, had not spoken. He now took his pipe from his lips. "Old Man, how's that yer Johnny gettin' on? Seems to me he didn't look so peart last time I seed him on the bluff heavin' rocks at Chinamen. Didn't seem to take much interest in it. Thar was a gang of 'em by yar yesterday,—drownded out up the river,—and I kinder thought o' Johnny, and how he'd miss 'em! May be now, we'd be in the way ef he wus sick?"

The father, evidently touched not only by this pathetic picture of Johnny's deprivation, but by the considerate delicacy of the speaker, hastened to assure him that Johnny was better and that a "little fun might 'liven him up." Whereupon Dick arose, shook himself, and saying, "I'm ready. Lead the way, Old Man: here goes," himself led the way with a leap, a characteristic howl, and darted out into the night. As he passed through the outer room he caught up a blazing brand from the hearth. The action was repeated by the rest of the party, closely following and elbowing each other, and before the astonished proprietor of Thompson's grocery was aware of the intention of his guests, the room was deserted.

The night was pitchy dark. In the first gust of wind their temporary torches were extinguished, and only the red brands dancing and flitting in the gloom like drunken will-o'-the-wisps indicated their whereabouts. Their way led up Pine-Tree Canyon, at the head of which a broad, low, bark-thatched cabin burrowed in the mountain-side. It was the home of the Old Man, and the entrance to the tunnel in which he worked when he worked at all. Here the crowd paused for a moment, out of delicate deference to their host, who came up panting in the rear.

"P'r'aps ye'd better hold on a second out yer, whilst I go in and see thet things is all right," said the Old Man, with an indifference he was far from feeling. The suggestion was graciously accepted, the door opened and closed on the host, and the crowd, leaning their backs against the wall and cowering under the eaves, waited and listened.

For a few moments there was no sound but the dripping of water from the eaves, and the stir and rustle of wrestling boughs above them. Then the men became uneasy, and whispered suggestion and suspicion passed from the one to the other. "Reckon she's caved in his head the first lick!" "Decoyed him inter the tunnel and barred him up, likely." "Got him down and sittin' on him." "Prob'ly bilin suthin to heave on us: stand clear the door, boys!" For just then the latch clicked, the door slowly opened, and a voice said, "Come in out o' the wet."

The voice was neither that of the Old Man nor of his wife. It was the voice of a small boy, its weak treble broken by that preternatural hoarseness which only vagabondage and the habit of premature self-assertion can give. It was the face of a small boy that looked up at theirs,—a face that might have been pretty and even refined but that it was darkened by evil knowledge from within, and dirt and hard experience from without. He had a blanket around his shoulders and had evidently just risen from his bed. "Come in," he repeated, "and don't make no noise. The Old Man's in there talking to mar," he continued, pointing to an adjacent room which seemed to be a kitchen, from which the Old Man's voice came in deprecating accents. "Let me be," he added, querulously, to Dick Bullen, who had caught him up, blanket and all, and was affecting to toss him into the fire, "let go o' me, you d——d old fool, d'ye hear?"

Thus adjured, Dick Bullen lowered Johnny to the ground with a smothered laugh, while the men, entering quietly, ranged themselves around a long table of rough boards which occupied the centre of the room. Johnny then gravely proceeded to a cupboard and brought out several articles which he deposited on the table. "Thar's whiskey. And crackers. And red herons. And cheese." He took a bite of the latter on his way to the table. "And sugar." He scooped up a mouthful en route with a small and very dirty hand. "And terbacker. Thar's dried appils too on the shelf, but I don't admire 'em. Appils is swellin'. Thar," he concluded, "now wade in, and don't be afeard. I don't mind the old woman. She don't b'long to *me.* S'long."

He had stepped to the threshold of a small room, scarcely larger than a closet, partitioned off from the main apartment, and holding in its dim recess a small bed. He stood there a moment looking at the company, his bare feet peeping from the blanket, and nodded.

"Hello, Johnny! You ain't goin' to turn in agin, are ye?" said Dick.

"Yes, I are," responded Johnny, decidedly.

"Why, wot's up, old fellow?"

"I'm sick."

"How sick!"

"I've got a fevier. And childblains. And roomatiz," returned Johnny, and vanished within. After a moment's pause, he added in the dark, apparently from under the bedclothes,—"And biles!"

There was an embarrassing silence. The men looked at each other, and at the fire. Even with the appetizing banquet before them, it seemed as if they might again fall into the despondency of Thompson's grocery, when the voice of the Old Man, incautiously lifted, came deprecatingly from the kitchen.

"Certainly! Thet's so. In course they is. A gang o' lazy drunken loafers, and that ar Dick Bullen's the ornariest of all. Didn't hev no more *sabe* than to come round yar with sickness in the house and no provision. Thet's what I said: 'Bullen,' sez I, 'it's crazy drunk you are, or a fool,' sez I, 'to think o' such a thing.' 'Staples,' I sez, 'be you a man, Staples, and 'spect to raise h——ll under my roof and invalids lyin' round?' But they would come,—they would. Thet's wot you must 'spect o' such trash as lays round the Bar."

A burst of laughter from the men followed this unfortunate exposure. Whether it was overheard in the kitchen, or whether the Old Man's irate companion had just then exhausted all other modes of expressing her contemptuous indignation, I cannot say, but a back door was suddenly slammed with great violence. A moment later and the Old Man reappeared, haply unconscious of the cause of the late hilarious outburst, and smiled blandly.

"The old woman thought she'd jest run over to Mrs. McFadden's for a sociable call," he explained, with jaunty indifference, as he took a seat at the board.

Oddly enough it needed this untoward incident to relieve the embarrassment that was beginning to be felt by the party, and their natural audacity returned with their host. I do not propose to record the convivialities of that evening. The inquisitive reader will accept the statement that the conversation was characterized by the same intellectual exaltation, the same cautious reverence, the same fastidious delicacy, the same rhetorical precision, and the same logical and coherent discourse somewhat later in the evening, which distinguish similar gatherings of the masculine sex in more civilized localities and under more favorable auspices. No glasses were broken in the absence of any; no liquor was uselessly spilt on floor or table in the scarcity of that article.

It was nearly midnight when the festivities were interrupted. "Hush," said Dick Bullen, holding up his hand. It was the querulous voice of Johnny from his adjacent closet: "O dad!"

The Old Man arose hurriedly and disappeared in the closet. Presently he reappeared. "His rheumatiz is coming on agin bad," he explained, "and he wants rubbin'." He lifted the demijohn of whiskey from the table and shook it. It was empty. Dick Bullen put down his tin cup with an embarrassed laugh. So did the others. The Old Man examined their contents and said hopefully, "I reckon that's enough; he don't need much. You hold on all o' you for a spell, and I'll be back"; and vanished in the closet with an old flannel shirt and the whiskey. The door closed but imperfectly, and the following dialogue was distinctly audible:—

"Now, Sonny, whar does she ache worst?"

"Sometimes over yar and sometimes under yer; but it's most powerful from yer to yer. Rub yer, dad."

A silence seemed to indicate a brisk rubbing. Then Johnny:

"Hevin' a good time out yer, dad?"

"Yes, sonny."

"To-morrer's Chrismiss,—ain't it?"

"Yes, Sonny. How does she feel now?"

"Better. Rub a little furder down. Wot's Chrismiss, anyway? Wot's it all about?"

"O, it's a day."

This exhaustive definition was apparently satisfactory, for there was a silent interval of rubbing. Presently Johnny again:

"Mar sez that everywhere else but yer everybody gives things to everybody Chrismiss, and then she jist waded inter you. She sez thar's a man they call Sandy Claws, not a white man, you know, but a kind o' Chinemin, comes down the chimbley night afore Chrismiss and gives things to chillern,—boys like me. Puts 'em in their butes! Thet's what she tried to play upon me. Easy now, pop, whar are you rubbin' to,—thet's a mile from the place. She jest made that up, didn't she, jest to aggrewate me and you? Don't rub thar. . . . Why, dad!"

In the great quiet that seemed to have fallen upon the house the sigh of the near pines and the drip of leaves without was very distinct. Johnny's voice, too, was lowered as he went on, "Don't you take on now, fur I'm gettin' all right fast. Wot's the boys doin' out thar?"

The Old Man partly opened the door and peered through. His guests were sitting there sociably enough, and there were a few silver coins and a lean buckskin purse on the table. "Bettin' on suthin,—some little game or 'nother. They're all right," he replied to Johnny, and recommenced his rubbing.

"I'd like to take a hand and win some money," said Johnny, reflectively, after a pause.

The Old Man glibly repeated what was evidently a familiar formula, that if Johnny would wait until he struck it rich in the tunnel he'd have lots of money, etc., etc.

"Yes," said Johnny, "but you don't. And whether you strike it or I win it, it's about the same. It's all luck. But it's mighty cur'o's about Chrismiss,—ain't it? Why do they call it Chrismiss?"

Perhaps from some instinctive deference to the overhearing of his guests, or from some vague sense of incongruity, the Old Man's reply was so low as to be inaudible beyond the room.

"Yes," said Johnny, with some slight abatement of interest, "I've heerd o' *him* before. Thar, that'll do, dad. I don't ache near so bad as I did. Now wrap me tight in this yer blanket. So. Now," he added in a muffled whisper, "sit down yer by me till I go asleep." To assure himself of obedience, he disengaged one hand from the blanket and, grasping his father's sleeve, again composed himself to rest.

For some moments the Old Man waited patiently. Then the unwonted stillness of the house excited his curiosity, and without moving from the bed, he cautiously opened the door with his disengaged hand, and looked into the main room. To his infinite surprise it was dark and deserted. But even then a smouldering log on the hearth broke, and by the upspringing blaze he saw the figure of Dick Bullen sitting by the dying embers.

"Hello!"

Dick started, rose, and came somewhat unsteadily toward him.

"Whar's the boys?" said the Old Man.

"Gone up the canyon on a little *pasear.* They're coming back for me in a minit. I'm waitin' round for 'em. What are you starin' at, Old Man?" he added with a forced laugh; "do you think I'm drunk?"

The Old Man might have been pardoned the supposition, for Dick's eyes were humid and his face flushed. He loitered and lounged back to the chimney, yawned, shook himself, buttoned up his coat and laughed. "Liquor ain't so plenty as that, Old Man. Now don't you git up," he continued, as the Old Man made a movement to release his sleeve from Johnny's hand. "Don't you mind manners. Sit jest whar you be; I'm goin' in a jiffy. Thar, that's them now."

There was a low tap at the door. Dick Bullen opened it quickly, nodded "Good night" to his host, and disappeared. The Old Man would have followed him but for the hand that still unconsciously grasped his sleeve. He could have easily disengaged it: it was small, weak, and emaciated. But perhaps because it *was* small, weak, and emaciated, he changed his mind, and, drawing his chair closer to the bed, rested his head upon it. In this defenceless attitude the potency of his earlier potations surprised him. The room flickered and faded before his eyes, reappeared, faded again, went out, and left him—asleep.

Meantime Dick Bullen, closing the door, confronted his companions. "Are you ready?" said Staples. "Ready," said Dick; "what's the time?" "Past twelve," was the reply; "can you make it?—it's nigh on fifty miles, the round trip hither and yon." "I reckon," returned Dick, shortly. "Whar's the mare?" "Bill and Jack's holdin' her at the crossin'." "Let 'em hold on a minit longer," said Dick.

He turned and re-entered the house softly. By the light of the guttering candle and dying fire he saw that the door of the little room was open. He stepped toward it on tiptoe and looked in. The Old Man had fallen back in his chair, snoring, his helpless feet thrust out in a line with his collapsed shoulders, and his hat pulled over his eyes. Beside him, on a narrow wooden bedstead, lay Johnny, muffled tightly in a blanket that hid all save a strip of forehead and a few curls damp with perspiration. Dick Bullen made a step forward, hesitated, and glanced over his shoulder into the deserted room. Everything was quiet. With a sudden resolution he parted his huge mustaches with both hands and stooped over the sleeping boy. But even as he did so a mischievous blast, lying in wait, swooped down the chimney, rekindled the hearth, and lit up the room with a shameless glow from which Dick fled in bashful terror.

His companions were already waiting for him at the crossing. Two of them were struggling in the darkness with some strange misshapen bulk, which as Dick came nearer took the semblance of a great yellow horse.

It was the mare. She was not a pretty picture. From her Roman nose to her rising haunches, from her arched spine hidden by the stiff *machillas* of a Mexican saddle, to her thick, straight, bony legs, there was not a line of equine grace. In her half-blind but wholly vicious white eyes, in her protruding under lip, in her monstrous color, there was nothing but ugliness and vice.

"Now then," said Staples, "stand cl'ar of her heels, boys, and up with you. Don't miss your first holt of her mane, and mind ye get your off stirrup *quick.* Ready!"

There was a leap, a scrambling struggle, a bound, a wild retreat of the crowd, a circle of flying hoofs, two springless leaps that jarred the earth, a rapid play and jingle of spurs, a plunge, and then the voice of Dick somewhere in the darkness, "All right!"

"Don't take the lower road back onless you're hard pushed for time! Don't hold her in down hill! We'll be at the ford at five. G'lang! Hoopa! Mula! GO!"

A splash, a spark struck from the ledge in the road, a clatter in the rocky cut beyond, and Dick was gone.

* * *

Sing, O Muse, the ride of Richard Bullen! Sing, O Muse of chivalrous men! the sacred quest, the doughty deeds, the battery of low churls, the fearsome ride and grewsome perils of the Flower of Simpson's Bar! Alack! she is dainty, this Muse! She will have none of this bucking brute and swaggering, ragged rider, and I must fain follow him in prose, afoot!

It was one o'clock, and yet he had only gained Rattlesnake Hill. For in that time Jovita had rehearsed to him all her imperfections and practised all her vices. Thrice had she stumbled. Twice had she thrown up her Roman nose in a straight line with the reins, and, resisting bit and spur, struck out madly across country. Twice had she reared, and, rearing, fallen backward; and twice had the agile Dick, unharmed, regained his seat before she found her vicious legs again. And a mile beyond them, at the foot of a long hill, was Rattlesnake Creek. Dick knew that here was the crucial test of his ability to perform his enterprise, set his teeth grimly, put his knees well into her flanks, and changed his defensive tactics to brisk aggression. Bullied and maddened, Jovita began the descent of the hill. Here the artful Richard pretended to hold her in with ostentatious objurgation and well-feigned cries of alarm. It is unnecessary to add that Jovita instantly ran away. Nor need I state the time made in the descent; it is written in the chronicles of Simpson's Bar. Enough that in another moment, as it seemed to Dick, she was splashing on the overflowed banks of Rattlesnake Creek. As Dick expected, the momentum she had acquired carried her beyond the point of balking, and, holding her well together for a mighty leap, they dashed into the middle of the swiftly flowing current. A few moments of kicking, wading, and swimming, and Dick drew a long breath on the opposite bank.

The road from Rattlesnake Creek to Red Mountain was tolerably level. Either the plunge in Rattlesnake Creek had dampened her baleful fire, or the art which led to it had shown her the superior wickedness of her rider, for Jovita no longer wasted her surplus energy in wanton conceits. Once she bucked, but it was from force of habit; once she shied, but it was from a new freshly painted meeting-house at the crossing of the county road. Hollows, ditches, gravelly deposits, patches of freshly springing grasses, flew from beneath her rattling hoofs. She began to smell unpleasantly, once or twice she coughed slightly, but there was no abatement of her strength or speed. By two o'clock he had passed Red Mountain and begun the descent to the plain. Ten minutes later the driver of the fast Pioneer coach was overtaken and passed by a "man on a Pinto hoss,"—an event sufficiently notable for remark. At half past two Dick rose in his stirrups with a great shout. Stars were glittering through the rifted clouds, and beyond him, out of the plain, rose two spires, a flagstaff, and a straggling line of black objects. Dick jingled his spurs and swung his *riata,* Jovita bounded forward, and in another moment they swept into Tuttleville and drew up before the wooden piazza of "The Hotel of All Nations."

What transpired that night at Tuttleville is not strictly a part of this record. Briefly I may state, however, that after Jovita had been handed over to a sleepy ostler, whom she at once kicked into unpleasant consciousness, Dick sallied out with the bar-keeper for a tour of the sleeping town. Lights still gleamed from a few saloons and gambling-houses; but, avoiding these, they stopped before several closed shops, and by persistent tapping and judicious outcry roused the proprietors from their beds, and made them unbar the doors of their magazines and expose their wares. Sometimes they were met by curses, but oftener by interest and some concern in their needs, and the interview was invariably concluded by a drink. It was three o'clock before this pleasantry was given over, and with a small waterproof bag of india-rubber strapped on his shoulders Dick returned to the hotel. But here he was waylaid by Beauty,—Beauty opulent in charms, affluent in dress, persuasive in speech, and Spanish in accent! In vain she repeated the invitation in "Excelsior," happily scorned by all Alpine-climbing youth, and rejected by this child of the Sierras,—a rejection softened in this instance by a laugh and his last gold coin. And then he sprang to the saddle and dashed down the lonely street and out into the lonelier plain, where presently the lights, the black line of houses, the spires, and the flagstaff sank into the earth behind him again and were lost in the distance.

The storm had cleared away, the air was brisk and cold, the outlines of adjacent landmarks were distinct, but it was half past four before Dick reached the meeting-house and the crossing of the county road. To avoid the rising grade he had taken a longer and more circuitous road, in whose viscid mud Jovita sank fetlock deep at every bound. It was a poor preparation for a steady ascent of five miles more; but Jovita, gathering her legs under her, took it with her usual blind, unreasoning fury, and a half-hour later reached the long level that led to Rattlesnake Creek. Another half-hour would bring him to the creek. He threw the reins lightly upon the neck of the mare, chirruped to her, and began to sing.

Suddenly Jovita shied with a bound that would have unseated a less practised rider. Hanging to her rein was a figure that had leaped from the bank, and at the same time from the road before her arose a shadowy horse and rider. "Throw up your hands," commanded this second apparition, with an oath.

Dick felt the mare tremble, quiver, and apparently sink under him. He knew what it meant and was prepared.

"Stand aside, Jack Simpson, I know you, you d——d thief. Let me pass or—"

He did not finish the sentence. Jovita rose straight in the air with a terrific bound, throwing the figure from her bit with a single shake of her vicious head, and charged with deadly malevolence down on the impediment before her. An oath, a pistol-shot, horse and highwayman rolled over in the road, and the next moment Jovita was a hundred yards away. But the good right arm of her rider, shattered by a bullet, dropped helplessly at his side.

Without slacking his speed he shifted the reins to his left hand. But a few moments later he was obliged to halt and tighten the saddle-girths that had slipped in the onset. This in his crippled condition took some time. He had no fear of pursuit, but looking up he saw that the eastern stars were already paling, and that the distant peaks had lost their ghostly whiteness, and now stood out blackly against a lighter sky. Day was upon him. Then completely absorbed in a single idea, he forgot the pain of his wound, and mounting again dashed on toward Rattlesnake Creek. But now Jovita's breath came broken by gasps, Dick reeled in his saddle, and brighter and brighter grew the sky.

Ride, Richard; run, Jovita; linger, O day!

For the last few rods there was a roaring in his ears. Was it exhaustion from loss of blood, or what? He was dazed and giddy as he swept down the hill, and did not recognize his surroundings. Had he taken the wrong road, or was this Rattlesnake Creek?

It was. But the brawling creek he had swam a few hours before had risen, more than doubled its volume, and now rolled a swift and resistless river between him and Rattlesnake Hill. For the first time that night Richard's heart sank within him. The river, the mountain, the quickening east, swam before his eyes. He shut them to recover his self-control. In that brief interval, by some fantastic mental process, the little room at Simpson's Bar and the figures of the sleeping father and son rose upon him. He opened his eyes wildly, cast off his coat, pistol, boots, and saddle, bound his precious pack tightly to his shoulders, grasped the bare flanks of Jovita with his bared knees, and with a shout dashed into the yellow water. A cry rose from the opposite bank as the head of a man and horse struggled for a few moments against the battling current, and then were swept away amidst uprooted trees and whirling drift-wood.

* * *

The Old Man started and woke. The fire on the hearth was dead, the candle in the outer room flickering in its socket, and somebody was rapping at the door. He opened it, but fell back with a cry before the dripping half-naked figure that reeled against the doorpost.

"Dick?"

"Hush! Is he awake yet?"

"No,—but, Dick?—"

"Dry up, you old fool! Get me some whiskey *quick!*"

The Old Man flew and returned with—an empty bottle! Dick would have sworn, but his strength was not equal to the occasion. He staggered, caught at the handle of the door, and motioned to the Old Man.

"Thar's suthin' in my pack yer for Johnny. Take it off. I can't."

The Old Man unstrapped the pack and laid it before the exhausted man.

"Open it, quick!"

He did so with trembling fingers. It contained only a few poor toys,—cheap and barbaric enough, goodness knows, but bright with paint and tinsel. One of them was broken; another, I fear, was irretrievably ruined by water; and on the third—ah me! there was a cruel spot.

"It don't look like much, that's a fact," said Dick, ruefully. . . ."But it's the best we could do. . . . Take 'em, Old Man, and put 'em in his stocking, and tell him—tell him, you know—hold me, Old Man—" The Old Man caught at his sinking figure. "Tell him," said Dick, with a weak little laugh,—"tell him Sandy Claus has come."

And even so, bedraggled, ragged, unshaven and unshorn, with one arm hanging helplessly at his side, Santa Claus came to Simpson's Bar and fell fainting on the first threshold. The Christmas dawn came slowly after, touching the remoter peaks with the rosy warmth of ineffable love. And it looked so tenderly on Simpson's Bar that the whole mountain as if caught in a generous action, blushed to the skies.

AN ENGLISH NEW YEAR

HENRY JAMES

From *English Hours* (Cambridge, MA: Riverside Press, 1905), 270–75.

Henry James's brief account of Christmas in England in 1878 (first published in January 1879) provides a compelling contrast to Washington Irving's opening paean to Christmas in the Old World. Though both men were Anglophiles who framed their literary careers around interpreting life across the Atlantic for American readers, this sketch shares little of Irving's nostalgic veneer, even if James's account of Christmas in a depressed England has its own fascinations. Though not explicitly named here, James's Christmas hosts were lawyer and politician Charles Milnes Gaskell and his wife, Mary Williams-Wynn, at their residence in Wakefield, Thornes House. In a letter to his sister Alice, written on New Year's Eve, he declared that he had been "very pleasantly occupied" by Gaskell's "beautiful and interesting library." The company, on the other hand, he found to be "of sufficient, but not of first class, interest."

It will hardly be pretended this year that the English Christmas has been a merry one, or that the New Year has the promise of being particularly happy. The winter is proving very cold and vicious—as if nature herself were loath to be left out of the general conspiracy against the comfort and self-complacency of man. The country at large has a sense of embarrassment and depression, which is brought home more or less to every class in the closely graduated social hierarchy, and the light of Christmas firesides has by no means dispelled the gloom. Not that I mean to overstate the gloom. It is difficult to imagine any combination of adverse circumstances powerful enough to infringe very sensibly upon the appearance of activity and prosperity, social stability and luxury, which English life must always present to a stranger. Nevertheless the times are distinctly of the kind synthetically spoken of as hard—there is plenty of evidence of it—and the spirits of the public are not high. The depression of business is extreme and universal; I am ignorant whether it has reached so calamitous a point as that almost hopeless prostration of every industry which it is assured us you have lately witnessed in America, and I believe the sound of lamentation is by no means so loud as it has been on two or three occasions within the present century. The possibility of distress among the lower classes has been minimised by the gigantic poor-relief system which is so characteristic a feature of English civilisation and which, under especial stress, is supplemented (as is the case at present) by private charity proportionately huge. I notice too that in some parts of the country discriminating groups of work-people have selected these dismal days as a happy time for striking. When the labouring classes rise to the recreation of a strike I suppose the situation may be said to have its cheerful side. There is, however, great distress in the North, and there is a general feeling of scant money to play with throughout the country. The "Daily News" has sent a correspondent to the great industrial regions, and almost every morning for the last three weeks a very cleverly executed picture of the misery of certain parts of Yorkshire and Lancashire has been served up with the matutinal tea and toast. The work is a good one, and, I take it, eminently worth doing, as it appears to have had a visible effect upon the purse-strings of the well-to-do. There is nothing more striking in England than the success with which an "appeal" is always made. Whatever the season or whatever the cause, there always appears to be enough money and enough benevolence in the country to respond to it in sufficient measure—a remarkable fact when one remembers that there is never a moment of the year when the custom of "appealing" intermits. Equally striking perhaps is the perfection to which the science of distributing charity has been raised—the way it has been analysed and organised and made one of the exact sciences. You perceive that it has occupied for a long time a foremost place among administrative questions, and has received all the light that experience and practice can throw upon it. Is there in this perception more of a lightened or more of an added weight for the brooding consciousness? Truly there are aspects of England at which one can but darkly stare.

I left town a short time before Christmas and went to spend the festive season in the North, in a part of the country with which I was unacquainted. It was quite possible to absent one's self from London without a sense of sacrifice, for the charms of the capital during the last several weeks have been obscured by peculiarly vile weather. It is of course a very old story that London is foggy, and this simple statement raises no blush on the face of Nature as we see it here. But there are fogs and fogs, and the folds of the black mantle have been during the present winter intolerably thick. The thickness that draws down and absorbs the smoke of the housetops, causes it to hang about the streets in impenetrable density, forces it into one's eyes and down one's throat, so that one is half-blinded and quite sickened—this form of the particular plague has been much more frequent than usual. Just before Christmas, too, there was a heavy snow-storm, and even a tolerably light fall of snow has London quite at its mercy. The emblem of purity is almost immediately converted into a sticky, lead-coloured mush, the cabs skulk out of sight or take up their stations before the lurid windows of a public-house, which glares through the sleety darkness at the desperate wayfarer with an air of vulgar bravado. For recovery of one's nervous balance the only course was flight—flight to the country and the confinement of one's vision to the large area of one of those admirable homes which at this season overflow with hospitality and good cheer. By this means the readjustment is effectually brought about—these are conditions that you cordially appreciate. Of all the great things that the English have invented and made a part of the credit of the national character, the most perfect, the most characteristic, the one they have mastered most completely in all its details, so that it has become a compendious illustration of their social genius and their manners, is the well-appointed, well-administered, well-filled country-house. The grateful stranger makes these reflections—and others besides—as he wanders about in the beautiful library of such a dwelling, of an inclement winter afternoon, just at the hour when six o'clock tea is impending. Such a place and such a time abound in agreeable episodes; but I suspect that the episode from which, a fortnight ago, I received the most ineffaceable impression was but indirectly connected with the charms of a luxurious fireside. The country I speak of was a populous manufacturing region, full of tall chimneys and of an air that is grey and gritty. A lady had made a present of a Christmas-tree to the children of a workhouse, and she invited me to go with her and assist at the distribution of the toys. There was a drive through the early dusk of a very cold Christmas Eve, followed by the drawing up of a lamp-lit brougham in the snowy quadrangle of a grim-looking charitable institution. I had never been in an English workhouse before, and this one transported me, with the aid of memory, to the early pages of "Oliver Twist." We passed through cold, bleak passages, to which an odour of suet-pudding, the aroma of Christmas cheer, failed to impart an air of hospitality; and then, after waiting a while in a little parlour appertaining to the superintendent, where the remainder of a dinner of by no means eleemosynary simplicity and the attitude of a gentleman asleep with a flushed face on the sofa seemed to effect a tacit exchange of references, we were ushered into a large frigid refectory, chiefly illumined by the twinkling tapers of the Christmas-tree. Here entered to us some hundred and fifty little children of charity, who had been making a copious dinner and who brought with them an atmosphere of hunger memorably satisfied—together with other traces of the occasion upon their pinafores and their small red faces. I have said that the place reminded me of "Oliver Twist," and I glanced through this little herd for an infant figure that should look as if it were cut out for romantic adventures. But they were all very prosaic little mortals. They were made of very common clay indeed, and a certain number of them were idiotic. They filed up and received their little offerings, and then they compressed themselves into a tight infantine bunch and, lifting up their small hoarse voices, directed a melancholy hymn toward their benefactress. The scene was a picture I shall not forget, with its curious mixture of poetry and sordid prose—the dying wintry light in the big, bare, stale room; the beautiful Lady Bountiful, standing in the twinkling glory of the Christmas-tree; the little multitude of staring and wondering, yet perfectly expressionless, faces.

CHRISTMAS EVERY DAY

WILLIAM DEAN HOWELLS

From *Christmas Every Day and Other Stories Told for Children* (New York: Harper & Brothers, 1892).

Arguably the central figure in American literary life in the last decades of the nineteenth century—as a deeply influential editor as well as a prolific author—William Dean Howells largely held a dim view of what he described as the "ghastly" state of Christmas literature in the late nineteenth century. Even in this example from his collection of stories for children, while it may seem that Howells succumbed to the lure of the holiday sketch, he really presented his young readers with a gentle critique of festive excess and the very tradition of the Christmas story itself. Its autobiographical framing is also clear: Howells largely worked at home and was closely involved in his children's lives. The little girl depicted here might be Mildred, his youngest daughter, who as well as writing poetry in her own right became Howells's literary executor and editor of his correspondence. Or more poignantly, she might be shaped by memories of Winifred, his oldest child, who had died in 1889.

The little girl came into her papa's study, as she always did Saturday morning before breakfast, and asked for a story. He tried to beg off that morning, for he was very busy, but she would not let him. So he began:

"Well, once there was a little pig—"

She put her hand over his mouth and stopped him at the word. She said she had heard little pig-stories till she was perfectly sick of them.

"Well, what kind of story *shall* I tell, then?"

"About Christmas. It's getting to be the season. It's past Thanksgiving already."

"It seems to me," her papa argued, "that I've told as often about Christmas as I have about little pigs."

"No difference! Christmas is more interesting."

"Well!" Her papa roused himself from his writing by a great effort. "Well, then, I'll tell you about the little girl that wanted it Christmas every day in the year. How would you like that?"

"First-rate!" said the little girl; and she nestled into comfortable shape in his lap, ready for listening.

"Very well, then, this little pig—Oh, what are you pounding me for?"

"Because you said little pig instead of little girl."

"I should like to know what's the difference between a little pig and a little girl that wanted it Christmas every day!"

"Papa," said the little girl, warningly, "if you don't go on, I'll *give* it to you!" And at this her papa darted off like lightning, and began to tell the story as fast as he could.

> Well, once there was a little girl who liked Christmas so much that she wanted it to be Christmas every day in the year; and as soon as Thanksgiving was over she began to send postal-cards to the old Christmas Fairy to ask if she mightn't have it. But the old fairy never answered any of the postals; and after a while the little girl found out that the Fairy was pretty particular, and wouldn't notice anything but letters—not even correspondence cards in envelopes; but real letters on sheets of paper, and sealed outside with a monogram—or your initial, anyway. So, then, she began to send her letters; and in about three weeks—or just the day before Christmas, it was—she got a letter from the Fairy, saying she might have it Christmas every day for a year, and then they would see about having it longer.

The little girl was a good deal excited already, preparing for the old-fashioned, once-a-year Christmas that was coming the next day, and perhaps the Fairy's promise didn't make such an impression on her as it would have made at some other time. She just resolved to keep it to herself, and surprise everybody with it as it kept coming true; and then it slipped out of her mind altogether.

She had a splendid Christmas. She went to bed early, so as to let Santa Claus have a chance at the stockings, and in the morning she was up the first of anybody and went and felt them, and found hers all lumpy with packages of candy, and oranges and grapes, and pocket-books and rubber balls, and all kinds of small presents, and her big brother's with nothing but the tongs in them, and her young lady sister's with a new silk umbrella, and her papa's and mamma's with potatoes and pieces of coal wrapped up in tissue-paper, just as they always had every Christmas. Then she waited around till the rest of the family were up, and she was the first to burst into the library, when the doors were opened, and look at the large presents laid out on the library-table—books, and portfolios, and boxes of stationery, and breastpins, and dolls, and little stoves, and dozens of handkerchiefs, and ink-stands, and skates, and snow-shovels, and photograph-frames, and little easels, and boxes of water-colors, and Turkish paste, and nougat, and candied cherries, and dolls' houses, and waterproofs—and the big Christmas-tree, lighted and standing in a waste-basket in the middle.

She had a splendid Christmas all day. She ate so much candy that she did not want any breakfast; and the whole forenoon the presents kept pouring in that the expressman had not had time to deliver the night before; and she went round giving the presents she had got for other people, and came home and ate turkey and cranberry for dinner, and plum-pudding and nuts and raisins and oranges and more candy, and then went out and coasted, and came in with a stomach-ache, crying; and her papa said he would see if his house was turned into that sort of fool's paradise another year; and they had a light supper, and pretty early everybody went to bed cross.

Here the little girl pounded her papa in the back, again.
"Well, what now? Did I say pigs?"
"You made them *act* like pigs."
"Well, didn't they?"
"No matter; you oughtn't to put it into a story."
"Very well, then, I'll take it all out."
Her father went on:

The little girl slept very heavily, and she slept very late, but she was wakened at last by the other children dancing round her bed with their stockings full of presents in their hands.

"What is it?" said the little girl, and she rubbed her eyes and tried to rise up in bed.

"Christmas! Christmas! Christmas!" they all shouted, and waved their stockings.

"Nonsense! It was Christmas yesterday."

Her brothers and sisters just laughed. "We don't know about that. It's Christmas to-day, anyway. You come into the library and see."

Then all at once it flashed on the little girl that the Fairy was keeping her promise, and her year of Christmases was beginning. She was dreadfully sleepy, but she sprang up like a lark—a lark that had overeaten itself and gone to bed cross—and darted into the library. There it was again! Books, and portfolios, and boxes of stationery, and breastpins—

"You needn't go over it all, papa; I guess I can remember just what was there," said the little girl.

Well, and there was the Christmas-tree blazing away, and the family picking out their presents, but looking pretty sleepy, and her father perfectly puzzled, and her mother ready to cry. "I'm sure I don't see how I'm to dispose of all these things," said her mother, and her father said it seemed to him they had had something just like it the day before, but he supposed he must have dreamed it. This struck the little girl as the best kind of a joke; and so she ate so much candy she didn't want any breakfast, and went round carrying presents, and had turkey and cranberry for dinner, and then went out and coasted, and came in with a—

"Papa!"
"Well, what now?"
"What did you promise, you forgetful thing?"
"Oh! oh yes!"

Well, the next day, it was just the same thing over again, but everybody getting crosser; and at the end of a week's time so many people had lost their tempers that you could pick up lost tempers anywhere; they perfectly strewed the ground. Even when people tried to recover their tempers they usually got somebody else's, and it made the most dreadful mix.

The little girl began to get frightened, keeping the secret all to herself; she wanted to tell her mother, but she didn't dare to; and she was ashamed to ask the Fairy to take back her gift, it seemed ungrateful and ill-bred, and she thought she would try to stand it, but she hardly knew how she could, for a whole year. So it went on and on, and it was Christmas on St. Valentine's Day and Washington's Birthday, just the same as any day, and it didn't skip even the First of April, though everything was counterfeit that day, and that was some *little* relief.

After a while coal and potatoes began to be awfully scarce, so many had been wrapped up in tissue-paper to fool papas and mammas with. Turkeys got to be about a thousand dollars apiece—

"Papa!"
"Well, what?"
"You're beginning to fib."
"Well, *two* thousand, then."

And they got to passing off almost anything for turkeys—half-grown humming-birds, and even rocs out of the *Arabian Nights*—the real turkeys were so scarce. And cranberries—well, they asked a diamond apiece for cranberries. All the woods and orchards were cut down for Christmas-trees, and where the woods and orchards used to be it looked just like a stubble-field, with the stumps. After a while they had to make Christmas-trees out of rags, and stuff them with bran, like old-fashioned dolls; but there were plenty of rags, because people got so poor, buying presents for one another, that they couldn't get any new clothes, and they just wore their old ones to tatters. They got so poor that everybody had to go to the poor-house, except the confectioners, and the fancy-store keepers, and the picture-book sellers, and the expressmen; and *they* all got so rich and proud that they would hardly wait upon a person when he came to buy. It was perfectly shameful!

Well, after it had gone on about three or four months, the little girl, whenever she came into the room in the morning and saw those great ugly, lumpy stockings dangling at the fire-place, and the disgusting presents around everywhere, used to just sit down and burst out crying. In six months she was perfectly exhausted; she couldn't even cry any more; she just lay on the lounge and rolled her eyes and panted. About the beginning of October she took to sitting down on dolls wherever she found them—French dolls, or any kind—she hated the sight of them so; and by Thanksgiving she was crazy, and just slammed her presents across the room.

By that time people didn't carry presents around nicely any more. They flung them over the fence, or through the window, or anything; and, instead of running their tongues out and taking great pains to write "For dear Papa," or "Mamma," or "Brother," or "Sister," or "Susie," or "Sammie," or "Billie," or "Bobbie," or "Jimmie," or "Jennie," or whoever it was, and troubling to get the spelling right, and then signing their names, and "Xmas, 18—," they used to write in the gift-books, "Take it, you horrid old thing!" and then go and bang it against the front door. Nearly everybody had built barns to hold their presents, but pretty soon the barns overflowed, and then they used to let them lie out in the rain, or anywhere. Sometimes the police used to come and tell them to shovel their presents off the sidewalk, or they would arrest them.

"I thought you said everybody had gone to the poor-house," interrupted the little girl.

"They did go, at first," said her papa; "but after a while the poor-houses got so full that they had to send the people back to their own houses. They tried to cry, when they got back, but they couldn't make the least sound."

"Why couldn't they?"

"Because they had lost their voices, saying 'Merry Christmas' so much. Did I tell you how it was on the Fourth of July?"

"No; how was it?" And the little girl nestled closer, in expectation of something uncommon.

> Well, the night before, the boys stayed up to celebrate, as they always do, and fell asleep before twelve o'clock, as usual, expecting to be wakened by the bells and cannon. But it was nearly eight o'clock before the first boy in the United States woke up, and then he found out what the trouble was. As soon as he could get his clothes on he ran out of the house and smashed a big cannon-torpedo down on the pavement; but it didn't make any more noise than a damp wad of paper; and after he tried about twenty or thirty more, he began to pick them up and look at them. Every single torpedo was a big raisin! Then he just streaked it up-stairs, and examined his fire-crackers and toy-pistol and two-dollar collection of fireworks, and found that they were nothing but sugar and candy painted up to look like fireworks! Before ten o'clock every boy in the United States found out that his Fourth of July things had turned into Christmas things; and then they just sat down and cried—they were so mad. There are about twenty million boys in the United States, and so you can imagine what a noise they made. Some men got together before night, with a little powder that hadn't turned into purple sugar yet, and they said they would fire off *one* cannon, anyway. But the cannon burst into a thousand pieces, for it was nothing but rock-candy, and some of the men nearly got killed. The Fourth of July orations all turned into Christmas carols, and when anybody tried to read the Declaration, instead of saying, "When in the course of human

events it becomes necessary," he was sure to sing, "God rest you, merry gentlemen." It was perfectly awful.

The little girl drew a deep sigh of satisfaction.

"And how was it at Thanksgiving?"

Her papa hesitated. "Well, I'm almost afraid to tell you. I'm afraid you'll think it's wicked."

"Well, tell, anyway," said the little girl.

Well, before it came Thanksgiving it had leaked out who had caused all these Christmases. The little girl had suffered so much that she had talked about it in her sleep; and after that hardly anybody would play with her. People just perfectly despised her, because if it had not been for her greediness it wouldn't have happened; and now, when it came Thanksgiving, and she wanted them to go to church, and have squash-pie and turkey, and show their gratitude, they said that all the turkeys had been eaten up for her old Christmas dinners, and if she would stop the Christmases, they would see about the gratitude. Wasn't it dreadful? And the very next day the little girl began to send letters to the Christmas Fairy, and then telegrams, to stop it. But it didn't do any good; and then she got to calling at the Fairy's house, but the girl that came to the door always said, "Not at home," or "Engaged," or "At dinner," or something like that; and so it went on till it came to the old once-a-year Christmas Eve. The little girl fell asleep, and when she woke up in the morning—

"She found it was all nothing but a dream," suggested the little girl.

"No, indeed!" said her papa. "It was all every bit true!"

"Well, what *did* she find out, then?"

"Why, that it wasn't Christmas at last, and wasn't ever going to be, any more. Now it's time for breakfast."

The little girl held her papa fast around the neck.

"You sha'n't go if you're going to leave it so!"

"How do you want it left?"

"Christmas once a year."

"All right," said her papa; and he went on again.

Well, there was the greatest rejoicing all over the country, and it extended clear up into Canada. The people met together everywhere, and kissed and cried for joy. The city carts went around and gathered up all the candy and raisins and nuts, and dumped them into the river; and it made the fish perfectly sick; and the whole United States, as far out as Alaska, was one blaze of bonfires, where the children were burning up their gift-books and presents of all kinds. They had the greatest *time!*

The little girl went to thank the old Fairy because she had stopped its being Christmas, and she said she hoped she would keep her promise and see that Christmas never, never came again. Then the Fairy frowned, and asked her if she was sure she knew what she meant; and the little girl asked her, Why not? and the old Fairy said that now she was behaving just as greedily as ever, and she'd better look out. This made the little girl think it all over carefully again, and she said she would be willing to have it Christmas about once in a thousand years; and then she said a hundred, and then she said ten, and at last she got down to one. Then the Fairy said that was the good old way that had pleased people ever since Christmas began, and she was agreed. Then the little girl said, "What're your shoes made of?" And the Fairy said, "Leather." And the little girl said, "Bargain's done forever," and skipped off, and hippity-hopped the whole way home, she was so glad.

"How will that do?" asked the papa.

"First-rate!" said the little girl; but she hated to have the story stop, and was rather sober. However, her mamma put her head in at the door, and asked her papa:

"Are you never coming to breakfast? What have you been telling that child?"

"Oh, just a moral tale."

The little girl caught him around the neck again.

"*We* know! Don't you tell *what,* papa! Don't you tell *what!*"

CHRISTMAS JENNY

MARY WILKINS FREEMAN

From *A New England Nun and Other Stories* (New York: Harper & Brothers, 1891), 160–77.

One of the most important authors in the local color tradition, Mary Wilkins Freeman wrote stories of New England life that were a staple of literary journals in the closing decade of the nineteenth century. Freeman was also a prolific creator of Christmas sketches, repeatedly returning to the season throughout her career. Her apparently gentle tales of marginal regional life, festive and otherwise, contain significant moments of subversion. This holiday sketch is no different, and features a typically compelling example of a Freeman heroine: older, independent, and quietly rebellious. Freeman depicts Christmas Jenny as a symbolically charged avatar of the season, connected through her evergreens to the deep roots of winter celebrations—a primal, nurturing Green Woman to rival the patriarchal dominance of Santa Claus.

The day before there had been a rain and a thaw, then in the night the wind had suddenly blown from the north, and it had grown cold. In the morning it was very clear and cold, and there was the hard glitter of ice over everything. The snow-crust had a thin coat of ice, and all the open fields shone and flashed. The tree boughs and trunks, and all the little twigs, were enamelled with ice. The roads were glare and slippery with it, and so were the door-yards. In old Jonas Carey's yard the path that sloped from the door to the well was like a frozen brook.

Quite early in the morning old Jonas Carey came out with a pail, and went down the path to the well. He went slowly and laboriously, shuffling his feet, so he should not fall. He was tall and gaunt, and one side of his body seemed to slant towards the other, he settled so much more heavily upon one foot. He was somewhat stiff and lame from rheumatism.

He reached the well in safety, hung the pail, and began pumping. He pumped with extreme slowness and steadiness; a certain expression of stolid solemnity, which his face wore, never changed.

When he had filled his pail he took it carefully from the pump spout, and started back to the house, shuffling as before. He was two thirds of the way to the door, when he came to an extremely slippery place. Just there some roots from a little cherry-tree crossed the path, and the ice made a dangerous little pitch over them.

Old Jonas lost his footing, and sat down suddenly; the water was all spilled. The house door flew open, and an old woman appeared.

"Oh, Jonas, air you hurt?" she cried, blinking wildly and terrifiedly in the brilliant light.

The old man never said a word. He sat still and looked straight before him, solemnly.

"Oh, Jonas, you ain't broke any bones, hev you?" The old woman gathered up her skirts and began to edge off the door-step, with trembling knees.

Then the old man raised his voice. "Stay where you be," he said, imperatively. "Go back into the house!"

He began to raise himself, one joint at a time, and the old woman went back into the house, and looked out of the window at him.

When old Jonas finally stood upon his feet it seemed as if he had actually constructed himself, so piecemeal his rising had been. He went back to the pump, hung the pail under the spout, and filled it. Then he started on the return with more caution than before. When he reached the dangerous place his feet flew up again, he sat down, and the water was spilled.

The old woman appeared in the door; her dim blue eyes were quite round, her delicate chin was dropped. "Oh, Jonas!"

"Go back!" cried the old man, with an imperative jerk of his head towards her, and she retreated. This time he arose more quickly, and made quite a lively shuffle back to the pump.

But when his pail was filled and he again started on the return, his caution was redoubled. He seemed to scarcely move at all. When he approached the dangerous spot his progress was hardly more perceptible than a scaly leaf-slug's. Repose almost lapped over motion. The old woman in the window watched breathlessly.

The slippery place was almost passed, the shuffle quickened a little—the old man sat down again, and the tin pail struck the ice with a clatter.

The old woman appeared. "Oh, Jonas!"

Jonas did not look at her; he sat perfectly motionless.

"Jonas, air you hurt? Do speak to me for massy sake!" Jonas did not stir.

Then the old woman let herself carefully off the step. She squatted down upon the icy path, and hitched along to Jonas. She caught hold of his arm—"Jonas, you don't feel as if any of your bones were broke, do you?" Her voice was almost sobbing, her small frame was all of a tremble.

"Go back!" said Jonas. That was all he would say. The old woman's tearful entreaties did not move him in the least. Finally she hitched herself back to the house, and took up her station in the window. Once in a while she rapped on the pane, and beckoned piteously.

But old Jonas Carey sat still. His solemn face was inscrutable. Over his head stretched the icy cherry-branches, full of the flicker and dazzle of diamonds. A woodpecker flew into the tree and began tapping at the trunk, but the ice-enamel was so hard that he could not get any food. Old Jonas sat so still that he did not mind him. A jay flew on the fence within a few feet of him; a sparrow pecked at some weeds piercing the snow-crust beside the door. Over in the east arose the mountain, covered with frosty foliage full of silver and blue and diamond lights. The air was stinging. Old Jonas paid no attention to anything. He sat there.

The old woman ran to the door again. "Oh, Jonas, you'll freeze, settin' there!" she pleaded. "Can't you git up? Your bones ain't broke, air they?" Jonas was silent.

"Oh, Jonas, there's Christmas Jenny comin' down the road—what do you s'pose she'll think?"

Old Jonas Carey was unmoved, but his old wife eagerly watched the woman coming down the road. The woman looked oddly at a distance: like a broad green moving bush; she was dragging something green after her, too. When she came nearer one could see that she was laden with evergreen wreaths—her arms were strung with them; long sprays of ground-pine were wound around her shoulders, she carried a basket trailing with them, and holding also many little bouquets of bright-colored everlasting flowers. She dragged a sled, with a small hemlock-tree bound upon it. She came along sturdily over the slippery road. When she reached the Carey gate she stopped and looked over at Jonas. "Is he hurt?" she sang out to the old woman.

"I dunno—he's fell down three times."

Jenny came through the gate, and proceeded straight to Jonas. She left her sled in the road. She stooped, brought her basket on a level with Jonas's head, and gave him a little push with it. "What's the matter with ye?" Jonas did not wink. "Your bones ain't broke, are they?"

Jenny stood looking at him for a moment. She wore a black hood, her large face was weather-beaten, deeply tanned, and reddened. Her features were strong, but heavily cut. She made one think of those sylvan faces with features composed of bark-wrinkles and knot-holes, that one can fancy looking out of the trunks of trees. She was not an aged woman, but her hair was iron-gray, and crinkled as closely as gray moss.

Finally she turned towards the house. "I'm comin' in a minute," she said to Jonas's wife, and trod confidently up the icy steps.

"Don't you slip," said the old woman, tremulously.

"I ain't afraid of slippin'." When they were in the house she turned around on Mrs. Carey, "Don't you fuss, he ain't hurt."

"No, I don't s'pose he is. It's jest one of his tantrums. But I dunno what I am goin' to do. Oh, dear me suz, I dunno what I am goin' to do with him sometimes!"

"Leave him alone—let him set there."

"Oh, he's tipped all that water over, an' I'm afeard he'll—freeze down. Oh, dear!"

"Let him freeze! Don't you fuss, Betsey."

"I was jest goin' to git breakfast. Mis' Gill she sent us in two sassage-cakes. I was goin' to fry 'em, an' I jest asked him to go out an' draw a pail of water, so's to fill up the tea-kittle. Oh, dear!"

Jenny sat her basket in a chair, strode peremptorily out of the house, picked up the tin pail which lay on its side near Jonas, filled it at the well, and returned. She wholly ignored the old man. When she entered the door his eyes relaxed their solemn stare at vacancy, and darted a swift glance after her.

"Now fill up the kittle, an' fry the sassages," she said to Mrs. Carey.

"Oh, I'm afeard he won't git up, an' they'll be cold! Sometimes his tantrums last a consider'ble while. You see he sot down three times, an' he's awful mad."

"I don't see who he thinks he's spitin'."

"I dunno, 'less it's Providence."

"I reckon Providence don't care much where he sets."

"Oh, Jenny, I'm dreadful afeard he'll freeze down."

"No, he won't. Put on the sassages."

Jonas's wife went about getting out the frying-pan, crooning over her complaint all the time. "He's dreadful fond of sassages," she said, when the odor of the frying sausages became apparent in the room.

"He'll smell 'em an' come in," remarked Jenny, dryly. "He knows there ain't but two cakes, an' he'll be afeard you'll give me one of 'em."

She was right. Before long the two women, taking sly peeps from the window, saw old Jonas lumberingly getting up. "Don't say nothin' to him about it when he comes in," whispered Jenny.

When the old man clumped into the kitchen, neither of the women paid any attention to him. His wife turned the sausages, and Jenny was gathering up her wreaths. Jonas let himself down into a chair, and looked at them uneasily. Jenny laid down her wreaths. "Goin' to stay to breakfast?" said the old man.

"Well, I dunno," replied Jenny. "Them sassages do smell temptin'."

All Jonas's solemnity had vanished, he looked foolish and distressed.

"Do take off your hood, Jenny," urged Betsey. "I ain't very fond of sassages myself, an' I'd jest as liv's you'd have my cake as not."

Jenny laughed broadly and good-naturedly, and began gathering up her wreaths again. "Lor,' I don't want your sassage-cake," said she. "I've had my breakfast. I'm goin' down to the village to sell my wreaths."

Jonas's face lit up. "Pleasant day, ain't it?" he remarked, affably.

Jenny grew sober. "I don't think it's a very pleasant day; guess you wouldn't if you was a woodpecker or a blue-jay," she replied.

Jonas looked at her with stupid inquiry.

"They can't git no breakfast," said Jenny. "They can't git through the ice on the trees. They'll starve if there ain't a thaw pretty soon. I've got to buy 'em somethin' down to the store. I'm goin' to feed a few of 'em. I ain't goin' to see 'em dyin' in my door-yard if I can help it. I've given 'em all I could spare from my own birds this mornin'."

"It's too bad, ain't it?"

"I think it's too bad. I was goin' to buy me a new caliker dress if this freeze hadn't come, but I can't now. What it would cost will save a good many lives. Well, I've got to hurry along if I'm goin' to git back to-day."

Jenny, surrounded with her trailing masses of green, had to edge herself through the narrow doorway. She went straight to the village and peddled her wares from house to house. She had her regular customers. Every year, the week before Christmas, she came down from the mountain with her evergreens. She was popularly supposed to earn quite a sum of money in that way. In the summer she sold vegetables, but the green Christmas traffic was regarded as her legitimate business—it had given her her name among the villagers. However, the fantastic name may have arisen from the popular conception of Jenny's character. She also was considered somewhat fantastic, although there was no doubt of her sanity. In her early youth she had had an unfortunate love affair, that was supposed to have tinctured her whole life with an alien element. "Love-cracked," people called her.

"Christmas Jenny's kind of love-cracked," they said. She was Christmas Jenny in midsummer, when she came down the mountain laden with green peas and string-beans and summer squashes.

She owned a little house and a few acres of cleared land on the mountain, and in one way or another she picked up a living from it.

It was noon to-day before she had sold all her evergreens and started up the mountain road for home. She had laid in a small stock of provisions, and she carried them in the basket which had held the little bunches of life-everlasting and amaranth flowers and dried grasses. The road wound along the base of the mountain. She had to follow it about a mile; then she struck into a cart-path which led up to the clearing where her house was.

After she passed Jonas Carey's there were no houses and no people, but she met many living things that she knew. A little field-mouse, scratching warily from cover to cover, lest his enemies should spy him, had appreciative notice from Jenny Wrayne. She turned her head at the call of a jay, and she caught a glimmer of blue through the dazzling white boughs. She saw with sympathetic eyes a woodpecker drumming on the ice-bound trunk of a tree. Now and then she scattered, with regretful sparseness, some seeds and crumbs from her parcels.

At the point where she left the road for the cart-path there was a gap in the woods, and a clear view of the village below. She stopped and looked back at it. It was quite a large village; over it hung a spraying net-work of frosty branches; the smoke arose straight up from the chimneys. Down in the village street a girl and a young man were walking, talking about her, but she did not know that.

The girl was the minister's daughter. She had just become engaged to the young man, and was walking with him in broad daylight with a kind of shamefaced pride. Whenever they met anybody she blushed, and at the same time held up her head proudly, and swung one arm with an airy motion. She chattered glibly and quite loudly, to cover her embarrassment.

"Yes," she said, in a sweet, crisp voice, "Christmas Jenny has just been to the house, and we've bought some wreaths. We're going to hang them in all the front windows. Mother didn't know as we ought to buy them of her, there's so much talk, but I don't believe a word of it, for my part."

"What talk?" asked the young man. He held himself very stiff and straight, and never turned his head when he shot swift, smiling glances at the girl's pink face.

"Why, don't you know? It's town-talk. They say she's got a lot of birds and rabbits and things shut up in cages, and half starves them; and then that little deaf-and-dumb boy, you know—they say she treats him dreadfully. They're going to look into it. Father and Deacon Little are going up there this week."

"Are they?" said the young man. He was listening to the girl's voice with a sort of rapturous attention, but he had little idea as to what she was saying. As they walked, they faced the mountain.

It was only the next day when the minister and Deacon Little made the visit. They started up a flock of sparrows that were feeding by Jenny's door; but the birds did not fly very far—they settled into a tree and watched. Jenny's house was hardly more than a weather-beaten hut, but there was a grape-vine trained over one end, and the front yard was tidy. Just before the house stood a tall pine-tree. At the rear, and on the right, stretched the remains of Jenny's last summer's garden, full of plough-ridges and glistening corn-stubble.

Jenny was not at home. The minister knocked and got no response. Finally he lifted the latch, and the two men walked in. The room seemed gloomy after the brilliant light outside; they could not see anything at first, but they could hear a loud and demonstrative squeaking and chirping and twittering that their entrance appeared to excite.

At length a small pink-and-white face cleared out of the gloom in the chimney-corner. It surveyed the visitors with no fear nor surprise, but seemingly with an innocent amiability.

"That's the little deaf-and-dumb boy," said the minister, in a subdued voice. The minister was an old man, narrow-shouldered, and clad in long-waisted and wrinkly black. Deacon Little reared himself in his sinewy leanness until his head nearly touched the low ceiling. His face was sallow and severely corrugated, but the features were handsome.

Both stood staring remorselessly at the little deaf-and-dumb boy, who looked up in their faces with an expression of delicate wonder and amusement. The little boy was dressed like a girl, in a long blue gingham pinafore. He sat in the midst of a heap of evergreens, which he had been twining into wreaths; his pretty, soft, fair hair was damp, and lay in a very flat and smooth scallop over his full white forehead.

"He looks as if he was well cared for," said Deacon Little. Both men spoke in hushed tones—it was hard for them to realize that the boy could not hear, the more so because every time their lips moved his smile deepened. He was not in the least afraid.

They moved around the room half guiltily, and surveyed everything. It was unlike any apartment that they had ever entered. It had a curious sylvan air; there were heaps of evergreens here and there, and some small green trees leaned in one corner. All around the room—hung on the walls, standing on rude shelves—were little rough cages and hutches, from which the twittering and chirping sounded. They contained forlorn little birds and rabbits and field-mice. The birds had rough feathers and small, dejected heads, one rabbit had an injured leg, one field-mouse seemed nearly dead. The men eyed them sharply. The minister drew a sigh; the deacon's handsome face looked harder. But they did not say what they thought, on account of the little deaf-and-dumb boy, whose pleasant blue eyes never left their faces. When they had made the circuit of the room, and stood again by the fireplace, he suddenly set up a cry. It was wild and inarticulate, still not wholly dissonant, and it seemed to have a meaning of its own. It united with the cries of the little caged wild creatures, and it was all like a soft clamor of eloquent appeal to the two visitors, but they could not understand it.

They stood solemn and perplexed by the fireplace. "Had we better wait till she comes?" asked the minister.

"I don't know," said Deacon Little.

Back of them arose the tall mantel-shelf. On it were a clock and a candlestick, and regularly laid bunches of brilliant dried flowers, all ready for Jenny to put in her basket and sell.

Suddenly there was a quick scrape on the crusty snow outside, the door flew open, and Jonas Carey's wife came in. She had her shawl over her head, and she was panting for breath.

She stood before the two men, and a sudden crust of shy formality seemed to form over her. "Good-arternoon," she said, in response to their salutations.

She looked at them for a moment, and tightened her shawl-pin; then the restraint left her. "I knowed you was here," she cried, in her weak, vehement voice; "I knowed it. I've heerd the talk. I knowed somebody was goin' to come up here an' spy her out. I was in Mis' Gregg's the other day, an' her husband came home; he'd been down to the store, an' he said they were talkin' 'bout Jenny, an' sayin' she didn't treat Willy and the birds well, an' the town was goin' to look into it. I knowed you was comin' up here when I seed you go by. I told Jonas so. An' I knowed she wa'n't to home, an' there wa'n't nothin' here that could speak, an' I told Jonas I was comin'. I couldn't stan' it nohow. It's dreadful slippery. I had to go on my hands an' knees in some places, an' I've sot down twice, but I don't care. I ain't goin' to have you comin' up here to spy on Jenny, an' nobody to home that's got any tongue to speak for her."

Mrs. Carey stood before them like a ruffled and defiant bird that was frighting herself as well as them with her temerity. She palpitated all over, but there was a fierce look in her dim blue eyes.

The minister began a deprecating murmur, which the deacon drowned. "You can speak for her all you want to, Mrs. Carey," said he. "We ain't got any objections to hearin' it. An' we didn't know but what she was home. Do you know what she does with these birds and things?"

"Does with 'em? Well, I'll tell you what she does with 'em. She picks 'em up in the woods when they're starvin' an' freezin' an' half dead, an' she brings 'em in here, an' takes care of 'em an' feeds 'em till they git well, an' then she lets 'em go again. That's what she does. You see that rabbit there? Well, he's been in a trap. Somebody wanted to kill the poor little cretur. You see that robin? Somebody fired a gun at him an' broke his wing.

"That's what she does. I dunno but it 'mounts to jest about as much as sendin' money to missionaries. I dunno but what bein' a missionary to robins an' starvin' chippies an' little deaf-an'-dumb children is jest as good as some other kinds, an' that's what she is.

"I ain't afeard to speak; I'm goin' to tell the whole story. I dunno what folks mean by talkin' about her the way they do. There, she took that little dumbie out of the poor-house. Nobody else wanted him. He don't look as if he was abused very bad, far's I can see. She keeps him jest as nice an' neat as she can, an' he an' the birds has enough to eat, if she don't herself.

"I guess I know 'bout it. Here she is goin' without a new caliker dress, so's to git somethin' for them birds that can't git at the trees, 'cause there's so much ice on 'em.

"You can't tell me nothin'. When Jonas has one of his tantrums she can git him out of it quicker'n anybody I ever see. She ain't goin' to be talked about and spied upon if I can help it. They tell about her bein' love-cracked. H'm, I dunno what they call love-cracked. I know that Anderson fellar went off an' married another girl, when Jenny jest as much expected to have him as could be. He ought to ha' been strung up. But I know one thing—if she did git kind of twisted out of the reg'lar road of lovin', she's in another one, that's full of little dumbies an' starvin' chippies an' lame rabbits, an' she ain't love-cracked no more'n other folks."

Mrs. Carey, carried away by affection and indignation, almost spoke in poetry. Her small face glowed pink, her blue eyes were full of fire, she waved her arms under her shawl. The little meek old woman was a veritable enthusiast.

The two men looked at each other. The deacon's handsome face was as severe and grave as ever, but he waited for the minister to speak. When the minister did speak it was apologetically. He was a gentle old man, and the deacon was his mouthpiece in matters of parish discipline. If he failed him he betrayed how feeble and kindly a pipe was his own. He told Mrs. Carey that he did not doubt everything was as it should be; he apologized for their presence; he praised Christmas Jenny. Then he and the deacon retreated. They were thankful to leave that small, vociferous old woman, who seemed to be pulling herself up by her enthusiasm until she reached the air over their heads, and became so abnormal that she was frightful. Indeed, everything out of the broad, common track was a horror to these men and to many of their village fellows. Strange shadows, that their eyes could not pierce, lay upon such, and they were suspicious. The popular sentiment against Jenny Wrayne was originally the outcome of this characteristic, which was a remnant of the old New England witchcraft superstition. More than anything else, Jenny's eccentricity, her possibly uncanny deviation from the ordinary ways of life, had brought this inquiry upon her. In actual meaning, although not even in self-acknowledgment, it was a witch-hunt that went up the mountain road that December afternoon.

They hardly spoke on the way. Once the minister turned to the deacon. "I rather think there's no occasion for interference," he said, hesitatingly.

"I guess there ain't any need of it," answered the deacon.

The deacon spoke again when they had nearly reached his own house. "I guess I'll send her up a little somethin' Christmas," said he. Deacon Little was a rich man.

"Maybe it would be a good idea," returned the minister. "I'll see what I can do."

Christmas was one week from that day. On Christmas morning old Jonas Carey and his wife, dressed in their best clothes, started up the mountain road to Jenny Wrayne's. Old Jonas wore his great-coat, and had his wife's cashmere scarf wound twice around his neck. Mrs. Carey wore her long shawl and her best bonnet. They walked along quite easily. The ice was all gone now; there had been a light fall of snow the day before, but it was not shoe-deep. The snow was covered with the little tracks of Jenny's friends, the birds and the field-mice and the rabbits, in pretty zigzag lines.

Jonas Carey and his wife walked along comfortably until they reached the cart-path, then the old man's shoestring became loose, and he tripped over it. He stooped and tied it laboriously; then he went on. Pretty soon he stopped again. His wife looked back. "What's the matter?" said she.

"Shoestring untied," replied old Jonas, in a half inarticulate grunt.

"Don't you want me to tie it, Jonas?"

Jonas said nothing more; he tied viciously.

They were in sight of Jenny's house when he stopped again, and sat down on the stone wall beside the path. "Oh, Jonas, what is the matter?"

Jonas made no reply. His wife went up to him, and saw that the shoestring was loose again. "Oh, Jonas, do let me tie it; I'd just as soon as not. Sha'n't I, Jonas?"

Jonas sat there in the midst of the snowy blackberry vines, and looked straight ahead with a stony stare.

His wife began to cry. "Oh, Jonas," she pleaded, "don't you have a tantrum to-day. Sha'n't I tie it? I'll tie it real strong. Oh, Jonas!"

The old woman fluttered around the old man in his great-coat on the wall, like a distressed bird around her mate. Jenny Wrayne opened her door and looked out; then she came down the path. "What's the matter?" she asked.

"Oh, Jenny, I dunno what to do. He's got another—tantrum!"

"Has he fell down?"

"No; that ain't it. His shoestring's come untied three times, an' he don't like it, an' he's sot down on the wall. I dunno but he'll set there all day. Oh, dear me suz, when we'd got most to your house, an' I was jest thinkin' we'd come 'long real comfort'ble! I want to tie it for him, but he won't let me, an' I don't darse to when he sets there like that. Oh, Jonas, jest let me tie it, won't you? I'll tie it real nice an' strong, so it won't undo again."

Jenny caught hold of her arm. "Come right into the house," said she, in a hearty voice. She quite turned her back upon the figure on the wall.

"Oh, Jenny, I can't go in an' leave him a-settin' there. I shouldn't wonder if he sot there all day. You don't know nothin' about it. Sometimes I have to stan' an' argue with him for hours afore he'll stir."

"Come right in. The turkey's most done, an' we'll set right down as soon as 'tis. It's 'bout the fattest turkey I ever see. I dunno where Deacon Little could ha' got it. The plum-puddin's all done, an' the vegetables is 'most ready to take up. Come right in, an' we'll have dinner in less than half an hour."

After the two women had entered the house the figure on the wall cast an uneasy glance at it without turning his head. He sniffed a little.

It was quite true that he could smell the roasting turkey, and the turnip and onions, out there.

In the house, Mrs. Carey laid aside her bonnet and shawl, and put them on the bed in Jenny's little bedroom. A Christmas present, a new calico dress, which Jenny had received the night before, lay on the bed also. Jenny showed it with pride. "It's that chocolate color I've always liked," said she. "I don't see what put it into their heads."

"It's real handsome," said Mrs. Carey. She had not told Jenny about her visitors; but she was not used to keeping a secret, and her possession of one gave a curious expression to her face. However, Jenny did not notice it. She hurried about preparing dinner. The stove was covered with steaming pots; the turkey in the oven could be heard sizzling. The little deaf-and-dumb boy sat in his chimney-corner, and took long sniffs. He watched Jenny, and regarded the stove in a rapture, or he examined some treasures that he held in his lap. There were picture-books and cards, and boxes of candy, and oranges. He held them all tightly gathered into his pinafore. The little caged wild things twittered sweetly and pecked at their food. Jenny laid the table with the best table-cloth and her mother's flowered china. The mountain farmers, of whom Jenny sprang, had had their little decencies and comforts, and there were china and a linen table-cloth for a Christmas dinner, poor as the house was.

Mrs. Carey kept peering uneasily out of the window at her husband on the stone wall.

"If you want him to come in you'll keep away from the window," said Jenny; and the old woman settled into a chair near the stove.

Very soon the door opened, and Jonas came in. Jenny was bending over the potato kettle, and she did not look around. "You can put his great-coat on the bed, if you've a mind to, Mrs. Carey," said she.

Jonas got out of his coat, and sat down with sober dignity; he had tied his shoestring very neatly and firmly. After a while he looked over at the little deaf-and-dumb boy, who was smiling at him, and he smiled back again.

The Careys stayed until evening. Jenny set her candle in the window to light them down the cart-path. Down in the village the minister's daughter and her betrothed were out walking to the church, where there was a Christmas-tree. It was quite dark. She clung closely to his arm, and once in a while her pink cheek brushed his sleeve. The stars were out, many of them, and more were coming. One seemed suddenly to flash out on the dark side of the mountain.

"There's Christmas Jenny's candle," said the girl. And it was Christmas Jenny's candle, but it was also something more. Like all common things, it had, and was, its own poem, and that was—a Christmas star.

LITTLE MISS SOPHIE

ALICE DUNBAR-NELSON

From *The Goodness of St. Rocque and Other Stories* (New York: Dodd, Mead and Co., 1899).

Alice Dunbar-Nelson achieved fame as a writer at an early age—fame that was only compounded by her (ultimately unhappy) marriage to fellow writer Paul Laurence Dunbar. This sketch is typical of much of her early work: stories rich in local color detail from New Orleans, her hometown. For much of the twentieth century, her frequent focus as a Black writer on white Creoles like the protagonist of this story meant that her work was critically adrift, not always included in challenges to the literary canon. In recent years, however, aspects of Dunbar-Nelson's generic and racial ambiguity have been reinterpreted in ways that frame her knowing use of local color traditions, including the use of Christmas, as social and cultural critique.

When Miss Sophie knew consciousness again, the long, faint, swelling notes of the organ were dying away in distant echoes through the great arches of the silent church, and she was alone, crouching in a little, forsaken black heap at the altar of the Virgin. The twinkling tapers shone pityingly upon her, the beneficent smile of the white-robed Madonna seemed to whisper comfort. A long gust of chill air swept up the aisles, and Miss Sophie shivered not from cold, but from nervousness.

But darkness was falling, and soon the lights would be lowered, and the great massive doors would be closed; so, gathering her thin little cape about her frail shoulders, Miss Sophie hurried out, and along the brilliant noisy streets home.

It was a wretched, lonely little room, where the cracks let the boisterous wind whistle through, and the smoky, grimy walls looked cheerless and unhomelike. A miserable little room in a miserable little cottage in one of the squalid streets of the Third District that nature and the city fathers seemed to have forgotten.

As bare and comfortless as the room was Miss Sophie's life. She rented these four walls from an unkempt little Creole woman, whose progeny seemed like the promised offspring of Abraham. She scarcely kept the flickering life in her pale little body by the unceasing toil of a pair of bony hands, stitching, stitching, ceaselessly, wearingly, on the bands and pockets of trousers. It was her bread, this monotonous, unending work; and though whole days and nights constant labour brought but the most meagre recompense, it was her only hope of life.

She sat before the little charcoal brazier and warmed her transparent, needle-pricked fingers, thinking meanwhile of the strange events of the day. She had been up town to carry the great, black bundle of coarse pants and vests to the factory and to receive her small pittance, and on the way home stopped in at the Jesuit Church to say her little prayer at the altar of the calm white Virgin. There had been a wondrous burst of music from the great organ as she knelt there, an overpowering perfume of many flowers, the glittering dazzle of many lights, and the dainty frou-frou made by the silken skirts of wedding guests. So Miss Sophie stayed to the wedding; for what feminine heart, be it ever so old and seared, does not delight in one? And why should not a poor little Creole old maid be interested too?

Then the wedding party had filed in solemnly, to the rolling, swelling tones of the organ. Important-looking groomsmen; dainty, fluffy, white-robed maids; stately, satin-robed, illusion-veiled bride, and happy groom. She leaned forward to catch a better glimpse of their faces. "Ah!"—

Those near the Virgin's altar who heard a faint sigh and rustle on the steps glanced curiously as they saw a slight black-robed figure clutch the railing and lean her head against it. Miss Sophie had fainted.

"I must have been hungry," she mused over the charcoal fire in her little room, "I must have been hungry"; and she smiled a wan smile, and busied herself getting her evening meal of coffee and bread and ham.

If one were given to pity, the first thought that would rush to one's lips at sight of Miss Sophie would have been, "Poor little woman!" She had come among the bareness and sordidness of this neighbourhood five years ago, robed in crape, and crying with great sobs that seemed to shake the vitality out of her. Perfectly silent, too, she was about her former life; but for all that, Michel, the quartee grocer at the corner, and Madame Laurent, who kept the rabbé shop opposite, had fixed it all up between them, of her sad history and past glories. Not that they knew; but then Michel must invent something when the neighbours came to him as their fountain-head of wisdom.

One morning little Miss Sophie opened wide her dingy windows to catch the early freshness of the autumn wind as it whistled through the yellow-leafed trees. It was one of those calm, blue-misted, balmy, November days that New Orleans can have when all the rest of the country is fur-wrapped. Miss Sophie pulled her machine to the window, where the sweet, damp wind could whisk among her black locks.

Whirr, whirr, went the machine, ticking fast and lightly over the belts of the rough jeans pants. Whirr, whirr, yes, and Miss Sophie was actually humming a tune! She felt strangely light to-day.

"Ma foi," muttered Michel, strolling across the street to where Madame Laurent sat sewing behind the counter on blue and brown-checked aprons, "but the little ma'amselle sings. Perhaps she recollects."

"Perhaps," muttered the rabbé woman.

But little Miss Sophie felt restless. A strange impulse seemed drawing her up town, and the machine seemed to run slow, slow, before it would stitch all of the endless number of jeans belts. Her fingers trembled with nervous haste as she pinned up the unwieldy black bundle of finished work, and her feet fairly tripped over each other in their eagerness to get to Claiborne Street, where she could board the up-town car. There was a feverish desire to go somewhere, a sense of elation, a foolish happiness that brought a faint echo of colour into her pinched cheeks. She wondered why.

No one noticed her in the car. Passengers on the Claiborne line are too much accustomed to frail little black-robed women with big, black bundles; it is one of the city's most pitiful sights. She leaned her head out of the window to catch a glimpse of the oleanders on Bayou Road, when her attention was caught by a conversation in the car.

"Yes, it's too bad for Neale, and lately married too," said the elder man. "I can't see what he is to do."

Neale! She pricked up her ears. That was the name of the groom in the Jesuit Church.

"How did it happen?" languidly inquired the younger. He was a stranger, evidently; a stranger with a high regard for the faultlessness of male attire.

"Well, the firm failed first; he didn't mind that much, he was so sure of his uncle's inheritance repairing his lost fortunes; but suddenly this difficulty of identification springs up, and he is literally on the verge of ruin."

"Won't some of you fellows who've known him all your lives do to identify him?"

"Gracious man, we've tried; but the absurd old will expressly stipulates that he shall be known only by a certain quaint Roman ring, and unless he has it, no identification, no fortune. He has given the ring away, and that settles it."

"Well, you're all chumps. Why doesn't he get the ring from the owner?"

"Easily said; but—it seems that Neale had some little Creole love-affair some years ago, and gave this ring to his dusky-eyed fiancée. You know how Neale is with his love-affairs, went off and forgot the girl in a month. It seems, however, she took it to heart,—so much so that he's ashamed to try to find her or the ring."

Miss Sophie heard no more as she gazed out into the dusty grass. There were tears in her eyes, hot blinding ones that wouldn't drop for pride, but stayed and scalded. She knew the story, with all its embellishment of heartaches. She knew the ring, too. She remembered the day she had kissed and wept and fondled it, until it seemed her heart must burst under its load of grief before she took it to the pawn-broker's that another might be eased before the end came,—that other her father. The little "Creole love affair" of Neale's had not always been poor and old and jaded-looking; but reverses must come, even Neale knew that, so the ring was at the Mont de Piété. Still he must have it, it was his; it would save him from disgrace and suffering and from bringing the white-gowned bride into sorrow. He must have it; but how?

There it was still at the pawn-broker's; no one would have such an odd jewel, and the ticket was home in the bureau drawer. Well, he must have it; she might starve in the attempt. Such a thing as going to him and telling him that he might redeem it was an impossibility. That good, straight-backed, stiff-necked Creole blood would have risen in all its strength and choked her. No; as a present had the quaint Roman circlet been placed upon her finger, as a present should it be returned.

The bumping car rode slowly, and the hot thoughts beat heavily in her poor little head. He must have the ring; but how—the ring—the Roman ring—the white-robed bride starving—she was going mad—ah yes—the church.

There it was, right in the busiest, most bustling part of the town, its fresco and bronze and iron quaintly suggestive of mediaeval times. Within, all was cool and dim and restful, with the faintest whiff of lingering incense rising and pervading the gray arches. Yes, the Virgin would know and have pity; the sweet, white-robed Virgin at the pretty flower-decked altar, or the one away up in the niche, far above the golden dome where the Host was.

Titiche, the busybody of the house, noticed that Miss Sophie's bundle was larger than usual that afternoon. "Ah, poor woman!" sighed Titiche's mother, "she would be rich for Christmas."

The bundle grew larger each day, and Miss Sophie grew smaller. The damp, cold rain and mist closed the white-curtained window, but always there behind the sewing-machine drooped and bobbed the little black-robed figure. Whirr, whirr went the wheels, and the coarse jeans pants piled in great heaps at her side. The Claiborne Street car saw her oftener than before, and the sweet white Virgin in the flowered niche above the gold-domed altar smiled at the little supplicant almost every day.

"Ma foi," said the slatternly landlady to Madame Laurent and Michel one day, "I no see how she live! Eat? Nothin', nothin', almos', and las' night when it was so cold and foggy, eh? I hav' to mek him build fire. She mos' freeze."

Whereupon the rumour spread that Miss Sophie was starving herself to death to get some luckless relative out of jail for Christmas; a rumour which enveloped her scraggy little figure with a kind of halo to the neighbours when she appeared on the streets.

November had merged into December, and the little pile of coins was yet far from the sum needed. Dear God! how the money did have to go! The rent and the groceries and the coal, though, to be sure, she used a precious bit of that. Would all the work and saving and skimping do good? Maybe, yes, maybe by Christmas.

Christmas Eve on Royal Street is no place for a weakling, for the shouts and carousels of the roisterers will strike fear into the bravest ones. Yet amid the cries and yells, the deafening blow of horns and tin whistles, and the really dangerous fusillade of fireworks, a little figure hurried along, one hand clutching tightly the battered hat that the rude merry-makers had torn off, the other grasping under the thin black cape a worn little pocketbook.

Into the Mont de Piété she ran breathless, eager. The ticket? Here, worn, crumpled. The ring? It was not gone? No, thank Heaven! It was a joy well worth her toil, she thought, to have it again.

Had Titiche not been shooting crackers on the banquette instead of peering into the crack, as was his wont, his big, round black eyes would have grown saucer-wide to see little Miss Sophie kiss and fondle a ring, an ugly clumsy band of gold.

"Ah, dear ring," she murmured, "once you were his, and you shall be his again. You shall be on his finger, and perhaps touch his heart. Dear ring, ma chère petite de ma coeur, chérie de ma coeur. Je t'aime, je t'aime, oui, oui. You are his; you were mine once too. To-night, just one night, I'll keep you—then—to-morrow, you shall go where you can save him."

The loud whistles and horns of the little ones rose on the balmy air next morning. No one would doubt it was Christmas Day, even if doors and windows were open wide to let in cool air. Why, there was Christmas even in the very look of the mules on the poky cars; there was Christmas noise in the streets, and Christmas toys and Christmas odours, savoury ones that made the nose wrinkle approvingly, issuing from the kitchen. Michel and Madame Laurent smiled greetings across the street at each other, and the salutation from a passer-by recalled the many-progenied landlady to herself.

"Miss Sophie, well, po' soul, not ver' much Chris'mas for her. Mais, I'll jus' call him in fo' to spen' the day with me. Eet'll cheer her a bit."

It was so clean and orderly within the poor little room. Not a speck of dust or a litter of any kind on the quaint little old-time high bureau, unless you might except a sheet of paper lying loose with something written on it. Titiche had evidently inherited his prying propensities, for the landlady turned it over and read,—

> LOUIS,—Here is the ring. I return it to you. I heard you needed it. I hope it comes not too late. SOPHIE.

"The ring, where?" muttered the landlady. There it was, clasped between her fingers on her bosom,—a bosom white and cold, under a cold happy face. Christmas had indeed dawned for Miss Sophie.

IV

Wrestling with the Reason for the Season

EXCERPT FROM

BEN HUR: A TALE OF THE CHRIST

LEW WALLACE

From *Ben Hur: A Tale of the Christ*
(New York: Harper & Brothers, 1880), 58–65.

One of the publishing sensations of the nineteenth century, and a multimedia juggernaut long after, Ben Hur *reimagined the relationship between religion and the novel for a wide swath of readers. Set against the backdrop of the Gospels and the life of Christ, Wallace's novel follows the life and conversion of Judah Ben-Hur, a Jewish prince. A beguiling blend of historical romance and meticulous research, the book even received the blessing of Pope Leo XIII and became a staple of Sunday schools across America. The extract below is taken from the long, standalone opening of the novel—also published separately as* The First Christmas *(1899)—which reimagines the canonical rudiments of the Nativity through Wallace's typical combination of intense textural detail and human drama.*

A mile and a half, it may be two miles, southeast of Bethlehem, there is a plain separated from the town by an intervening swell of the mountain. Besides being well sheltered from the north winds, the vale was covered with a growth of sycamore, dwarf-oak, and pine trees, while in the glens and ravines adjoining there were thickets of olive and mulberry; all at this season of the year invaluable for the support of sheep, goats, and cattle, of which the wandering flocks consisted.

At the side farthest from the town, close under a bluff, there was an extensive *mârâh,* or sheepcot, ages old. In some long-forgotten foray, the building had been unroofed and almost demolished. The enclosure attached to it remained intact, however, and that was of more importance to the shepherds who drove their charges thither than the house itself. The stone wall around the lot was high as a man's head, yet not so high but that sometimes a panther or a lion, hungering from the wilderness, leaped boldly in. On the inner side of the wall, and as an additional security against the constant danger, a hedge of the rhamnus had been planted, an invention so successful that now a sparrow could hardly penetrate the overtopping branches, armed as they were with great clusters of thorns hard as spikes.

The day of the occurrences which occupy the preceding chapters, a number of shepherds, seeking fresh walks for their flocks, led them up to this plain; and from early morning the groves had been made ring with calls, and the blows of axes, the bleating of sheep and goats, the tinkling of bells, the lowing of cattle, and the barking of dogs. When the sun went down, they led the way to the *mârâh,* and by nightfall had everything safe in the field; then they kindled a fire down by the gate, partook of their humble supper, and sat down to rest and talk, leaving one on watch.

There were six of these men, omitting the watchman; and afterwhile they assembled in a group near the fire, some sitting, some lying prone. As they went bareheaded habitually, their hair stood out in thick, coarse, sunburnt shocks; their beard covered their throats, and fell in mats down the breast; mantles of the skin of kids and lambs, with the fleece on, wrapped them from neck to knee, leaving the arms exposed; broad belts girthed the rude garments to their waists; their sandals were of the coarsest quality; from their right shoulders hung scrips containing food and selected stones for slings, with which they were armed; on the ground near each one lay his crook, a symbol of his calling and a weapon of offence.

Such were the shepherds of Judea! In appearance, rough and savage as the gaunt dogs sitting with them around the blaze; in fact, simple-minded, tender-hearted: effects due, in part, to the primitive life they led, but chiefly to their constant care of things lovable and helpless.

They rested and talked; and their talk was all about their flocks, a dull theme to the world, yet a theme which was all the world to them. If in narrative they dwelt long upon affairs of trifling moment; if one of them omitted nothing of detail in recounting the loss of a lamb, the relation between him and the unfortunate should be remembered: at birth it became his charge, his to keep all its days, to help over the floods, to carry down the hollows, to name and train; it was to be his companion, his object of thought and interest, the subject of his will; it was to enliven and share his wanderings; in its defence he might be called on to face the lion or robber—to die.

The great events, such as blotted out nations and changed the mastery of the world, were trifles to them, if perchance they came to their knowledge. Of what Herod was doing in this city or that, building palaces and gymnasia, and indulging forbidden practises, they occasionally heard. As was her habit in those days, Rome did not wait for people slow to inquire about her; she came to them. Over the hills along which he was leading his lagging herd, or in the fastnesses in which he was hiding them, not unfrequently the shepherd was startled by the blare of trumpets, and, peering out, beheld a cohort, sometimes a legion, in march; and when the glittering crests were gone, and the excitement incident to the intrusion over, he bent himself to evolve the meaning of the eagles and gilded globes of the soldiery, and the charm of a life so the opposite of his own.

Yet these men, rude and simple as they were, had a knowledge and a wisdom of their own. On Sabbaths they were accustomed to purify themselves, and go up into the synagogues, and sit on the benches farthest from the ark. When the chazzan bore the *Torah* round, none kissed it with greater zest; when the sheliach read the text, none listened to the interpreter with more absolute faith; and none took away with them more of the elder's sermon, or gave it more thought afterwards. In a verse of the Shema they found all the learning and all the law of their simple lives—that their Lord was One God, and that they must love him with all their souls. And they loved him, and such was their wisdom, surpassing that of kings.

While they talked, and before the first watch was over, one by one the shepherds went to sleep, each lying where he had sat.

The night, like most nights of the winter season in the hill country, was clear, crisp, and sparkling with stars. There was no wind. The atmosphere seemed never so pure, and the stillness was more than silence; it was a holy hush, a warning that heaven was stooping low to whisper some good thing to the listening earth.

By the gate, hugging his mantle close, the watchman walked; at times he stopped, attracted by a stir among the sleeping herds, or by a jackal's cry off on the mountain-side. The midnight was slow coming to him; but at last it came. His task was done; now for the dreamless sleep with which labor blesses its wearied children! He moved towards the fire, but paused; a light was breaking around him, soft and white, like the moon's. He waited breathlessly. The light deepened; things before invisible came to view; he saw the whole field, and all it sheltered. A chill sharper than that of the frosty air—a chill of fear—smote him. He looked up; the stars were gone; the light was dropping as from a window in the sky; as he looked, it became a splendor; then, in terror, he cried,

"Awake, awake!"

Up sprang the dogs, and, howling, ran away.

The herds rushed together bewildered.

The men clambered to their feet, weapons in hand.

"What is it?" they asked, in one voice.

"See!" cried the watchman, "the sky is on fire!"

Suddenly the light became intolerably bright, and they covered their eyes, and dropped upon their knees; then, as their souls shrank with fear, they fell upon their faces blind and fainting, and would have died had not a voice said to them,

"Fear not!"

And they listened.

"Fear not: for behold, I bring you good tidings of great joy, which shall be to all people."

The voice, in sweetness and soothing more than human, and low and clear, penetrated all their being, and filled them with assurance. They rose upon their knees, and, looking worshipfully, beheld in the centre of a great glory the appearance of a man, clad in a robe intensely white; above its shoulders towered the tops of wings shining and folded; a star over its forehead glowed with steady lustre, brilliant as Hesperus; its hands were stretched towards them in blessing; its face was serene and divinely beautiful.

They had often heard, and, in their simple way, talked, of angels; and they doubted not now, but said, in their hearts, The glory of God is about us, and this is he who of old came to the prophet by the river of Ulai.

Directly the angel continued:

"For unto you is born this day, in the city of David, a Saviour, which is Christ the Lord!"

Again there was a rest, while the words sank into their minds.

"And this shall be a sign unto you," the annunciator said next. "Ye shall find the babe, wrapped in swaddling-clothes, lying in a manger."

The herald spoke not again; his good tidings were told; yet he stayed awhile. Suddenly the light, of which he seemed the centre, turned roseate and began to tremble; then up, far as the men could see, there was flashing of white wings, and coming and going of radiant forms, and voices as of a multitude chanting in unison,

"Glory to God in the highest, and on earth peace, good-will towards men!"

Not once the praise, but many times.

Then the herald raised his eyes as seeking approval of one far off; his wings stirred, and spread slowly and majestically, on their upper side white as snow, in the shadow vari-tinted, like mother-of-pearl; when they were expanded many cubits beyond his stature, he arose lightly, and, without effort, floated out of view, taking the light up with him. Long after he was gone, down from the sky fell the refrain in measure mellowed by distance, "Glory to God in the highest, and on earth peace, good-will towards men."

When the shepherds came fully to their senses, they stared at each other stupidly, until one of them said, "It was Gabriel, the Lord's messenger unto men."

None answered.

"Christ the Lord is born; said he not so?"

Then another recovered his voice, and replied, "That is what he said."

"And did he not also say, in the city of David, which is our Bethlehem yonder. And that we should find him a babe in swaddling-clothes?"

"And lying in a manger."

The first speaker gazed into the fire thoughtfully, but at length said, like one possessed of a sudden resolve, "There is but one place in Bethlehem where there are mangers; but one, and that is in the cave near the old khan. Brethren, let us go see this thing which has come to pass. The priests and doctors have been a long time looking for the Christ. Now he is born, and the Lord has given us a sign by which to know him. Let us go up and worship him."

"But the flocks!"

"The Lord will take care of them. Let us make haste."

Then they all arose and left the *mârâh.*

* * *

Around the mountain and through the town they passed, and came to the gate of the khan, where there was a man on watch.

"What would you have?" he asked.

"We have seen and heard great things to-night," they replied.

"Well, we, too, have seen great things, but heard nothing. What did you hear?"

"Let us go down to the cave in the enclosure, that we may be sure; then we will tell you all. Come with us, and see for yourself."

"It is a fool's errand."

"No, the Christ is born."

"The Christ! How do you know?"

"Let us go and see first."

The man laughed scornfully.

"The Christ indeed! How are you to know him?"

"He was born this night, and is now lying in a manger, so we were told; and there is but one place in Bethlehem with mangers."

"The cave?"

"Yes. Come with us."

They went through the court-yard without notice, although there were some up even then talking about the wonderful light. The door of the cavern was open. A lantern was burning within, and they entered unceremoniously.

"I give you peace," the watchman said to Joseph and the Beth-Dagonite. "Here are people looking for a child born this night, whom they are to know by finding him in swaddling-clothes and lying in a manger."

For a moment the face of the stolid Nazarene was moved; turning away, he said, "The child is here."

They were led to one of the mangers, and there the child was. The lantern was brought, and the shepherds stood by mute. The little one made no sign; it was as others just born.

"Where is the mother?" asked the watchman.

One of the women took the baby, and went to Mary, lying near, and put it in her arms. Then the bystanders collected about the two.

"It is the Christ!" said a shepherd, at last.

"The Christ!" they all repeated, falling upon their knees in worship. One of them repeated several times over,

"It is the Lord, and his glory is above the earth and heaven."

And the simple men, never doubting, kissed the hem of the mother's robe, and with joyful faces departed. In the khan, to all the people aroused and pressing about them, they told their story; and through the town, and all the way back to the *mârâh,* they chanted the refrain of the angels, "Glory to God in the highest, and on earth peace, good-will towards men!"

The story went abroad, confirmed by the light so generally seen; and the next day, and for days thereafter, the cave was visited by curious crowds, of whom some believed, though the greater part laughed and mocked.

MIRACLE JOYEUX

FRANK NORRIS

From *McClure's Magazine*, December 1898.

Most famous for his brutal, naturalistic stories of contemporary American life—particularly McTeague *(1899), with its account of urban poverty, jealousy, greed, and murder—Frank Norris might seem an unlikely candidate for a sentimental sketch of the young Christ. Norris's debt to Wallace's* Ben Hur *is clear, but tensions are discernible in his theological vision. In an early version of this story, first published in San Francisco's* The Wave *in 1897, the youthful Jesus uses his powers to blind two rivals who each demand a miracle from him. When he submitted the story to* McClure's, *they asked for a rewrite in order to include the story in their Christmas edition, and "Miracle Joyeux" was the result. After Norris's untimely death in 1902, the story was retitled* The Joyous Miracle *and was rereleased as a festive gift book in 1906.*

Mervius had come to old Jerome's stone built farmhouse, across the huge meadow where some half-dozen of the neighboring villagers pastured their stock in common. Old Jerome had received a certain letter, which was a copy of another letter, which in turn was a copy of another letter, and so on and so on, nobody could tell how far. Mervius would copy this letter and take it back to his village, where it would be copied again and again and yet again, and copies would be made of these copies, till the whole countryside would know the contents of that letter pretty well by heart. It was in this way, indeed, that these people made their literature. They would hand down the precious documents to their children, and that letter's contents would become folk-lore, become so well known that it would be repeated orally. It would be a legend, a mythos; perhaps by and by, after a long time, it might gain credence and become even history.

But in that particular part of the country this famous letter was doubly important, because it had been written by a man whom some of the peasants and laborers and small farmers knew. "I knew him," said old Jerome, when Mervius had come in and the two had sat down on either side of the oak table in the brick paved kitchen. Mervius—he was past seventy himself—slipped his huge wooden sabots and let his feet rest on the warm bricks near the fireplace, for the meadow grass had been cold.

"Yes, I knew him," said Jerome. "He took the name of Peter afterwards. He was a fisherman, and used to seine fish over in the big lake where the vineyards are. He used to come here twice a week and sell me fish. He was a good fisherman. Then the carpenter's son set the whole country by the ears, and he went away with him. I missed his fish. Mondays and Wednesdays he came, and his fish were always fresh. They don't get such fish nowadays."

"I'll take the letter you have," said Mervius—"the copy, that is—and my wife will transcribe it; I—I am too old, and my eyes are bad. This carpenter's son now—as you say, he set the people by the ears. It is a strange story."

Old Jerome put his chin in the air. "He was the son of a carpenter, nothing else. We all knew his people; you did, and I. His father built the bin where I store my corn, and some stalls in my brother's barn in the next village. The son was a dreamer; any one could have told he would have perished in the end. The people were tired of him, a mild lunatic. That was all."

Mervius did not answer directly. "I have read this letter," he said, "this fisherman's letter. The man who looks after my sheep loaned me a copy. Peter was not always with the man, the carpenter's son. One thing he has left out—one thing that I saw."

"That *you* saw!" exclaimed old Jerome.

Mervius nodded.

"I saw this man once."

"The carpenter's son?"

"Yes, once, and I saw him smile. You notice this letter never makes record of him smiling."

"I know."

"I saw him smile."

"As how?"

Mervius wrapped his lean, old arms under the folds of his blouse, and resting his elbows on his knees, looked into the fire. Jerome's crow paced gravely in at the door, and perched on his master's knee. Jerome fed him bits of cheese dipped in wine.

"It was a long time ago," said Mervius; "I was a lad. I remember I and my cousin Joanna—she was a little girl of seven then—used to run out to the cow stables early of the cold mornings, and stand in the fodder on the floor of the stalls to warm our feet. I had heard my father tell of this man, this carpenter's son. Did you ever hear," he added, turning to old Jerome, "did you ever hear when you were a boy—hear the older people speak of the 'White Night'? At midnight it grew suddenly light, as though the sun had risen out of season. In fact, there *was* a sun, or star—something. The chickens all came down from their roosts, the oxen lowed, the cocks crew, as though at daybreak. It was light for hours. Then towards four o'clock the light faded again. It happened in midwinter. Yes, they called it the 'White Night.' It was strange. You know the followers of this man claim that he was born on that night. My father knew some shepherds who told a strange story . . . however.

"For the children of our village—that is to say, my little cousin Joanna, my brother Simon, the potter's little son, Septimus, a lad named Joseph, whose father was the olive presser of the district, and myself—the village bleach-green was the playground.

"This bleach-green was a great meadow by the brook, on the other side my father's sheepfolds. It belonged to the fuller of the village. After weaving, the women used to bring here their webs of cloth to be whitened. Many a time I have seen the great squares and lengths of cloth covering the meadow, till you would have said the snow had fallen.

"It was that way on a holiday, when the five of us children were at our play along the banks of the little brook. Across the brook was the road that led to the city, and back of us the bleach-green was one shimmer of white, great spreads and drifts of white cloth, billowing and rippling like shallow pools of milk, as the breeze stirred under them. They were weighted down at the corners with huge, round stones. It was a pretty sight. I have never forgotten that bleach-green.

"I remember that day we had found a bank of clay, and the potter's son, Septimus, showed us how to model the stuff into pots and drinking-vessels, and afterwards even into the form of animals: dogs, fishes, and the lame cow that belonged to the widow at the end of the village. Simon made a wonderful beast, that he assured us was a lion, with twigs for legs, while I and Septimus patted and pinched our lump of clay to look like the great he-pig that had eaten a litter of puppies the week past—a horror that was yet the talk of all the village.

"Joanna—she was younger than all the rest of us—was fashioning little birds, clumsy, dauby little lumps of wet clay without much form. She was very proud of them, and set them in a row upon a stick, and called for us to look at them. As boys will, we made fun of her and her little, clumsy clay birds, because she was a girl, and Simon, my brother, said:

"'Hoh, those aren't like birds at all. More like bullfrogs, I guess. *I'll* show you.'

"He and the rest of us took to making all manner of birds—pigeons, hawks, chickens, and the like. Septimus, the potter's son, executed a veritable masterpiece, a sort of peacock with tail spread which was very like, and which he swore he would take to his father's kiln to have baked. We all exclaimed over this marvel, and gathered about Septimus, praising him and his handiwork, and poor little Joanna and her foolish dauby lumps were forgotten. Then, of course, we all made peacocks, and set them in a row, and compared them with each other's. Joanna sat apart looking at us through her tears, and trying to pretend that she did not care for clay peacocks, that the ridicule of a handful of empty-headed boys did not hurt her, and that her stupid little birds were quite as brave as ours. Then she said, by and by, timid-like and half to herself, 'I think my birds are pretty, too."

"'Hoh,' says Septimus, 'look at Joanna's bullfrogs! Hoh! You are only a girl. What do you know! You don't know *anything.* I think you had better go home. We don't like to play with girls.'

"She was too brave to let us see her cry, but she got up, and was just about going home across the bleach-green—in the green aisles between the webs of cloth—when Simon said to me and to the others:

"'Look, quick, Mervius, here comes that man that father spoke about, the carpenter's son who has made such a stir.' And he pointed across the brook, down the road that runs from the city over towards the lake, the same lake where you say this Peter used to fish. Joanna stopped, and looked where he pointed; so did we all. I saw the man, the carpenter's son, whom Simon meant, and knew at once that it was he."

Old Jerome interrupted: "You had never seen him before. How did you know it was he?"

Mervius shook his head. "It was he. How could *I* tell? I don't know. I knew it was he."

"What did he look like?" asked Jerome, interested.

Mervius paused. There was a silence. Jerome's crow looked at the bright coals of the fire, his head on one side.

"Not at all extraordinary," said Mervius at length. "His face was that of a peasant, sun-browned, touched, perhaps, with a certain calmness. That was all. A face that was neither sad nor glad, calm merely, and not unusually or especially pleasing. He was dressed as you and I are now—as a peasant—and his hands were those of a worker. Only his head was bare."

"Did he wear his beard?"

"No, that was afterward. He was younger when I saw him, about twenty-one maybe, and his face was smooth. There was nothing extraordinary about the man."

"Yet you knew it was he."

"Yes," admitted Mervius, nodding his head. "Yes, I knew it was he. He came up slowly along the road near the brook where we children were sitting. He walked as any traveler along those roads might, not thoughtful nor abstracted, but minding his steps and looking here and there about the country. The prettier things, I noted, seemed to attract him, and I particularly remember his stopping to look at a cherry-tree in full bloom and smelling at its blossoms. Once, too, he stopped and thrust out of the way a twig that had fallen across a little ant heap. When he had come opposite us, he noticed us all standing there and looking at him quietly from across the brook, and he came down and stood on the other bank and asked us for a drink. There was a cup in an old bucket not far away that was kept there for those who worked on the bleach-green. I ran to fetch it, and when I had come back, he, the carpenter's son, had crossed the brook, and was sitting on the bank, and all the children were about him. He had little Joanna on his knee, and she had forgotten to cry. He drank out of the cup I gave him, and fell to asking us about what we had been doing. Then we all cried out together, and showed him our famous array of clay peacocks."

"And you were that familiar with him?" said old Jerome.

"He seemed like another child to us," answered Mervius. "We were all about him, on his shoulders, on his knees, in his arms, and Joanna in his lap—she had forgotten to cry."

"'See, see my birds,' she said. I tell you she had her arms around his neck. 'See, they said they were not pretty. They are pretty, aren't they, quite as pretty as theirs?'

"'Prettier, prettier,' he said. 'Look now.' He set our little clay birds before him in a row. First mine, then Simon's, then those of Joseph and of Septimus, then one of little Joanna's shapeless little lumps. He looked at them, and at last touched the one Joanna had made with his finger-tip, then—Did you ever see when corn is popping, how the grain swells, swells, swells, then bursts forth into whiteness? So it was then. No sooner had that little bird of Joanna, that clod of dust, that poor bit of common clay, felt the touch of his finger, than it awakened into life and became a live bird—and white, white as the sunshine, a beautiful little white bird that flew upward on the instant, with a tiny, glad note of song. We children shouted aloud, and Joanna danced and clapped her hands. And then it was the carpenter's son smiled. He looked at her as she looked up at that soaring white bird, and smiled, smiled just once, and then fell calm again.

"He rose to go, but we hung about him, and clamored for him to stay.

"'No,' he said, as he kissed us all, 'I must go, go up to the city.' He crossed the brook, and looked back at us.

"'Can't we go with you?' we cried to him. He shook his head.

"'Where I am going you cannot go. But,' he added, 'I am going to make a place for just such as you.'

"'And you'll come again?' we cried.

"'Yes, yes, I shall come again.'

"Then he went away, though often looking back and waving his hand at us. What we said after he had gone I don't know. How we felt I cannot express. Long time and in silence we stood there watching, until his figure vanished around a bend in the road. Then we turned and went home across the bleach-green, through the green aisles between the webs of white cloth. We never told what had happened. That was just for ourselves alone. The same evening we heard of a great wonder that had been worked at a marriage in a town near by, water turned to wine, and a little later another, a man blind from his birth suddenly made to see. What did we care? He had not smiled upon those others, those people at the marriage, that crowd in the market-place. What did we care?"

* * *

Mervius stopped, and slipped his feet back into his sabots, and rose. He took the letter from Jerome, and put it in the pocket of his blouse.

"And you saw that?"

Mervius nodded, but old Jerome shook his head in the manner of one who is not willing to be convinced.

"He was a dreamer with unspeakable pretensions. Why, his people were laboring folk in one of the villages beyond the lake. His father was a carpenter, and built my corn-bin. The son was a fanatic. His wits were turned."

"But this thing I saw," said Mervius at the door. "I saw it, who am speaking to you."

Jerome put his chin in the air.

". . . A dreamer. . . . We were well rid of him. . . . But I was sorry when Peter went away. . . . Mondays and Wednesdays he came, and his fish were always fresh."

A CHRISTMAS SERMON
AND
WHAT I WANT FOR CHRISTMAS

ROBERT G. INGERSOLL

From *The Works of Robert Ingersoll,* ed. C. P. Farrell (New York: Ingersoll Publishers, 1900), vols. 7: 263–64; 11: 375–76.

"The Great Agnostic," Robert Ingersoll was one of the most popular, and controversial, orators of the late nineteenth century. He was a lawyer and a politician, and achieved renown in those fields, but it was his public criticisms of organized religion which made him most famous. To his friend Walt Whitman, Ingersoll was "the man of men [. . .]. He is never passionate in the outward sense, yet every sentence is a thrust in itself—a dagger—a gleam—a fire—a torch, vital and vitalizing—full of pulse, power, magnificent potencies." In these two examples of his formidable rhetorical skills, Ingersoll turns his attention to the emotive topic of Christmas, offering alternative visions of the season that reach back to a pre-Christian vision of winter festivities, and look forward to a millennial vision of its possibilities.

A CHRISTMAS SERMON (1891)

The good part of Christmas is not always Christian—it is generally Pagan; that is to say, human, natural.

Christianity did not come with tidings of great joy, but with a message of eternal grief. It came with the threat of everlasting torture on its lips. It meant war on earth and perdition hereafter.

It taught some good things—the beauty of love and kindness in man. But as a torch-bearer, as a bringer of joy, it has been a failure. It has given infinite consequences to the acts of finite beings, crushing the soul with a responsibility too great for mortals to bear. It has filled the future with fear and flame, and made God the keeper of an eternal penitentiary, destined to be the home of nearly all the sons of men. Not satisfied with that, it has deprived God of the pardoning power.

And yet it may have done some good by borrowing from the Pagan world the old festival called Christmas.

Long before Christ was born the Sun-God triumphed over the powers of Darkness. About the time that we call Christmas the days begin perceptibly to lengthen. Our barbarian ancestors were worshipers of the sun, and they celebrated his victory over the hosts of night. Such a festival was natural and beautiful. The most natural of all religions is the worship of the sun. Christianity adopted this festival. It borrowed from the Pagans the best it has.

I believe in Christmas and in every day that has been set apart for joy. We in America have too much work and not enough play. We are too much like the English.

I think it was Heinrich Heine who said that he thought a blaspheming Frenchman was a more pleasing object to God than a praying Englishman. We take our joys too sadly. I am in favor of all the good free days—the more the better.

Christmas is a good day to forgive and forget—a good day to throw away prejudices and hatreds—a good day to fill your heart and your house, and the hearts and houses of others, with sunshine.

* * *

WHAT I WANT FOR CHRISTMAS (1897)

If I had the power to produce exactly what I want for next Christmas, I would have all the kings and emperors resign and allow the people to govern themselves.

I would have all the nobility drop their titles and give their lands back to the people. I would have the Pope throw away his tiara, take off his sacred vestments, and admit that he is not acting for God—is not infallible—but is just an ordinary Italian. I would have all the cardinals, archbishops, bishops, priests and clergymen admit that they know nothing about theology, nothing about hell or heaven, nothing about the destiny of the human race, nothing about devils or ghosts, gods or angels. I would have them tell all their "flocks" to think for themselves, to be manly men and womanly women, and to do all in their power to increase the sum of human happiness.

I would have all the professors in colleges, all the teachers in schools of every kind, including those in Sunday schools, agree that they would teach only what they know, that they would not palm off guesses as demonstrated truths.

I would like to see all the politicians changed to statesmen,—to men who long to make their country great and free,—to men who care more for public good than private gain—men who long to be of use.

I would like to see all the editors of papers and magazines agree to print the truth and nothing but the truth, to avoid all slander and misrepresentation, and to let the private affairs of the people alone.

I would like to see drunkenness and prohibition both abolished.

I would like to see corporal punishment done away with in every home, in every school, in every asylum, reformatory, and prison. Cruelty hardens and degrades, kindness reforms and ennobles.

I would like to see the millionaires unite and form a trust for the public good.

I would like to see a fair division of profits between capital and labor, so that the toiler could save enough to mingle a little June with the December of his life.

I would like to see an international court established in which to settle disputes between nations, so that armies could be disbanded and the great navies allowed to rust and rot in perfect peace.

I would like to see the whole world free—free from injustice—free from superstition.

This will do for next Christmas. The following Christmas, I may want more.

V

Happy Christmas to All?

EXCERPT FROM

THE GHOST DANCE WAR

CHARLES ALEXANDER EASTMAN

"The Ghost Dance War" (1890) taken from *From the Deep Woods to Civilization* (Boston: Little, Brown, and Co., 1916), 104–15.

Charles Alexander Eastman (Santee Sioux) was born on a reservation in Minnesota. Named Hakadah at birth—"pitiful last," because of his mother's death following his arrival—then Ohíyesa ("always wins"), he changed his name to Charles Eastman after his family's conversion to Christianity. Educated at both Dartmouth College and Boston University, Eastman became a doctor. While working as a physician for the Bureau of Indian Affairs he was posted to South Dakota, where he was a witness to the aftermath of the Wounded Knee massacre of hundreds of Lakota men, women, and children in December 1890. It is that ordeal, and its grim contrast with Christmas celebrations on the reservation, that Eastman recounts here—for as well as his medical career and a variety of political activities, he was a prolific and pioneering author who attempted to communicate his experiences of American Indian life to a wide audience.

The Christmas season was fast approaching, and this is perhaps the brightest spot in the mission year. The children of the Sunday Schools, and indeed all the people, look eagerly forward to the joyous feast; barrels and boxes are received and opened, candy bags made and filled, carols practiced, and churches decorated with ropes of spicy evergreen.

Anxious to relieve the tension in every way within his power, Mr. Cook and his helpers went on with their preparations upon even a larger scale than usual. Since all of the branch stations had been closed and the people called in, it was planned to keep the Christmas tree standing in the chapel for a week, and to distribute gifts to a separate congregation each evening. I found myself pressed into the service, and passed some happy hours in the rectory. For me, at that critical time, there was inward struggle as well as the threat of outward conflict, and I could not but recall what my "white mother" had said jokingly one day, referring to my pleasant friendships with many charming Boston girls, "I know one Sioux who has not been conquered, and I shall not rest till I hear of his capture!"

I had planned to enter upon my life work unhampered by any other ties, and declared that all my love should be vested in my people and my profession. At last, however, I had met a woman whose sincerity was convincing and whose ideals seemed very like my own. Her childhood had been spent almost as much out of doors as mine, on a lonely estate high up in the Berkshire hills; her ancestry Puritan on one side, proud Tories on the other. She had been moved by the appeals of that wonderful man, General Armstrong, and had gone to Hampton as a young girl to teach the Indians there. After three years, she undertook pioneer work in the West as teacher of a new camp school among the wilder Sioux, and after much travel and study of their peculiar problems had been offered the appointment she now held. She spoke the Sioux language fluently and went among the people with the utmost freedom and confidence. Her methods of work were very simple and direct. I do not know what unseen hand had guided me to her side, but on Christmas day of 1890, Elaine Goodale and I announced our engagement.

Three days later, we learned that Big Foot's band of ghost dancers from the Cheyenne river reservation north of us was approaching the agency, and that Major Whiteside was in command of troops with orders to intercept them.

Late that afternoon, the Seventh Cavalry under Colonel Forsythe was called to the saddle and rode off toward Wounded Knee creek, eighteen miles away. Father Craft, a Catholic priest with some Indian blood, who knew Sitting Bull and his people, followed an hour or so later, and I was much inclined to go too, but my fiancée pointed out that my duty lay rather at home with our Indians, and I stayed.

The morning of December 29th was sunny and pleasant. We were all straining our ears toward Wounded Knee, and about the middle of the forenoon we distinctly heard the reports of the Hotchkiss guns. Two hours later, a rider was seen approaching at full speed, and in a few minutes he had dismounted from his exhausted horse and handed his message to General Brooke's orderly. The Indians were watching their own messenger, who ran on foot along the northern ridges and carried the news to the so-called "hostile" camp. It was said that he delivered his message at almost the same time as the mounted officer.

The resulting confusion and excitement was unmistakable. The white teepees disappeared as if by magic and soon the caravans were in motion, going toward the natural fortress of the "Bad Lands." In the "friendly" camp there was almost as much turmoil, and crowds of frightened women and children poured into the agency. Big Foot's band had been wiped out by the troops, and reprisals were naturally looked for. The enclosure was not barricaded in any way and we had but a small detachment of troops for our protection. Sentinels were placed, and machine guns trained on the various approaches.

A few hot-headed young braves fired on the sentinels and wounded two of them. The Indian police began to answer by shooting at several braves who were apparently about to set fire to some of the outlying buildings. Every married employee was seeking a place of safety for his family, the interpreter among them. Just then General Brooke ran out into the open, shouting at the top of his voice to the police: "Stop, stop! Doctor, tell them they must not fire until ordered!" I did so, as the bullets whistled by us, and the General's coolness perhaps saved all our lives, for we were in no position to repel a large attacking force. Since we did not reply, the scattered shots soon ceased, but the situation remained critical for several days and nights.

My office was full of refugees. I called one of my good friends aside and asked him to saddle my two horses and stay by them. "When general fighting begins, take them to Miss Goodale and see her to the railroad if you can," I told him. Then I went over to the rectory. Mrs. Cook refused to go without her husband, and Miss Goodale would not leave while there was a chance of being of service. The house was crowded with terrified people, most of them Christian Indians, whom our friends were doing their best to pacify.

At dusk, the Seventh Cavalry returned with their twenty-five dead and I believe thirty-four wounded, most of them by their own comrades, who had encircled the Indians, while few of the latter had guns. A majority of the thirty or more Indian wounded were women and children, including babies in arms. As there were not tents enough for all, Mr. Cook offered us the mission chapel, in which the Christmas tree still stood, for a temporary hospital. We tore out the pews and covered the floor with hay and quilts. There we laid the poor creatures side by side in rows, and the night was devoted to caring for them as best we could. Many were frightfully torn by pieces of shells, and the suffering was terrible. General Brooke placed me in charge and I had to do nearly all the work, for although the army surgeons were more than ready to help as soon as their own men had been cared for, the tortured Indians would scarcely allow a man in uniform to touch them. Mrs. Cook, Miss Goodale, and several of Mr. Cook's Indian helpers acted as volunteer nurses. In spite of all our efforts, we lost the greater part of them, but a few recovered, including several children who had lost all their relatives and who were adopted into kind Christian families.

On the day following the Wounded Knee massacre there was a blizzard, in the midst of which I was ordered out with several Indian police, to look for a policeman who was reported to have been wounded and left some two miles from the agency. We did not find him. This was the only time during the whole affair that I carried a weapon; a friend lent me a revolver which I put in my overcoat pocket, and it was lost on the ride. On the third day it cleared, and the ground was covered with an inch or two of fresh snow. We had feared that some of the Indian wounded might have been left on the field, and a number of us volunteered to go and see. I was placed in charge of the expedition of about a hundred civilians, ten or fifteen of whom were white men. We were supplied with wagons in which to convey any whom we might find still alive. Of course a photographer and several reporters were of the party.

Fully three miles from the scene of the massacre we found the body of a woman completely covered with a blanket of snow, and from this point on we found them scattered along as they had been relentlessly hunted down and slaughtered while fleeing for their lives. Some of our people discovered relatives or friends among the dead, and there was much wailing and mourning. When we reached the spot where the Indian camp had stood, among the fragments of burned tents and other belongings we saw the frozen bodies lying close together or piled one upon another. I counted eighty bodies of men who had been in the council and who were almost as helpless as the women and babes when the deadly fire began, for nearly all their guns had been taken from them. A reckless and desperate young Indian fired the first shot when the search for weapons was well under way, and immediately the troops opened fire from all sides, killing not only unarmed men, women, and children, but their own comrades who stood opposite them, for the camp was entirely surrounded.

It took all of my nerve to keep my composure in the face of this spectacle, and of the excitement and grief of my Indian companions, nearly every one of whom was crying aloud or singing his death song. The white men became very nervous, but I set them to examining and uncovering every body to see if one were living. Although they had been lying untended in the snow and cold for two days and nights, a number had survived. Among them I found a baby of about a year old warmly wrapped and entirely unhurt. I brought her in, and she was afterward adopted and educated by an army officer. One man who was severely wounded begged me to fill his pipe. When we brought him into the chapel he was welcomed by his wife and daughters with cries of joy, but he died a day or two later.

Under a wagon I discovered an old woman, totally blind and entirely helpless. A few had managed to crawl away to some place of shelter, and we found in a log store near by several who were badly hurt and others who had died after reaching there. After we had dispatched several wagon loads to the agency, we observed groups of warriors watching us from adjacent buttes; probably friends of the victims who had come there for the same purpose as ourselves. A majority of our party, fearing an attack, insisted that some one ride back to the agency for an escort of soldiers, and as mine was the best horse, it fell to me to go. I covered the eighteen miles in quick time and was not interfered with in any way, although if the Indians had meant mischief they could easily have picked me off from any of the ravines and gulches.

All this was a severe ordeal for one who had so lately put all his faith in the Christian love and lofty ideals of the white man. Yet I passed no hasty judgment, and was thankful that I might be of some service and relieve even a small part of the suffering. An appeal published in a Boston paper brought us liberal supplies of much needed clothing, and linen for dressings. We worked on. Bishop Hare of South Dakota visited us, and was overcome by faintness when he entered his mission chapel, thus transformed into a rude hospital.

After some days of extreme tension, and weeks of anxiety, the "hostiles," so called, were at last induced to come in and submit to a general disarmament. Father Jutz, the Catholic missionary, had gone bravely among them and used all his influence toward a peaceful settlement. The troops were all recalled and took part in a grand review before General Miles, no doubt intended to impress the Indians with their superior force.

In March, all being quiet, Miss Goodale decided to send in her resignation and go East to visit her relatives, and our wedding day was set for the following June.

RABBI ELIEZER'S CHRISTMAS

ABRAHAM CAHAN

From *Scribner's Magazine,* December 1899.

Fleeing persecution both political and anti-Semitic, Abraham Cahan left Russia in 1882. Making his way to New York, he remained a committed socialist while also becoming a writer, in both Yiddish and English, for a variety of publications—most notably the Jewish Daily Forward, *a publication that he helped to found and edited from 1903 to 1946. Alongside his political journalism, Cahan was also a popular novelist and short-story writer who fictionalized the lives of Jewish immigrants like himself for a wide American audience, tracing the potent tensions thrown up by the pull between assimilation and the preservation of cultural and religious identity. This story, in which the bestowing of a charitable gift at Christmastime creates an existential crisis for its recipient, is a powerful case in point. It also reflects a potent contemporary debate at the time that Cahan was writing, prompted by a question posed by St. Louis Rabbi Solomon H. Sonneschien in 1883: "Can the American Jew Keep Christmas?"*

One of the two well-dressed strangers who were picking their way through the Ghetto—a frail, sharp-featured little Gentile woman with grayish hair—brought herself and her tall companion to a sudden halt.

"Look at that man!" she said, with a little gasp of ecstasy, as she pointed out an elderly Jew who sat whispering over an open book behind a cigarette-stand. "Don't you think there is a lion effect in his face? Only he is so pathetic."

The other agreed, phlegmatically, that the man was perfectly delightful, but this was not enough.

"You say it as if the woods were full of such faces," the nervous little woman protested. "A more exquisite head I never saw. Why, it's classic, it's a perfect—tragedy. His eyes alone would make the fortune of a beginning artist. I must telegraph Harold about him."

"Yes, there is pathos in his eyes," the Head Worker of the College Settlement assented, with dawning interest.

"Pathos! Why, they are full of martyrdom. Just look at the way his waxen face shapes itself out of that sea of white hair and beard, Miss Colton. And those eyes of his—doesn't it seem as if they were looking out of a tomb half a mile away? We must go up and speak to him. He looks like a lion in distress."

Miss Bemis was out with her list of "deserving cases," mostly Irish, which Miss Colton had prepared for her as she had done the year before. This time, however, her effervescent enthusiasm was not exclusively philanthropic. She had recently become infatuated with a literary family and had been hunting after types ever since.

When the two came up to the old man's stand they found that besides cigarettes it was piled with candy and Yiddish newspapers, and that part of the brick wall back of it was occupied by an improvised little bookcase filled with poorly bound volumes.

Miss Colton, who spoke German and had taken special pains to learn the dialect of the Ghetto, acted as her friend's interpreter.

"How much are these cigarettes?" she asked, for a beginning, as she took up a package decorated with a picture of Captain Dreyfus.

"Cigarettes?" the old man asked, with a perplexed smile which made his sallow face sadder than ever.

"Yes, these cigarettes."

"How many? One, two, three, or the whole package?" he inquired, timidly.

"Of course, the whole package. Why, do you find it strange for women to buy cigarettes?"

"Not at all. Who says it is strange?" he answered, with apologetic vehemence. "Quite a few of my customers are ladies."

"Do they smoke?"

"They? What business has a woman to smoke? But then she may have a husband or a sweetheart who smokes."

Miss Bemis bought the Dreyfus package and one bearing a likeness of Karl Marx. By this time the old man's bashfulness had worn off, and he said, in answer to questions, that his name was Eliezer (Rabbi Eliezer people called him, out of respect for his voluminous gray beard and piety); that he had been in America two years and that he was all alone in the world.

"And how much does your stand bring you?"

For an answer he drew a deep sigh and made a gesture of despair. After a short silence he said:

"I sit freezing like a dog from six in the morning to eleven in the night, as you see. And what do I get for my pains? When I make five dollars I call it an extra good week. If I had a larger stock I might make a little more. It's America, not Russia. If one would do business one must have all kinds of goods. But then it's a sin to grumble. I am not starving—praised be the All High for that."

Speaking of his bookcase, he explained that it was a circulating library.

"Silly stuff, that," he said with contempt. "Nothing but lies—yarns about how a lad fell in love with a girl and such-like nonsense. Yet, I must keep this kind of trash. Ah, this is not what I came to America for. Was I not happy at home? Did I want for anything? Birds' milk, perhaps. I was a *sopher.** I was poor, but I never went hungry, and people showed me respect. And so I lived in peace until the black year brought to our town a man who advised me to go to America. He saw me make a *Misrach*—a

*A writer of parchment scrolls of the Pentateuch, or some other section of the Old Testament.

kind of picture which pious Jews keep on the east wall of their best room. I fitted it up with beautiful pillars, two lions supporting the tables of the Law and all kinds of trappings, you know. Well, all this lots of people could do, but what nobody could do and I can is to crowd the whole of Deuteronomy into a circle the size of a tea-glass." A sparkle came into his dark brown eyes; an exalted smile played about his lips; but, this only deepened the gloom of his face. "I would just take a glass, stand it on the paper upside down, trace the brim and—set to work. People could hardly read it—so tiny were the letters; but I let everybody look at them through a magnifying glass and they saw every word. And how well written! Just like print. 'Well,' says that man, 'Rabbi Eliezer,' says he, 'you have hands of gold, but sense you have none. Why throw yourself away upon a sleepy town like this? Just you go to America, and pearls will be showered on you.'" After a little pause Rabbi Eliezer waved his hand at his wares and said, with a bitter smile: "Well, here they are, the pearls."

"And what became of your pictures?" asked Miss Colton.

"My pictures? Better don't ask about them, good lady," the old man answered, with a sigh. "I sat up nights to make one, and when it was finished I got one dollar for it, and that was a favor. My lions looked like potatoes, they said. 'As to your Deuteronomy—it isn't bad, but this is America, and such things are made by machine and sold five cents apiece.' The merchant showed me some such pictures. Well, the lions were rather better than mine, and the letters even smaller—that I won't deny—but do you know how they were made? By hand? Not a bit. They write big words and have them photographed by a tricky sort of thing which makes them a hundred times smaller than they are—do you understand? 'Ah, but that's machine-work—a swindle,' says I, 'while I make every letter with my own hands, and my words are full of life.' 'Bother your hands and your words!' said the merchant. 'This isn't Russia,' says he. 'It's America, the land of machines and of "hurry up!"' says he, and there you are!" The old man's voice fell. "Making letters smaller, indeed!" he said, brokenly. "Me, too, they have made a hundred times smaller than I was. A pile of ashes they have made of me. A fine old age! Freezing like a dog, with no one to say a kind word to you," he concluded, trying to blink away his tears and to suppress the childlike quiver of his lips.

Miss Bemis was tingling with compassion and with something very like the sensation of an entomologist come upon a rare insect.

"Ask him how much money it would take to bring his stock up to the standard," she said, peremptorily.

Rabbi Eliezer's cadaverous face turned red, as he answered, bashfully:

"How much! Fifteen dollars, perhaps! I wish I had ten."

As Miss Bemis opened her handbag, the old scroll-writer's countenance changed colors and he looked as if he did not know what to do with his eyes.

* * *

The two Gentile women had no sooner left the cigarette-stand than the market-people came crowding about Rabbi Eliezer.

"How much did she give you?" they inquired, eagerly.

"How much! It is not quite a hundred dollars—you may be sure of that," he replied, all flushed with excitement.

"Why should you be afraid to tell us how much? We aren't going to take it away from you, are we?"

"Afraid! What reason have I to be afraid? But then—what matters it how much she gave me?"

One of the fishwives said she knew the taller of the two ladies.

"She belongs in that Gentile house on the next block where they fuss around with children and teach them to be ladies, you know," she explained. "They are all Gentiles over there, but good as diamonds. How much did she give you, Rabbi Eliezer?" she concluded, confidentially.

Rabbi Eliezer made no reply. He was struggling to look calm, but he could not. The twenty-dollar bill in his bosom-pocket was the largest sum he had ever handled. Every time a passer-by stopped at his stand he would leap to his feet, all in a flutter, and wait upon him with feverish eagerness; and at the same time he was so absent-minded that he often offered his customer the wrong article. Again and again he put his hand to his breast, to make sure that the twenty dollars were safe. Now it occurred to him that there might be a hole in his pocket; now he asked himself if he was positive that he had put the precious piece of paper into his purse. He distinctly remembered having done so, yet at moments his mind seemed to be a blank. "With these begrudging creatures around, one might truly lose one's mind," he complained to himself.

He pictured the increased stock and library, and the display he would make of it. All this would only take about fifteen dollars, so that he could well afford a new praying-shawl for himself. His old one was all patches, and how could he expect any attention at the synagogue? Wouldn't his fellow-worshippers be surprised! "I see you are doing good business, Rabbi Eliezer," they would say. Yes, he would get himself a new praying-shawl and a new hat. His skull-cap in which he worshipped at the synagogue was also rather rusty, but a new one cost only twenty-five cents, and this was now a trifle. Suddenly it became clear to him that he had no recollection of putting the twenty-dollar bill into his purse. His heart sank. Under the pretence of rearranging some books he hastily took out his dilapidated purse. The twenty-dollar bill was there—green on one side and brown on the other.

"Been counting the money the Gentile woman gave you?" asked a market-woman, archly.

"Not at all," he murmured, coloring.

"Foolish man that you are, does anybody begrudge you?" a carrot-pedler put in. "Out with it—how much?"

This time Rabbi Eliezer somehow felt hurt.

"What do you want of me? Do I owe anything?" he flamed out.

"You need not be excited, nor stuck up, either, even if a Gentile woman did make you a Christmas present—in honor of her God's birth," snapped the other.

"That's what it was—a present in honor of their God," seconded a remnant-pedler.

Rabbi Eliezer was in a rage.

"You say it all because your eyes are creeping out of your heads with envy," he said, with flashing eyes. "Well, she gave me twenty dollars. There now!"

The quarrel blew over, but Rabbi Eliezer was left with a wound in his heart. The green-and-brown piece of paper now seemed to smell of the incense and to have something to do with the organ-sounds which came from the Polish church in his birthplace. He was horrified. Nestling in his bosom-pocket right against his heart, was something *treife* (impure), unholy, loathsome. And this loathsome thing was so dear to that heart of his—woe to him! . . . What a misfortune that it should all have happened on Christmas of all other days! Had the good-hearted Gentile woman only come one day sooner, all would have gone well. Or, had there been nobody around to see him receive the Christmas present. . . . Anyhow, she never said it was a Christmas present, did she? Rabbi Eliezer also reminded himself of the Christmas gifts which thousands of American Jews exchanged with their Christian friends, and even among themselves; but the thought had no comfort to offer him. What if so-called Jews who shave their beards and smoke on the Sabbath do exchange Christmas presents? Shall he, an old man with one foot in his grave, follow their godless example? Woe is him, has it come to that? He was firmly determined to return the Gentile woman her money, and felt much relieved. He knew all the while that he would not do it, however, and little by little his heart grew heavy again. "Ah, it was the black year which brought me the Gentile ladies and their twenty dollars!" he exclaimed in despair.

At last, after hours of agony, he hit upon a plan. He would call at the Gentile House, as he described the College Settlement to himself, and ask whether the money had been given to him in honor of Christmas. He would not say: "Was it a Christmas present?" for that would be too dangerous a question to ask. Instead he would put it like this: "I am a poor man, but I am a Jew, and a Jew must not accept any presents in honor of a Gentile faith. I took the money because the kindly lady gave me it. It wasn't meant for a Christmas present, was it?" To be sure, the good woman would understand his trouble and whether it was a Christmas present or not, she would say that it was not.

It seemed such a trifling thing to do, and yet when he found himself in front of the little two-story building—the only exception in a block of towering tenement-houses—his heart sank with fear lest the well-dressed lady should say, Yes, it was a Christmas present.

"Why should I bother them, anyhow? Is it not enough that they gave me such a pile of money?" he said to himself, with an insincere sense of decency, and turned back. He had not gone many blocks when he retraced his steps. When he came in sight of the brown-stone stoop he slackened his pace. Never in his life had he called at the house of *pritzim* (noble folk), and he now felt, with a rush of joy, that he had not the courage to ring the door-bell. Finally when he had nerved himself up to the feat, his heart beat so violently that he was afraid he could not speak.

A minute later he was in the presence of Miss Colton. He recognized her, yet she seemed much younger and taller.

"Well, what can I do for you, Rabbi Eliezer?" she asked, with a friendly radiance which did his heart good.

"I come to ask you something, lady," he said, with a freedom of manner which was a surprise to himself. "People tell me it was a Christmas present that lady gave me. I am a Jew, you know, and I must not take any Christmas presents. I don't care if other Jews do or not."

He could not go on. He felt that it was not the speech he had prepared, and that it might cost him the twenty dollars. He was dying to correct it, but he could not speak. After a pause he blurted out:

"If I had received the money yesterday or to-morrow it would be another matter, but to-day—"

Miss Colton burst into laughter.

"Of course, it wasn't a Christmas present," she said. "The good lady never meant it for one, for didn't she know you were a Jew, and a pious one? But since you are worried about it let me have the twenty dollars and you call to-morrow morning, and I shall give them to you in the lady's name as a fresh present. Will that mend the matter?"

Rabbi Eliezer said it would, and left the College Settlement with his heart in his throat.

The next thing he did was to inquire of the Jews in the neighborhood whether Miss Colton was good pay. Everybody said she was good in every way, and Rabbi Eliezer went to the evening services at his synagogue in high spirits. Still, during the Eighteen Blessings he caught himself thinking of the twenty dollars and the Gentile God, and had to say it all over again.

By the time he got back to his stand the markets were in full blast. The sidewalks and the pavement were bubbling with men and women and torches. Hundreds of quivering lights stretched east and west, north and south—two restless bands of fire crossing each other in a blaze and losing themselves in a medley of flames, smoke, fish, vegetables, Sabbath-loaves, muslin and faces.

"Fish, fish, living fish—buy fish, dear little housewives! Dancing, tumbling, wriggling, screaming fish in honor of the Sabbath! Potatoes as big as your fist! A bargain in muslin! Buy a calico remnant—calico as good as silk, sweet little housewives!"

Rabbi Eliezer, whose place of business was in the heart of this babel, sat behind his stand, musing. He was broken in body and spirit. That he should have been in a fever of anxiety, humiliating himself and deceiving his God—and all because he was so poor that twenty dollars appeared like a fortune to him—suddenly seemed a cruel insult to his old age. He burst out muttering a psalm, and whatever the meaning of the Hebrew words his lips uttered, his shaking voice and doleful intonation prayed Heaven to forgive him and to take pity on his last years on earth.

The reddish torch-light fell upon his waxen cheeks and white beard. His eyes shone with a dull, disconsolate lustre. As he went on whispering and nodding his beautiful old head, amid the hubbub of the market, a pensive smile overspread his face. His heart was praying for tears. "I am so unhappy, so unhappy!" he said to himself in an ecstasy of woe. And at the same time he felt that hanging somewhere far away in the background was a disagreeable little question: Will the Gentile lady pay him the twenty dollars?

GENERAL WASHINGTON: A CHRISTMAS STORY

PAULINE HOPKINS

From *Colored American Magazine*, December 1900.

Born into a family with a long and prominent activist history, Pauline Hopkins was herself a groundbreaking figure in an extraordinary variety of spheres: she was a playwright, an actress, and a singer; a journalist and a prolific fiction writer; a political campaigner and a public intellectual. This story was published in the Colored American Magazine, *a pioneering Black literary periodical that was the first of its kind in America. Hopkins joined the staff of the magazine when it launched in 1900, the only woman to be invited to do so. As well as publishing numerous stories and serialized novels in its pages, she eventually edited the magazine. Though long neglected, Hopkins has been recognized as a vital figure in American literary history whose generically innovative work (including "Talma Gordon," a pioneering detective story) tangled tirelessly with the most pressing issues of the day facing Black Americans.*

I.

General Washington did any odd jobs he could find around the Washington market, but his specialty was selling chitlins.

General Washington lived in the very shady atmosphere of Murderer's Bay in the capital city. All that he could remember of father or mother in his ten years of miserable babyhood was that they were frequently absent from the little shanty where they were supposed to live, generally after a protracted spell of drunkenness and bloody quarels when the police were forced to interfere for the peace of the community. During these absences, the child would drift from one squalid home to another wherever a woman—God save the mark!—would take pity upon the poor waif and throw him a few scraps of food for his starved stomach, or a rag of a shawl, apron or skirt, in winter, to wrap about his attenuated little body.

One night the General's daddy being on a short vacation in the city, came home to supper; and because there was no supper to eat, he occupied himself in beating his wife. After that time, when the officers took him, the General's daddy never returned to his home. The General's mammy? Oh, she died!

General Washington's resources developed rapidly after this. Said resources consisted of a pair of nimble feet for dancing the hoe down, shuffles intricate and dazzling, and the Juba; a strong pair of lungs, a wardrobe limited to a pair of pants originally made for a man, and tied about the ankles with strings, a shirt with one gallows, a vast amount of "brass," and a very, very small amount of nickel. His education was practical: "Ef a corn-dodger costs two cents, an' a fellar hain't got de two cents, how's he gwine ter git de corn-dodger?"

General Washington ranked first among the knights of the pavement. He could shout louder and hit harder than any among them; that was the reason they called him "Buster" and "the General." The General could swear, too; I am sorry to admit it, but the truth must be told.

He uttered an oath when he caught a crowd of small white aristocrats tormenting a kitten. The General landed among them in quick time and commenced knocking heads at a lively rate. Presently he was master of the situation, and marched away triumphantly with the kitten in his arms, followed by stones and other missiles which whirled about him through space from behind the safe shelter of back yards and street corners.

The General took the kitten home. Home was a dry-goods box turned on end and filled with straw for winter. The General was as happy as a lord in summer, but the winter was a trial. The last winter had been a hard one, and Buster called a meeting of the leading members of the gang to consider the advisability of moving farther south for the hard weather. "'Pears lak to me, fellers, Wash'nton's heap colder'n it uster be, an' I'se mighty onscruplus 'bout stoppin' hyar."

"Bisness am mighty peart," said Teenie, the smallest member of the gang, "s'pose we put off menderin' tell after Chris'mas; Jeemes Henry, fellers, it hain't no Chris'mas fer me outside ob Wash'nton."

"Dat's so, Teenie," came from various members as they sat on the curbing playing an interesting game of craps.

"Den hyar we is tell after Chris'mas, fellers; then dis sonny's gwine ter move, sho, hyar me?"

"De gang's wid yer, Buster; move it is." It was about a week before Chris'mas, and the weather had been unusually severe. Probably because misery loves company—nothing could be more miserable than his cat—Buster grew very fond of Tommy. He would cuddle him in his arms every night and listen to his soft purring while he confided all his own hopes and fears to the willing ears of his four-footed companion, occasionally poking his ribs if he showed any signs of sleepiness.

But one night poor Tommy froze to death. Buster didn't—more's the wonder—only his ears and his two big toes. Poor Tommy was thrown off the dock into the Potomac the next morning, while a stream of salt water trickled down his master's dirty face, making visible, for the first time in a year, the yellow hue of his complexion. After that the General hated all flesh and grew morose and cynical.

Just about a week before Tommy's death, Buster met the fairy. Once, before his mammy died, in a spasm of reform she had forced him to go to school, against his better judgment, promising the teacher to go up and "wallop" the General every day if he thought Buster needed it. This gracious offer was declined with thanks. At the end of the week the General left school for his own good and the good of the school. But in that week he learned something about fairies; and so, after she threw him the pinks that she carried in her hand, he called her to himself "the fairy."

Being Christmas week, the General was pretty busy. It was a great sight to see the crowds of people coming and going all day long about the busy market; wagon loads of men, women and children, some carts drawn by horses, but more by mules. Some of the people well-dressed, some scantily clad, but all intent on getting enjoyment out of this their leisure season. This was the season for selling crops and settling the year's account. The store-keepers, too, had prepared their most tempting wares, and the thoroughfares were crowded.

"I 'clare to de Lord, I'se done busted my ol' man, shure," said one woman to another as they paused to exchange greetings outside a store door.

"N'em min'," returned the other, "he'll wurk fer mo'. Dis is Chris'mas, honey."

"To be sure," answered the first speaker, with a flounce of her ample skirts.

Meanwhile her husband pondered the advisability of purchasing a mule, feeling in his pockets for the price demanded, but finding them nearly empty. The money had been spent on the annual festival.

"Ole mule, I want yer mighty bad, but you'll have to slide dis time; it's Chris'mas, mule." The wise old mule actually seemed to laugh as he whisked his tail against his bony sides and steadied himself on his three sound legs.

The venders were very busy, and their cries were wonderful for ingenuity of invention to attract trade: "Hellow, dar, in de cellar, I'se got fresh aggs fer de 'casion; now's yer time fer agg-nogg wid new aggs in it."

There were the stalls, too, kept by venerable aunties and filled with specimens of old-time southern cheer: Coon, corn-pone, possum fat and hominy; there was piles of gingerbread and boiled chestnuts, heaps of walnuts and roasting apples. There were great barrels of cider, not to speak of something stronger. There were terrapin and the persimmon and the chinquapin in close proximity to the succulent viands—chine and spare-rib, sausage and crackling, savory souvenirs of the fine art of hog-killing. And everywhere were faces of dusky hue; Washington's great negro population bubbled over in every direction.

The General was peddling chitlins. He had a tub upon his head and was singing in his strong childish tones:

> "Here's yer chitlins, fresh an' sweet,
> Young hog's chitlins hard to beat,
> Methodis chitlins, jes' been biled,
> Right fresh chitlins, dey ain't spiled,
> Baptis' chitlins by de pound,
> As nice chitlins as ever was foun,"

"Hyar, boy, duzyer mean ter say dey is real Baptis' chitlins, sho nuff?"

"Yas, mum."

"How duz you make dat out?"

"De hog raised by Mr. Robberson, a hard-shell Baptis', mum."

"Well, lem-me have two poun's."

"Now," said a solid-looking man as General finished waiting on a crowd of women and men, "I want some o' de Methodess chitlins you's bin hollerin' 'bout."

"Hyar dey is, ser."

"Take 'em all out o' same tub?"

"Yas, ser. Only dair leetle mo' water on de Baptis' chitlins, an' dey's whiter."

"How you tell 'em?"

"Well, ser, two hog's chitlins in dis tub an one ob de hogs raised by Unc. Bemis, an' he's a Methodes', ef dat don't make him a Methodes hog nuthin' will."

"Weigh me out four pounds, ser."

In an hour's time the General had sold out. Suddenly at his elbow he heard a voice:

"Boy, I want to talk to you."

The fairy stood beside him. She was a little girl about his own age, well wrapped in costly velvet and furs; her long, fair hair fell about her like an aureole of glory; a pair of gentle blue eyes set in a sweet, serious face glanced at him from beneath a jaunty hat with a long curling white feather that rested light as thistle-down upon the beautiful curly locks. The General could not move for gazing, and as his wonderment grew his mouth was extended in a grin that revealed the pearly whiteness of two rows of ivory.

"Boy, shake hands."

The General did not move; how could he?

"Don't you hear me?" asked the fairy, imperiously:

"Yas'm," replied the General meekly. "Deed, missy, I'se 'tirely too dirty to tech dem clos o' yourn."

Nevertheless he put forth timidly and slowly a small paw begrimed with the dirt of the street. He looked at the hand and then at her; she looked at the hand and then at him. Then their eyes meeting, they laughed the sweet laugh of the free-masonry of childhood.

"I'll excuse you this time, boy," said the fairy, graciously, "but you must remember that I wish you to wash your face and hands when you are to talk with me; and," she added, as though inspired by an afterthought, "it would be well for you to keep them clean at other times, too."

"Yas'm," replied the General.

"What's your name, boy?"

"Gen'r'l Wash'nton," answered Buster, standing at attention as he had seen the police do in the courtroom.

"Well, General, don't you know you've told a story about the chitlins you've just sold?"

"Tol' er story?" queried the General with a knowing look.

"Course I got to sell my chitlins ahead ob de oder fellars, or lose my trade."

"Don't you know it's wicked to tell stories?"

"How come so?" asked the General, twisting his bare toes about in his rubbers, and feeling very uncomfortable.

"Because, God says we musn't."

"Who's he?"

The fairy gasped in astonishment. "Don't you know who God is?"

"No'pe; never seed him. Do he live in Wash'nton?"

"Why, God is your Heavenly Father, and Christ was His son. He was born on Christmas Day a long time ago. When He grew a man, wicked men nailed Him to the cross and killed Him. Then He went to heaven, and we'll all live with Him some day if we are good before we die. O I love Him; and you must love Him, too, General."

"Now look hyar, missy, you kayn't make this chile b'lieve nufin lak dat."

The fairy went a step nearer the boy in her eagerness:

"It's true; just as true as you live."

"Whar'd you say He lived?"

"In heaven," replied the child, softly.

"What kin' o' place is heaven?"

"Oh, beautiful!"

The General stared at the fairy. He worked his toes faster and faster.

"Say, kin yer hab plenty to eat up dar?"

"O, yes; you'll never be hungry there."

"An' a fire, an' clos?" he queried in suppressed, excited tones.

"Yes; it's all love and plenty when we get to heaven, if we are good here."

"Well, missy, dat's a pow'ful good story, but I'm blamed ef I b'lieve it." The General forgot his politeness in his excitement.

"An' ef it's true, tain't only fer white fo'ks; you won't fin' nary n——r dar."

"But you will; and all I've told you is true. Promise me to come to my house on Christmas morning and see my mother. She'll help you, and she will teach you more about God. Will you come?" she asked eagerly, naming a street and number in the most aristocratic quarter of Washington. "Ask for Fairy, that's me. Say quick; here is my nurse."

The General promised.

"Law, Miss Fairy, honey; come right hyar. I'll tell yer mawmaw how you's done run 'way from me to talk to dis dirty little monkey. Pickin' up sech trash fer ter talk to."

The General stood in a trance of happiness. He did not mind the slurring remarks of the nurse, and refrained from throwing a brick at the buxom lady, which was a sacrifice on his part. All he saw was the glint of golden curls in the winter sunshine, and the tiny hand waving him good-bye.

"An' her name is Fairy! Jes' ter think how I hit it all by my lonesome."

Many times that week the General thought and puzzled over Fairy's words. Then he would sigh:

"Heaven's where God lives. Plenty to eat, warm fire all de time in winter; plenty o' clos', too, but I'se got to be good. 'Spose dat means keepin' my face an' han's clean an' stop swearin' an' lyin'. It kayn't be did."

The gang wondered what had come over Buster.

II.

The day before Christmas dawned clear and cold. There was snow on the ground. Trade was good, and the General, mindful of the visit next day, had bought a pair of second-hand shoes and a new calico shirt.

"Git onter de dude!" sang one of the gang as he emerged from the privacy of the dry-goods box early Christmas Eve.

The General was a dancer and no mistake. Down at Dutch Dan's place they kept the old-time Southern Christmas moving along in hot time until the dawn of Christmas Day stole softly through the murky atmosphere. Dutch Dan's was the meeting place of the worst characters, white and black, in the capital city. From that vile den issued the twin spirits murder and rapine as the early winter shadows fell; there the criminal entered in the early dawn and was lost to the accusing eye of justice. There was a dance at Dutch Dan's Christmas Eve, and the General was sent for to help amuse the company.

The shed-like room was lighted by oil lamps and flaring pine torches. The center of the apartment was reserved for dancing. At one end the inevitable bar stretched its yawning mouth like a monster awaiting his victims. A long wooden table was built against one side of the room, where the game could be played to suit the taste of the most expert devotee of the fickle goddess.

The room was well filled, early as it was, and the General's entrance was the signal for a shout of welcome. Old Unc' Jasper was tuning his fiddle and blind Remus was drawing sweet chords from an old banjo. They glided softly into the music of the Mobile shuffle. The General began to dance. He was master of the accomplishment. The pigeon-wing, the old buck, the hoe-down and the Juba followed each other in rapid succession. The crowd shouted and cheered and joined in the sport. There was hand-clapping and a rhythmic accompaniment of patting the knees and stamping the feet. The General danced faster and faster:

"Juba up and juba down,
Juba all aroun' de town;
Can't you hyar de juba pat?
Juba!"

sang the crowd. The General gave fresh graces and new embellishments. Occasionally he added to the interest by yelling, "Ain't dis fin'e!" "Oh, my!" "Now I'm gittin' loose!" "Hol' me, hol' me!"

The crowd went wild with delight.

The child danced until he fell exhausted to the floor. Someone in the crowd "passed the hat." When all had been waited upon the bar-keeper counted up the receipts and divided fair—half to the house and half to the dancer. The fun went on, and the room grew more crowded. General Wash'nton crept under the table and curled himself up like a ball. He was lucky, he told himself sleepily, to have so warm a berth that cold night; and then his heart glowed as he thought of the morrow and Fairy, and wondered if what she had said were true. Heaven must be a fine place if it could beat the floor under the table for comfort and warmth. He slept. The fiddle creaked, the dancers shuffled. Rum went down their throats and wits were befogged. Suddenly the General was wide awake with a start. What was that?

"The family are all away to-night at a dance, and the servants gone home. There's no one there but an old man and a kid. We can be well out of the way before the alarm is given. 'Leven sharp, Doc. And, look here, what's the number agin?"

Buster knew in a moment that mischief was brewing, and he turned over softly on his side, listening mechanically to catch the reply. It came. Buster sat up. He was wide awake then. They had given the street and number where Fairy's home was situated.

III.

Senator Tallman was from Maryland. He had owned slaves, fought in the Civil War on the Confederate side, and at its end had been returned to a seat in Congress after reconstruction, with feelings of deeply rooted hatred for the Negro. He openly declared his purpose to oppose their progress in every possible way. His favorite argument was disbelief in God's handiwork as shown in the Negro.

"You argue, suh, that God made 'em. I have my doubts, suh. God made man in His own image, suh, and that being the case, suh, it is clear that he had no hand in creating n——s. A n——r, suh, is the image of nothing but the devil." He also declared in his imperious, haughty, Southern way: "The South is in the saddle, suh, and she will never submit to the degradation of Negro domination; never, Suh."

The Senator was a picture of honored age and solid comfort seated in his velvet armchair before the fire of blazing logs in his warm, well-lighted study. His lounging coat was thrown open, revealing its soft silken lining, his feet were thrust into gayly embroidered fur-lined slippers. Upon the baize covered table beside him a silver salver sat holding a decanter, glasses and fragrant mint, for the Senator loved the beguiling sweetness of a mint julep at bedtime. He was writing a speech which in his opinion would bury the blacks too deep for resurrection and settle the Negro question forever. Just now he was idle; the evening paper was folded across his knees; a smile was on his face. He was alone in the grand mansion, for the festivities of the season had begun and the family were gone to enjoy a merry-making at the house of a friend. There was a picture in his mind of Christmas in his old Maryland home in the good old days "befo' de wah," the great ball-room where giggling girls and matrons fair glided in the stately minuet. It was in such a gathering he had met his wife, the beautiful Kate Channing. Ah, the happy time of youth and love! The house was very still; how loud the ticking of the clock sounded. Just then a voice spoke beside his chair:

"Please, sah, I'se Gen'r'l Wash'n ton."

The Senator bounded to his feet with an exclamation:

"Eh! Bless my soul, suh; where did you come from?"

"Ef yer please, boss, froo de winder." The Senator rubbed his eyes and stared hard at the extraordinary figure before him. The Gen'r'l closed the window and then walked up to the fire, warmed himself in front, then turned around and stood with his legs wide apart and his shrewd little gray eyes fixed upon the man before him.

The Senator was speechless for a moment; then he advanced upon the intruder with a roar warranted to make a six-foot man quake in his boots:

"Through the window, you black rascal! Well, I reckon you'll go out through the door, and that in quick time, you little thief."

"Please, boss, it hain't me; it's Jim the crook and de gang from Dutch Dan's."

"Eh!" said the Senator again.

"What's yer cronumter say now, boss? 'Leven is de time fer de perfahmance ter begin. I reckon'd I'd git hyar time nuff fer yer ter call de perlice."

"Boy, do you mean for me to understand that burglars are about to raid my house?" demanded the Senator, a light beginning to dawn upon him.

The General nodded his head:

"Dat's it, boss, ef by 'buglers' you means Jim de crook and Dutch Dan."

It was ten minutes of the hour by the Senator's watch. He went to the telephone, rang up the captain of the nearest station, and told him the situation. He took a revolver from a drawer of his desk and advanced toward the waiting figure before the fire.

"Come with me. Keep right straight ahead through that door; if you attempt to run I'll shoot you."

They walked through the silent house to the great entrance doors and there awaited the coming of the police. Silently the officers surrounded the house. Silently they crept up the stairs into the now darkened study. "Eleven" chimed the little silver clock on the mantel. There was the stealthy tread of feet a moment after, whispers, the flash of a dark lantern,—a rush by the officers and a stream of electricity flooded the room. "It's the n——r did it!" shouted Jim the crook, followed instantly by the sharp crack of a revolver. General Washington felt a burning pain shoot through his breast as he fell unconscious to the floor. It was all over in a moment. The officers congratulated themselves on the capture they had made—a brace of daring criminals badly wanted by the courts.

When the General regained consciousness, he lay upon a soft, white bed in Senator Tallman's house. Christmas morning had dawned, clear, cold and sparkling; upon the air the joy-bells sounded sweet and strong: "Rejoice, your Lord is born." Faintly from the streets came the sound of merry voices: "Chris'mas gift, Chris'mas gift."

The child's eyes wandered aim lessly about the unfamiliar room as if seeking and questioning. They passed the Senator and Fairy, who sat beside him and rested on a copy of Titian's matchless Christ which hung over the mantel. A glorious stream of yellow sunshine fell upon the thorn-crowned Christ.

> "God of Nazareth, see!
> Before a trembling soul
> Unfoldeth like a scroll
> Thy wondrous destiny!"

The General struggled to a sitting position with arms out stretched, then fell back with a joyous, awesome cry:

"It's Him! It's Him!"

"O General," sobbed Fairy, "don't you die, you're going to be happy all the rest of your life. Grandpa says so."

"I was in time, little Missy; I tried mighty hard after I knowed whar' dem debbils was a-comin' to."

Fairy sobbed; the Senator wiped his eyeglasses and coughed. The General lay quite still a moment, then turned himself again on his pillow to gaze at the pictured Christ.

"I'm a-gittin' sleepy, missy, it's so warm an' comfurtable here. 'Pears lak I feel right happy sence Ise seed Him." The morning light grew brighter. The face of the Messiah looked down as it must have looked when He was transfigured on Tabor's heights. The ugly face of the child wore a strange, sweet beauty. The Senator bent over the quiet figure with a gesture of surprise.

The General had obeyed the call of One whom the winds and waves of stormy human life obey. Buster's Christmas Day was spent in heaven.

* * *

For some reason, Senator Tallman never made his great speech against the Negro.

MERRY CHRISTMAS IN THE TENEMENTS

JACOB A. RIIS

From *Out of Mulberry Street: Stories of Tenement Life in New York City* (New York: The Century Co., 1898), 1–46.

*Growing up in Denmark, Jacob Riis was encouraged in his English studies by his father, a newspaper editor, who made his son read the works of Charles Dickens. This proved to be prescient. After Riis emigrated to America in 1870, and following his own experiences of poverty, he became one of the most famous documenters of Gilded Age urban deprivation. As a police reporter working in the toughest neighborhoods of New York, Riis pioneered the use of flash photography in an attempt to record and publicize the squalor that he found there. Those iconic images, and the work that contained them—*How The Other Half Lives: Studies among the Tenements of New York *(1890)—remain his most enduring legacy. But Riis was a prolific writer working in a variety of genres, and, perhaps thanks to his childhood association with Dickens, frequently centered Christmas in his work—including* Is There a Santa Claus? *(1904), a book for children. This sketch, first published in the Christmas edition of the* Century *in 1897, presents a rich, panoramic, impressionistic portrait of seasonal life in the city as the twentieth century beckoned.*

It was just a sprig of holly, with scarlet berries showing against the green, stuck in, by one of the office boys probably, behind the sign that pointed the way up to the editorial rooms. There was no reason why it should have made me start when I came suddenly upon it at the turn of the stairs; but it did. Perhaps it was because that dingy hall, given over to dust and draughts all the days of the year, was the last place in which I expected to meet with any sign of Christmas; perhaps it was because I myself had nearly forgotten the holiday. Whatever the cause, it gave me quite a turn.

I stood, and stared at it. It looked dry, almost withered. Probably it had come a long way. Not much holly grows about Printing-House Square, except in the colored supplements, and that is scarcely of a kind to stir tender memories. Withered and dry, this did. I thought, with a twinge of conscience, of secret little conclaves of my children, of private views of things hidden from mamma at the bottom of drawers, of wild flights when papa appeared unbidden in the door, which I had allowed for once to pass unheeded. Absorbed in the business of the office, I had hardly thought of Christmas coming on, until now it was here. And this sprig of holly on the wall that had come to remind me,—come nobody knew how far,—did it grow yet in the beech-wood clearings, as it did when I gathered it as a boy, tracking through the snow? "Christ-thorn" we called it in our Danish tongue. The red berries, to our simple faith, were the drops of blood that fell from the Saviour's brow as it drooped under its cruel crown upon the cross.

Back to the long ago wandered my thoughts: to the moss-grown beech in which I cut my name and that of a little girl with yellow curls, of blessed memory, with the first jack-knife I ever owned; to the story-book with the little fir tree that pined because it was small, and because the hare jumped over it, and would not be content though the wind and the sun kissed it, and the dews wept over it and told it to rejoice in its young life; and that was so proud when, in the second year, the hare had to go round it, because then it knew it was getting big,—Hans Christian Andersen's story that we loved above all the rest; for we knew the tree right well, and the hare; even the tracks it left in the snow we had seen. Ah, those were the Yule-tide seasons, when the old Domkirke shone with a thousand wax candles on Christmas eve; when all business was laid aside to let the world make merry one whole week; when big red apples were roasted on the stove, and bigger doughnuts were baked within it for the long feast! Never such had been known since. Christmas to-day is but a name, a memory.

A door slammed below, and let in the noises of the street. The holly rustled in the draught. Some one going out said, "A Merry Christmas to you all!" in a big, hearty voice. I awoke from my reverie to find myself back in New York with a glad glow at the heart. It was not true. I had only forgotten. It was myself that had changed, not Christmas. That was here, with the old cheer, the old message of good-will, the old royal road to the heart of mankind. How often had I seen its blessed charity, that never corrupts, make light in the hovels of darkness and despair! how often watched its spirit of self-sacrifice and devotion in those who had, besides themselves, nothing to give! and as often the sight had made whole my faith in human nature. No! Christmas was not of the past, its spirit not dead. The lad who fixed the sprig of holly on the stairs knew it; my reporter's note-book bore witness to it. Witness of my contrition for the wrong I did the gentle spirit of the holiday, here let the book tell the story of one Christmas in the tenements of the poor.

It is evening in Grand Street. The shops east and west are pouring forth their swarms of workers. Street and sidewalk are filled with an eager throng of young men and women, chatting gaily, and elbowing the jam of holiday shoppers that linger about the big stores. The street-cars labor along, loaded down to the steps with passengers carrying bundles of every size and odd shape. Along the curb a string of pedlers hawk penny toys in push-carts with noisy clamor, fearless for once of being moved on by the police. Christmas brings a two weeks' respite from persecution even to the friendless street-fakir. From the window of one brilliantly lighted store a bevy of mature dolls in dishabille stretch forth their arms appealingly to a troop of factory-hands passing by. The young men chaff the girls, who shriek with laughter and run. The policeman on the corner stops beating his hands together to keep warm, and makes a mock attempt to catch them, whereat their shrieks rise shriller than ever. "Them stockin's o' yourn'll be the death o' Santa Claus!" he shouts after them, as they dodge. And they, looking back, snap saucily, "Mind yer business, freshy!" But their

Holiday Shoppers on Avenue A, illustration from
"Merry Christmas in the Tenements."

laughter belies their words. "They giv' it to ye straight that time," grins the grocer's clerk, come out to snatch a look at the crowds; and the two swap holiday greetings.

At the corner, where two opposing tides of travel form an eddy, the line of push-carts debouches down the darker side street. In its gloom their torches burn with a fitful glare that wakes black shadows among the trusses of the railroad structure overhead. A woman, with worn shawl drawn tightly about head and shoulders, bargains with a pedler for a monkey on a stick and two cents' worth of flitter-gold. Five ill-clad youngsters flatten their noses against the frozen pane of the toy-shop, in ecstasy at something there, which proves to be a milk wagon, with driver, horses, and cans that can be unloaded. It is something their minds can grasp. One comes forth with a penny goldfish of pasteboard clutched tightly in his hand, and, casting cautious glances right and left, speeds across the way to the door of a tenement, where a little girl stands waiting. "It's yer Chris'mas, Kate," he says, and thrusts it into her eager fist. The black doorway swallows them up.

Across the narrow yard, in the basement of the rear house, the lights of a Christmas tree show against the grimy window-pane. The hare would never have gone around it, it is so very small. The two children are busily engaged fixing the goldfish upon one of its branches. Three little candles that burn there shed light upon a scene of utmost desolation. The room is black with smoke and dirt. In the middle of the floor oozes an oil-stove that serves at once to take the raw edge off the cold and to cook the meals by. Half the window panes are broken, and the holes stuffed with rags. The sleeve of an old coat hangs out of one, and beats drearily upon the sash when the wind sweeps over the fence and rattles the rotten shutters. The family wash, clammy and gray, hangs on a clothes-line stretched across the room. Under it, at a table set with cracked and empty plates, a discouraged woman sits eying the children's show gloomily. It is evident that she has been drinking. The peaked faces of the little ones wear a famished look. There are three—the third an infant, put to bed in what was once a baby-carriage. The two from the street are pulling it around to get the tree in range. The baby sees it, and crows with delight. The boy shakes a branch, and the goldfish leaps and sparkles in the candle-light.

"See, sister!" he pipes; "see Santa Claus!" And they clap their hands in glee. The woman at the table wakes out of her stupor, gazes around her, and bursts into a fit of maudlin weeping.

The door falls to. Five flights up, another opens upon a bare attic room which a patient little woman is setting to rights. There are only three chairs, a box, and a bedstead in the room, but they take a deal of careful arranging. The bed hides the broken plaster in the wall through which the wind came in; each chair-leg stands over a rat-hole, at once to hide it and to keep the rats out. One is left; the box is for that. The plaster of the ceiling is held up with pasteboard patches. I know the story of that attic. It is one of cruel desertion. The woman's husband is even now living in plenty with the creature for whom he forsook her, not a dozen blocks away, while she "keeps the home together for the childer." She sought justice, but the lawyer demanded a retainer; so she gave it up, and went back to her little ones. For this room that barely keeps the winter wind out she pays four dollars a month, and is behind with the rent. There is scarce bread in the house; but the spirit of Christmas has found her attic. Against a broken wall is tacked a hemlock branch, the leavings of the corner grocer's fitting-block; pink string from the packing-counter hangs on it in festoons. A tallow dip on the box furnishes the illumination. The children sit up in bed, and watch it with shining eyes.

"We're having Christmas!" they say.

The lights of the Bowery glow like a myriad twinkling stars upon the ceaseless flood of humanity that surges ever through the great highway of the homeless. They shine upon long rows of lodging-houses, in which hundreds of young men, cast helpless upon the reef of the strange city, are learning their first lessons of utter loneliness; for what desolation is there like that of the careless crowd when all the world rejoices? They shine upon the tempter setting his snares there, and upon the missionary and the Salvation Army lass, disputing his catch with him; upon the police detective going his rounds with coldly observant eye intent upon the outcome of the contest; upon the wreck that is past hope, and upon the youth pausing on the verge of the pit in which the other has long ceased to struggle. Sights and sounds of Christmas there are in plenty in the Bowery.

Juniper and tamarack and fir stand in groves along the busy thoroughfare, and garlands of green embower mission and dive impartially. Once a year the old street recalls its youth with an effort. It is true that it is largely a commercial effort—that the evergreen, with an instinct that is not of its native hills, haunts saloon-corners by preference; but the smell of the pine woods is in the air, and—Christmas is not too critical—one is grateful for the effort. It varies with the opportunity. At "Beefsteak John's" it is content with artistically embalming crullers and mince-pies in green cabbage under the window lamp. Over yonder, where the mile-post of the old lane still stands,—in its unhonored old age become the vehicle of publishing the latest "sure cure" to the world,—a florist, whose undenominational zeal for the holiday and trade outstrips alike distinction of creed and property, has transformed the sidewalk and the ugly railroad structure into a veritable bower, spanning it with a canopy of green, under which dwell with him, in neighborly good-will, the Young Men's Christian Association and the Gentile tailor next door.

In the next block a "turkey-shoot" is in progress. Crowds are trying their luck at breaking the glass balls that dance upon tiny jets of water in front of a marine view with the moon rising, yellow and big, out of a silver sea. A man-of-war, with lights burning aloft, labors under a rocky coast. Groggy sailormen, on shore leave, make unsteady attempts upon the dancing balls. One mistakes the moon for the target, but is discovered in season. "Don't shoot that," says the man who loads the guns; "there's a lamp behind it." Three scared birds in the window recess try vainly to snatch a moment's sleep between shots and the trains that go roaring overhead on the elevated road. Roused by the sharp crack of the rifles, they blink at the lights in the street, and peck moodily at a crust in their bed of shavings.

The dime museum gong clatters out its noisy warning that "the lecture" is about to begin. From the concert-hall, where men sit drinking beer in clouds of smoke, comes the thin voice of a short-skirted singer, warbling, "Do they think of me at home?" The young fellow who sits near the door, abstractedly making figures in the wet track of the "schooners," buries something there with a sudden restless turn, and calls for another beer. Out in the street a band strikes up. A host with banners advances, chanting an unfamiliar hymn. In the ranks marches a cripple on crutches. Newsboys follow, gaping. Under the illuminated clock of the Cooper Institute the procession halts, and the leader, turning his face to the sky, offers a prayer. The passing crowds stop to listen. A few bare their heads. The devoted group, the flapping banners, and the changing torch-light on upturned faces, make a strange, weird picture. Then the drum-beat, and the band files into its barracks across the street. A few of the listeners follow, among them the lad from the concert hall, who slinks shamefacedly in when he thinks no one is looking.

Down at the foot of the Bowery is the "panhandlers' beat," where the saloons elbow one another at every step, crowding out all other business than that of keeping lodgers to support them. Within call of it, across the square, stands a church which, in the memory of men yet living, was built to shelter the fashionable Baptist audiences of a day when Madison Square was out in the fields, and Harlem had a foreign sound. The fashionable audiences are gone long since. To-day the church, fallen into premature decay, but still handsome in its strong and noble lines, stands as a missionary outpost in the land of the enemy, its builders would have said, doing a greater work than they planned. To-night is the Christmas festival of its English-speaking Sunday-school, and the pews are filled. The banners of United Italy, of modern Hellas, of France and Germany and England, hang side by side with the Chinese dragon and the starry flag—signs of the cosmopolitan character of the congregation. Greek and Roman Catholics, Jews and joss-worshippers, go there; few Protestants, and no Baptists. It is easy to pick out the children in their seats by nationality, and as easy to read the story of poverty and suffering that stands written in more than one mother's haggard face, now beaming with pleasure at the little ones' glee. A gayly decorated Christmas tree has taken the place of the pulpit. At its foot is stacked a mountain of bundles, Santa Claus's gifts to the school. A self-conscious young man with soap-locks has just been allowed to retire, amid tumultuous applause, after blowing "Nearer, my God, to thee" on his horn until his cheeks swelled almost to bursting. A trumpet ever takes the Fourth Ward by storm. A class of little girls is climbing upon the platform. Each wears a capital letter on her breast, and has a piece to speak that begins with the letter; together they spell its lesson. There is momentary consternation: one is missing. As the discovery is made, a child pushes past the doorkeeper, hot and breathless. "I am in 'Boundless Love,'" she says, and makes for the platform, where her arrival restores confidence and the language.

In the audience the befrocked visitor from up-town sits cheek by jowl with the pigtailed Chinaman and the dark-browed Italian. Up in the gallery, farthest from the preacher's desk and the tree, sits a Jewish mother with three boys, almost in rags. A dingy and threadbare shawl partly hides her poor calico wrap and patched apron. The woman shrinks in the pew, fearful of being seen; her boys stand upon the benches, and applaud with the rest. She endeavors vainly to restrain them. "Tick, tick!" goes the old clock over the door through which wealth and fashion went out long years ago, and poverty came in.

Loudly ticked the old clock in time with the doxology, the other day, when they cleared the tenants out of Gotham Court down here in Cherry Street, and shut the iron doors of Single and Double Alley against them. Never did the world move faster or surer toward a better day than when the wretched slum was seized by the health officers as a nuisance unfit longer to disgrace a Christian city. The snow lies deep in the deserted passageways, and the vacant floors are given over to evil smells, and to the rats that forage in squads, burrowing in the neglected sewers. The "wall of wrath" still towers above the buildings in the adjoining Alderman's Court, but its wrath at last is wasted.

It was built by a vengeful Quaker, whom the alderman had knocked down in a quarrel over the boundary line, and transmitted its legacy of hate to generations yet unborn; for where it stood it shut out sunlight and air from the tenements of Alderman's Court. And at last it is to go, Gotham Court and all; and to the going the wall of wrath has contributed its share, thus in the end atoning for some of the harm it wrought. Tick! old clock; the world moves. Never yet did Christmas seem less dark on Cherry Hill than since the lights were put out in Gotham Court forever.

In "The Bend" the philanthropist undertaker who "buries for what he can catch on the plate" hails the Yule-tide season with a pyramid of green made of two coffins set on end. It has been a good day, he says cheerfully, putting up the shutters; and his mind is easy. But the "good days" of The Bend are over, too. The Bend itself is all but gone. Where the old pigsty stood, children dance and sing to the strumming of a cracked piano-organ propelled on wheels by an Italian and his wife. The park that has come to take the place of the slum will curtail the undertaker's profits, as it has lessened the work of the police. Murder was the fashion of the day that is past. Scarce a knife has been drawn since the sunlight shone into that evil spot, and grass and green shrubs took the place of the old rookeries. The Christmas gospel of peace and good-will moves in where the slum moves out. It never had a chance before.

The children follow the organ, stepping in the slush to the music, bareheaded and with torn shoes, but happy; across the Five Points and through "the Bay,"—known to the directory as Baxter Street,—to "the Divide," still Chatham Street to its denizens, though the aldermen have rechristened it Park Row. There other delegations of Greek and Italian children meet and escort the music on its homeward trip. In one of the crooked streets near the river its journey comes to an end. A battered door opens to let it in. A tallow dip burns sleepily on the creaking stairs. The water runs with a loud clatter in the sink: it is to keep it from freezing. There is not a whole window pane in the hall. Time was when this was a fine house harboring wealth and refinement. It has neither now. In the old parlor downstairs a knot of hard-faced men and women sit on benches about a deal table, playing cards. They have a jug between them, from which they drink by turns. On the stump of a mantel-shelf a lamp burns before a rude print of the Mother of God. No one pays any heed to the hand-organ man and his wife as they climb to their attic. There is a colony of them up there—three families in four rooms.

"Come in, Antonio," says the tenant of the double flat,—the one with two rooms,—"come and keep Christmas." Antonio enters, cap in hand. In the corner by the dormer-window a "crib" has been fitted up in commemoration of the Nativity. A soap-box and two hemlock branches are the elements. Six tallow candles and a night-light illuminate a singular collection of rarities, set out with much ceremonial show. A doll tightly wrapped in swaddling-clothes represents "the Child." Over it stands a ferocious-looking beast, easily recognized as a survival of the last political campaign,—the Tammany tiger,—threatening to swallow it at a gulp if one as much as takes one's eyes off it. A miniature Santa Claus, a pasteboard monkey, and several other articles of bric-à-brac of the kind the tenement affords, complete the outfit. The background is a picture of St. Donato, their village saint, with the Madonna "whom they worship most." But the incongruity harbors no suggestion of disrespect. The children view the strange show with genuine reverence, bowing and crossing themselves before it. There are five, the oldest a girl of seventeen, who works for a sweater, making three dollars a week. It is all the money that comes in, for the father has been sick and unable to work eight months and the mother has her hands full: the youngest is a baby in arms. Three of the children go to a charity school, where they are fed, a great help, now the holidays have come to make work slack for sister. The rent is six dollars—two weeks' pay out of the four. The mention of a possible chance of light work for the man brings the daughter with her sewing from the adjoining room, eager to hear. That would be Christmas indeed! "Pietro!" She runs to the neighbors to communicate the joyful tidings. Pietro comes, with his new-born baby, which he is tending while his wife lies ill, to look at the maestro, so powerful and good. He also has been out of work for months, with a family of mouths to fill, and nothing coming in. His children are all small yet, but they speak English.

"What," I say, holding a silver dime up before the oldest, a smart little chap of seven—"what would you do if I gave you this?"

"Get change," he replies promptly. When he is told that it is his own, to buy toys with, his eyes open wide with wondering incredulity. By degrees he understands. The father does not. He looks questioningly from one to the other. When told, his respect increases visibly for "the rich gentleman."

They were villagers of the same community in southern Italy, these people and others in the tenements thereabouts, and they moved their patron saint with them. They cluster about his worship here, but the worship is more than an empty form. He typifies to them the old neighborliness of home, the spirit of mutual help, of charity, and of the common cause against the common enemy. The community life survives through their saint in the far city to an unsuspected extent. The sick are cared for; the dreaded hospital is fenced out. There are no Italian evictions. The saint has paid the rent of this attic through two hard months; and here at his shrine the Calabrian village gathers, in the persons of these three, to do him honor on Christmas eve.

Where the old Africa has been made over into a modern Italy, since King Humbert's cohorts struck the up-town trail, three hundred of the little foreigners are having an uproarious time over their Christmas tree in the Children's Aid Society's school. And well they may, for the like has not been seen in Sullivan Street in this generation. Christmas trees are rather rarer over here than on the East Side, where the German leavens the lump with his loyalty to home traditions. This is loaded with silver and gold and toys without end, until there is little left of the original green. Santa Claus's sleigh must have been upset in a snow-drift over here, and righted by throwing the cargo overboard, for there is at least a wagon-load of things that can find no room on the tree. The appearance of "teacher" with a double armful of curly-headed dolls in red, yellow, and green Mother-Hubbards, doubtful how to dispose of them, provokes a shout of approval, which is presently quieted by the principal's bell. School is "in" for the preliminary exercises. Afterward there are to be the tree and ice-cream for the good children. In their anxiety to prove their title clear, they sit so straight, with arms folded, that the whole row bends over backward. The lesson is brief, the answers to the point.

"What do we receive at Christmas?" the teacher wants to know. The whole school responds with a shout, "Dolls and toys!" To the question, "Why do we receive them at Christmas?" the answer is not so prompt. But one youngster from Thompson Street holds up his hand. He knows. "Because we always get 'em," he says; and the class is convinced: it is a fact. A baby wails because it cannot get the whole tree at once. The "little mother"—herself a child of less than a dozen winters—who has it in charge, cooes over it, and soothes its grief with the aid of a surreptitious sponge-cake evolved from the depths of teacher's pocket. Babies are encouraged in these schools, though not originally included in their plan, as often the one condition upon which the older children can be reached. Some one has to mind the baby, with all hands out at work.

The school sings "Santa Lucia" and "Children of the Heavenly King," and baby is lulled to sleep.

"Who is this King?" asks the teacher, suddenly, at the end of a verse. Momentary stupefaction. The little minds are on ice-cream just then; the lad nearest the door has telegraphed that it is being carried up in pails. A little fellow on the back seat saves the day. Up goes his brown fist.

"Well, Vito, who is he?"

"McKinley!" shouts the lad, who remembers the election just past; and the school adjourns for ice-cream.

It is a sight to see them eat it. In a score of such schools, from the Hook to Harlem, the sight is enjoyed in Christmas week by the men and women who, out of their own pockets, reimburse Santa Claus for his outlay, and count it a joy, as well they may; for their beneficence sometimes makes the one bright spot in lives that have suffered of all wrongs the most cruel,—that of being despoiled of their childhood. Sometimes they are little Bohemians; sometimes the children of refugee Jews; and again, Italians, or the descendants of the Irish stock of Hell's Kitchen and Poverty Row; always the poorest, the shabbiest, the hungriest—the children Santa Claus loves best to find, if any one will show him the way. Having so much on hand, he has no time, you see, to look them up himself. That must be done for him; and it is done. To the teacher in the Sullivan-street school came one little girl, this last Christmas, with anxious inquiry if it was true that he came around with toys.

"I hanged my stocking last time," she said, "and he didn't come at all." In the front house indeed, he left a drum and a doll, but no message from him reached the rear house in the alley. "Maybe he couldn't find it," she said soberly. Did the teacher think he would come if she wrote to him? She had learned to write.

Together they composed a note to Santa Claus, speaking for a doll and a bell—the bell to play "go to school" with when she was kept home minding the baby. Lest he should by any chance miss the alley in spite of directions, little Rosa was invited to hang her stocking, and her sister's, with the janitor's children's in the school. And lo! on Christmas morning there was a gorgeous doll, and a bell that was a whole curriculum in itself, as good as a year's schooling any day! Faith in Santa Claus is established in that Thompson-street alley for this generation at least; and Santa Claus, got by hook or by crook into an Eighth-Ward alley, is as good as the whole Supreme Court bench, with the Court of Appeals thrown in, for backing the Board of Health against the slum.

But the ice-cream! They eat it off the seats, half of them kneeling or squatting on the floor; they blow on it, and put it in their pockets to carry home to baby. Two little shavers discovered to be feeding each other, each watching the smack develop on the other's lips as the acme of his own bliss, are "cousins"; that is why. Of cake there is a double supply. It is a dozen years since "Fighting Mary," the wildest child in the Seventh Avenue school, taught them a lesson there which they have never forgotten. She was perfectly untamable, fighting everybody in school, the despair of her teacher, till on Thanksgiving, reluctantly included in the general amnesty and mince-pie, she was caught cramming the pie into her pocket, after eying it with a look of pure ecstasy, but refusing to touch it. "For mother" was her explanation, delivered with a defiant look before which the class quailed. It is recorded, but not in the minutes, that the board of managers wept over Fighting Mary, who, all unconscious of having caused such an astonishing "break," was at that moment engaged in maintaining her prestige and reputation by fighting the gang in the next block. The minutes contain merely a formal resolution to the effect that occasions of mince-pie shall carry double rations thenceforth. And the rule has been kept—not only in Seventh-Avenue, but in every industrial school—since. Fighting Mary won the biggest fight of her troubled life that day, without striking a blow.

It was in the Seventh-Avenue school last Christmas that I offered the truant class a four-bladed penknife as a prize for whittling out the truest Maltese cross. It was a class of black sheep, and it was the blackest sheep of the flock that won the prize. "That awful Savarese," said Miss Haight, in despair. I thought of Fighting Mary, and bade her take heart. I regret to say that within a week the hapless Savarese was black-listed for banking up the school door with snow, so that not even the janitor could get out and at him.

Within hail of the Sullivan-street school camps a scattered little band, the Christmas customs of which I had been trying for years to surprise. They are Indians, a handful of Mohawks and Iroquois, whom some ill wind has blown down from their Canadian reservation, and left in these West-Side tenements to eke out such a living as they can, weaving mats and baskets, and threading glass pearls on slippers and pin-cushions, until, one after another, they have died off and gone to happier hunting-grounds than Thompson street. There were as many families as one could count on the fingers of both hands when I first came upon them, at the death of old Tamenund, the basket maker. Last Christmas there were seven. I had about made up my mind that the only real Americans in New York did not keep the holiday at all, when, one Christmas eve, they showed me how. Just as dark was setting in, old Mrs. Benoit came from her Hudson Street attic—where she was known among the neighbors, as old and poor as she, as Mrs. Ben Wah, and was believed to be the relict of a warrior of the name of Benjamin Wah—to the office of the Charity Organization Society, with a bundle for a friend who had helped her over a rough spot—the rent, I suppose. The bundle was done up elaborately in blue cheese-cloth, and contained a lot of little garments which she had made out of the remnants of blankets and cloth of her own from a younger and better day. "For those," she said, in her French patois, "who are poorer than myself"; and hobbled away. I found out, a few days later, when I took her picture weaving mats in her attic room, that she had scarcely food in the house that Christmas day and not the car fare to take her to church! Walking was bad, and her old limbs were stiff. She sat by the window through the winter evening, and watched the sun go down behind the western hills, comforted by her pipe. Mrs. Ben Wah, to give her her local name, is not really an Indian; but her husband was one, and she lived all her life with the tribe till she came here. She is a philosopher in her own quaint way. "It is no disgrace to be poor," said she to me, regarding her empty tobacco-pouch; "but it is sometimes a great inconvenience." Not even the recollection of the vote of censure that was passed upon me once by the ladies of the Charitable Ten for surreptitiously supplying an aged couple, the special object of their charity, with army plug, could have deterred me from taking the hint.

Very likely, my old friend Miss Sherman, in her Broome-street cellar,—it is always the attic or the cellar,—would object to Mrs. Ben Wah's claim to being the only real American in my note-book. She is from Down East, and says "stun" for stone. In her youth she was lady's-maid to a general's wife, the recollection of which military career equally condones the cellar and prevents her holding any sort of communication with her common neighbors, who add to the offence of being foreigners the unpardonable one of being mostly men. Eight cats bear her steady company, and keep alive her starved affections. I found them on last Christmas eve behind barricaded doors; for the cold that had locked the water-pipes had brought the neighbors down to the cellar, where Miss Sherman's cunning had kept them from freezing. Their tin pans and buckets were even then banging against her door. "They're a miserable lot," said the old maid, fondling her cats defiantly; "but let 'em. It's Christmas. Ah!" she added, as one of the eight stood up in her lap and rubbed its cheek against hers, "they're innocent. It isn't poor little animals that does the harm. It's men and women that does it to each other." I don't know whether it was just philosophy, like Mrs. Ben Wah's, or a glimpse of her story. If she had one, she kept it for her cats.

In a hundred places all over the city, when Christmas comes, as many open-air fairs spring suddenly into life. A kind of Gentile Feast of the Tabernacles possesses the tenement districts especially. Green-embowered booths stand in rows at the curb, and the voice of the tin trumpet is heard in the land. The common source of all the show is down by the North River, in the district known as "the Farm." Down there Santa Claus establishes headquarters early in December and until past New Year. The broad quay looks then more like a clearing in a pine forest than a busy section of the metropolis. The steamers discharge their loads of fir trees at the piers until they stand stacked mountain-high, with foot-hills of holly and ground-ivy trailing off toward the land side. An army-train of wagons is engaged in carting them away from early morning till late at night; but the green forest grows, in spite of it all, until in places it shuts the shipping out of sight altogether. The air is redolent with the smell of balsam and pine. After nightfall, when the lights are burning in the busy market, and the homeward-bound crowds with baskets and heavy burdens of Christmas greens jostle one another with good-natured banter,—nobody is ever cross down here in the holiday season,—it is good to take a stroll through the Farm, if one has a spot in his heart faithful yet to the hills and the woods in spite of the latter-day city. But it is when the moonlight is upon the water and upon the dark phantom forest, when the heavy breathing of some passing steamer is the only sound that breaks the stillness of the night, and the watchman smokes his only pipe on the bulwark, that the Farm has a mood and an atmosphere all its own, full of poetry, which some day a painter's brush will catch and hold.

Into the ugliest tenement street Christmas brings something of picturesqueness, of cheer. Its message was ever to the poor and the heavy-laden, and by them it is understood with an instinctive yearning to do it honor. In the stiff dignity of the brownstone streets up-town there may be scarce a hint of it. In the homes of the poor it blossoms on stoop and fire-escape, looks out of the front window, and makes the unsightly barber-pole to sprout overnight like an Aaron's rod. Poor indeed is the home that has not its sign of peace over the hearth, be it but a single sprig of green. A little color creeps with it even into rabbinical Hester street, and shows in the shop-windows and in the children's faces. The very feather dusters in the peddler's stock take on brighter hues for the occasion, and the big knives in the cutler's shop gleam with a lively anticipation of the impending goose "with fixin's"—a concession, perhaps, to the commercial rather than the religious holiday. Business comes then, if ever. A crowd of ragamuffins camp out at a window where Santa Claus and his wife stand in state, embodiment of the domestic ideal that has not yet gone out of fashion in these tenements, gazing hungrily at the announcement that "A silver present will be given to every purchaser by a real Santa Claus.—M. Levitsky." Across the way, in a hole in the wall, two cobblers are pegging away under an oozy lamp that makes a yellow splurge on the inky blackness about them, revealing to the passer-by their bearded faces, but nothing of the environment save a single sprig of holly suspended from the lamp. From what forgotten brake it came with a message of cheer, a thought of wife and children across the sea waiting their summons, God knows. The shop is their house and home. It was once the hall of the tenement; but to save space, enough has been walled in to make room for their bench and bed. The tenants go through the next house. No matter if they are cramped; by and by they will have room. By and by comes the spring, and with it the steamer. Does not the green branch speak of spring and of hope? The policeman on the beat hears their hammers beat a joyous tattoo past midnight, far into Christmas morning. Who shall say its message has not reached even them in their slum?

Where the noisy trains speed over the iron highway past the second-story windows of Allen Street, a cellar door yawns darkly in the shadow of one of the pillars that half block the narrow sidewalk. A dull gleam behind the cobweb-shrouded window pane supplements the sign over the door, in Yiddish and English: "Old Brasses." Four crooked and mouldy steps lead to utter darkness, with no friendly voice to guide the hapless customer. Fumbling along the dank wall, he is left to find the door of the shop as best he can. Not a likely place to encounter the fastidious from the Avenue! Yet ladies in furs and silk find this door and the grim old smith within it. Now and then an artist stumbles upon them, and exults exceedingly in his find. Two holiday shoppers are even now haggling with the coppersmith over the price of a pair of curiously wrought brass candlesticks. The old man has turned from the forge, at which he was working, unmindful of his callers roving among the dusty shelves. Standing there, erect and sturdy, in his shiny leather apron, hammer in hand, with the firelight upon his venerable head, strong arms bared to the elbow, and the square paper cap pushed back from a thoughtful, knotty brow, he stirs strange fancies. One half expects to see him fashioning a gorget or a sword on his anvil. But his is a more peaceful craft. Nothing more warlike is in sight than a row of brass shields, destined for ornament, not for battle. Dark shadows chase one another by the flickering light among copper kettles of ruddy glow, old-fashioned samovars, and massive andirons of tarnished brass. The bargaining goes on. Overhead the nineteenth century speeds by with rattle and roar; in here linger the shadows of the centuries long dead. The boy at the anvil listens open-mouthed, clutching the bellows-rope.

In Liberty Hall a Jewish wedding is in progress. Liberty! Strange how the word echoes through these sweaters' tenements, where starvation is at home half the time. It is as an all-consuming passion with these people, whose spirit a thousand years of bondage have not availed to daunt. It breaks out in strikes, when to strike is to hunger and die. Not until I stood by a striking cloak-maker whose last cent was gone, with not a crust in the house to feed seven hungry mouths, yet who had voted vehemently in the meeting that day to keep up the strike to the bitter end,—bitter indeed, nor far distant,—and heard him at sunset recite the prayer of his fathers: "Blessed art thou, O Lord our God, King of the world, that thou hast redeemed us as thou didst redeem our fathers, hast delivered us from bondage to liberty, and from servile dependence to redemption!"—not until then did I know what of sacrifice the word might mean, and how utterly we of another day had forgotten. But for once shop and tenement are left behind. Whatever other days may have in store, this is their day of play.

The bridegroom, a cloak-presser in a hired dress suit, sits alone and ill at ease at one end of the hall, sipping whiskey with a fine air of indifference, but glancing apprehensively toward the crowd of women in the opposite corner that surround the bride, a pale little shop-girl with a pleading, winsome face. From somewhere unexpectedly appears a big man in an ill-fitting coat and skullcap, flanked on either side by a fiddler, who scrapes away and away, accompanying the improvisator in a plaintive minor key as he halts before the bride and intones his lay. With many a shrug of stooping shoulders and queer excited gesture, he drones, in the harsh, guttural Yiddish of Hester Street, his story of life's joys and sorrows, its struggles and victories in the land of promise. The women listen, nodding and swaying their bodies sympathetically. He works himself into a frenzy, in which the fiddlers vainly try to keep up with him. He turns and digs the laggard angrily in the side without losing the metre. The climax comes. The bride bursts into hysterical sobs, while the women wipe their eyes. A plate, heretofore concealed under his coat, is whisked out. He has conquered; the inevitable collection is taken up.

The tuneful procession moves upon the bridegroom. An Essex Street girl in the crowd, watching them go, says disdainfully: "None of this humbug when I get married." It is the straining of young America at the fetters of tradition. Ten minutes later, when, between double files of women holding candles, the couple pass to the canopy where the rabbi waits, she has already forgotten; and when the crunching of a glass under the bridegroom's heel announces that they are one, and that until the broken pieces be reunited he is hers and hers alone, she joins with all the company in the exulting shout of "Mozzel tov!" ("Good luck!"). Then the *dupka,* men and women joining in, forgetting all but the moment, hands on hips, stepping in time, forward, backward, and across. And then the feast. The ceremony is over, and they sit at the long tables by squads and tribes. Those who belong together sit together. There is no attempt at pairing off for conversation or mutual entertainment at speech-making or toasting. The business in hand is to eat, and it is attended to. The bridegroom, at the head of the table, with his shiny silk hat on, sets the example; and the guests emulate it with zeal, the men smoking big, strong cigars between mouthfuls. "Gosh! ain't it fine?" is the grateful comment of one curly-headed youngster, bravely attacking his third plate of chicken-stew. "Fine as silk," nods his neighbor in knickerbockers. Christmas, for once, means something to them that they can understand. The crowd of hurrying waiters make room for one bearing aloft a small turkey adorned with much tinsel and many paper flowers. It is for the bride, the one thing not to be touched until the next day—one day off from the drudgery of housekeeping; she, too, can keep Christmas.

A group of bearded, dark-browed men sit apart, the rabbi among them. They are the orthodox, who cannot break bread with the rest, for fear, though the food be kosher, the plates have been defiled. They brought their own to the feast, and sit at their own table, stern and justified. Did they but know what depravity is harbored in the impish mind of the girl yonder, who plans to hang her stocking overnight by the window! There is no fireplace in the tenement. Queer things happen over here, in the strife between the old and the new. The girls of the College Settlement, last summer, felt compelled to explain that the holiday in the country which they offered some of these children was to be spent in an Episcopal clergyman's house, where they had prayers every morning. "Oh," was the mother's indulgent answer, "they know it isn't true, so it won't hurt them."

The bell of a neighboring church tower strikes the vesper hour. A man in working-clothes uncovers his head reverently, and passes on. Through the vista of green bowers formed of the grocer's stock of Christmas trees a passing glimpse of flaring torches in the distant square is caught. They touch with flame the gilt cross towering high above the "White Garden," as the German residents call Tompkins Square. On the sidewalk the holy-eve fair is in its busiest hour. In the pine-board booths stand rows of staring toy dogs alternately with plaster saints. Red apples and candy are hawked from carts. Peddlers offer colored candles with shrill outcry. A huckster feeding his horse by the curb scatters, unseen, a share for the sparrows. The cross flashes white against the dark sky.

In one of the side streets near the East River has stood for thirty years a little mission church, called Hope Chapel by its founders, in the brave spirit in which they built it. It has had plenty of use for the spirit since. Of the kind of problems that beset its pastor I caught a glimpse the other day, when, as I entered his room, a rough-looking man went out.

"One of my cares," said Mr. Devins, looking after him with contracted brow. "He has spent two Christmas days of twenty-three out of jail. He is a burglar, or was. His daughter has brought him round. She is a seamstress. For three months, now, she has been keeping him and the home, working nights. If I could only get him a job! He won't stay honest long without it; but who wants a burglar for a watchman? And how can I recommend him?"

A few doors from the chapel an alley sets into the block. We halted at the mouth of it.

"Come in," said Mr. Devins, "and wish Blind Jennie a Merry Christmas." We went in, in single file; there was not room for two. As we climbed the creaking stairs of the rear tenement, a chorus of children's shrill voices burst into song somewhere above.

"This is her class," said the pastor of Hope Chapel, as he stopped on the landing. "They are all kinds. We never could hope to reach them; Jennie can. They fetch her the papers given out in the Sunday-school, and read to her what is printed under the pictures; and she tells them the story of it. There is nothing Jennie doesn't know about the Bible."

The door opened upon a low-ceiled room, where the evening shades lay deep. The red glow from the kitchen stove discovered a jam of children, young girls mostly, perched on the table, the chairs, in one another's laps, or squatting on the floor; in the midst of them, a little old woman with heavily veiled face, and wan, wrinkled hands folded in her lap. The singing ceased as we stepped across the threshold.

"Be welcome," piped a harsh voice with a singular note of cheerfulness in it. "Whose step is that with you, pastor? I don't know it. He is welcome in Jennie's house, whoever he be. Girls, make him to home." The girls moved up to make room.

"Jennie has not seen since she was a child," said the clergyman, gently; "but she knows a friend without it. Some day she shall see the great Friend in his glory, and then she shall be Blind Jennie no more."

The little woman raised the veil from a face shockingly disfigured, and touched the eyeless sockets. "Some day," she repeated, "Jennie shall see. Not long now—not long!" Her pastor patted her hand. The silence of the dark room was broken by Blind Jennie's voice, rising cracked and quavering: "Alas! and did my Saviour bleed?" The shrill chorus burst in:

> It was there by faith I received my sight,
> And now I am happy all the day.

The light that falls from the windows of the Neighborhood Guild, in Delancey Street, makes a white path across the asphalt pavement. Within, there is mirth and laughter. The Tenth Ward Social Reform Club is having its Christmas festival. Its members, poor mothers, scrubwomen,—the president is the janitress of a tenement near by,—have brought their little ones, a few their husbands, to share in the fun. One little girl has to be dragged up to the grab-bag. She cries at the sight of Santa Claus. The baby has drawn a woolly horse. He kisses the toy with a look of ecstatic bliss, and toddles away. At the far end of the hall a game of blindman's-buff is starting up. The aged grand-mother, who has watched it with growing excitement, bids one of the settlement workers hold her grandchild, that she may join in; and she does join in, with all the pent-up hunger of fifty joyless years. The worker, looking on, smiles; one has been reached. Thus is the battle against the slum waged and won with the child's play.

Tramp! tramp! comes to-morrow upon the stage. Two hundred and fifty pairs of little feet, keeping step, are marching to dinner in the Newsboys' Lodging-house. Five hundred pairs more are restlessly awaiting their turn upstairs. In prison, hospital, and almshouse to-night the city is host, and gives of her plenty. Here an unknown friend has spread a generous repast for the waifs who all the rest of the days shift for themselves as best they can. Turkey, coffee, and pie, with "vegetubles" to fill in. As the file of eagle-eyed youngsters passes down the long tables, there are swift movements of grimy hands, and shirt-waists bulge, ragged coats sag at the pockets. Hardly is the file seated when the plaint rises: "I ain't got no pie! It got swiped on me." Seven despoiled ones hold up their hands.

The superintendent laughs—it is Christmas eve. He taps one tentatively on the bulging shirt. "What have you here, my lad?"

"Me pie," responds he, with an innocent look; "I wuz scart it would get stole."

A little fellow who has been eying one of the visitors attentively takes his knife out of his mouth, and points it at him with conviction.

"I know you," he pipes. "You're a p'lice commissioner. I seen yer picter in the papers. You're Teddy Roosevelt!"

The clatter of knives and forks ceases suddenly. Seven pies creep stealthily over the edge of the table, and are replaced on as many plates. The visitors laugh. It was a case of mistaken identity.

Farthest down-town, where the island narrows toward the Battery, and warehouses crowd the few remaining tenements, the sombre-hued colony of Syrians is astir with preparation for the holiday. How comes it that in the only settlement of the real Christmas people in New York the corner saloon appropriates to itself all the outward signs of it? Even the floral cross that is nailed over the door of the Orthodox church is long withered and dead; it has been there since Easter, and it is yet twelve days to Christmas by the belated reckoning of the Greek Church. But if the houses show no sign of the holiday, within there is nothing lacking. The whole colony is gone a-visiting. There are enough of the unorthodox to set the fashion, and the rest follow the custom of the country. The men go from house to house, laugh, shake hands, and kiss one another on both cheeks, with the salutation, "Every year and you are safe," as the Syrian guide renders it into English; and a non-professional interpreter amends it: "May you grow happier year by year." Arrack made from grapes and flavored with aniseed, and candy baked in little white balls like marbles, are served with the indispensable cigarette; for long callers, the pipe.

In a top-floor room of one of the darkest of the dilapidated tenements, the dusty window-panes of which the last glow in the winter sky is tinging faintly with red, a dance is in progress. The guests, most of them fresh from the hillsides of Mount Lebanon, squat about the room. A reed-pipe and a tambourine furnish the music. One has the centre of the floor. With a beer jug filled to the brim on his head, he skips and sways, bending, twisting, kneeling, gesturing, and keeping time, while the men clap their hands. He lies down and turns over, but not a drop is spilled. Another succeeds him, stepping proudly, gracefully, furling and unfurling a handkerchief like a banner. As he sits down, and the beer goes around, one in the corner, who looks like a shepherd fresh from his pasture, strikes up a song—a far-off, lonesome, plaintive lay. "'Far as the hills,'" says the guide; "a song of the old days and the old people, now seldom heard." All together croon the refrain. The host delivers himself of an epic about his love across the seas, with the most agonizing expression, and in a shockingly bad voice. He is the worst singer I ever heard; but his companions greet his effort with approving shouts of "Yi! yi!" They look so fierce, and yet are so childishly happy, that at the thought of their exile and of the dark tenement the question arises, "Why all this joy?" The guide answers it with a look of surprise. "They sing," he says, "because they are glad they are free. Did you not know?"

The bells in old Trinity chime the midnight hour. From dark hallways men and women pour forth and hasten to the Maronite church. In the loft of the dingy old warehouse wax candles burn before an altar of brass. The priest, in a white robe with a huge gold cross worked on the back, chants the ritual. The people respond. The women kneel in the aisles, shrouding their heads in their shawls; the surpliced acolyte swings his censer; the heavy perfume of burning incense fills the hall.

The band at the anarchists' ball is tuning up for the last dance. Young and old float to the happy strains, forgetting injustice, oppression, hatred. Children slide upon the waxed floor, weaving fearlessly in and out between the couples—between fierce, bearded men and short-haired women with crimson-bordered kerchiefs. A Punch-and-Judy show in the corner evokes shouts of laughter.

Outside the snow is falling. It sifts silently into each nook and corner, softens all the hard and ugly lines, and throws the spotless mantle of charity over the blemishes, the shortcomings. Christmas morning will dawn pure and white.